Leah Fleming was born in Lancashire and is married with three sons and a daughter. She writes from an old farmhouse in the Yorkshire Dales and an olive grove in Crete.

You can follow Leah on Twitter at @LeahleFleming or on Facebook where she has her own page.

For more information about Leah's work please visit www.leahfleming.co.uk.

The Captain's Daughter

LEAH FLEMING

**SIMON &
SCHUSTER**

London · New York · Sydney · Toronto · New Delhi

A CBS COMPANY

First published in Great Britain by Simon & Schuster UK Ltd, 2012
This paperback edition published by Simon & Schuster UK Ltd, 2012
A CBS COMPANY

1 3 5 7 9 10 8 6 4 2

Simon & Schuster UK Ltd
1st Floor
222 Gray's Inn Road
London WC1X 8HB

www.simonandschuster.co.uk

Simon & Schuster Australia, Sydney
Simon & Schuster India, New Delhi

A CIP catalogue record for this book is available from the British Library

ISBN 978-0-85720-344-1
E-book ISBN 978-0-85720-343-4

Typeset by Hewer Text UK Ltd, Edinburgh
Printed and bound in Great Britain by CPI Group (UK) Ltd, Croydon, CR0 4YY

In memory of all the lives lost on 15th April 1912.

Part 1

1912–1914

1

England, April 1912

They were far too early. Standing amid a pile of cases, carpetbags and parcels, one eye on the terracotta clock tower, straining for the distant roar of an engine, the smell of burning coal, the soot and heat that heralded the arrival of the London train into Trinity Street, May Smith watched as the platform began filling with travellers. Some carried briefcases, others parcels, all were intent on their business. She looked over at her husband, dressed in his best second-hand tweed overcoat and trilby, holding Ellen, who was bundled into her new bonnet and coat, and wrapped in a shawl against the cool breeze funnelling down the platform from the moors, her eyes wide with uncertainty at the bustle around them. So many new noises for her to take in; for them all to take in: porters rattling trolleys loaded with boxes, carriage doors slamming, the whistles on the wind from the opposite platform.

Their train must come soon. This was the early train the businessmen caught, in their smart suits and bowler hats, the train that carried Lancashire cottons down to the city. She wanted to shout out like a child, 'Guess where we're going? You'll never believe it,' but of course, she kept silent, exhilarated yet ashamed of her excitement.

These people were used to travelling, unlike her, all dressed up in her sensible three-quarter-length navy-blue jacket, nipped in at the waist and flared out over her long serge skirt, her over-polished boots, her fair hair neatly coiled under a black straw boater with a wide brim. Everything on her back was serviceable, designed not to show the dirt and last their long journey, or so she hoped.

May ran over her list in her head once again: a tin box of sandwiches and apples, a bottle of milk for Ellen, some fancy biscuits and boiled sweets in case they felt sick, a picture book, clean napkins and a damp facecloth in a toilet bag for the journey.

Their papers and documents were safe in the leather attaché case Joe had been given as a leaving present from the mill. In their trunk was the fine pair of Horrocks cotton sheets embroidered with their initials, which the girls in the weaving shed had given her on her last day at work. Nestled safely in their folds were gifts for Uncle George in Idaho: a newspaper from his old hometown, studio portraits, a fancy tea caddy and a signed Bible from their Sunday school class.

'It's late,' May whispered, but Joe just laughed.

'It's you who had us here too early. Look, the signal on the track has changed. Any minute now . . .' He was peering over the platform edge, making her nervous.

'Step back,' she urged. 'Ellen will be scared. Not to mention me.' The locomotives terrified her; they looked like great black dragons breathing fire. She felt the gust of wind, the blast of heat on her cheeks, the deafening roar as the monster thundered into the station, screeching to a halt in a cloud of steam.

'You have got all our tickets?' she asked Joe once again.

Ellen burst into tears at the noise.

'Give her here!' May insisted, wrapping her arms round the screaming child. 'Hush, it's only a puffa train come to take us to a new world. Say bye-bye to Bolton. We're off on our adventure.'

They piled into the second-class compartment, Joe checking

their trunk was wheeled into the guard's van before settling himself down. Ellen continued to protest.

'She'll soon settle,' May said, smiling at the passengers who looked at them with dismay. There was nothing for it but to shove a biscuit in Ellen's hand and hope for the best. It did the trick and within a few seconds she was contentedly munching away.

May stared back at their companions, riled. She had as much right as they had to be sitting here. She and Joe might be orphans, but they had a sponsor in America willing to give them a new life. They might not have much in the way of possessions, but they had each other and a lovely little daughter, who was as bright as a new penny. They were young, with all their lives before them. She wanted to pinch herself yet again at this change in fortune, this chance to start anew.

May caught her reflection in the carriage window and smiled. She might not be a beauty but she had rosy cheeks, a sturdy body and she wasn't afraid of hard work, the very type of girl to flourish in the New World, if reports were correct. It was a blessing little Ellen had her daddy's fair curls and sea-blue eyes. Not that they'd ever seen the sea, mind, but they would soon.

Suddenly carriage doors were slamming, and whistles signalled the train's imminent departure. The carriage juddered, jolting May forward.

For a second her optimism vanished and she felt only panic. *Why are we leaving all we know? What are we doing?* She wanted to stop the train, to get out and go home to everything familiar and comforting. She almost shot out of her seat but fell back when she saw Joe staring out of the window with that determined look on his face. He had been so proud when he'd received an invitation from his relatives in America to join their carpentry business. How could she let him down? She'd walk to the ends of the earth with him.

It wasn't that they disliked their northern cotton town. It had sheltered both of them, in their tiny cottage on the edge of the moors, given them useful training and sent them out first into service and then into the mill where they had met. They were childhood sweethearts, married when Joe's apprenticeship had ended. But she'd always known that Joe had wanted more for his family, that he was restless to prove himself and she was happy to encourage his ambition. Who wouldn't want a life free from chimney smoke for their daughter, a chance to meet people from all over the world who, like them, were risking everything to start afresh? It took courage to leave all you'd ever known, and she was no coward. But that wave of panic still unsettled her. What if it all went wrong? What if this Uncle George was a tyrant? What if . . . ?

Stop fretting, she chided herself and looked up at the suitcase labels she had printed and tied on so carefully: Mr and Mrs Joseph Smith, RMS *Titanic*, Southampton. That would soon be their next port of call.

2

The cathedral bells tolled out across the city as the family gathered by the West Door, lining up to walk behind the cortège. Celestine Parkes was glad of the black lace veil hiding her grief from view as she clung onto her father's arm and watched as her brothers shouldered the coffin. It wouldn't be a heavy burden; her mother, Louisa, had shrunk to skin and bone in the final days of her illness.

Celeste could not forgive herself for her late arrival, her chance to say goodbye irretrievably lost. The ship from New York had been delayed by storms, but they had postponed the funeral until she finally arrived back at the family home in Lichfield. It had been a shock to see her once-beautiful mother reduced to a skeletal stranger.

Now the wind whipped across Cathedral Close, dead leaves cart-wheeling on the cobbles as the mourners stood before the dean, who had come to escort them into the echoing nave.

Celeste looked up at Lichfield Cathedral's trio of spires, those Three Ladies of the Vale piercing a bright March sky. She glanced across at the elegant houses circling the Close in salmon-pink sandstone. How familiar it all was in early spring, with daffodils poking through the grass, the sharp air straight from the Fens catching her breath. Coming home in springtime always moved her, especially the sight of blossom, of buds opening, and the green grass of the parks and fields. Easter in the cathedral was always special but this year it would be tinged with the sorrow of their loss.

For a second she thought of her own home and her beloved son, so far away across the ocean. She couldn't help but consider the long return journey to come, but quickly dismissed such weary thoughts. She had other things to think about right now.

She touched her long woollen coat with the fox fur collar, which she wore over her mother's beaded mourning dress with her black gloves. It was comforting to feel her mother's shape in these sleeves and to catch the familiar scent of lavender water in the fabric. Her felt hat, hiding the wildness of her auburn curls, was pinned with her grandmother's jet hatpins. Celeste had had little time to buy suitable mourning attire and she only hoped she had chosen well. Louisa Forester had always looked so elegant and her daughter wanted to honour her in death as she had loved her in life.

Celeste had treasured her mother's lively letters, with all their news of the cathedral, the clergy and the Theological College scholars' antics. They'd been such a precious link with home. Then the handwriting had begun to crawl, roaming carelessly across the page, and her father had taken to writing, explaining that her mother was not feeling well enough to lift the pen, hinting it was time their daughter came home before the illness took its inevitable toll.

I didn't say goodbye to you, she had cried every night since her return. Now there would be some comfort in this service. As a bishop's daughter, Louisa would be given every dignity and honour and would be interred in the grassy mound close to the cathedral.

But where *will I mourn you when I return home?* Celeste wondered sadly.

'I am the resurrection and the life . . .' The soothing words boomed out as she clutched her father's hand and tried not to weep.

Why have you left us? How can I do my duty without your strength and love to guide me?

Later, when it was all over and they had sipped tea and nibbled cold meats in the refectory of the Theological College, Celeste returned with her brothers to Red House, their home in Streethay. It was here their father made his announcement.

'Now you're all together, I want to tell you that I'm not going to stay here. There's a place for me in Vicar's Close. I want to be near your mother and closer to the town, too, to be of service.'

'We can't stay here without you,' said Selwyn, a lawyer, who travelled into Birmingham each day.

'Of course you can. One day you'll marry and your wife won't want an old man to look after. Bertram's at university, he needs a billet in the vacations, and Celeste too if she ever manages to bring her family to visit,' he said, looking to the smiling picture of his grandson Roddy, which took pride of place on the mantelpiece. 'Your mother loved that photo,' he said softly. He shook himself from his reverie and continued, 'Celestine, my dear, you must take some of her things back with you.'

Celeste was in no mood for dismantling the home, with all its sacred memories. There would be a time for that.

Her father carried on, though, unaware of her distress. 'You must take her table linen,' he insisted. 'Your mother embroidered so beautifully. She would want you to have it.'

With tears in her eyes, Celeste fingered the tablecloth, now covered with vases of flowers and condolence cards. 'Thank you,' she murmured. 'But not now.'

At last her father caught her mood and held her hand. 'Don't worry, your mother is always in your heart,' he comforted her. 'She'll never leave you. You'll all carry on as she would have done, I'm sure. She taught you well. And you have the joy of a loving family to return to, my dear.'

He was right. She had been taught well and knew that duty and others must come first before selfish needs. So she swallowed back her tears and stared out of the window onto the lawn in its first flush of green. If only Lichfield didn't look so beautiful at this time of year... She should have spoken out then, but always something held her back. This was no time to burden an old man with her troubles. No matter how terrible they might be.

3

Her first sight of London and its magnificent buildings filled May with awe. She stared up at Big Ben with disbelief and caught a glimpse of the Tower of London from the bridge. They stayed overnight in a boarding house close to St Paul's that was none too clean. One look at the landlady's grubby face and May immediately turned over the mattresses to inspect them for bugs. Ellen couldn't settle in the strange surroundings and they had a restless night. If this was what it was going to be like, May said, it would be one hell of a long sea voyage. They'd be wrecks by the end of it. Joe laughed and whirled her around the room in excitement. She couldn't help but laugh back up at him. His spirit and enthusiasm were infectious.

Early the next morning, they treated themselves to a cab to Waterloo Station, sending postcards to friends at the mill before they left. May stared in wonder at the queues of omnibuses, horses and carts, and men pushing barrows. She had never seen such a huge city bustling in the early morning light. Where did all these folk come from?

To think, the next big city would be New York!

When they finally reached Waterloo to catch the boat train, May didn't think she had ever seen such a crush of humanity – men and women carrying suitcases and bags, small children lagging behind. She desperately clung onto Joe and Ellen for fear of being separated. The smoke, steam, soot and noise swept them along into the waiting carriages bound for Southampton. Tired, dishevelled, one among hundreds, May felt a familiar surge of pride that Joe had enough about him to want more for his family than the backstreets of a cotton town.

But as the train rattled on the tracks, taking them further and further from everything they had ever known, she felt uneasy again. How would they fare in a strange country? What would the weather be like? Would they fit in? What if the baby got sick? It was all such a risk. As the train drew into Southampton harbour she saw the grey sea and glimpsed the tall ship with the White Star ensign flying on its mast. It rose high above the trees and houses, and her heart thudded. There was no turning back now. They must trust themselves to the ship's crew to carry them across the ocean and to their new life.

When they reached the docking shed May saw the *Titanic*'s great bulk, its four funnels rising above them, and an involuntary shiver crept down her spine. The funnels were painted cream, tipped with black rings and crowning a wall of cast iron a hundred feet tall, rearing up like a steel mountain.

'How on earth can that thing float?' she croaked as they joined the embarkation queue making its way onto C Deck. She was so in awe of the scale of the vessel that would be their home for the next week that she stumbled over the skirt of the woman in front, who turned round and glared.

'Had a good trip?' Joe laughed, but May wasn't amused.

'My feet don't want to board this ship,' she whispered.

'Stuff and nonsense,' Joe replied, reading her mind. 'God himself couldn't sink this ship!'

'I hope you know what we're doing, Joe. It's such a long way to go.' She pulled her coat around her tightly.

'Just look for yourself, the water's deep enough to hold her up. The *Titanic*'s brand new, and we are lucky to be sailing on her. The papers say her Third Class is as good as First on other ships. They say she has every safety feature known to man. She's unsinkable. Don't go worrying, May.'

Their tickets were checked off and they were inspected for signs of fever and lice by a man in a white coat and spectacles, which May found utterly shaming. They could strip her down to her chemise and not find anything but clean Lancashire cotton.

Guided by stewards, they followed the queue onto C Deck. Despite herself May felt a shiver of fear as they descended lower into the ship along a narrow warren of corridors. She'd never liked the water much, not even a ride on the boating lake in Queens Park, though Joe had made her learn to swim up at the reservoirs at Belmont. He'd taught her a half-decent breast stroke one bank holiday at the Blue Lagoon. Splashing and protesting, she'd hated feeling the water up her nose and in her eyes, and had strained to keep her head out of it.

Down in the bowels of the ship they were directed to a neat pine-panelled cabin with bunks, one of many along a linoleum-tiled corridor with steel walls now as wide as a high street. The passage was crowded with noisy families, racing children excit-edly calling to one another in a babble of foreign languages. The air was filled with strange aromas: spices, tobacco smoke, sweat, all mixed with the smell of fresh paint.

Inside the cabin May sat down on the bunk and instinctively tested it for size. 'A proper mattress this time,' she noted. Everything was new: the sheets, the towels, the flooring. 'I can't breathe in here,' she said. 'It's clean but . . .' She couldn't imagine how she'd spend seven nights cooped up in this wooden box of a room, clean as it was. It smelled like a coffin. She shuddered again and then looked over at Ellen, who was crawling around the floor, exploring. Another one with a thirst for adventure. She needed to pull herself together. At least they weren't forced to share with strangers.

'Right then,' she rallied herself, 'let's get on deck. I'll feel better when I get some fresh air.'

Weaving in and out of a maze of passages and stairs, May eyed the ship's quarters with wonder, almost forgetting her misgivings. 'It's like a town all of its own,' she exclaimed, peering into every open space. There was a huge dining room with long wooden tables and solid captain's chairs like the ones in the church vestry. The floors were laid with patterned lino that smelled new and gluey. There was a room for smokers somewhere above but here was a large saloon with comfortable armchairs and a piano in the corner. Everything was polished and sparkling, with framed pictures on the walls and pot plants standing in corners. There wasn't a speck of dust to be found. It was all most satisfactory and yet . . . She couldn't help feeling it was far too big and they were accommodated far too low in the water.

Joe carried Ellen down corridors and up stairs in search of some open space on deck where they could look at the seagulls. 'It won't be long now before we're off,' he shouted, and May saw the genuine excitement etched on his face. She turned and watched other passengers hugging their relatives, saying goodbye, with something close to envy. She and Joe had hardly one blood relative between them. All their hopes were pinned on 'Uncle' George in Idaho. As happy as their little family was, it would be wonderful to have a sense of belonging to something bigger.

It was strange to think they might never see England again, never see the Union Jack flying or hear good Lancashire voices calling to one another on the pavements. Where would she find a decent cup of tea? She'd heard they only drank coffee in the States. Joe was pointing out ships on the other berths to Ellen, hanging over the side and watching a crane hoist up a beautiful black and gold saloon car. There was such wealth on board higher up in the First Class apartments though May knew the likes of them would be kept well away from such important passengers. They would be living on board in two different worlds but she didn't care as long as they all arrived safely in New York.

May turned towards Joe and felt the breeze on Ellen's cold cheeks. Time to go indoors. She didn't want to watch the ship sliding away from her homeland or see the teary farewells from relatives pausing for one last glimpse of their loved ones. It had been a long day and she wanted to explore further below deck. If she got lost there were stewards to help her and she'd memorized their cabin number. Depending on the weather there would be seven nights to endure, she thought with a sigh. She hoped she could hold on until Wednesday.

Later that evening Joe was pacing up and down the little cabin, impatient. 'Why do you huddle in here like a hermit crab when there's so much to explore? There's a piano playing, and singing, we can listen to the orchestra, have a bite to eat. I've never seen so many choices on the menu: pies, pastries, salads. We should fill up our bellies while we can,' he advised.

'You go on,' May replied, groaning from her bunk. 'My stomach's not up to it. I don't fancy moving about. It's thronged with people now. We don't know anyone and half the people I've seen don't speak a word of English since we picked up that lot at Cherbourg. What a racket they make.'

'We're all in the same boat, love,' Joe smiled. 'Everyone's wanting to make a fresh start in the New World. Don't begrudge them their chances.'

'I'm not, it's just I feel safe here. I can't explain it but I just feel safe with all my things around me.'

'No one's going to steal anything.'

'You never know.'

'Oh, May, you are funny. Here we are on the high seas – where would they run to? And what have we got to be stolen?'

'There's those lovely sheets I was given,' she argued, knowing she was being a worry guts.

'With our initials on them? Don't be daft! They probably have far nicer ones of their own. Come on, let's give Ellen some fresh air before we turn in for the night.'

'I've had this funny feeling in the pit of my belly ever since I saw the size of the *Titanic*,' May argued. 'I can't shift it. You go and let me rest.'

'Now you're being morbid; that's not like you,' Joe replied. 'Fresh air will do you good.'

'I suppose you're right, lying here won't change anything, but I wish I didn't feel so worried.' May put on her woollen jacket and muffler and pinned on her beret with the pompom on the top, tying Ellen into her plaid shawl.

'That's better. Let's go and see the stars and make a wish.' Joe took her hand.

May smiled up at her husband. She must trust in Joe's good common sense. He was the sort of man that was handed nothing but blows in life, no parents, no money, no education. Now he was going to make something of himself, no matter what. How could she not love a man like that?

Despite her misgivings May slept well on that first night out at sea. The meals in the dining room were delicious and settled her stomach. It was such a treat to be cooked for and waited on, and it gave her and Joe a chance to wander round on deck and let Ellen toddle between them. After they docked in Ireland, there'd be nothing but the grey open sea between them and their final destination. She must try to relax and enjoy this once-in-a-lifetime voyage.

It was cold and she was glad of her thick jacket and Joe's over-coat. Ellen had layers of knitted wool with a felted coat, bonnet and firm leather boots given to her by a neighbour for when she started to walk properly. It was strange to think she'd spend her first birthday thousands of miles away from the place where she had been born.

May looked up with wonder at the stars stretched across the

sky. Where would they be this time next week? 'Do you think we're doing the right thing?'

Joe nodded and smiled, dismissing her edginess. 'It's been a smooth ride so far. We're in safe hands.' He pointed up where the captain, with his distinctive white beard, strode on deck inspecting his crew, then watching over them from his perch. 'He's the best captain or he wouldn't be steering this ship on its maiden voyage, now, would he? Enjoy it, we won't be doing this again in our lifetime, will we?'

4

Celestine looked up through her black veil at the ship that would be taking her back to America. Her shoes felt like lead as she stepped along the First Class gangway, her brother storming ahead, dying to inspect the transatlantic liner from bow to stern.

'Wait for me!' she called.

Selwyn turned and grinned. 'Come on, slow coach, I want to see what all the bally fuss is about this *Titanic*, and Father wants you to meet that old dear, the archdeacon's aunt ...'

'My chaperone. Honestly, can't a married woman be allowed on board without a guardian? I hope Mrs Grant isn't as awful as the one I had coming over. She could see I was worried about Mama but she insisted on talking throughout the entire journey.'

'Grover was quite insistent you were not to travel unaccompanied,' Selwyn replied. 'Though why he couldn't accompany you himself beats me. We all wanted to meet little Roddy too. Poor Mama never got to see him ...'

'I know, but my husband's a very busy man.'

'It was your mother's funeral, for pity's sake! You could have done with some support on the journey over, especially in the circumstances.' Selwyn was not one to mince his words. It was one of the things Celestine loved about him.

'You've all looked after me so well. I'm fine. Of course, I'd like to have my own family around me but Grover said funerals are not for children.'

'He could have made the effort, Sis.'

'I know . . . it's just . . .' How could she explain that Grover didn't take much interest in England or her family? He had his own parents close by and was insistent that Roddy's routine must not be disturbed. Her only thought now was to return to her son and settle back into the daily routine, and to do that she must climb onto this monster whale's back to go west, home to Akron, Ohio.

Selwyn helped her settle herself into her cabin, making sure she could spread herself out and not be disturbed. If the voyage were as bad as her crossing five weeks ago, she was in for a painful time and would spend most of it in her cabin.

Because of a coal strike that had caused disruption to shipping schedules, she'd been given an alternative berth on the *Titanic* for her return to New York. She ought to be thrilled to be on its maiden voyage with all the razzmatazz in Southampton, but her heart was heavy to be leaving her family behind. She wondered when she would see them again. If she would ever see her father again. He'd looked so frail, so broken after her mother's death.

The First Class apartments were on the upper decks; state rooms and private cabins were connected by corridors laid with thick, plush carpets. Her cabin was well lit with electric lamps, and she had a brass-railed bed with sumptuous soft linens and an eiderdown. The walls were lined with panels of flock wallpaper like a fine hotel room, and fresh flowers everywhere; the scents of hothouse lilies, freesias and jasmine barely disguised the odour of newly decorated paintwork. There were even excellent stewardesses at her beck and call with the push of a button on the wall. If only she could get away from the smell of paint and glue, which made her feel queasy. It was a pity her sea legs were so poor. Sea travel was a luxurious business these days.

They met up with the elderly widow Mrs Grant at the top of the grand staircase by the wonderful carved clock. Selwyn stood to admire the elegant sweep of the stairs and the great latticed glass dome, which allowed light to shine down the carved oak balustrades. 'Not one for sliding down, Sis?' he smiled. 'I've never seen anything like it.'

Ada Grant was going out to visit her sister in Pennsylvania for the summer. There wasn't time to get very well acquainted before the whistle blew, but Celeste promised to take tea with her later.

It was time for Selwyn to leave the ship but Celeste clutched his hand. Tears welled and she clung to him. 'I wish I could stay longer.'

'Steady on, old girl. Mama's at peace now.'

How she wanted to cry out to him, finally to tell him the truth. 'I know and I must return. Roddy needs me but . . . You will look after Papa for me.' She felt sick to her stomach, knowing that her bereaved father and two brothers thought her so fortunate to be married to a wealthy businessman with a darling little boy and a lovely house. They knew only what she wanted them to know. She couldn't let them worry.

'Goodbye and good luck.' Selwyn hugged her. '*Bon voyage* and all that, and don't leave it so long next time. Roddy will be in long pants before we get to meet him.' With that he was gone, striding down the corridor and off the ship.

Celestine looked after him, bereft. She didn't think she'd ever felt so entirely alone.

What she needed now was fresh air and one last lingering look at the dockside. She must take her leave of her country. 'Be British and stomach your sorrow,' she chided herself, thinking of her father's words when he'd caught her crying in her room the evening before. She hadn't had the heart to tell him the real reason for her tears.

Wrapping herself in her new black coat and pinning the black hat and veil firmly over her face, she made her way down the panelled corridor with its two-toned blue carpet. There seemed to be smiling stewards around every corner to guide her out onto the promenade deck.

The ship was stirring into life, and she wanted to watch it turning out of the dock to face up the river to Southampton and out towards Cherbourg, seventy miles across the Channel. France would be their next port of call.

A crowd had gathered at the railings as the whistles blasted over the city. People were climbing up poles and through windows, waving them off from every vantage point along the coastline, shouting and cheering them on their way. How she wished she was a little girl again at the seaside at Sidmouth, watching as the tall sailing ships floated across the water. Roddy would have loved all this. He was nearly three and such a chatterbox. She'd bought him picture books of London and postcards of the *Titanic* and a toy yacht to help her explain to him where she'd been all this time.

The *Titanic* drifted slowly from the dock, pulled out by little tugs and manoeuvred into a position so she was facing downriver.

There were other big liners tied up at their berths like a stable of restless horses, but as the ship passed there was a sudden swell of water, and Celeste could see one of the liners jerk from its mooring.

'The ropes on the *New York* have snapped!' shouted one of the sailors working behind her.

'It's going to crash into us!' screamed a passenger.

'Bloody hell, what a start to a maiden voyage!' another shouted across to the officer looking on in shock.

All eyes were fixed on the *New York*. Its stern was arcing outwards, drawing to them. But below, a little tug was coming to the rescue, gathering up its loose rope, gaining control of the errant steed, somehow pulling it away as the captain on the bridge above them was steering the ship out of danger, edging it slowly out of the path of the oncoming liner. They seemed to be going backwards.

'Drama over. That was a close call!' A sigh of relief went round the onlookers but Celeste overheard a steward mutter under his breath, 'I didn't like this ship before, and now I like it even less. It can't even get into the water without causing trouble.'

She smiled to herself. Sailors were a superstitious lot and she didn't have time for such folly. You made your own fortunes, she thought. It was the one thing she agreed with Grover about. No point in dwelling on misfortunes that didn't happen. There were enough of them that did. The danger had been averted by skill and science. It boded well for their journey.

Now they were on their way, delayed for only an hour or so. It was time to explore the rest of this floating palace but first she must take tea with her chaperone. Mrs Grant was waiting in the Café Parisienne.

'Isn't this modern? It's like an open veranda and the wicker trelliswork with the ivy is so realistic, don't you think? They've thought of everything. It's all light and air and sea views. Isn't this journey going to be fun?'

Celeste tried to look enthused but all she could think of was Selwyn on his way home and what might be waiting for her in Akron, Ohio.

Later she strolled around the freshly painted deck, enjoying the familiar strains of music from the ship's orchestra playing in an open gallery nearby. She'd seen signs to a gymnasium and both a swimming bath and a Turkish bath down below deck. She found her way to the reading room to seek a quiet corner to read her Edith Wharton novel: *The House of Mirth*. She must make the most of her remaining time alone. This perhaps would be where she took her refuge, among the soft armchairs and the writing tables. The room was decorated in a Georgian style with moulded panelled walls painted white, simple fittings and a bay window overlooking the promenade deck letting in even more light. Here she could sink into a chair and escape into her book.

But as the waters drew them further and further from the

shore, she felt a peculiar churning in her stomach. It was time to head for the safety of her four-poster bed until this feeling passed. All this luxury didn't make for happiness but it certainly made misery more comfortable.

5

It was Sunday morning and May had heard there was a church service taking place somewhere on the upper decks. She asked a steward exactly where it was being held.

'It's only for First and Second Class passengers, ma'am,' he said, eyeing her up and down.

'Well, I am Church of England so where do I worship then?' she replied, refusing to be cowed by his abrupt manner.

'I'll go and see,' he sighed. 'Wait here.'

She was feeling brighter now she'd got used to the pitch of the ship, and Joe had told her to go and have some time to herself while he looked after Ellen. She looked respectable enough, spruced up in her Sunday best. Why shouldn't she be in church along with the best of them?

Judging by the to-ing and fro-ing, her request had caused a bit of a fuss, but eventually a steward escorted her upstairs, unlocking some screens onto the upper decks to let her into the holy of holies. 'You were right, ma'am. The service is for everyone.'

No odours of stew, gravy or stale sweat clouded the air here. Instead, May smelled the wafting perfume of fresh arum lilies, carnations and cigar smoke, and felt the thickest of rich-patterned carpets at her feet. She was underdressed and self-conscious, but no one seemed even to notice her as they promenaded around the decks. The steward pressed her on apace until they came to a sumptuous dining saloon with leather chairs in rows and a rostrum at the far end.

'Stay in these back rows, please, madam. They are reserved for visitors.' By that May knew he meant the steerage passengers, and she was relieved to see she was not the only brave soul to venture forth into this strange uncharted territory. In fact there were rows of visitors, and sitting next to her was another woman wearing a dowdy coat and plain hat. Soon the room filled up with the rich and famous, according to her neighbour, who, by her own admission, was here only to gawp and gossip.

'Are you here to see how the other half live then? Just look at those hats. I bet each one of them would cost our men a year's wages? Still, they do put on a show for us; they say the richest men in the world are on board, Astor, the Guggenheims . . . and I bet some of them fancy women aren't their wives. I saw one carrying a dog with a diamond collar, I ask you.' She rattled off who they all were and who was related to whom; names that meant nothing to May.

Then the captain arrived along with several members of the crew armed with hymn sheets, which were passed along the rows. He led them through a simple service that wouldn't offend anyone. The singing was polite and muted, but May loved a good hymn and when it came to 'O God, our help in ages past' she couldn't help but sing out, her strong soprano voice betraying her enthusiasm until people turned round to see where the noise was coming from. She blushed and lowered her voice.

She sneaked a closer look at Captain Smith. He was older than she expected, with his silver hair and portly figure. May couldn't help but think about the congregation gathering back at her parish church in Deane. Another wave of panic flooded her at the thought of them all in church without her. Here she was, a stranger among strangers in a steel ship at the mercy of the waves. Tomorrow the girls from the mill would be lining up at their machines for the new week without her. Would any of them miss her?

Still, it was her chance to glimpse into a world where passengers wore furs, exquisite hats, velvet coats and fine leather boots. A restless pampered toddler, dressed in silks and swansdown, was whisked away by her maidservant. May was glad she hadn't brought Ellen, not least because her homespun clothes would have looked shabby in contrast. Alone, there was time to drink in her surroundings and gaze on the congregation at leisure.

She had never seen such sumptuous rooms. The wall panelling was decorated with beautifully carved flowers and leaves. Joe would know how it was done. And above her head electric domes of light hung from ceilings of ornate white plasterwork.

No wonder there were stewards at each door to make sure the likes of her were promptly escorted back to their rightful deck. They might all be equal under the Lord, she smiled ruefully, but on board this British ship it was everyone in their proper station. She was honoured just to be in the same room as these grand people, if only for a few minutes. She didn't mind being set apart. It was only right and proper. These gentlefolk had paid much more for their tickets so they deserved all this finery. It was a different world up here in First Class. Would America be as class bound or was it truly the land of the free?

Celeste attended morning service in the First Class dining room. She caught glimpses of the famous in their seats at the front: wealthy American hostesses from Boston and Philadelphia; the cream of New York society, the Astors, Guggenheims, Wideners; Walter Douglas, founder of the Quaker Oats factory, a familiar face from the pages of Akron's *Beacon Journal*, returning from Paris with his wife. Some of the wealthiest men in the world were aboard. Grover would be impressed by her fellow passengers. It was more like a ballroom than a church assembly. The captain did his best using the ship's order of service sheets to cater for a broad church sort of worship but it made her feel even more homesick.

She couldn't help but think of the vaulting roof of Lichfield Cathedral, the peal of its bells ringing through the morning air, the organ's great basso profundo, the parade of choirboys in their white and scarlet robes and the dean in his gold vestments.

This service was perfectly acceptable, though. At least they'd allowed other classes of passenger to attend. She'd heard one young woman singing her heart out in the back row, in tune and on time, although she'd made a quick diminuendo when she realized this was no Evangelical Revival tent but a polite token to Sunday worship. At the end of the service, the back rows were rushed out from view as if their presence would somehow offend the sensibilities of the First Class passengers. Pity, Celeste smiled; she would like to have had a good look at the girl with the golden voice and thank her for raising the quality of their singing, if only for a few verses. She looked like a nice woman.

It was proving to be a long voyage with only Mrs Grant for company, and a novel about a young girl struggling to fit into New York society at the turn of the new century was hardly cheering reading.

If only there were some like minds to talk to over the dining table, not the usual mixture of wealthy travellers reliving their exotic adventures in Europe, dropping names like croutons into their soup, or Ada Grant chattering on about her relatives and their children.

Celeste wondered what it was like for that girl with the lovely voice down below in steerage, and was glad she had managed to cross the golden gates into this pampered cocoon. What must she make of all this luxury and privilege that was making Celeste feel so uncomfortable? It was all too much on this ship so aptly named *Titanic*. Why couldn't she just relax and enjoy the experience of being cosseted? Why did she feel so uneasy?

'So what's it like up there in the gods?' Joe asked over lunch, slurping his soup with gusto.

'Another world. You've never seen the like: acres of thick carpets – it was like walking on air – and the women dressed like mannequins in a shop window, weighed down with so many pearls and gems. But they can't sing for toffee.'

Joe grinned. 'I bet you showed them how.'

'I tried but I got stared at and so I shut up. I enjoyed it, though, seeing how the other half lives. We got a bum's rush as soon as it was over, though, in case we ran off with the silver. I'm glad I'm back down here.'

'That's a relief. Don't want you getting no fancy ideas. It might be a log cabin for us when we get out west.'

'At least we'll all be equal out there. How do folks get to be so rich that they can spend thousands on a ticket? I'm sure they're no happier than us. There was one poor widow all in black who looked as if she was about to burst into tears any minute and she wasn't a day older than me. I don't know what I'd do if anything happened to you. You won't ditch me for some rich American fancy woman, will you?'

Joe grabbed her hand, laughing. 'I don't know where you think all this stuff up, May. You and me are stuck together like glue, and that's a promise. We'll never be apart. Not until our dying day.'

6

For Celeste it was proving to be an uneventful Sunday. She was feeling squeamish and picked at her luncheon while old Mrs Grant struggled with fearful indigestion. In her mind Celeste was preparing herself for the rigours of her marriage and duties in Akron. The thought filled her with dread. There was only Roddy's welcome to look forward to.

She spent the afternoon listening to the orchestra, promenading the decks for fresh air before it was time to prepare for yet another dress parade in the dining room.

She was still wearing her mother's black silk two-piece with the jet-beaded collar and cuffs. It smelled of home and Father's pipe smoke. Who was there here to notice that she was wearing the same dress each evening? She was in mourning, after all; it was hardly a time to be the belle of the ball. Defiant though she felt, faced with all the fuss of dining rituals, she did make a valiant effort to dress her hair without the aid of a lady's maid or stewardess. The damp air had turned the loose ends into a frizz of curls.

She still wasn't hungry but listened to the restful serenades and waltzes, music designed to instil a sense of calm. The livelier numbers would be reserved for the dancing later.

The orchestra lifted her mood until she saw the menu presented so beautifully before them, and her heart sank. No one could eat ten courses, though Mrs Grant made a valiant

attempt to work her way through each one. She would undoubt-
edly suffer again later, Celeste grimaced. She settled for the
Consommé Olga, the poached salmon with mousseline sauce,
the sauté of chicken, but couldn't face the entrée of lamb, beef
or duckling. She skipped the Punch Romaine, tasted the roast
squab and cold asparagus vinaigrette but the pâté de foie gras
defeated her. There was just room left for the peaches in
Chartreuse jelly. She resolutely stuck to water, refusing any of
the wines chosen for each course. Rich wine went to her head
and made her weepy.

Grover would have insisted she had his money's worth but
Grover wasn't here, she thought defiantly.

By ten o'clock Mrs Grant was half asleep and Celeste amused
herself listening to the chatter and laughter around her, the clink
of glasses, savouring the noise before another night descended
and she'd be alone with her increasingly dark thoughts. The
glitter of diamonds flashing in the lamplight, the scent of Parisian
perfume, the shimmer of silk and feathers was a feast for the eyes.
Everyone around her looked so relaxed and glamorous but
Celeste could take no pleasure in this ambience. Her heart was
not in the First Class dining room, with its gilded opulence and
Louis Seize décor, but was yearning for what she had left behind.

She'd had enough of sitting with Mrs Grant, who was hard of
hearing and wanted to regale her with gossip.

'It's like a club, you know; they all gather in Paris,
Cairo . . . wherever. Captain Smith is their favourite so that's
why they're all here now. They only travel on his ship. He's
never had an accident . . .'

'What about the incident before we left Southampton?'
Celeste asked.

'There you see, it didn't turn into anything and that's because
Captain Smith is so lucky.'

There was no use arguing, and Celeste was horribly bored,
trying not to yawn. Once again it annoyed her that she – a

respectable married woman – was unable to sit alone. She didn't want any unnecessary attention from some of the single men who were ogling her table with interest. They'd gathered a coterie of giggling females to their side but still had time to give her the glad eye, mourning or not. She'd have to fend them off for three more nights.

When Celeste returned to her cabin, a stewardess came to help her undress. She laughed when Celeste clutched her full stomach and groaned.

'You've not seen anything yet, madam. We're coming to the "Devils Hole" where the icebergs float and the water boils.'

'Oh, don't tell me that!' Celeste said laughing. 'I'll never sleep now.'

'You will, I assure you – there's nothing like a rich meal, fresh air and Mr Hartley's band music in your ears to send you off.'

Celeste did indeed nod off but woke about midnight, her stomach protesting at her gluttony. She felt a small shudder, a shake, a jerk, enough for her crystal water jug to rattle and her tumbler to slide along the mahogany surface. Then the engine seemed to judder to a stop like a train pulling into a station. Was she still dreaming? She turned back, irritable at being woken, and drifted back to sleep. Suddenly there were noises in the corridor, not party revellers but the sound of rapid footfall, and the echoing bangs of doors opening and closing in haste. Instantly she was wide awake, alert to trouble.

'What's going on?' she called out, wrapping her Japanese silk kimono over her nightdress as she opened the door. She was thinking about deaf Mrs Grant down the corridor. Did she know what was happening?

'The ship's hit an iceberg,' someone called across.

'No! Not at all . . . no panic,' the same stewardess who had helped her undress hours before called. 'There's nothing to be alarmed about but we would like you all to make your way up on deck as a precaution. Wrap up warmly, please, and take your life jacket too. I'll assist you if you are unable to reach.'

Celeste threw on her black jacket, tugged her skirt over her nightdress, found her thick coat and her fur tippet, and pulled on her boots. Without thinking, she took her purse, a photo of Roddy and the rings Grover had given her. Everything else could wait for her return.

She followed a line of hastily dressed passengers, wondering where they were being led. She'd felt nothing at all to suggest a crash, but suddenly the corridors were lined with stewards checking them over and pointing the way to the boat deck. What on earth was going on? Why were they disturbing them in the middle of the night? She felt her stomach lurch with fear. Could the unthinkable possibly be true? Was this just a safety drill or something much more serious?

7

May had never spent such a jolly Sunday night. Her feet had tapped to the music in the saloon, accordions, banjos, the clatter of clogs and boots on the wooden floor, couples spinning around in foreign dances, while children slid across the floor like they did in any church hall, getting in everyone's way.

She and Joe took a stroll on deck before bed to look at the stars but it was too chilly to stay out long, especially with a sleeping baby over Joe's shoulder.

'What a stretch of stars! Look, Orion's Belt,' Joe said, pointing to a shape of twinkling stars. 'And there's the North Star, the sailor's special compass point. You feeling a bit more relaxed now, my love?'

'A bit, but let's turn in. Another night can be ticked off,' May replied. She couldn't wait to be back on dry land. If she never sailed again, it would be too soon.

'I don't want to forget a minute of this journey. Who'd have thought it, you and me on the high seas? I don't regret it for all the tea in China.'

'I hope we don't regret it,' she replied darkly.

'What's that supposed to mean? Are you having second thoughts about leaving?'

'Of course not . . . but a week at sea. It's too long, too cold and too far from land.' There was no use pretending she wasn't still feeling nervous. She knew the worst part of the voyage was to come. In the bar, there had been talk of icebergs and waves as high as church steeples. Wild talk, fuelled by drink, May knew, but she couldn't help but think there must be a grain of truth in the tall tales.

'Where's your sense of adventure? Don't be such a wet blanket.'

'I'm sorry but it's how I feel,' she said, close to tears now. 'Don't laugh at me. I can't help it.'

'I know, and I love you just the same for being a worrywart,' Joe said, hugging her and stroking her cheek. 'You are cold. Sorry, love. Let's go down and I'll warm you up good and proper.' They both laughed.

'None of your sauce, young man, I'm a respectable married woman, I'll have you know.'

'And I'm a married man, so that's all right then.'

May slept deeply, sated from lovemaking, fresh air and rich food, and Ellen continued to sleep soundly in her cot even when May was woken by noises in the corridor outside. Doors were banging; then there was a knock on their own door. Joe got up to open it and May's anxiey only increased when he took his time returning.

'What's going on? Is it drunks?' she called out. 'I'll give 'em what for if they wake the baby!'

'Nowt . . . just something about a bit of a bump with ice. We've all got to get dressed and put on life jackets . . . just in case,' Joe assured her. 'Better wrap up warm, love. It'll be parky up there.'

'What time is it? I didn't feel anything, did you?' she said, struggling to her feet, aware the floor wasn't quite level. 'What are they playing at, messing us about like this?'

'Just get dressed and do as you're told. Get Ellen togged up well. Can't have her getting a chill now, can we?' His voice was calm but May sensed Joe was rattled.

May grabbed everything she could lay her hands on, pulling on a cardigan, jacket and a warm skirt over her nightgown. Struggling into her boots, and tying up her hair, she shoved on her bonnet. She wasn't going to get her best straw wet. They'd soon be back down.

'Have you got our money, Joe?'

'Don't worry, it's all in my wallet together with the ticket and George's address. Follow me and don't let me out of your sight. It's probably just a practice drill.'

They tried not to wake Ellen but she stirred and cried as they piled on her clothes. May's heart was thumping. What if this wasn't a drill? What if it was for real?

In the corridor it was bedlam. People were yelling in a babble of foreign tongues, shoving and pushing forward. The ship lurched forward again and everyone screamed. They were going in the wrong direction, surely? May had memorized her bearings and knew that to get up on deck they must turn the other way. She pushed against the crowd but it was no use. They were forced along with everyone else and found themselves lined up in one of the dining rooms where everyone was checked for life jackets.

'What's going on?' Joe shouted to a steward.

'Nothing to worry about . . . We scraped past an iceberg and took in a little water. The captain wants the women and children to go up to the lifeboat area as a precaution. There's just a bit of a queue, don't panic.'

The ship was making funny grinding noises, lights flickered on and off and a scream went up for the wrought-iron doors to be opened but the stewards stayed firm.

'For the love of mercy, let the women and kiddies up on deck!' shouted an old Irishman.

'Not until I get my orders,' shouted one of the stewards on the other side. May saw the raw panic on his face and knew the worst was happening.

'We'll never get off this ship, Joe, if we wait for him,' she whispered. 'I just know it. Like I knew there was something wrong with this ship the minute I clapped eyes on her. Now will you believe me? We can't wait here ... If we want to live, we need to go. Now.'

8

The First Class passengers were herded down their corridors and assembled on the promenade deck, where officers were patrolling up and down directing them to various muster stations. Could this really be happening? Celeste wondered. She hadn't seen Mrs Grant but there was no reason to think she hadn't been woken by the stewards, as she herself had been. Then to her horror a stoker burst in on them, his face covered in soot, burns and blood, holding up a stump of a hand, its fingers blown off. He was speechless, just shaking his fist.

The nearest officer ran to move him aside. 'Not here!' he bellowed, but one of the passengers shot forward.

'Is there any danger?' he asked the injured man, holding his wife and his little boy back from the terrible sight.

'Danger, I should bloody say so!' screamed the man. 'It's hell on earth down there. This ship is sinking!'

Celeste felt the grip of sickening fear. This was real. The officers turned quickly into guards ordering them efficiently to muster points, letting no one else through. It was past one o'clock in the morning and the night was bitterly cold, the stars bright.

Celeste continued to look out for Mrs Grant, but couldn't see her. 'I have to go back,' she said, trying to return down the stairs. 'There's an old lady, she can't hear ...' But she was pushed forward out onto the boat deck, where the ropes on the arched davits holding up the lifeboats were being unravelled.

'We're not going in there, are we?' asked one of the women.

'I have to find Mrs Grant,' Celeste repeated to no one in particular before turning back again. 'She might not have heard the instructions.'

An officer barred her path. 'You're going nowhere, miss.'

'But she's old and extremely deaf!'

'The stewards will see to her. You stay exactly where you are now!'

What could she do but comply? She stood huddled with the other women not half as well covered as she was, some with small children wrapped in blankets to keep off the chill.

'Lower the boats!' cried a host of voices.

'Women and children first!' shouted one of the officers, looking grave. 'Only women and children!'

Celeste watched husbands and fathers stepping back instinctively, making no protest, pushing their families towards the lifeboats. Some of the wives clung to their men, refusing to move any closer to the dangling boats.

'You go on, dearest . . . I'll follow in the men's boat later . . . Please, think of the children,' said one man, lifting a sleeping child into the arms of a seaman in the boat, knowing his wife would have no option but to follow.

Celeste felt herself drawn back with the men. She was not going to be the first to get into the fragile wooden vessels, not when the old lady was nowhere to be seen yet. Then a young man, seeing the empty spaces, pushed forward from the back, ready to leap on board. The officers instantly hauled him back. 'Not now, son! Ladies and children first.'

Two lifeboats were lowered down out of sight. Celeste was appalled to see one was almost empty. Still she couldn't move, her eyes constantly searching through the crowds for Mrs Grant.

When the third boat was half full, a sailor caught her arm. 'Time to go, lady,' he ordered.

Celeste froze on the spot. 'I can't!'

'You can and you will,' he said, and wrapping both arms round her waist he dragged her forward and almost threw her into the lifeboat. She landed with a crunch but quickly gathered herself and took a seat. Looking up, she saw some of her fellow passengers standing back with their husbands, shaking their heads as she was being lowered down, past the other decks. There were people hanging out of portholes desperately waving for help but the descending boat didn't stop to take them on board.

She daren't look at the drop. The boat swung violently and children cried out in fear. They landed on the sea with a great slap and she saw the icebergs looming like blue mountains, one with a twin peak, beautiful but sinister, and felt their chill on the frozen water. Only as they rowed away did she see the unnatural angle of the great ship, its electric lights glowing from every deck and porthole. Only then did she hear the ragtime music played by Mr Hartley's band shift into more sombre tunes coming floating over the air. Only then did she realize she was saved, while all those remaining were doomed. And only then, when she felt the stinging of her ankle and the last bars of the haunting music, did she finally realize that this was no dream but a nightmare about to begin.

9

Clutching Ellen to his chest, Joe pushed May back in the direction from which they'd come and they gradually made their way through the maze of corridors, through an unlocked door and up onto the deck above. There were people standing around in queues and May could hear music somewhere above them. There were no lifeboats on this deck.

A man in uniform opened another gate into First Class and ordered the women to make for the grand stairs to the upper deck, but the men forced their way through, not wanting to be separated from their terrified families.

They were walking through a terrible fairyland. Chandeliers swayed, beautiful carpets ran as far as the eye could see and there was hardly a soul about. Stewards rushed to and fro, pointing them ever upwards. Joe's eyes were out on stalks. This was another world. There were men in evening dress, smoking, ignoring the stampede, the frantic cries for directions; some were playing cards as if there were all the time in the world to finish their game as the large gilded clock on the mantelpiece struck two o'clock.

May could feel the ship lurch at an alarming angle. Precious glassware was smashing around them, table lights were knocked over, chairs were sliding away. Through the golden lounge and the Palm Court they continued. Up above she could hear ragtime music playing. Where *was* everyone?

'I don't like this, Joe.'

'Just keep moving, love. I've got Ellen safe. Better to do what they say. I'm sure it's all organized up top.'

Suddenly they felt a rush of cold air as they found themselves up on the boat deck among a crowd of people clinging to each other, crying.

'Where are the lifeboats?' said Joe, staring up at the empty davits.

'You may well ask, laddie,' replied a gruff Scottish voice. 'They've all gone ... not enough for the likes of us.'

The ship lurched deeper again. May clung to Joe, trying not to panic.

'What do we do now?' She couldn't bear to think of what lay ahead. The thought of swimming in the dark water was terrifying, but to stay and drown ...

'There's boats on the port side,' yelled a passenger. 'Come on, follow me!' It was hard straining against the slope, trying to stay together. When they reached the other side, they found no lifeboats but some men were trying to release some collapsible boats without success.

'Go back to starboard. There's collapsibles there,' ordered a seaman, pointing at May and the baby in surprise. 'Women and kiddies should've gone ages ago!'

Joe tugged May back from the crowd but she remained rigid. 'This is no good ... there's nowt left for us, is there?' she cried as panic rose in her throat. How long before the vessel would tip into the sea, throwing them all into the freezing water?

'There's got to be boats. They wouldn't leave us in danger ... not with little kiddies!' Joe cried grim-faced, clasping Ellen closer. Struggling to stand upright as the ship pitched once more, he yelled, 'We're going to jump, May. Ellen's safe with me. I've tied her into my coat. We must go now while there're lifeboats close enough to pull us in!'

'I'm not going anywhere without you!' she screamed, her eyes wide in terror at the sight of the sea edging ever closer towards them.

10

Celeste watched the drama unfolding, her eyes locked onto the stricken ship as it slid further and further towards its final descent. She didn't even feel the chill in the air as her heart pounded at the sight of men leaping into the water and trying to swim.

'We've got to get away before it sucks us all in,' screamed a woman clutching her Pekinese dog to her chest. 'We don't want them scrabbling into the boat and capsizing us.'

'But we must rescue people! This boat's not full,' Celeste insisted. 'There's plenty of space. We can't just row away and leave them.'

'I'm not having steerage passengers sitting next to me,' the woman continued. 'You never know what you might catch.'

Celeste couldn't believe what she was hearing. This very woman had sat in the same row as her that morning, sharing her hymn sheet. They had sung 'Eternal Father, strong to save'.

'Don't listen to her nonsense,' Celeste yelled. 'We have to help these poor souls.'

But the men rowed faster away from the ship with determined looks on their faces.

The noise of the doomed passengers, the screams, the roar of spluttering engines grew ever louder. Floating debris bobbed around them, the wreckage of deck chairs, baggage, planks of wood torn from the decks, terrible reminders of what had once been this ship, clogging up the path to safety for those still thrashing towards them in the water.

'Oh, stop! Please, in the name of all that's merciful, stop. We have to wait for them. What if it was your wife or child or husband? Would you leave them to die?' Celeste yelled, hoping to shame the sailors into turning round.

One by one the men slowly lifted their oars and the lifeboat began to drift towards the sinking ship. Celeste bowed her head in relief. Perhaps now there was a chance of saving more lives.

11

May froze with panic at the choices before them. The sea was slowly creeping up, deck after deck submerged, and her ears were filled with the screams of the frantic passengers scrambling for safety. Others were kneeling, praying, holding hands, waiting to be saved by a miracle that would never come.

'We're going to have to make a jump for it, love.' Joe grabbed her hand.

'I can't!' She was shaking with terror but Joe was adamant.

'Jump! For Ellen's sake. She deserves a chance. Hold my hand and we'll jump together. Only God can save us now,' he coaxed. The surface of the water lapped ever closer.

'But I can't swim.'

'Yes, you can. I taught you. The jacket'll hold you up. You must try.'

'I can't.'

'We can together. We didn't come all this way to die like rats.'

His words were stirring up fury in her. Die? Who said anything about dying? This was not how they were going to end their lives, thrown into the vast ocean. She could see what had happened to those who had jumped first. The water was full of floating life jackets with no life left in them. But Joe was right: they had to jump. They were going into the sea one way or another.

'Hold my hand and good luck, but if luck's not on our side, I'll see you in paradise. No one will separate us there.'

A wave rose from nowhere, washing over them, throwing them clear of the ship. The frozen water pierced May with icy darts, taking her breath clean away as she spluttered for the surface, her eyes searching in the dark for Joe.

She tried to scream, thrashing in her clumsy effort to stay afloat. The jacket miraculously held her up. The roar of the rising water in her eardrums drowned out all coherent sound. Her arms were like useless propellers and the weight of her clothes impeded her limbs as she thrashed away from the ship. She had to keep sight of them but it was so dark, and she was so very cold.

In slow motion she thought she saw an outline, a head, but there were so many people in the water, some face down, floating like flotsam. Then her limbs tried to swim, suddenly freed in a frenzy of panic, but they were like lead weights, her strokes powerless to propel her forward as the icy water held her in its iron vice. She gasped for breath and bobbed on the water, desperately searching for Joe. He was drifting further and further from her grasp. She paddled on like an automaton, using every last ounce of her body's strength. She caught another glimpse of Joe's head bobbing and little Ellen floating away like a bundle of rags on the surface. May tried desperately to catch up with them. Ellen was slipping out of reach and Joe's head had suddenly disappeared. She must reach her baby. 'I'm coming!' she tried to yell but her mouth was filling with salt water, muffling her cries, choking her. She was starting to feel drowsy and limp, her hope ebbing, her efforts weakening.

There was only darkness and death, empty faces with eyes staring up at the cruel stars. The water was awash with barrels, bottles, trunks, coal scuttles, plant pots, deck chairs. She couldn't push past them, she couldn't find Joe.

'Take me now, pull me under, Lord,' she prayed. What was the point of living if they'd gone ahead without her? 'I'm coming! I'm coming.' Her voice was getting weaker but the life jacket held her firm in its grip as she floated further and further from the spot where she last saw her family. Her fingers were numb, too cold to grasp the surrounding debris; lifebelts drifted by, useless, as the chill began to squeeze the life out of her. The light faded from her eyes and her voice was reduced to a whisper as she gave herself up to the sea.

12

The lifeboat edged further into the wreckage and a torch was shone through the gloom to search for any survivors.

'There's one here! Her lips are moving. She's just a slip of a thing.' The sailor hooked the floating body closer to the side and another member of the crew helped pull her into the boat.

Celeste forgot her own chill as she stepped across to help rub life into the girl. Her eyes opened briefly and she tried to shake her head, muttering words of protest.

'No, no ... baby's in the water ... Go and find them! Joe ... Let me go!' Celeste hurriedly covered her with a spare blanket. 'No,' the girl whispered. 'Go back ... my baby ... Let me go ... Joe, we're coming.' She tried to sit up, her hand rigid, her clenched fingers unable to point.

'Put her down in the bottom with the dead one. Look at the state of her. She's not going to last long.'

'No, I'll look after her,' Celeste insisted. 'She's got a baby in the water. For God's sake, stop and find it.'

'Shut that bloody woman up, will you!' said a voice from under a shawl.

'We'll never get away if we keep picking up waifs and strays! They'll capsize us all!' the woman with the dog ranted once again.

'You shut up, you selfish bitch! Call yourself a Christian?

Don't be so cruel,' Celeste barked back with such confidence and vehemence she surprised herself. 'This poor soul's lost everything and you just sit there with your pet dog on your lap. We must go back and find more of them.'

'I'm sorry, ma'am, this is as far as we can go. The ship's going down now and we don't want to be sucked down with it,' the crewman was shouting. 'We've found some. How this one managed to survive so long beats me, but enough's enough. I can't risk the rest of us. Row on!'

The girl was shivering, crying as Celeste wrapped another blanket around her. 'Sit tight, now . . . Be British, be brave, you're safe here.' The warmth of human touch in the darkness was all she could offer. 'We must all stay calm.'

It was while she was nursing the girl that there came another commotion from the water and an arm stretched out, dumping a sodden blanket into the lap of a shaking boy. 'Take the child!' a gruff voice shouted. Celeste thought she caught sight of a white beard in the lantern light.

'It's the captain . . . Sir! Captain Smith. We can take you aboard,' yelled a sailor, reaching out to the man in the water.

The arm hovered for a second and then withdrew. 'Good luck, lads, do your duty.'

Silence followed.

'Give the bairn to its ma,' the sailor shouted, and suddenly the bundle was passed down the boat into the girl's arms, swathed in dry blankets. The girl clung to the baby with relief, suddenly roused from her stupor, groping in the darkness for the baby's face, fingering her frozen cheek, listening for every breath. She cried with relief on hearing the baby whimper.

God in His mercy had reunited them! Celeste thought. What a wonderful thing to see amidst the horrors of the night. What if this had been Roddy? Thank goodness she had not brought him on her travels. For once Grover was right to withhold his consent. How could she ever have lived with herself if he had been lost?

Celeste strained to see in the darkness, leaning over the boat's side, knowing so many babies and their families were in the icy water. How many more would survive the night? One thing was sure, after this terrifying ordeal, after what she had just seen, life would never be the same for her again.

13

May clutched her baby for dear life, barely able to believe, through her stupor, that such a miracle had happened. Now, relief jolted her back into life, the numbness replaced by a stinging pain. In the darkness she could feel the baby was warm, alive, her breathing soft as she slept. If only she could peel back the layers and kiss her downy cheek, but the chill off the Atlantic was too raw for her safely to disturb the blankets.

She smelled of the sea, oil, salt. She looked up to see stars shooting across the midnight-blue sky and thanked God her darling girl had been saved. There was mercy after all.

'How can such a terrible thing be happening on such a beautiful night?' whispered the girl by her side, her auburn hair trailing under her black hat. Together they watched the ship rising up in its death throes, silhouetted against the sky like a black finger accusing the heavens of a great treachery. Then came more terrible screams as passengers threw themselves off the vessel, swimming, thrashing, drowning, crying for their mothers, to God, to the saints for mercy. May knew she'd be hearing those voices for as long as she lived.

'Go back, please, go back!' the women both cried. 'My husband's in the sea ...' May insisted.

'So is half the ship,' yelled one of their crew. 'We've done our bit. It's too dangerous. All hope is lost now.'

May turned her back. She couldn't bear to watch any longer

as she nuzzled the baby into her chest, trying to blot out the cries.

'For God's sake, help them!' the woman next to her cried out. 'Have you no hearts?'

'Shut up! You've got your bairn. We can't take on any more, we'll capsize.'

'Save your strength, lady, it's going to be a long night,' a hoarse voice ordered.

The girl in black slumped forward, silently shivering as they watched two funnels of the great leviathan collapse. The ship was snapping in two, one half slipping underwater, the other rearing up like a pointing finger before it slid smoothly into the deep as if it was the most natural thing in the world. May rocked her baby back and forth, grateful for the warmth and comfort of her.

If Ellen was safe there was hope for Joe too, May reasoned. Her heart lightened at this thought. *Yea though I walk through the valley of the shadow of death, I will fear no evil,* she prayed for those lost souls, trusting Joe must be on another lifeboat. She looked up again and strained to listen as the watery screams grew fainter. There followed an awesome silence.

'They're all gone,' whispered the young woman next to her. 'Their pain is over, but ours is only beginning, I fear. The crew didn't mean to shout at you. Fear makes us do terrible things. Thank God your baby is safe. Come on, chaps, row us to the other boats. Someone out there must be looking for us.'

'Aye aye, lady, they will that, and all the boats must stick together,' shouted the sailor in charge of their lifeboat as the lantern swung slowly across the prow.

Soon they made a silent flotilla of bobbing boats strung together like toy ships on a great millpond. Slowly the dawn was breaking. May had never felt so cold. Somehow the baby slept on. Hours went by when there was nothing but ice and the lapping of the oars on the water. She felt the chill numbing all sensation in her limbs. It was hard not to drift into sleep. In her mind's eye she could see Joe swimming, being lifted into a lifeboat, alive out there just as she was, searching, praying they would soon be united. She clung to this hope like a life raft.

'Keep awake, everyone. Don't go to sleep or you might not wake up,' a warning went out. It was hard not to surrender to sleep, to blissful ignorance, but May was on guard, watching for any change in her baby's breathing. Every time her head nodded she jerked it back. Then suddenly there were shouts of a light on the horizon, a real light this time, not a false dawn, and a rocket arced into the night sky.

'They're coming! Look over there; a ship is coming! Wake up! We're saved!'

14

Celeste tried to coax her frozen limbs back to life. For a few precious minutes she'd held the baby girl for the mother while she rubbed her icy hands and tried to thaw them. How could a baby sleep through such drama? She had no idea what a miracle child she was. Had it really been the captain who'd saved her? He had made no attempt to rescue himself.

'About bloody time!' shouted an old lady with a shawl round her head that 'she' no longer bothered using to conceal the beard on 'her' chin: another spineless wonder who had jumped ship to save his skin, Celeste thought, sickened. How she despised such cowards, along with the woman who edged herself away from the mother and baby as if she suspected they had fleas.

Celeste watched the chunks of iceberg all around them, transfixed by the beauty of the growlers. As the sun rose they sparkled like jewels, among them the monster that had caused the disaster. How cruel was nature in bringing them so low with such magnificence.

The sea began to swell and toss them from side to side as if to challenge this rescue attempt. The ship was coming closer. Celeste wrapped her own dry blanket round the baby. How had it come to this?

'Are you all right?' she whispered to May. 'Shall I take the baby?'

'Thank you, but no. You have been so kind. I don't even know your name.'

'My name is Celestine Parkes. I was on my way home. And this little one?' she asked, touching the baby's arm.

'This is Ellen and I am May Smith. My husband, Joe, will be on another lifeboat. We're heading out to the Midwest and he's got the address and everything.'

The poor girl was not taking in what had happened to them at all, Celeste realized. The chances of her husband being picked up would be slim. 'How will you manage?'

'We'll get by,' May Smith whispered to the baby in her lap. 'We'll be all right.'

Only as the dawn light brightened and the ship on the horizon loomed large did May relax her grip of the blankets that swaddled Ellen so securely. She was so tiny, she thought, as if she had shrunk in the water, and still she slept on. Better not disturb her. When Joe met up with them she'd have such a story to tell him: how she was dragged from the water half dead and the baby rescued not five minutes later. She felt so tired and weary and her whole body ached as she shivered. One glimpse of her daughter would bring her back to life.

As the light flooded into the lifeboat she pulled back the blankets framing her tiny face to see if she was awake.

The eyes staring back at her shone like coal. Eyes she'd never seen in her life before. Ellen's eyes were blue. Swallowing the scream that rose in her throat she pulled the blanket back down over the face again to blot out the discovery, her heart thumping with horror. This isn't her, she thought in horror. It's not my baby!

No one was taking any notice of May; they were too busy cheering on the rescue ship. She looked again, only to see those strange eyes peeking out from a lace bonnet, piercing her soul. She examined the baby's face minutely to make sure she wasn't dreaming. From what she could see of its clothes under the swaddle of blankets, they were different from Ellen's too.

May sat back shaking as the great ocean liner steamed towards them. This wasn't right. This was not how it should be: *The Lord gives and the Lord takes but not from me. Is this His idea of a joke, this gift of life from the sea? Was this the captain's last act of courage, to put a stranger's baby in my lap? Where is my own baby? I want her back.*

She stared behind her to all that was gone, to the murderous sea so calm and treacherous and then at the face staring up at her, wide-eyed, questioning: Who are you? This baby was all there was, this child of the sea, someone's daughter or son.

What do I do? Oh, please God, what do I do now?

Celeste watched the ship racing towards them with mounting excitement. She sighed with relief that their ordeal was almost over. If she lived for a hundred years she would never forget what she'd seen this night. Her escape had been smooth, plenty of time to pile on warm clothes on top of her nightdress, a walk over planks into a descending lifeboat. They'd been warned early by the stewards in First Class, handed life jackets and ushered quickly to safety. She had seen the look in the stewardess's eyes that made her obey her orders, a grimace of a smile and that hesitancy when she asked what was happening.

But what she had just witnessed was obscene, unspeakable suffering. This was the greatest ship on earth on its maiden voyage and yet a hazard of nature had ripped it apart. Amidst the horror had she really seen a baby restored to its mother's arms by the captain? She'd seen a silver beard and white hair – was it really him? Poor man, whoever he was. How could she ever forget him tugging away the arms that would have rescued him? And those final words?

Thank God she hadn't brought Roddy. How she longed to have him in her arms now but he'd be back home, tucked up in his bed, with his nursemaid, Susan, in the next room. Grover would be in his office burning the midnight oil or out on the town somewhere. With God knows who, she thought grimly.

The sea began to swell again, throwing them from side to side.

For a brief second she felt panic, to be close and yet so far from safety. Would she ever see her little boy again? She watched the girl next to her hugging her child, moaning from the chill, calling out the name of her lost husband over and over again. Pain was etched on her stricken face.

At least Celeste's new coat was keeping them both warm, and the fox fur tippet was now wrapped around the girl. She'd pinned her purse into her coat lining alongside her rings and the photos of Roddy she'd brought to show to Papa. How futile possessions seemed now, she reflected.

She looked at the pathetic procession of lifeboats. Why were so many only half full? She'd assumed earlier that other passengers had been on the other side of the ship being loaded up, following behind them but now she realized just how few survivors there appeared to be. So many must have been trapped, so many of the Third Class passengers left to fend for themselves. It wasn't right.

At least their crew had eventually had the heart to linger, pulling out three swimmers before the poor girl whose agony tore at her heart. The young mother was about her own age, a tiny thing, her accent northern. It would be Celeste's duty to see them safely aboard the rescue ship. She would also see that she got good treatment for her frozen hands. A clergyman's daughter knew her responsibilities. It would take her mind off her own sad thoughts.

Mother's funeral seemed far off now. At least she'd been laid to rest with dignity, unlike all those poor frozen souls thrashing in the ice until they thrashed no more and gave up in despair. She hoped what they said about drowning was true, that it was like sleep in the end.

The steerage passengers had been called up too late, anyone could see that; one rule for the rich and another for the poor. It was shameful.

What were her meagre problems now compared to the

women who had watched their husbands drown? She must grit her teeth and return to Akron, to the smell of its chemical factories, back to darling Roddy, back to Grover and the difficulties of their marriage. Her brief respite was over: a funeral and a shipwreck, not much of a holiday.

She had been spared for a purpose. She must swallow any discontent and fear for herself. Shocked as she was, she knew she must bear witness to what she had seen and ask for answers. Why had this disaster happened? How many had died needlessly? Who would be accountable for all this slaughter? But first she must take these two survivors under her wing. It was the proper thing to do and would take her mind off an unholy thought growing inside her.

Celeste looked back to where the *Titanic* had sunk. If her husband had accompanied her, he would now be resting fathoms deep under the ocean. Grover liked to think he was a gentleman. Would he have stepped back like the other husbands and done his duty? She couldn't be sure. How could she be thinking such a terrible thought at such a time? But it was there in her mind and would not be dislodged.

'It's the *Carpathia*! She's come for us.' A weak cheer went up as the big liner steamed to their rescue. Soon they would be safe. Celeste turned to her companion, wondering how on earth they'd get the children and the injured up the ladders to safety. She knew she would stay with her two charges until they did.

17

May sat by the railings on board the *Carpathia*, looking out across the silver expanse of water, alongside the other widows, praying there would be more boats to come. They'd been hoisted up in nets like cargo. She had been too weak and too cold to climb the ropes. Some were frozen in shawls and nightclothes, others dressed in furs clutching bedraggled, bewildered children, wrapped in blankets. All were equal in their suffering here.

There was an eerie silence punctuated by survivors scrabbling from deck to deck asking for news of their kin. 'Have you seen . . . ? Which lifeboat were you in? Did you see my husband?' The foreign women huddled in groups trying to understand their predicament while interpreters waved their arms, pointing out to sea and shaking their heads. May could hear the women screaming when they realized that they were now alone in the world with only the clothes they stood up in.

May sat back in a deck chair, cocooned in blankets, refusing to go below deck. She would sleep outside, if need be. How could she face the bowels of a ship again? She sipped strange coffee laced with spirits, warming her hands on the mug, the searing pain coursing through her fingers as they came back to life.

The girl in the fine coat had never left her side, fetching and carrying for her like a servant until she felt embarrassed. She couldn't even recall her name. Was it Ernestine something? No, no matter . . . She was too tired to think.

She should have spoken up then, told her the truth about the baby, but she couldn't let go of it. The panic of having empty arms overwhelmed her when a nurse came out to take the baby below for a medical examination. May had tried to follow but, overcome with anxiety, had sunk sobbing onto her deck chair. Now the child was back on her lap, clean and dry, and none the worse for her experience, they said. 'Her.' So, a baby girl, then, May noted. The power of those chocolate eyes bore into her heart as she smiled and the baby, wary at first, responded with a toothy grin. This poor little mite would know nothing of their ordeal, remember none of what went before. But May would remember this night for the rest of her life. She knew she would never be able to put it behind her.

Only yesterday she was snug with Joe in their cabin on the way to a new life, and then came those terrifying moments on deck before they were separated. Were Joe and Ellen gone? How cruel it was not to be able to say goodbye to them. There were no tender words of farewell, no kisses, just a frantic thrashing in the water in a desperate bid for life. Was she the only one left now to fend for herself? Her heart was numb with terror. The *Titanic* was indeed a monster swallowing every precious thing she possessed. Out there in the water, Joe and Ellen lay frozen, and in her heart she knew she would never see them again. She had lost her truest friend, her soul mate and their darling child, the flesh of her flesh. She clutched the rails desperately hoping for sight of another boat on the horizon.

She heard other women telling their stories to the crew of the *Carpathia* over and over again as if to make some sense of the terrible night's drama.

Suddenly she heard the din of screaming voices as a mother was pulling a baby from the arms of another woman. 'That's my child! You have my Philly! Give him to me!'

The other woman, a foreigner, was clinging to the child. '*Non! Non! Mio bambino!*'

Then an officer came to separate them. 'What's going on?'

'That woman has my son, Phillip. He was thrown in a lifeboat without me. She has my son!'

A crowd gathered, staring at the two crying women, who were quickly bustled out of sight by the crew. 'Captain Rostron will sort this out in private,' said the officer, who took the screaming baby in his arms and disappeared with it down the stairs, the women howling after him.

Unnerved by the scene, May knew she must take off the baby's lace bonnet and force herself to walk around so people could admire the child's lustrous dark hair and someone might lay claim to her.

'Isn't she lovely, and not a mark on her,' said one couple, who were clinging to each other.

'The captain rescued her himself and put her into the boat after me but he didn't stop. The sailor told me, didn't he?' She looked around for her new friend from the lifeboat to confirm her story but she was out of earshot.

'Did you hear that? Captain Smith saved the baby. He deserves a medal,' said another woman, patting the baby's curls.

May walked round every corner of the deck showing off the child, but no one claimed her as their own So it began right there, the slow realization that she could keep the little orphan. The baby was younger than Ellen, dark-eyed and olive-skinned but perfect.

May found some shelter to unpeel the blankets and examine the dry new layette given to her by passengers on the *Carpathia*. She couldn't help but marvel at its quality. It was fit for a princess, made from fine lawn and merino wool, a lacy jacket and pretty ruffled bonnet, all donated willingly. Her kind befriender promised the baby's original clothes were being laundered for her.

Discreetly, she opened the baby's napkin, shaking with anxiety, but to her utter relief she saw the baby was indeed a girl. The temptation was growing stronger now. Why should she not keep her? A baby needed a mother, not an orphanage full of other children. She should know, she'd been in one herself, later brought up in Cottage Homes outside the town and put into service without a relative who cared for her welfare until she met Joe. What would Joe make of it all? Suddenly she realized he would not be there to help her. *Oh, Joe, what shall I do?* Her mind was numb. She wept into her blanket, knowing she was alone in making this momentous decision.

The icy numbness of the night was wearing off into an aching in all her joints.

She knew when the baby had been declared unharmed by her experience, she should have spoken up to the ship's doctor and confessed her mistake. But still she couldn't spit out the words that would separate them. Perhaps later, when they docked, she would tell the truth, but she knew in her heart the deed was done.

'You were given to me, the captain's gift. It's meant to be, you and me. Mum's the word!' she whispered into the baby's ear. The baby was already nudging May's chest for milk, fidgeting in her blankets and staring up at her in hunger.

'Ella wants a feed,' smiled her new friend, Celeste Parkes. The name suddenly came back to May.

'I've no milk left,' May muttered. Her own child had been weaned months ago.

'I'm not surprised, the shock alone will have stopped your breast milk,' Celeste replied. 'Let me find her a bottle.'

Out of earshot, May bent over the baby. 'I'm not giving you to no strangers after all we've been through together. I'll be taking care of you from now on.'

The ship was heading back towards the site of the disaster. The passengers were warned not to stay on deck and it was raining, but May still refused to go below. She could see white objects bobbing on the horizon: wreckage and bodies. She turned her back on the sea. There was no point tormenting herself. Joe was never coming back, nor little Ellen. She felt sick at the thought of them out there somewhere at the mercy of the waves. How could she leave them and sail away? *How can I live without you both? What shall I do now?*

Suddenly she knew she hadn't the courage to go on to Idaho alone. She couldn't go back to Bolton either. How could she explain the change in Ella's size and colouring? Ella. Mrs Parkes had misheard her name but this suited May. Ella Smith was close enough to the name on her own baby's birth certificate but different enough not to cause a shard of pain to pierce her heart every time she uttered it. Already she was proving adept in planning this terrible deceit.

Her mind was racing now. The two of them must go as far away from the sea as possible and from the memory of this terrible night, somewhere where no one knew them, where she could start over, and live this lie.

Hanging over the railings, she sobbed into the wind. *I have to do this, fill this emptiness in my heart with a bigger secret.* There was no hope for her now, only a lifetime of pain, but Ella was a remedy of sorts. May could hardly breathe for the ache in her ribs, that wave of relief to be alive, yet guilt, fury and loss were drowning her at the same time. She must turn aside from her own grief and live for this baby in her arms. In the purple twilight between darkness and daylight, she stared out to sea, wild-eyed, bewildered like a frightened child watching the sea crash against the ship, her eyes searching for something that was no longer there.

It came to her then that this was the most she could make of life now, a lonely journey carrying such a momentous secret in her heart, crippled with pain and guilt, with only this tiny mite in her arms. Numb as she was, part of her mind was alert, reasoning her actions. *God be with you, my darlings. I hope you understand there's a little one here who needs me now. You will remain in my heart for as long as I live but now I have another purpose.* She had survived to take care of this baby. Ella would be her reason to live.

18

Later on that long morning came the muster roll of survivors.

'Your name?' said the officer, consulting his list, making sure every rescued passenger was accounted for.

'Mary Smith, but I am called May,' said May, hesitating, looking at Celeste. 'My husband, Joseph Smith, is twenty-seven, tall and dark. He's a carpenter.' She looked up hopefully.

He didn't meet her eye. 'The baby?'

'Ellen Smith ... little Ella, we call her. The captain saved her,' she added almost proudly.

'She's right, ask the fireman on our lifeboat. He tried to drag him in ... but he swam off,' Celeste added.

'I see. And you are ...?'

'Celestine Parkes, Mrs Grover Parkes from Akron, Ohio. I was with this lady in the same lifeboat. Do you have a Mrs Grant on board?'

The officer shook his head. 'We've not mustered everyone yet. The *Carpathia* will sweep over the site and then return to New York so I suggest you go down into the dining room and take instruction from there,' he ordered. 'There will be a service of remembrance shortly.'

'But this lady needs new clothes, as you can see,' Celeste insisted.

'The women passengers aboard will see to that when you go below deck. This is no place to be out with a baby,' he insisted. 'Everything you need is down there.'

'Thank you,' Celeste muttered as the officer rushed to another group of survivors.

May was reluctant to descend. 'I can't go down there. I can't move.'

'I'll help you down. Let me take little Ella. She's such a picture,' she said. 'So dark . . . not a bit like you.' Celeste paused, hoping she didn't take offence. May was the sort of girl you would never notice in a crowd. Celeste could read the panic on her face as she relived terrible memories.

'Joe was dark. They said there was gypsy blood way back when the weavers walked,' May replied, not looking at her. It was an effort to say her husband's name out loud.

'Really? Those eyes are as dark as coal. My son, Roderick, is so fair his eyes are almost silver. He's safe at home with his father. I was back in England attending my mother's funeral in Lichfield.' Celeste stopped in her tracks. She didn't normally tell strangers her business but they were hardly strangers now. They had shared the worst a person could face. 'Do call me Celeste . . . I'm afraid my parents got carried away. I was the last, the only girl in a tribe of brothers, and my mother thanked the heavens for my appearance!'

'I'm sorry about your mother. It must be a wrench to live so far from home,' May replied as she gingerly took one step at a time below deck.

'Papa is well cared for with the other retired clergyman in Cathedral Close. I have to go back to be with my little boy. He's only two and I've missed him so much.'

'We were heading out to somewhere in Idaho. I had the address but it's gone now. Where's Akron?' May, clutching the baby, edged down the corridor to a door opening into a vast dining room where people were sitting around looking lost.

'It's in Ohio, close to a city called Cleveland. It's not exactly pretty or ancient, like Lichfield, but I suppose I call it home. America is huge; you'll get used to it.'

'Oh, no, I'm going back to England. I can't stay here, not now,' May replied.

'Don't make any decisions yet. See how things turn out.'

'But I want to go back. There's nothing for us here. This was Joe's dream, never mine.' Her lip trembled. She'd never felt so alone, so far away from all she knew. 'They'll give us a return ticket, won't they?'

'I'm sure they will.' Celeste could see the panic on her face and wanted to comfort her. 'Don't look so worried. I'll help you. The White Star Line must compensate you for your loss. Now I must go in search of news of Mrs Grant . . . I do hope she survived.'

'Thank you, you've been so kind.' May started to shake again and Celeste found her a corner to sit down. 'Joe had such plans. I can't believe this is happening. What did we do to deserve this, Celestine?'

'We did nothing but trust ourselves to the good offices of the White Star Line. They will have to account in a court of law for all this. Now you must rest. You'll feel more yourself with fresh clothes and a warm bath. I'll go with Ella and see if my old lady was rescued. Your baby's safe with me and may possibly tug some heartstrings for information.'

'No!' May shouted. 'I mean, please, the baby stays with me. I don't want to let her out of my sight.' May clutched the bundle of blankets for dear life. 'Thank you kindly, ma'am, but we'll stay put.'

The poor girl couldn't let Ella out of her sight. It must be the shock, Celeste thought as she went back on deck. Looking up, she saw that the ship's flag flew at half mast. Soon they would all be gathering down below for the remembrance service. She didn't envy the person having to lead such a sorrowful gathering but the dead must be honoured.

19

May was glad to be alone, away from prying questions, however kindly meant. Celeste's offer to take Ella had rattled her resolve. Should she disappear, take Ella to the purser's office and confess her mistake? Should she give up the baby and hide away from the world with just her grief for company? She could claim her dreadful error was brought about by shock. There would be no harm done and she needn't face the lady again. Celestine. What a name to have to cart around.

She kept bouncing the baby on her knee, barely hoping someone would recognize her but no one did, walking past with dazed looks on their faces. *She has no one and you have no one, where's the harm in passing her off as your own?* The battle for and against keeping Ella raged in May's mind like a fever. They had to salvage something out of this terrible event. If Ella was orphaned, she might be adopted by rich Americans and given every luxury far beyond May's means. What did she have? She had nothing to offer her but love.

But what if the baby was dumped in an orphanage? They would do their best for her but house mothers were busy and surrounded by needy children. There was never enough attention to go around. May could all too easily recall the pushing and shoving, the second-hand toys, the same grey uniform and regimented routines. Even hair was bobbed and cropped to save time. No one was going to cut off these beautiful black curls.

May took a deep breath. What was done was done. There was no going back now.

20

After the remembrance service, the survivors crowded together in the First Class saloon. May and Celeste stood in silence with the other shocked passengers and crew. It was whispered that some survivors had died on the ship and would be buried later in the afternoon. Celeste, who'd had no information so far, made for the purser's office to check once again if anyone had heard of Mrs Grant. The news was good. She was somewhere in the ship's infirmary suffering from exposure. Celeste rushed to visit her but the old lady was asleep under sedation. Then she made for the laundry, collected Ella's dry clothes and was given a bright dress from one of the *Carpathia*'s passengers, a soft woollen garment with darted bodice that fitted her like a glove. She swapped it for her own black garment, which was pressed and sponged down. Instinctively Celeste knew that May, so recently widowed, would prefer to wear mourning rather than the brighter colour, and Celeste was willing to pass on to her the warm and dry black dress.

She clutched the baby clothes and sniffed the fresh scent of clean laundry. How could plain little May have produced such a beauty? How she longed for a chance to have another child of her own but Grover was adamant that one son and heir was an elegant sufficiency.

Their life in Akron seemed so far away. She thought back to when they'd met in London, at a dinner party given by her grandfather, a retired bishop, in London, for visiting American Episcopalians. Grover had been on a business trip for the Diamond Rubber Company and had come along with a friend, sweeping her off her feet with roses and gifts, putting a ring on her finger before she had a chance to blink, and had her on the first ship to New York. It all seemed such a long time ago.

All marriages take time to settle down, but theirs was taking longer than most. Their worlds were far apart but Roddy was such a joy. She must wire to tell them she was safe but how would Grover understand what she'd just been through? The screams of those drowning souls would echo in her ears for the rest of her days. The sight of the sinking ship flashed before her eyes as if it was still happening. How could things ever be the same after this?

As Celeste passed through the dining room she noticed a group of women sitting round on the floor, wrapped in furs and paisley shawls, listening to a large woman holding forth.

'Now, ladies, we can't just sit here and do nothing. Before we leave this ship we must form a committee and make some firm resolutions. This disaster is going to shake the world and heads must roll for what went on last night. Here are all these poor souls without a stitch on their backs, not a cent in their pockets. Who's going to see they get justice? How will they make out when we dock in New York if we don't get to work right now?'

'But, Mrs Brown, the White Star Line is responsible for their welfare, not us,' said another lady, standing by her side.

The stout woman shook her head and held up her hand. 'I've known what it's like not to have a dime to my name. America can make men rich or make beggars of them. I was lucky, my husband struck gold, but I know one thing: if you don't shout, you don't get!'

Celeste moved closer. The woman was on fire with indignation, voicing just the sort of sentiments she was feeling herself. Surprisingly she felt bold enough to add her tuppence worth.

'You're so right. I was on a boat where a poor woman was dragged from the sea. Everything she possesses is gone – her husband, their tickets, their money. Her baby was rescued, praise the Lord, but she is destitute.'

Mrs Brown turned towards the new arrival and smiled. 'There, you see . . . Welcome. Don't you just love that accent? Come and join us, sister. We need women like you to stand up and be counted. Who will thank Captain Rostron and the crew of the *Carpathia* if we don't? Who will see that the immigrants get recompensed, if not us? When we land, it's going to be chaos at first. Everyone will want to help now, but when the poor souls disperse, someone has to follow up and see that their needs are met.'

'But, Margaret, dear, isn't it too soon to be taking responsibility for such things? The government will want to do that,' said a First Class passenger wrapped in fox furs.

'Ethel, the government is an ass! Pardon my French. It's women who do the caring. Always have, always will. We must make sure that no one goes hungry because of this disaster. Kids must get a proper education. How many pas have been lost, rich ones as well as poor? How many orphans has the *Titanic* made? Who'll bury those poor frozen bodies of the poor? It all needs a woman's compassion. Charity can be awful cold. I'll pass round a paper. Sign your names, add your addresses and what you are prepared to do and give for the unfortunates amongst us.'

'But some of us have lost everything too,' one woman sobbed.

'I know, sister, but the good Lord helps those who help themselves. It's better to get organized now, before we all scatter to the far corners of this great country of ours. You must spread the word, sisters! Tell your story and get the tins rattling. Doing something is better than weeping into your coffee.'

Celeste started to clap, enthused by Margaret Brown's rousing words. She couldn't stand by and not get involved, not when she had seen how bad things were for the sick and destitute on board. There were those so shocked they wandered around like ghosts. How would they ever stand up for themselves?

When the impromptu meeting dispersed, Mrs Brown made her way to Celeste, a beaming smile on her face. 'And where're you heading, sister?'

'Back to Akron, Ohio. I like what you said. I'd like to help,' Celeste replied.

'I heard there are some poor folks heading for Rubber Town who lost their menfolk. We lost Walter Douglas of Quaker Oats fame. His wife is over there, do you know her?' She pointed to a woman weeping in a corner. 'Still in shock but she'll come round. I want to make sure we thank the crew properly, not just some letter but a real token of our appreciation,' she added.

'Like a medal, perhaps?' Celeste offered.

'You've got it! A medal struck for each of the crew presented at a ceremony . . . not now, of course. It'll take some organizing . . . you interested?' Margaret Brown fixed her with a look that demanded no excuses.

'But I live in Ohio.'

'So? I'm out west . . . There are trains. We'll hold another meeting before we leave. Welcome aboard. You are . . . ?'

'Mrs Grover Parkes.'

'But who are you? First names only on my watch . . .'

'Celestine Rose . . . Celeste . . .' She hesitated, nervous now about what she was letting herself in for.

'What a heavenly name,' Margaret Brown chuckled as she led her round the room chatting to other supporters. 'You're English. There's a lot of them on board, see if you can corner them and don't take no for an answer. If they won't help, at least get a donation off them or an address where we can badger them later with our appeal.'

Celeste sighed at this gutsy larger-than-life lady who was making a beeline for the Astor contingent. The confidence was bursting out of her.

If only she could be more like that, she mused. If only she didn't feel every ounce of her own self worth had been ground out of her over these past years by Grover's constant criticism. He'd take one look at Mrs Brown and dismiss her as an interfering do-gooder with more money than sense. Well, he was wrong. She was the sort of woman who got things done and Celeste would be sticking close to her no matter what, hoping some of that brash, go-getting confidence might rub off on herself.

21

May was dozing when Celeste returned and she awoke with a start. She fingered the two-piece black dress folded over Celeste's arm with a sigh. 'How can I ever thank you? What lovely cloth.'

Celeste said nothing about how important it was to Grover that she dressed to suit her station in life. She must always look like a suitable consort to a successful businessman, clad in only the best fabrics and trimmings. Appearance was everything to Grover, Celeste thought darkly. And as the *Titanic* so terribly demonstrated, appearances could be deceptive.

'Let's see how it fits you. We can always take up the hem.'

May hung back. 'There are women walking round in skirts made out of blankets over there. This is too good for me.'

'Nonsense. Here are the baby's clothes, all spick and span. The lace on her nightdress is exquisite. It's hand done, and the bonnet too . . . Are you a lacemaker?'

May looked up. 'Oh, that,' she said flatly. 'It was a gift. I was once in service in Lostock outside Bolton to the wife of a cotton mill owner. When she heard about the baby, she gave me a load of stuff. It must be one of hers.' May amazed herself with the speed and confidence with which she concocted this dreadful lie. She'd never seen such fancy lace in her life.

'They look like heirlooms. I haven't seen anything like it before.'

'I suppose it is rather grand for a little 'un,' May blushed. 'I'll be right now, I reckon. Go and get yourself some tea. You've been so kind. We'll manage somehow.'

Celeste was not easily shifted, however. 'We started this together so we'll finish it too. I have all the time in the world. You need help and information. I can find you a place to stay in New York. You've enough on your plate with Ella to see to.'

'Are you always this bossy?' May smiled, revealing a row of crooked teeth.

'Only when I'm right,' the lady replied, smiling. 'I surprise myself sometimes. I'd like you to get those hands checked over again.' She took hold of May's hands and inspected the swollen fingers. 'A warm bath might ease them. I can see to Ella. She's such a darling, how old is she?'

'A year in May,' May answered swiftly and then wished she hadn't.

'Really? She's very small. Roddy was twice her size at that age.'

'She was a seven monther, a tiny thing at birth and so she is a bit behind others.' How could she let such lies trip off her tongue?

'I'd love a little girl. Perhaps one day . . .' Celeste looked wistful and far away. 'Roddy's nearly three. They grow so fast, don't they? Don't forget to wire your family back home to tell them that you are safe.'

'We've no family, not now, not ever. There were just the three of us. Ella's all I've got left.'

'Oh, that's terrible and so unfair. I'm so sorry. But there's your relative in Idaho.'

'Uncle George? I've never met him. He bought the ticket for us but Joe had everything in his coat.' Tears were welling up in her eyes now. 'I don't even know exactly where we were going. Isn't that terrible? Joe did everything like that. I didn't really want to come.' The tears flowed down her cheeks unchecked.

'Let it out, May. You need to cry. You've held yourself together so bravely. If this Uncle George sponsored you, officials will have his address. I'll make sure they know.'

'I don't deserve your kindness, Celeste. I'm making a fool of myself,' May sniffed.

'Don't be silly. They're holding a special burial service for those who've died on the ship. I think we should go. It will help. My father's a clergyman and he says saying goodbye helps. Standing side by side together we can support each other.'

'Oughtn't you to be up there?' May looked to where many First Class passengers were gathered in groups, talking, smoking.

'May, we're in this together.' Celeste held out her hand. It was too much for May and she cried again.

'Joe's never coming back, is he?'

'There's always hope. Maybe another ship picked survivors up.'

May sighed and swallowed her tears. 'He's gone. I can feel it here,' she whispered, touching her heart. 'I should have gone with them.'

'Don't say that! Think of Ella. She needs you more than ever now.'

May fingered the baby's head and whispered, 'You're right. Every baby needs a mother. I may not be your flesh and blood,' she sighed, looking into the little stranger's eyes, 'but I'll do my best.'

22

Lower Manhattan

He was going to be late for his shift but Angelo Bartolini lingered, putting the finishing touches to his apartment off Baxter Street. He'd been counting off the days on his Holy Saints calendar. He couldn't wait to see Maria again, and meet his new baby daughter, but he didn't want her to be disappointed with the two rooms so he was giving them a lick of paint.

His uncle Salvi and aunt Anna had helped him furnish the tiny home with a bed, a crib, a table, two chairs and a cabin chest for their clothes. It had to be finished before their arrival on Wednesday. As he stood back to admire his handiwork, he smiled. This was as grand as a palace, with new lace curtains waiting to be hung, and a bowl of fresh fruit from Salvi's stall on Mulberry Street. Everything had to be perfect for their reunion.

He fingered the postcard in his dungarees pocket. There was a picture of the most magnificent ship in the world; his wife and baby were travelling to New York in style to begin their new life together. It was such a good omen for their future happiness.

How long they'd put off this reunion, first because of the baby and then because he wanted only the best for his wife. They would not be sharing rooms with anyone else. The Mulberry District was noisy, dusty, full of their compatriots trying to scratch a living. The streets of New York might be paved with gold but it was the Italians who had to do the paving.

The bustle of the streets was shocking to him at first, so different from their Tuscan village. Buildings towered over him and he could hardly breathe in the stale air. The heat, the smells, the crush of bodies lying on the floor, all of it was unbearable. It was tough, but Angelo survived long enough to see the opportunities in the New York streets. He helped Salvi's friend on a building site as a stevedore, up scaffolding where he caught the breeze off the Hudson. He had a natural head for heights and found steady work and regular pay.

His original idea had been to make money and eventually return home to Italy but Maria had begged to join him to see America for herself. He missed her so much he couldn't argue and, scrimping and saving, he'd got together the fare, found rooms and now – finally – his dream was coming true.

For his beautiful wife nothing was too good, and he clung to his crucifix and crossed himself, praying to the Saints that they would settle in this new life. He'd seen such pitiful sights in the back streets, widows and children picking rags, living in cubbyholes in stairwells.

When he was eight storeys high working on tenement sites by day, he could see where families perched in shacks on the rooftops, lying on the roof in the heat of the night, unable to breathe in the sweating streets of downtown.

How many hopes and dreams died right there after an outbreak of typhoid fever? He wasn't going to bring his family to squalor, not after the beautiful Tuscan countryside they'd been used to. He wanted only the best for them. With reluctance, he put down his brush and rushed out into the streets to start the working day.

Later, as Angelo worked suspended above the Manhattan streets, his mind kept drifting to all the preparations still to be made. There would be a family feast. Anna and her daughters would see to that, but he must go to the grocery store and fill the cupboard.

'Angelo! Careful!' someone warned. His concentration was drifting away from safety by the sight of someone running down Mulberry Street, shouting. The word '*Titanico*' drifted up and he saw women in aprons and smocks gathering in Mulberry Bend, men frantically turning pages of newspapers.

'What's going on?' he shouted to his workmate. Rocco shrugged his shoulders but another of his gang yelled across to them. 'They're saying a ship's gone down ... the *Titanic*'s gone down ...'

Angelo went ice cold, throwing his tool bag over his shoulder as he shinned down the scaffold and raced after the crowds. The blood was pulsing in his temples and he was sweating with anxiety. On the corner he saw the newspaper heading on a billboard and sank to his knees with joy. '*TITANIC* SUNK; ALL SAVED!' If it was in the paper it must be true. The newspapers wouldn't lie.

Nevertheless, Angelo kept on running, following the news-hungry crowd to the queue gathering outside the White Star Line office on Broadway, spilling across to Bowling Green Park opposite. Everyone wanted news, any news, but the rumours going round gave no comfort and Angelo's English seemed to have frozen in his panic and he couldn't catch just what was being said.

'*Per favore* ... please, what news?' he kept repeating, cap in hand, trying not to shake. Faces that had been relieved at first later reappeared full of strain. '*Molti morti* ... many dead. She is sunk, we think, but the rescue ship is coming in tonight. There's still hope ...'

He daren't move from the queue in case there was more news and eventually a list of survivors was pinned to the board. The day gradually darkened and news of the *Carpathia*'s unexpected return spread from mouth to mouth. Only relatives of passengers could go down to the harbour to claim their loved ones.

'*Per favore*, what I do?' he kept asking anyone who would listen. You wait, you pray, you stay calm and you hope, said the voice in his head. But how could he stay calm knowing his wife and baby were on that ship?

Long before dark, crowds began to gather in their thousands by Pier 54 waiting for the tragedy to unfold, spectators wanting a ringside seat. The police had prepared barriers. Only those with relatives on board were given chits with permission to wait closer in. Clutching his yellow ticket, shivering in the rain, Angelo was led with the others towards the harbour docking bays. The streets, already bursting with onlookers, curious and anxious to see the ship's return, backed up with even more people. Rich and poor stood shoulder to shoulder, all greedy for a sighting of the rescue ship, while ambulances, limousines and cabs lined up with hearses. The sight of the black vehicles chilled Angelo's very bones.

Alongside the nurses and doctors were the black-robed nuns of the Sisters of Charity and the familiar priests of Old St Patrick's Cathedral, who held out their hands in support and comfort.

'Now then, Angelo, have a brave heart. All shall be well.' Father Bernardo gave his blessing as he saw him.

There was a woman standing in front of him already keening in a high-pitched voice, tearing at her clothes, unable to control her grief. Angelo moved away from her, unnerved. It made him feel sick to his stomach.

It wasn't very long ago that he'd made this voyage himself, a stranger tossing about on the ocean, wondering what the hell he was doing leaving his beloved country. Now he was standing on this dark wet night, praying his wife and daughter were both safe on board, praying this nightmare would end with his arms around them.

Across the water every small boat seemed to be making its way to the Ambrose Light to await the first glimpse of the rescue ship. The sea was choppy but the mist and fog were lifting ahead. A cry went up that the *Carpathia* was on the horizon, a huge black hulk with one smoking chimney silhouetted in the far distance. 'Ship ahoy!' went through the crowds straining for a sighting.

Angelo stamped the life back into his feet through his wet shoes and hugged himself, trying not to shiver. He clutched the crucifix round his neck as a talisman. *Oh please, God, keep them safe.*

23

Buffeted by strong gusts and pelting rain, after a long journey delayed by fog, the *Carpathia* chugged through the storm, through the narrow straits into New York Harbour. May and Celeste stared out over the choppy waters, watching a line of small boats sounding their welcome. Reporters were holding up cardboard messages asking questions and offering to pay for survivors' stories. Flashlights exploded from photographers straining to get the first pictures of the *Titanic* survivors. On deck, neither of them spoke but looked out with dull eyes on the spectacle as the ship edged ever closer to the pier head.

'We're going to be a big attraction,' Celeste said eventually, but May wasn't listening, lost in her own thoughts. This should have been the most exciting moment of her life. Joe would have been hanging over the edge, pointing out the city skyline. But she felt nothing now, seeing those tall buildings and bridges dotted along the night sky, nothing but an aching weariness. She didn't want to be an object of pity or curiosity. All she wanted to do was to catch the first boat back to England, but that wouldn't be possible for days. She had only the borrowed clothes on her back and the bundle of her own garments. There was nothing in her pockets to pay for even a meal.

Survivors were summoned to muster points. There were over seven hundred of them squeezed on board. Now they were to be divided up according to their tickets. Celeste would be getting off first, leaving for her life back home far away. May would have to fend for herself.

As if reading her mind Celeste linked her arm through May's. 'Don't worry, I'm not leaving you, I'll stay here and see you settled. We have to find you lodgings. If Akron wasn't so far away, I'd take you home with me.'

May looked at this unlikely friend – so tall, so striking with her wild auburn hair, strong chin and sparkling blue eyes – and wanted to cry with relief. 'You've been so kind, but you must go back to your husband and little boy,' she said. She felt a fraud. What would she think of her if she knew the truth about Ella? She would run a mile.

'A few more days won't hurt. I'm not leaving you and Ella to be bundled into some flea-bitten hostel. I'll find us a decent place. There's bound to be somewhere now our Relief Committee's in charge of things. Americans are wonderful at organizing in emergencies, full of pioneer spirit, and we've collected thousands of dollars on board already.'

Celeste was soon ushered away but turned back to May and waved. 'I'll wait at the gate for you.' May was not so sure. Once she was in her husband's loving arms, she'd be whisked away and that would be the end of this strange friendship. It would be better if she stuck to her own plan and kept to herself. They'd be just ships that passed in the night, and those words shook her with their poignancy. She heard rumours on board that there were other ships that had not come to their rescue. If they had, more people would have been saved.

There was always the chance that Ella would have a family waiting at the gate to seize her too. May had thought about that on the seemingly endless voyage on the *Carpathia* and had her story ready for them. Better Celeste knew nothing about any of that.

It wasn't until 11 p.m., nearly an hour after Celeste left the ship, that the Third Class survivors disembarked after being checked over, processed like pieces of paper, given tickets and chits for aid and some dollars to spend. Suddenly May felt nervous clinging to the gangplank, afraid to leave the ship. Her legs wouldn't budge and she felt nauseous.

'I can't go,' she whispered to the stewardess behind her.

'Yes, you can,' came the order. 'There's nothing for you here, dear.'

Oh yes there was: the last precious link with Joe. If she left the *Carpathia*, she would be leaving Joe and Ellen behind for ever. How could she arrive in a foreign land without them? Once again, the enormity of what she was doing overwhelmed her. Was there someone on the quay waiting for Ella and her family? Someone who might recognize this baby? There were so many fathers lost that night, but what if the mother was travelling alone and her husband was waiting here, desperate for a sighting of his family?

She clutched Ella tightly, covering her hair with the bonnet. *I can't let you go now . . .* But she knew that she might have to.

Angelo bent over the barrier waving a tattered snapshot of his beloved, the one he carried next to his heart. 'My wife . . . wife. Have you seen my wife?' he shouted in Italian. 'Maria Elisabetta Bartolini! I'm here, over here!'

'Stand by the B gate, boy . . . They come through the letters of their surname. Over there,' said a porter, pointing towards a line of gates that filtered out the passengers. 'This is W for Wagner,' he added.

'*Non capisco . . .*' Angelo was confused now. 'No understand. *Dove Titanico?* Where is the big ship.'

'This is the *Carpathia,* friend. It picked up the survivors. If she's not on here . . .' The porter shook his head. 'I'm sorry.'

Angelo began to cry. 'No, no . . . My wife, my baby, where are they? How can I live without them? She must be here. Mother of God, please help me!'

24

As they disembarked slowly down the gangway, May managed to unlock her stiff limbs and descend, seeing waving crowds of onlookers had been held back. None of them was allowed close enough to pry on those tender moments of reunion that had come for the lucky ones. Reluctantly she pulled back Ella's lacy bonnet to reveal her face and the winsome smile that would warm the coldest of hearts. She walked slowly around the edge of the passengers to the barriers, shuffling in line past the relatives' enclosure, listening in dread for shouts of recognition. Slowly and deliberately she showed off her baby to the crowds but no one stopped her or claimed the baby as their own. There were men holding photographs, shouting in foreign languages as they passed by.

Ella began to cry, frightened by the noise and the bright lights and the sheer crush of humanity surrounding her. May's heart was in her mouth. She'd got her story word-perfect: she'd say she'd been given charge of this baby by the captain, no less, and his special orders were to release her only to a parent or relative. But still no one came forward as she lingered, her arms shaking in case someone rushed out to claim her at the last minute. She paused one more time and then passed through the S gate. She heaved a sigh of relief.

Then she saw Celeste standing with a man in an overcoat and a bowler hat. She assumed it was her husband, come to meet her from the boat.

'At last! I'm sorry they made you wait, but there were so many of us to process,' Celeste smiled, holding her arms out to Ella.

'Is this Mr Parkes?' May asked as the man whipped off his hat, smiling.

'No, ma'am, I'm Jack Bryden.' She shook his hand. He paused, waiting for Celeste to explain further.

'This is one of my husband's managers, sent to escort me home. I've told him I'm not ready to leave yet. I shall stay here until you're ready to leave yourself.'

'But you must go. Your family will be desperate to see you,' May protested, seeing the man looked anxious, gripping his hat.

'Grover is very busy, too busy to make this trip himself, evidently. Mr Bryden will kindly wait a day or two, I'm sure. I've just heard the terrible news, May. Only seven hundred of us survived. Fifteen hundred people drowned. I can't take it in. All those families who need help. I've work to do here and a meeting to attend before I can head home.'

'But, madam, I had express instructions to escort you on the train back home right away. The family are anxious to have you back.'

'I'm sure they are. Thank you, Jack, but as I said, I have pressing business here.'

There was an edge to Celeste's voice that May hadn't heard before. She was shocked at the number of souls lost: all those other widows and orphans like herself. Suddenly she felt sick and faint with exhaustion.

'I have to sit down.'

'No worries, we have a taxi waiting,' said Mr Bryden. 'I came down in the railcar with a young man from Akron. I want to see if he found his family. Did you come across any Wells folks from Cornwall?'

Both women shook their heads. There'd been too many

survivors scattered over the *Carpathia* to remember many names.

'Let's get out of this sad place. They've organized some decent hotels for us and I think little Ella needs a change of diaper,' Celeste ordered, taking May by the arm.

When the ship emptied, the gangplank came up and a hush fell over the lingering crowds; there were only stragglers left. Angelo was so caught up in shouting that his voice was hoarse. If he held his photo up high or shoved closer to the front, perhaps Maria would see her own face and know he was here waiting and turn back to find him.

Everyone was pacing about, including doctors and nurses pushing empty invalid chairs. Angelo had watched the passengers disembark: women clad in furs, wearing hats, shaken, but still proud. There was a rush of lucky relatives screaming with joy. Many were whisked away into the arms of husbands and wives; others leaning on walking sticks, their faces suntanned, slumped with shock.

Hundreds of walking heroes and heroines poured off the ship, shouting names into the ranks of people. It was the numbers Angelo couldn't fathom. Nearly two-and-a-half thousand had been on board *Titanic*, but only seven hundred had returned on the rescue ship. The numbers changed like whispers in a game. Surely they must be wrong?

His arm was aching from holding up his photograph. There was still a trickle of steerage passengers passing through the B section. No one looked at him. Their eyes were dull with exhaustion and fear. He waited and waited until the last straggler had passed through. No one else was coming. He must find the passenger list and check for sure. Could this be true? Was there no one else left on the ship? His wife and baby were lost and it was all his fault. If he had gone back home to Italy, as planned, he could have brought them himself. How would he tell their family back home this grim news?

His legs were trembling as he scoured the arrival space, searching, searching . . . There must be some mistake. He ran to each arrival gate, begging the stewards to look at his picture. They had to be here somewhere. 'Please . . . please, my wife, my *bambina*,' he pleaded until the officials shooed him away.

'They've all gone, sonny. Go home. There's only crew left.'

'But are you sure? Look at my wife.'

He ran out into the rain, crying, 'Maria!' before collapsing in a heap like a drunken man, his eyes blinded by tears. A lady in a black veil helped him to his feet. He trudged out into the cold night, passing others collapsed in grief, men with beards crying out to the heavens. It was only then he saw something on the floor, a *scarpetta*, a baby shoe in lacework, the sort his mamma and Maria made, a pattern he would recognize anywhere.

He picked it up and examined it closely. Yes, it was finely executed Italian lace over a little cloth shoe, the sort of shoes women in his village made for their babies. He had lived surrounded by lacework all his life. It was how the women earned extra money in the marketplace. It was one of the designs from their region. His heart leaped.

Angelo smiled with sheer relief. He must have missed them in the crowd. They'd arrived and passed him by. That was it. He shoved the baby shoe in his pocket and made for the welfare stand, his feet now dancing with relief. Holy Mother of God, they were not lost after all!

'Maria, Alessia, where are you? I am here. I've been waiting. Look, Baby has lost her shoe. I've got her shoe,' he shouted into the crowd.

'Come on now, son,' said a priest he didn't know, trying to comfort him. 'It's just a shoe. Don't take on so.'

'No, it is my baby's shoe. I know it. It is . . . They go to my address.'

Angelo was pushing his way through the crowds fuelled by a surge of hope now. When he got to Baxter Street they would be there. Locked out, cross maybe, but alive. It was wet and cold. He must hurry. He didn't want to lose them again.

In the days that followed, May and Celeste were overwhelmed with kindness and offers of help. The stalwart matrons of the Women's Relief Committee arrived with endless boxes of provisions. In fact kindness was a poor choice of word for the sympathy showed to them all.

'Look at these!' May shouted across the room. 'They're new!' Clothes were arriving in all shapes and sizes, good-quality garments, some brand new from stores that had donated racks of blouses, cardigans, trousers, a box of corsets and underwear, gloves and stockings. There were garters and suspenders, even hairpins and boots of all sizes, each with laces or button hooks inside them, and a box of discreet sanitary napkins, for which May was grateful. The stress had brought on her monthlies early.

There was a scrabble as women tried on dresses and shoes, shouting for the right size.

For a moment they were just women let loose in a toy store. Suitcases were given to each of them, along with a sympathy card from well-wishers. In fact, hundreds of cards and letters had been sent to the Star Hotel in Clarkson Street, where May was staying with Celeste, along with many other stranded survivors.

'There's a memorial service tonight in the cathedral. We should go,' Celeste suggested.

'It won't be for the likes of me. Besides, I'm not leaving Ella with strangers.'

'Why not for you? And bring her with you. It'll help the cause if the congregation see the real widows and orphans who need their money.'

'I'm not a charity case or a freak show,' May snapped in irritation.

'Don't be so touchy. They only want to help and feel needed. Everyone wants to help the survivors. One look at Ella will open their purses wide.'

'I'd rather not.'

Celeste turned away and bit her lip. 'Please yourself, I'm only trying to help.'

May could see Celeste was hurt.

'You've been so kind but I think you ought to be heading back to see your little boy. Mr Bryden called in twice while you were out. I hope you don't mind me saying . . . but he seems to think he'll be in trouble if you don't leave soon. He told me Mr Parkes wants you back as soon as possible and doesn't like being checked.'

'He can wait a little longer. I'm needed here too. I'll telephone Grover and explain.'

From where May was standing it was as if Celeste was enjoying every minute of her stay in New York, going to meetings, talking to newspapermen, stirring up comment. She didn't have to earn a living or worry about the future. They came from different worlds and it was beginning to show.

'You go to the service. I'm tired. I'll be no company for anyone tonight. It takes every ounce of strength just to get through the day.'

Downtown Manhattan had been taken over with *Titanic* Disaster events; special services of remembrance had been organized in every district; Episcopal, Presbyterian, Catholic churches opening their doors in hospitality. Celeste frequently disappeared to give interviews on behalf of the Women's Relief Committee in the city to try to raise more funds while interest was high.

There was camaraderie among the survivors, a dazed exhausted retelling of their stories. Everyone huddled in groups but May had clung only to Celeste for comfort at first. Now she realized she must fend for herself.

Ella was being fractious, sensing all the change and fuss. No longer so docile or sleepy, she watched everyone with those huge eyes. She was dressed like a little princess, fussed over and handed round like a doll, which May knew was giving comfort to the other widows even though she desperately wanted to keep the baby to herself.

The welfare officers arrived to take their details and informed May of a passage home the following week on the *Celtic*, if she chose to return.

'Is there anyone you wish us to inform?' the officer asked.

May shook her head. 'All I love lies at the bottom of the sea,' she replied, and he bowed his head in sympathy. 'Liverpool will be fine. I can make my own way after that.'

Celeste was having none of it. 'No, she will not. Mrs Smith will fill in all the forms and get what she and her child are entitled to from the White Star Line and the relief funds. You must send a forwarding address to keep them informed. May, you must understand that as a dependant you'll certainly be making a claim for support. She has no husband now and no belongings, nothing. Her sponsor in Idaho has been informed but Mrs Smith has no desire to stay on in America now.'

May hadn't the energy or confidence to speak up for herself. She just wanted to disappear. 'I just want to go home but I can't think what to do now. I can't go back to Bolton, not without Joe. I don't want to see the faces of folk who knew us both. I haven't got an idea in my head.'

'Well, I have,' said Celeste. 'I've got an idea. If you really want a fresh start, I think I've got the answer but not before I've shown you some of the sites of this great city. You must see Central Park.'

'Do I have to?'

'It will do you good.'

When Celeste had an idea it was hard not to listen. How could May explain this was no holiday but a living nightmare, filling in time until she could return back to her own country? She didn't want to stroll in the park. It should be Joe who should be on her arm, not some stranger, kind as she was. She didn't want Ella being fussed over and photographed – for reasons she must keep to herself.

May still couldn't believe that no one in this past week, on board ship or on dry land, had laid claim to the baby. Holding Ella took her mind off Ellen, who visited her dreams every night, holding out her hands to be picked up when she fell in her little black leather boots. She woke crying out and it was always Celeste who came to her bedside.

'It's only a dream. Ella is safe. You are safe. Go back to sleep.'

Safe, May thought bitterly. If she only knew . . .

26

Angelo raced through the streets, alive to the thought that his family would be waiting in the rain. He was exhausted, it was the worst day of his life, but now there was hope. What if they got lost, or worse? The last few steps were agony. Breathless, he shouted, 'Maria, I'm back ...' Then he saw Uncle Salvi's face peering down at him, worried and drawn.

'Oh, Angelo, we heard the news. We've been waiting.'

'Are they not here yet?' he said, collapsing on the stairwell. 'She has the address. She will come.'

They waited for an hour in silence, Angelo pacing the floor in agony. 'Just another hour and they will come. It's a big city. Maria wouldn't leave me.'

'It's late now. You must come home with me. It is no time to be alone.'

'No, I have to be here in case she comes. She's travelled so far. I can't let her down now.'

'She's not coming, Angelo. She wasn't there, was she?'

'But I have Baby's shoe, look. Tuscan lace ... I'd know it anywhere. Did we not bring a whole package over to sell to the lace shops? Please, a little longer, Salvi.'

It was dawn when he was led like a child weeping, muttering to himself as Salvi took him back to the shop, to Anna and into the bosom of his family. Dr Fortuna called and, seeing the state of him, administered a sleeping draught. They let him sleep on the sofa, not wanting him to return to the empty rooms.

'I have to go. There might be news,' he pleaded. Visitors called with cakes and flowers and condolences. He had a strange fever, hot and cold, breathless. He couldn't work or think, crying out for his wife.

Father Bernardo came every day to comfort him, offering Mass for their souls.

'Your heart is breaking but it will heal. Only prayer will ease your pain. They are in a better place,' he offered.

Angelo did not want to hear this. 'But I want them with me. I know they are out there somewhere. I have put cards in the shops and the Italian newspaper. Look,' he said, brightening, 'there's a woman coming to see me. She says she saw Maria on the ship with our baby. She is sure it is my Maria but she has to come a long way to talk to me so I sent her dollars for the train.'

'What's her name?' Bernardo asked. 'Let me see the letter.'

'Signora Bruno . . . look.'

'Did she come?'

'Not yet, but any day soon.'

The priest sighed. 'I don't think whoever wrote this will be coming. They've got your dollars. There's always those who prey on suffering. The city is rife with hustlers claiming to be survivors needing cash, asking for favours, giving false hope to desperate people, telling lies for their own ends. I'm so sorry.'

'I'm not giving up, Father. I have my baby's shoe. She's here. I know she is. She has been kidnapped or worse . . .' He was back up pacing the floor.

'Stop this, son. It's grief talking. It's been over a week now. You must face the truth. They didn't survive.'

Angelo put his hands over his ears. 'I'm not listening. They're alive, my baby lives. Someone has stolen her.'

'Oh, Angelo, listen to yourself. You are talking like a madman.

This will not make your pain any easier. Come to Mass, to the memorial, see others like you who are trying to be brave.'

'How can I pray to a God who destroys families?' he said, turning on the priest in anger.

'He didn't sink the *Titanic*. From what I hear, it sank itself. He calmed the sea and kept the survivors safe. They say the ocean was like a millpond. Don't blame God, blame the ship's design,' the priest answered, trying to calm him. 'You must carry on as Maria would want you to.'

'What is there to live for now, you tell me?' Angelo beat his chest.

'Son, you have life and breath while others have none. The why of it all is a mystery too big for me to fathom; how some are saved and some lost. We'll be finding out soon enough. There's to be an inquiry into the sinking. The truth will out. Until then, be brave. Salvi and Anna are so worried about you. I told them it's early days but you are strong and young. Don't let me down. Accept what must be borne, son.'

Angelo nodded politely. These words made sense in his head but not in his heart. It was still too full of hope.

27

Celeste and May made an emotional farewell at the quayside before the *Celtic* sailed. What was left of the *Titanic*'s returning crew would not be on board. They had been immediately separated from the other survivors, impounded to make witness statements, and were not allowed to return straight away. Celeste had offered her own statement to the officials but no one had seemed interested in her story. She had added the story of the captain's heroism and the rescued baby but couldn't recall the names of other witnesses on the lifeboat to verify her account.

'How can I thank you?' May cried, clinging to her. 'You saved our lives. I shall never forget you.'

'We're sisters now.' Celeste found herself crying too. 'Sisters of the *Titanic*, bound by what we saw that night. You must write and tell me how you get on in Lichfield. Promise to write and maybe, God willing, I'll come over with Roddy and we'll meet again. When I write to you I will think of home. You will be my special link.'

'I expect you will be very busy with your committees. You don't have to write, you know. I shall never forget your kindness. Oh, and tell your husband, thank you for letting you be by my side. He must be desperate to see you.'

'I will write and I'll send you a photograph of Roderick and you must send me a portrait of Ella and yourself. We must never let people forget what happened to the *Titanic*. You must tell people at home what you saw and heard, all of it, good and bad. It must never happen again.'

They both looked up at the liner and May shivered with apprehension.

Celeste felt herself hesitating. Why did she not want May to leave? 'You don't have to go so soon. You can stay on and build up your strength before you face another sea voyage. I know what you are thinking: how can I get on another boat?'

May tried to be brave, and attempted a smile. 'I just want to go home and get away from here. There's no future for us here. We'll manage now you've given me an opening. We're better off in our own country, I reckon.'

'Here.' Celeste smiled, shoving a silver hip flask into her hand. 'Someone gave it to me on board for Dutch courage. Take it. It'll warm you through and help you sleep. It's good French brandy.'

'Thanks, but I've never tasted spirits in my life so I'll not start now. I'll manage with sweet tea and cocoa.' May handed it back.

'You are such a brave woman. I'm proud to have met you. How do you stay so calm?' Celeste had tears in her eyes.

'She gives me the strength to carry on.' May nodded to the sleeping baby. 'She comes first. We'll be fine. You'd better go. Everyone's been so kind but the sooner we board, the sooner we'll be off. No long goodbyes. Thanks from the bottom of my heart. You've been a pal. You needn't have bothered with me but you did. You saved my life, keeping me warm and awake on that lifeboat. There are no words I can say to thank you for that.'

'I mean it, May, write to me. Tell me how things are, paint me pictures of my home town. I would be so grateful for your correspondence. I do get homesick sometimes.'

'I'll do my best. Never had much use for pen and paper, just lists and stuff like that. I've never had anyone to write to before but I'll give it a try. I just hope this thing floats better than the other.' May glanced up with a wry smile on her face. 'I never thought I'd make a joke like that. What's happening to me?'

'Change, that's what. None of us will ever be the same because of what happened. But we survived and we will continue to. Look how brave you've been, and so determined, going back over the very ocean that . . .' she hesitated. 'Good luck and *bon voyage.*' Celeste felt tears welling up as she kissed the baby and then hugged May tightly. 'Go on before I make a fool of myself. I will never forget your courage and will to make a new life after such a tragedy. God be with you on your journey. You've given me so much to think about.'

May walked away and Celeste stood until she was just a speck in the distance, then lost amongst the bustle of the docks. 'Will we ever meet again?' she sighed, turning towards the gate.

28

Every day since his recovery, Angelo took his well-trodden path to the offices of the White Star Line. Surely, someone somewhere had news? He'd heard of mistakes on the passenger lists. The clerk with the furrowed brow and weary eyes looked up and sighed heavily on recognizing Angelo.

'Not you again, son. Now listen, I've told you before, if we had any more news we'd send you a wire. We have your address.' The clerks had been sympathetic at first, but over the weeks they grew impatient as Angelo pleaded daily for them to recheck the survivors list. 'They embarked at Cherbourg, your wife and baby, but they didn't make it. The numbers all tally. Sadly they're not on any list.'

'But I heard some gave false names.'

'Rumours and press speculation, that's all. You have to accept they went down like so many other poor souls on that night.'

'But look at this shoe ... My wife was skilled with lacework, like my mother. In our region they make special lace and she told me she was bringing it over to New York to sell. No one else could do this work, no one.'

'Maybe someone bought it from her on the ship, one of the passengers. Maybe it got stolen. There are all manner of possibilities,' the clerk replied, deliberately turning to the mountain of paperwork on his desk and thereby signalling to Angelo that he considered the conversation closed.

People behind him started tutting impatiently. Angelo knew his dishevelled appearance – the days' worth of beard growth, his wild-eyed stare – made him look deranged. He could quite see how he would be mistaken for a madman. In truth he questioned his own sanity. He turned round to show the little shoe to the other folk in the queue.

'Who would steal a baby's shoe?' he asked them.

'There are passengers who'd steal the fleas off a dog, given half a chance,' muttered a man behind him.

'I'm sorry,' said the clerk. 'Go home and write to your folks, wherever they live, that the news is bad.'

'How can I tell her mamma that I caused her daughter's death? It was me who said it would be a good life here. It will kill them to discover this.'

'Look, sonny, face facts. They're gone and you have to break the news as best you can.'

'What if they are wandering the streets looking for me?'

The clerk took off his horn-rimmed glasses and wiped them, shaking his head. 'You Italians have your own newspapers and shops. They'd find you.'

'I've stuck cards everywhere I can: in the church, lodging houses, on billboards, even on the sidewalks. I have this feeling. I must keep looking just in case someone knows something,' Angelo pleaded. He couldn't give up, not now. He was haunted by the thought of Maria and the child stuck in the city somewhere, alone in a foreign land, unable to make themselves understood.

'Your effort does you credit, but we've also done everything we can at this end. Talk to your priests and city folk, but you have to face the truth.'

'What is true? They say that the ship went down with only enough lifeboats for half the passengers, that Third Class were left until it was too late . . . I've heard rumours, people shot on deck. Can you imagine what my wife went through and with no one to help her?' He was shouting now.

'Calm down, rumours won't help you. What happened happened, and that is what the public inquiry is for, to make sure nothing like this ever happens again.'

Someone listening interrupted. 'And how many steerage men have been called to bear witness? Only three out of hundreds, I've heard. It was mass slaughter. How can this boy ever get justice? It's a disgrace!'

'I am not judge or jury. I'm just doing my job. So don't take it out on me. You have to get on with your life. There's many worse off than you.' The clerk was rattled by the support Angelo was getting. 'Any more of this and I'll call the manager.'

There was nothing more to say, but Angelo pulled out the tiny shoe once again, showing it to the audience. 'I will have to live with this for the rest of my life. I killed my baby,' he whispered. 'And I didn't even get to hold her. She was born after I left.' He pulled out a tattered photo. 'This is all I have, this photo of my Maria and Alessia.'

'Such a pretty name,' said a woman pityingly.

'It was my grandmother's name,' he said, crossing himself.

'Now go and find yourself a stall, have a coffee and calm down,' the clerk said. 'You can't keep taking time off work to come here.'

'How can a man work when he's lost his world? Why did this have to happen to us? What did they do to deserve such an end?'

'Beats me, son, beats me. What sort of an Almighty lets some live and some die? I'm sorry but you must go. There's others waiting in the queue.'

As Angelo turned to leave the clerk hesitated. 'Good luck! Maybe one day the truth will out.'

Someone patted him on the back. Another squeezed his arm. None of it comforted him.

Fingering the shoe in his pocket Angelo bent his head and

pulled his cap over his face to hide his distress. He would never stop looking for Maria and Alessia. But first he needed more than strong coffee if he was going to write a letter home that would break all their hearts.

29

The journey back to Akron was a sullen affair. Celeste stared out of the window while Jack Bryden chattered on about the Wells family who'd lost both their men in the sinking. They were now five days later than planned, partly out of Celeste's defiance and disappointment that Grover hadn't rushed to New York to greet her. It might have made their reunion easier if he had been waiting, full of concern for her safety. All those cries of raw emotion she'd witnessed brought home how unmissed she had been, how life in Akron went on smoothly without her. Even Roddy sometimes saw more of his nursemaid, Susan, than he did of his mother. All that must change. All she'd got was poor Jack waiting in his mackintosh as if she was a mere client visitor to the Diamond Rubber Company. She'd wanted to scream at him but you didn't shoot the messenger. What was she thinking? Where was this fierce rage coming from?

Those meetings with Margaret Brown and her friends had filled her with zeal. She must continue her campaigning no matter what, and then there was the *Carpathia* reception to organize. She had telephoned Grover two nights earlier with their change of plan. He informed her that a welcome home soiree in her honour had now had to be rescheduled. He was clearly far from pleased about this delay. There would be a car waiting for them at the train station.

Celeste thought once again of May on the high seas and

hoped her journey back was trouble free. How brave she was to trust herself to another ship. How would she find life in the Midlands? Would she settle there? She shook her head to clear her mind, her thoughts spiralling. She must concentrate on her duties. Only the thought of Roddy's welcome warmed her heart.

As they drew into the driveway of the large house off Portage Hill, its ivy-clad turrets in each corner making it look more like a fortress than a home, she wondered what sort of reception would be waiting for her. Looking up, she saw Grover staring at her from an upstairs window, and she shivered.

The maid was standing at the door. 'Welcome home, Mrs Parkes. We are so glad you are safe.'

'Thank you, Minnie,' Celeste smiled. 'Where's Master Roddy?'

'Out with his nurse. We didn't know what time the train would arrive. The Master told Susan to take him out into the sunshine. I'm sure they won't be long.'

Celeste felt bitter disappointment stinging her.

'The Master's in the study. He'll see you in there when you're ready.'

Celeste's heart sank at this command. She was in disgrace. Everything had its price, and staying in New York would be viewed by Grover as defiance of the first order. With leaden feet she climbed the wide oak staircase to his study like a child before the headmaster. Her new-found courage was fast deserting her.

'At last. Close the door.' Grover strode across the room from the window. The look on his face would melt steel.

'How dare you arrive so late? I gave Bryden strict orders to bring you straight home, and you defy me,' he roared, his florid face growing even redder.

'I know, I'm sorry, but there were people I needed to help, survivors. It was terrible, Grover. You wouldn't have believed your own eyes. I couldn't desert them.'

'I don't want to hear your excuses.' He dismissed her with a wave of his hand. 'You were able to desert your own family for weeks. *That* didn't bother you.'

'My mother died. I had to go back.'

'You took your time to return. Go and get changed. We need to leave soon.'

'I want to see Roddy first. I've missed him so much.'

'He's out with Susan. She's more a mother to him than you are. He'll barely even notice you're back.'

'How can you say that? I wanted to take him with me to England but you wouldn't let me. My mother never even got to see him. Now it's too late.' She was close to tears. She was arguing and she knew that was unwise when Grover was in this mood.

'Do as I say and get those drab things off. You look like a common shop worker.'

'I'm in mourning.'

'Not here, you're not. Black doesn't become you.'

'It suits my mood after what I saw, what I've been through,' she snapped.

The blow to her shoulder knocked her sideways into the bureau. She staggered.

'I will not stand for disobedience in this house,' Grover roared. 'You ignore my instructions, my driver, my timetable. You know what happens when you do that.' He was standing over her with flint in his grey eyes. Celeste tried to stand upright.

'I nearly drowned and you expect me to dress up for a party? Grover, please ...'

'You should be grateful. My mother has been preparing this soiree for days. The cream of Akron society will want to hear your story first-hand.'

Celeste touched her shoulder, which hurt terribly. She felt dizzy and disoriented with the speed of her fall. 'I'm tired. I don't feel like celebrating anything.'

'What you feel and what you want is of no importance,' Grover barked.

'Please, another night,' she pleaded.

'Go to the bedroom. You need to be taught a lesson, one you won't forget in a hurry.'

Celeste saw the furious gleam in his eye and knew what was coming next. 'Oh, not now, please. Can't you see I'm hurt? For the love of God, don't take me now.'

'You are my wife and I won't be denied my rights. Get to the bedroom before I drag you by the hair. I would've thought by now you'd know who is master in this house. I will not be made to look foolish by a disobedient wife.'

30

May kept to her cabin on the *Celtic,* out of sight from prying eyes. She knew the other passengers were dying to ask her questions about her experience and to pet the baby. There were toys for Ella; a First Class passenger sent a beautiful teddy bear for her to play with and a doll dressed in pink velvet with gold lace ribbons. People meant well but May was too exhausted to appreciate it. There were at least five other female survivors on board, some with children, and she'd seen they were fussed over and passed around as if they were famous. She avoided their company when she could. People wanted them to pose for photographs but she shied away from the fuss and attention from the start. Slowly people were starting to get the message.

She'd been upgraded to Second Class and was sure that Celeste had something to do with this. She didn't deserve such a friend, one who'd saved her life. Their few days in New York she would never forget, riding in a carriage around Central Park, tasting ice-cream sodas, shopping in Macy's, trying not to gawp at the luxuries on the counters and the elegant ladies in cartwheel hats who sipped tea in the restaurant and admired Ella. It wasn't real. Nothing had been real since they'd set sail nearly two weeks ago. Could it really have been such a short time since she'd sailed into a new world, seen the bustle, noise and dust of the city? It wasn't for the likes of her. She was pleased to be heading home. If not to her real home, then to her own country where all would be more familiar.

Not for the first time she wondered if she was in some strange dream waiting to wake up. In a matter of days, she'd travelled from Bolton to London, Southampton to New York, and now back again into the unknown; days and days of living in borrowed clothes, carrying a baby she hardly knew. Then in the small hours of darkness reality dawned, the pain hit and her mind felt like it would explode. It was as much as she could do to make up a bottle for the baby.

Ella suckled on it unheeding. As long as she was fed and changed, she was no bother. *I have taken someone else's baby. God forgive me!* Willingly at first she'd clung to this child just for comfort but now there was no going back. She was her responsibility. For better or worse.

'I don't know you,' she whispered in the baby's ear. Ella grinned with such an appealing smile, and May shook her head. The innocence of the young. 'But we've plenty of time to get to know each other, lass.' There were days ahead to sit in peace, sing nursery rhymes and walk the decks before they must face the years to come.

Ella looked so different from Ellen, petite limbed, with long delicate fingers, and so dark skinned. She was foreign, no mistake about that. There'd been so many nations on board in steerage, families, women in headscarves jabbering away. Did this baby understand one word she was saying?

Everything they were wearing was new, from her black coat with the velvet trim, the smart hat and handbag, her calf-skin boots, her corset and shift. Only her careworn face was the same, but ravaged by sorrow, pale and drawn.

In her pocket was Celeste's letter of introduction to one of the clergymen of Lichfield Cathedral, Celeste's own father, Canon Forester. He would help her find a suitable position, her friend had insisted. What was a canon? The only cannon she knew was the gun that stood in the park. She'd no idea even where Lichfield was except it was somewhere close to Birmingham, and she'd never been inside a cathedral in her life.

Every time the ship's engine shuddered or went silent, she felt the panic rise. What if it happened again? The icebergs were still out there. She could hardly bear to go on deck to look. It was hard to sleep shut up in a cabin, however comfortable it might be.

When Ella woke for her dawn milk, May dressed her warmly and forced herself to walk her up and down the deck, looking out to sea. There was no one around to stare at them but crew, who smiled and left her to her own thoughts. They sensed she wanted no fuss, no reminders of what had happened to them.

Celeste may want to publicize their experience, to tell the world what had happened, but she never would as long as she lived and she'd begged her friend not to tell the canon too much of their story; only that she had been widowed by the disaster.

'Please,' she'd insisted, 'I don't want us to be pitied and pointed out in the street.' That was the only condition she'd asked in accepting this kind offer of help. Anonymity. The chance to start afresh. Celeste had had no option but to agree.

On 25 April, under a gull-grey sky, the ship slipped into the Western Approaches; that part of the Atlantic that heralded the coast of England was getting closer and soon they would be reaching Liverpool. There was one last task May decided she must do.

If this was to be a new start for both of them, then all reminders of this terrible experience must be destroyed: her salt-stiffened nightdress, the baby's clothes, nothing that could identify them as passengers of the *Titanic*. She pulled out her own things and the baby's clothes, stuffed them in the pocket of her new coat and took them on deck. When nobody was watching, she dropped her own clothes down into the water. They fluttered on the breeze at first, ballooned and then floated away like swollen bodies in the water. She turned away horrified at such a terrible reminder.

Then she fingered Ella's gown with that beautiful lacy border, the bonnet, the one little shoe. The other had been lost somewhere that day they'd gone ashore in New York. She hadn't noticed the lace's intricate pattern before. It was a frieze of Noah's Ark with animals two by two, dogs, horses, deer and a dove with outspread wings. Such fine work. As she touched the texture, she knew this lace had been made with love and pride.

The two of them had found an ark of safety in the lifeboat and then on the *Carpathia*. They were still at the mercy of the waves and water. Reaching over the side of the ship, May noticed how the swell of water frothed into hundreds of white holes with patterns like lace.

How could she watch these beautiful tiny clothes float away and sink like her own little girl must have done? She shoved them back into her pocket. These were not for the sea. They must be kept. They weren't hers to destroy, but Ella must know nothing of the secrets they held. All May knew was that you don't throw love away, however painful the memories.

31

The candelabras glittered, the diamonds shone on bracelets and ear drops. Dinner had gone well enough although Celeste hadn't been able to eat a thing. How could she with her ribs so bruised, chafing against the tightness of her corset. It was agony to bend or twist but she must smile and be the perfect guest. Formally and precisely seated were the usual stuffy line-up of masters of industry that had sprung up in the past few years in the city, including partners from the Roetzel and Andress law firm. One of the B. F. Goodrich Company rubber magnates was sitting opposite her. Everyone wanted to hear her dramatic tale.

'Isn't it terrible about Walter Douglas?' The Akron newspapers had been full of the loss on board of the founder of the Quaker Oats Company. 'Poor Mahala was left with nothing but a fur coat on her back. And John Jacob Astor, Guggenheim, and that poor Strauss couple, all of whom died . . . You must have met some of them in First Class, Celestine?'

She paused before replying, seeing Grover giving her a pointed look. She smiled, nodding. 'Those gentlemen were all so brave,' she said. 'They won't be forgotten for their courage. I met some of their wives at the Relief Committee.'

'I hear the steerage men behaved like brutes,' said Grover's mother, Harriet, as she stuffed another piece of cherry pie into her mouth.

'That's not what I saw,' Celeste snapped back. 'There were many gentlemen of all classes waving their children off and kissing their wives, knowing they'd never see them again. Most of the steerage passengers weren't allowed on deck until near the end when there were no lifeboats left. Women and children too. The poor souls were left to die, abandoned. Fifty-three children died that night in steerage. Fifty-three. Only one in First Class and that was because she refused to leave her parents.' She knew now that she had their full attention and could have turned their stomachs with even more harrowing details but this was neither the time nor the place. They wanted stories of heroism, nothing to disturb their night's sleep. 'But we raised ten thousand dollars on the ship alone for their immediate relief,' she added proudly.

And besides, Grover had said earlier that she mustn't go on about her experience at dinner. He'd not been impressed with her account.

'*Titanic!*' he'd said angrily. 'I am sick of the damned ship, nothing but news of it on every page of the *Tribune*. Everyone knows the score now so don't bang on about it on your high-and-mighty drum at the dinner tonight.'

'But it was terrible, Grover,' she'd protested. 'I'll never forget what I saw. I was so lucky to survive.'

'What was all this business I heard from Bryden about sorting out that widow from steerage? There was an army of do-gooders to do that.'

'May and I sat together in the lifeboat. She lost her husband and everything they possessed in the world. How could I not do my duty?' Celeste said, trying not to raise her voice. She'd heard Susan bringing Roddy back a few minutes before. She longed to see him but knew she must wait for Grover to dismiss her. To rile him risked him keeping Roddy from her for even longer. 'Besides, I wanted to help Mrs Brown with the survivors' fund.'

'Always the parson's daughter,' he sneered. 'Thank God I had more sense than to let you take my son. If anything had happened to him . . .' She could hear the threat in his voice.

The beating that followed was no surprise. She'd angered him and so she must be punished. He'd withheld Roddy until the last moment before they left for the dinner. She was too sore to pick him up and he had cried when he saw her, hiding behind Susan at first until she had produced a little package of toys. It broke her heart not to stay. It was all her fault for not returning when demanded.

Now she looked at the eager faces of Harriet's guests and swiftly changed the subject.

'Enough about me, what's been happening while I was away?' Celeste was soon subjected to all the local gossip, but when the women retired to the drawing room while the men took their port they took up the subject again. 'Did you see Madeleine Astor? They say she is in a *delicate* condition . . .'

'I saw her on the *Carpathia*, looking dreadful, and yes, she is pregnant.'

'Only eighteen, not married five minutes to a man twice her age . . . and him a married man when they met . . . Still, what will be will be, and we mustn't speak ill of the dead.'

'Did you see many bodies? How terrible for you to be shoved onto a boat with all the Third Class riffraff! How relieved you must be to be home and dry and back amongst your own.'

Oh shut up, she wanted to say to these silly women, over-stuffed into their evening gowns, their double chins wobbling, flesh bursting out of their low bodices. You have no idea how the world lives outside the few miles around here. Once your approval mattered to me, but not now. None of this mattered now, she sighed. I'll never belong here. I'm too English, too different, too young to be sitting here gossiping with puffed-up women who care only for show and status and haven't grasped anything of the horror I experienced. Why should they? It's all like some cinematograph drama on the silver screen to them. I

don't want to be here, her heart cried out. I want to take Roddy
and run.

She'd never felt so alone, so trapped, so frustrated. She'd
watched Grover drinking steadily all night, his eyes flashing with
fury as the attention kept being drawn back to his wife's story.

The carriage would soon come and he'd paw her all the way
home, expecting his reward in the bedroom. Not the gentle
caresses of a lover but a rushed brutal entry, a grunt and then it
would be over and she'd be left sore, feeling used and degraded
once more.

How had it come to this? His tender caresses had quickly
changed into attacks, even on their honeymoon in Paris. Once
they were married, it was as if Grover had become a different
person, criticizing her for the smallest thing: the way she dressed,
her hairstyle, her accent, her background. He talked of moulding
her into a suitable wife as if she was a piece of clay.

At first she had been too shocked, too frightened to resist or
protest. But this terrible secret she must endure. His assault
earlier was only a sample of what was to come if she disobeyed
again.

In the early hours of the morning she'd lie awake listening to
his snores, feeling desperate and helpless to move in case he
woke and she'd have to be subjected to it all over again.

Now, sipping coffee, pretending she was enjoying herself and
trying not to wince in pain, she realized she couldn't live like
this any more. Tonight a plan had formed in her mind. Listening
to all that talk, to the spurious gossip, she knew there might be a
way to take control. When they reached the house on Portage
Hill, she'd offer Grover some of the fine whiskey she'd brought
him back from New York and sit him down. She'd slip away, take
her time undressing, knowing he was tired, drunk and ready to
sleep. She would slip into Roddy's nursery, careful not to disturb
Susan next door. She would lock the door and find some blankets and a cushion for the daybed in there. Tonight she would be

safe, and if Grover complained she'd explain that he was so tired she thought it better for him to sleep it off on the sofa.

Something that Harriet Parkes had said after dinner had made her think. 'You ought to write it all down, my dear, before you forget the details.' Why should she stay silent about what had happened on the *Titanic*? Why shouldn't she tell her own story, raise funds for the needy *Titanic* immigrants from Cornwall, arriving in Akron, by all accounts? The papers were full of the story of Margaret Brown, the socialite who had rowed one of the lifeboats herself. She was now a friend and Celeste was determined to attend every Titanic Survivors' Committee, no matter what she had to do to get there.

She thought about May and Ella on the high seas. Would her plan work out for them? What would the Lancashire girl have made of all the glitz and falseness of tonight's gaudy spectacle? Celeste was not going to keep silent. There must be ways to stir up debate. What had happened was awful but preventable, of that she was sure.

Back home, in the nursery, she lit a candle, found a writing pad and pencil and began to write down every detail she could recall of that night while it was still fresh in her mind: conversations, scenes, out it all poured onto the paper. She felt such a surge of energy and resolve as she wrote her account of that fateful night, not only for Roddy to read when he was older but to withstand time as a piece of history. Something was shifting within herself as she realized she was no long Grover's doormat to be trampled on, but a woman of worth who had survived a cruel disaster and would never be put down again. She slept soundly for the first time in days.

32

Angelo sat slumped in a backstreet bar knocking back glass after glass of bourbon. He could never drink enough to dull the ache inside. What was the point of going home? The tiny apartment was as he'd left it on that April morning weeks ago, gathering dust, but it was somewhere to flop down when he staggered back in the early hours, somewhere to sleep off his hangover and hide from Aunt Anna, who screamed at him to tidy the place up.

'What for?' he yelled back. 'Who is there to see my mess but me?'

'You will bring rats if you leave food everywhere. Look at you, you've not shaved for days, nor worked. How will you pay the rent? They can't keep a man on who never shows up. Maria would be ashamed of you.'

'Don't you dare speak her name! You never even met her.'

'Salvi says she was beautiful and proud. You soil her memory with all this . . .' She flung her hands around in despair, picking up his dirty shirts as she swept round the room.

'Go away, I can do my own washing.'

'*Bah!* You want people to think Bartolinis are filthy pigs? The family name must be honoured. We have a business to run. Drinking solves nothing.'

'I'll do what I want,' he snapped.

'We worry about you. You are family. We can't let you sink to the gutter.'

'Why did I ever come to this rotten country? It has taken all that I had, all I loved. There's nothing for me here.'

'Then go back to Italy with your tail between your legs, tell them your sad story. Start again on the farm. Anything. But don't waste your life.'

'Leave me alone.'

Anna left him with her suggestion buzzing through his head. Go back to the village, back to his brother, his old mother and Maria's parents. But how would he face them?

He'd dragged himself out to Rizzi's bar and drank until there were no coins left in his pocket. There was no shame in returning home, but something was stopping him.

Angelo pushed his way through the crowd into the street. Here he was his own boss. Anna was as bad as his mother nagging him: do this, do that. Go home, no! Here he could do as he pleased, be invisible, drink what he wanted, when he wanted. Here he could hide from friends and family. He'd never go back! It smacked of failure and defeat. For better or worse, he was staying put.

33

Even before the train drew up in Trent Valley Station, May caught sight of the three cathedral spires. The Three Ladies of the Vale, Celeste had called them. She noticed that the cottages around the track were made of red brick, not the Accrington shiny brick of Lancashire but a softer blue with a pinky hue. Despite her anxiety at arriving in a place where she would be a complete stranger, May was glad that everything looked unfamiliar.

Ella was fast asleep, worn out by their journey. They were helped off the train onto the platform by a soldier in khaki. He was on his way to his regiment at Whittington Barracks, just outside the city. He'd been taken with Ella's antics on the long ride from Liverpool and had pushed a shilling into her little palm. The kindness of strangers, May mused, and her thoughts automatically strayed back to Celeste.

The spring day was bright and green leaves sparkled in the sunshine. It was more like being in the country, May thought, as she admired the church spires that replaced the mill chimneys she was used to back home. It was all so different from Bolton with its rows of terraced streets.

Thankfully there was an omnibus to take them from the station into town, and before long they alighted in the Market Square. May found a café to slake her thirst, fixing her dusty appearance before she took the short walk up Dam Street to

Cathedral Close. It was all very quaint, like a picture book. She saw Minster Pool, heard the quack of ducks and stood in wonder at the cherry trees decked out in pink blossom. Across the pool there were high brick buildings with gardens leading down to the water's edge. Here was fresh air, cobbled streets and old-world buildings, a world away from what she'd known before. Perhaps Celeste was right, this was a new place and they could settle here.

In her pocket were Celeste's instructions and her father's address, but try as she might she couldn't find the house. She walked round the outside of the cathedral to where the West Door rose up to a wall full of statues. She asked directions from a passing woman with a wicker basket, who pointed out an archway into a tiny little square with higgledy-piggledy low houses facing a vegetable patch.

'Who're you looking for?' she asked, smiling at Ella, who'd now woken.

'Canon Forester,' May said.

'Number four. He's the one with the daughter who was on the *Titanic*. She was saved, praise the Lord! Terrible, wasn't it?'

May nodded but said nothing. You couldn't miss the bill-boards, their sensational headlines screaming news of the disaster. '*TITANIC* BODIES SALVAGED FROM SEA. BOUND FOR HALIFAX' – each paper wanted to outdo the others in lurid details. But no one would get anything out of her. As far as they were concerned she'd never set foot on the ship.

'What a bonny baby,' said the woman, patting Ella's curls and looking from her to May with surprise. May was getting used to this response everywhere she and Ella went, be it on the train, the bus, or in the café in the square.

May took her leave with a nod of the head and made towards the door, hoping it was the right one. She knocked. A white-haired man with a lined but kindly face opened the door and smiled.

'Ah ha! I think I know who you might be. Come in ... come in, Mrs Smith. I hope you had a pleasant journey.'

'You know about me?'

'Of course. My daughter, Celeste, cabled to us. How is my unsinkable daughter?' His eyes twinkled and May sensed a generous man.

'I can't begin to tell you just what a friend she has been to me ...'

'Just like her dear mother. Sit down. I'll make some tea. My lady's not been in today so you see I'm in a bit of a muddle,' he apologized, trying to clear piles of books and papers to make room for May to sit down.

May placed Ella down on a chair, surrounding her with battered dusty cushions. 'Let me help. If you show me where everything is I can ...' The room was a clutter of books and newspapers and cuttings. Not one surface was visible.

'I've been cutting out all the articles about the sinking. I was wondering if you were both mentioned but so far no ... I'll send them to Celeste. I am very sorry for your loss, Mrs Smith.'

'We were on our way to Idaho ... to start a new life.' May felt the tears that were never far from the surface welling up but she must hold back her despair.

'What a blessing you have the child for comfort.'

'Yes,' she replied quickly, anxious there wouldn't be too many questions. 'She's my priority now. My poor husband had such dreams for her future. He wanted her to have a good education so I will do whatever I can to give her those chances. I have to work for both of us now and that's why I'm here.' Having said her piece she busied herself putting some cups and saucers on a tray while Canon Forester set the kettle to boil.

'I realize that. Have no fear, there's always work for honest folk in Lichfield. I'm sure I can get you fixed up. Have you any special training?'

'I was briefly in service and then in the cotton mills. I can get references but it may take some time,' she offered, knowing this would risk her address being known up north.

'My daughter's word is good enough for me. She's a shrewd judge of character as a rule.' He paused as if thinking about something in particular and sighed. 'Let's have some tea and I can tell you of some options that might work for you both.'

While Canon Forester poured out two cups, May pulled a rusk out of her bag for Ella. 'I have to fit work around my baby. I can't ... won't farm her out to strangers ... not now.'

'I'm sure we'll find a way around that. Once people know your circumstances ...'

'No!' she said, alarmed, almost dropping her teacup at his words. 'Please, sir, I don't want anyone knowing about all that ... It's better if no one knows. I've seen how some of the survivors get no peace from the newspapers.'

'It won't last, my dear. Memories are short but at least the *Titanic* Relief Fund is cashing in on public sympathy while it can. It has raised thousands already. People *want* to help. They want to show their support. But I understand your wish for privacy. The place I've got in mind is the Theological College across the Close. They're always in need of staff to help with meals, or in the laundry. I've had a word with the principal's wife, Mrs Phillips, and she's willing to show you round and explain your duties. There may be rooms where you can lodge nearby.'

May nodded with relief. 'Thank you, it sounds like work I could do.' She sipped her tea. Whoever was keeping house for him needed a lesson in washing up. The little kitchen was none too clean and several of the cups were chipped.

When they'd finished their tea, Canon Forester escorted May and Ella across to the college principal's house, where a maid told them the mistress was in the cathedral somewhere.

'I can wait,' May said, not sure if this was the right time for her to be interviewed.

'Why don't we go into the cathedral and I can show you around? I can introduce you right there. No time like the present,' said Canon Forester, not waiting for her reply.

May smiled. How like Celeste he was with his brisk no-nonsense manner.

They entered by a side door and May immediately felt the dampness of cool stones, looked about her in awe and saw the high vaulted ceiling. The silence was overwhelming.

'Can I sit for a while?' she whispered.

'Of course. I won't disturb you. I'll go and see if I can find Mrs Phillips.'

May sat with bowed head, Ella on her lap. There was something about the echoing vastness of the space that made her want to cry. She was so utterly weary. It was time to find a safe refuge. Was Lichfield the place? Was she worthy to be here? Just how dishonest was she being?

One day at a time, one slow step in front of another was all she could manage.

Ella must have a good life far away from any chilly orphanage. Here was as good a place as any. The truth about her history would never be known nor would it benefit anyone to start poking around. Her real story was lost with the ship. The lies of this new life were all in a good cause.

May saw the old man and a stout woman making their way towards her with purpose, their feet echoing on the stone flags. She braced herself to face them knowing this was her and Ella's only chance.

Ella was an orphan and nothing made up for the loss of a mother's tender care. But here was she, a mother without a child, willing to take on the precious task. Like ewe and lamb, they were, she smiled. Why shouldn't they be together?

She stood up to greet them. 'Hello, Mrs Phillips. I'm May Smith and this is my daughter, Ella. I do hope you can help us.'

34

The *Titanic* Survivors' Committee waited until the *Carpathia* arrived from Naples to settle in her berth on the pier in New York. How different from her last historic voyage in the darkness, Celeste mused, following the line of silk dresses and fine hats up the gangplank, not without a shudder of fear. How could she ever go aboard a ship again?

Yet May had gone willingly into the unknown only days after the disaster. So she must swallow her fear. For goodness' sake, this was only a visit, one long overdue. Margaret Brown was holding the silver cup they'd had engraved and many of the survivors were going to be present: Frederic Seward, Karl Behr, the tennis ace, and Mr Frauenthal, a German industrialist, were accompanying them.

They waited until all the passengers were off the ship and Captain Rostron summoned his crew. There were still over two hundred of the original crew, with some familiar faces lining up. Officers and engineers stood at their head, while the captain waited to receive the cup from the Survivors' Committee. Rank and file together, smart officers in navy next to nut-brown sailors, coal-smudged stokers and firemen, all were present and correct.

Celeste felt proud to be part of the Survivors' Committee. It had taken subterfuge to get this time away, chaperoned, of course, by Harriet Parkes, who was peeved not to be part of the actual ceremony, hoping for a chance to be seen with the great and the good of New York society.

It was this ambition that had persuaded Grover that it would do the directors of the Diamond Rubber Company no harm to make a generous donation to their cause.

Celeste's mother-in-law had scoured the Cleveland dress-makers' shops for something to wear that befitted the occasion. Celeste refused to wear anything but black. She was still in mourning for her own mother when out of sight of Grover, but forced to wear muted lilac and grey around the house.

The more she saw and read of Margaret Brown in the papers, now the nation's heroine, the more she admired her go-getting determination to make sure this organization was up and running before they left the ship. The sums raised now totalled hundreds of thousands of dollars. Celeste had been fundraising herself, holding sales of hand-made craftwork, paintings and tea parties, a soiree of musical entertainment, echoing similar evenings held in New York.

She'd been so busy she'd hardly had time to brood on how bad things were with Grover, and then there were the letters from Father saying how well 'Little May', as he called her, was settling into Cathedral Close.

What a hard worker she is, nothing is too much trouble. She's even taken over my chores, turning my muddled nest into a haven of polished tidiness so now I can't find a thing, but she means well. Her baby's the delight of the ladies of the Close, who know nothing of what brought them here. It keeps the newspapers from bothering her and I respect that. She's like a little mouse scuttling across the cobbles, skin and bone, but she seems happy enough. You did well in bringing her here. I suspect that she might turn out to be an angel in disguise …

May's first letter was a little more reticent, written in the careful neat handwriting of a child.

Dear Mrs Parkes

I hope this finds you as it finds me, as well as can be expected. Your father has been a Christian gentleman to us. I am well suited with my position in the Theological College. I have found rooms in Dam Street close by with a Mrs Allsop who says she used to help your mother with washing. She minds Ella while I am on duty. It is not ideal but I need to work and Baby can't come with me.

Everything around here is flat, which makes taking Ella out easy enough. My landlady found me a stroller to put her in.

Your father is in good spirits. I've sorted out his place to his satisfaction, I hope. Book readers spread themselves out a bit, don't they? Your brother Selwyn called to check me over and asked after you.

Yours sincerely

Mary Smith (May)

PS. I forgot to say thank you for Ella's birthday present. You shouldn't have. The dress is very pretty. She's sent you this portrait in return. Sorry I look so startled by the flash.

Celeste sighed as she recalled the letter. How she wished she was back in Lichfield at cherry blossom time, walking Roddy around Minster Pool, taking tea in the marketplace. She envied May but she could live vicariously through her letters and imagine herself there.

The silver-gilt loving cup with two handles was passed to Captain Rostron in appreciation of his heroism and efficient service in rescuing the survivors so promptly. There was also a framed set of resolutions from the women survivors, the ones they'd decided on that first gathering in the salon on the night of 17 April. They offered their profound thanks to the entire crew.

'You went at full speed into a dangerous sea as soon as you heard of the disaster. But for your heroism none of us would have survived.'

Celeste saw the captain was almost overcome by the praise.

'Thank you,' he mumbled, bowing his head. Then he took a deep breath. 'I don't know how to express my thanks for this tribute ... for the honour you've accorded me ... for this splendid cup of good fellowship. I tried to do my duty, first, as a sailor and, second, as a man towards my fellow men. It is not I who deserves this credit but my crew. I want to thank them for their loyalty, their valour and their trust. And I offer you the thanks of myself, my wife and my family. For generations to come this moment will be spoken of proudly by my descendants.'

Then, the chairman of the Survivors' Committee, Mr Seward, turned to the crew.

'When we saw the *Carpathia* coming to us as out of the dawn, we gave our heartfelt thanks. As a token of this, we'd like to present each one of you with a medal.' Celeste had seen the medals: six gold ones for the officers, silver and bronze for the rest. It was a bas-relief copy of the *Carpathia* speeding to their rescue. On the back an inscription read, 'Presented to the captain and crew in recognition of their gallant and heroic services.'

Everyone clapped and Celeste felt a lump form in her throat when she saw the young female steward who'd helped them so generously step forward and curtsy. She thought of the crew of the *Titanic*, who had been taken away for the official inquiry; it was rumoured that they had had their pay docked from the very minute the ship had sunk. They were dependent on charitable donations too. Then she thought of all those at the bottom of the ocean who would never receive anything more from this life.

Harriet was appeased when they attended the Memorial Concert on the Sunday at the Moulin Rouge Theatre, Broadway. What a line-up of artists: United States Army bands from the forts close to New York, navy bands from Brooklyn Navy Yard, children's orchestras, and some of the finest music in town. It was a great spectacle and hearts were lifted.

'You're not going to leave us in the lurch now, Celeste, are you?' Margaret Brown singled her out, strolling over to them at the interval. 'Your daughter-in-law's been such a loyal supporter of our cause, Mrs Parkes.'

Harriet blushed. 'Of course not. She will make herself useful where she can. She's already collected hundreds of dollars from her husband's corporation, the Diamond Rubber Company.'

'Is that so? I'm glad to hear it because we've gotten a big task ahead if we're to recompense those who have lost everything. So we'll see you at the next meeting, then, Celeste? We've got an idea for a special memorial statue as well as national monuments.'

Celeste nodded as Margaret winked.

'Is that the unsinkable Molly Brown?' Harriet gawped, staring after her.

'Shush, don't call her that! No one who knows her calls her Molly. She hates it. She is a one-woman powerhouse and never lets up. If anyone can raise a statue it'll be her and I bet it'll be a whoppa!'

'Don't be coarse, dear, it doesn't suit you,' said Harriet, eyeing the larger-than-life woman in her picture hat and outrageous silk dress. 'She's a bit of a rough diamond but rich as Croesus. She's not your type, surely? All that brash showy style.'

'That woman's heart is bigger than the ship that tried to sink her, pure gold, and a kind heart is all that matters, don't you think? I'll do anything I can to help her.' Celeste was determined to have the last word, leaving her mother-in-law speechless as she strode off.

35

Dear May

How lovely to receive your letter. I want two pages next time, please. How is Lichfield? Did you get to the Greenhill Bower parades at Whitsuntide? I have always loved the processions and the sports but most of all the fair. Everyone is dressed in summer frills with picture hats. There is always such a jolly atmosphere and of course the streets are full of visitors. We don't have anything quite like that in Akron, just a circus now and then and the church bazaar.

We presented the cup and medals to Captain Rostron. Harriet, my mother-in-law, insisted on coming as my chaperone. She was very impressed with all the hats and jewels. Now we are planning a national monument. If I promise to let her come with me on these trips so she can go shopping, I think Grover won't object to us disappearing once a month.

He is very protective of me, which is a bore sometimes but I am determined to be involved in the fund-raising campaign and will do all it takes.

Have you been to Red House yet? It's where I grew up. The garden is lovely at this time of the year with all its pinks and purples. My brothers will be on their walking holiday in Scotland, I expect. Is Ella walking now? Roddy has a scooter and we'll take him to the Great Lakes soon. He is growing so

fast he's soon to be britched and have his hair cropped. I'm
dreading him not being a baby any more.

Do write soon.

Your true friend across the water,

Celeste

May clutched her letters as she hurried into Cathedral Close on
this chill November morning. It was Monday, her day to 'do' for
Canon Forester and the cathedral seemed to loom above her
under a glowering sky threatening snow. She was glad she'd
wrapped Ella warmly in leggings and a thick coat.

She didn't like leaving her baby in Mrs Allsop's care but her
landlady was kindly enough and would wheel Ella out to
Market Street in her pram when she was shopping. Mondays
were always difficult but she could fit in the canon before her
duties at the college. She insisted Mrs Allsop walked Ella
around the Close so May could wave to her from the college
window or make an excuse to pop outside and hold her. Ella
would howl when she put her down, making May feel terrible
for leaving her, but May knew she must do her job no matter
what. They had to live.

Ella was toddling now, gabbling away and thriving in the
Staffordshire air. Her curls bobbed under her bonnet and she
was the object of so much attention with her coal-black eyes
always sparkling. She was such a smiley child. Would her own
baby have got the same attention, May wondered.

Not a day went by when she didn't ache for her own child,
recalling how they used to walk round Queens Park watching
the nursemaids with their fancy prams, or take a tram together
out to the countryside at Barrow Bridge, and sit on the grass
with ice-cream cones. How short their happiness had been.
But she must quietly bear the pain of her nightly dreams in
which she would see her baby's face drifting away on the
waves, fading out of her reach. Once she woke crying out, and

Ella was standing in her cot staring at her with those huge black eyes full of tears.

Don't think about any of it now, she scolded herself as she scuttled across the cobbles.

Without the Foresters she'd have been lost, but now she was safely established in this historic city as a domestic help, looking after all the young clergymen in training. She cleaned their rooms, did their laundry, and helped out in the refectory when she was needed. They kept funny hours but she had a room and kitchen off Dam Street and could nip in and out in the evening when Ella was in her cot, knowing old Mrs Allsop would oblige if she cried.

This letter was going to change things for the better but she needed the canon to check it over first. Her reading was fine but some of the sentences took a bit of swallowing, and what was this about opening a bank account? Celeste would be so knowledgeable about things like that, coming from a world where banks and lawyers and long words were so natural, a world May had never known before.

She would write again before Christmas and include a card and a little gift of knitted mittens for Roddy. It was hard at first to know what to write but it was getting easier and she had started to enjoy gossiping on paper.

And now she was looking forward to sharing some news of her own. Thanks to Canon Forester's encouragement she'd applied to the *Titanic* Relief Fund in London, explaining her circumstances. None of it was lies. She was a widow with a child to support.

'It's your entitlement to compensation and if you don't ask, Mrs Smith, you won't get it, and it would make all the difference to your comfort and Ella's,' the canon had insisted.

She wondered what sort of a muddle the old man had got himself into since her last visit. He had been staying with his son Selwyn in the family house outside the city for a while but he wouldn't stay there long, preferring to live in the little cottage behind the Close.

No one knew May's circumstances, not even the college principal and his wife. It was better that way, but this letter altered everything.

She'd almost been tempted to send a note with Christmas cards to Bolton friends, explaining her new circumstances, and went as far as choosing some pretty ones in the newsagent's. But what if they wrote back wanting her to visit? She put the cards back and hurried out of the shop, knowing it was better to remain silent.

The canon examined the letter with his glasses tipped over his nose. 'You're going to get fifteen shillings and sixpence a week, with three shillings for the child. They've enclosed a cheque with back payments. You must get this in the bank at once.'

'But I haven't got a bank account. How do I get one?' she asked. People like her didn't have bank accounts. Her spare cash was kept in a tea caddy on the mantelpiece. This was uncharted territory.

'Just present this to the bank on the corner of Market Street, sign the forms and they'll give you a proper book. They'll keep the money safe. It gives you options,' he smiled.

May looked up from her polishing. 'To do what?'

'To find your own place to live. You could rent a little cottage perhaps.'

'But who will look after Ella then?'

'You could afford to pay for proper care or work fewer hours.'

'I have to work,' May answered. 'I can't sit at home twiddling my thumbs, I wasn't brought up to be idle.' The thought of all those unoccupied hours stretching ahead terrified her.

'Bringing up a youngster keeps a woman busy enough, I'd have thought,' the canon replied. 'You don't seem very pleased to have a regular income,' he added, seeing the anxious look on her face.

'I'm sorry. It's all a bit above me, banks, cheques . . . What'll people think?'

'Who's to know except a bank clerk, and discretion is their byword.'

'So how long will this money go on?' she asked, trying to keep busy as she listened.

'Until you leave this world, my dear, or remarry. It will see Ella through school for as long as she chooses.'

'I won't be marrying again but it just seems too good to be true,' May sighed, her hands furiously scrubbing the tiles. How did he manage to get the floor so filthy?

'Think what you've lost, Mrs Smith. No money in the world can compensate for this tragedy, now can it?'

May wiped her forehead and shrugged. 'You're right but I've never had so much money in my life.'

'Then let it work for you and Ella. Claim your due and let's hear no more of it. Money gives you choices, my dear, and it will be there for you in the future whatever that may bring.'

36

Christmas 1912

Dear Celeste

I hope my parcel arrives before Christmas. It is getting
colder here. The wind is a lazy one, one as goes through you,
not round you, as my Joe used to say. I miss him so much now
this season is upon us. I took Ella to see Father Christmas but
she cried at his white beard. I've got a bit of good news. The
Titanic Relief Fund are giving us a pension, regular. I have a
bank book, which worried me but the same clerk always helps
me and is sworn to secrecy about money matters, so I am told.

I've enclosed for Roddy some warm mittens I knitted. I
expect you get a lot of snow over there. The lavender sachets
come from the flowers in Red House, to remind you of the
garden and help you sleep. Your brother said to help myself so I
did. Mr Selwyn is a bit of a card. He keeps calling me Queen
of the May. He made a little wheelbarrow for Ella to push,
which was kind of him.

Your father is on his rounds of mercy delivering to the poor
of the parish. I'm getting used to how they do things in the
Close and the services, though I go to St Chad's myself. No,
I've not been back to Bolton. I'd rather leave that part of my
life behind. Yes, I watched the Sheriff's Ride round the bound-
aries of the city, all those ladies on their mounts riding side

saddle. What a sight, and the buckets of horse droppings left behind! The gardeners were chasing after them with shovels. I'd be scared to death to ride but perhaps one day Ella will ride a pony. I saw the picture of you on one.

Must get on with my baking. I'm making mince pies for your father. The cook in the college showed me how.

All the best for the season to you and yours,

May and Ella

'Oh, look, Roddy, aren't those lovely? We'll put some string on them so they won't get lost,' said Celeste, unwrapping May's parcel and sniffing the lavender. It was the only present still left under the huge fir tree in the hall.

Roddy was wide-eyed with wonder at all his gifts, dashing from one to the other while the servants looked on. Susan had the day off so Celeste had her son all to herself after they went to church.

Grover's parents were due any minute for the Christmas lunch. How she longed for mince pies, the pastry melting round the spiced fruit, such an English tradition. But she would have to make do with a version of plum pudding that never quite tasted of home.

'Look, Grover, May's sent such thoughtful gifts and she's applied for the *Titanic* Relief Fund. I'm so pleased . . . Now she can go about building a life for herself. Look how Ella's grown,' said Celeste, trying to interest her husband in the Christmas card.

Once dinner was over, she knew they'd all sit together with nothing much to say and she didn't want him emptying the whiskey decanter.

Grover glanced at the formal shot of May sitting posed in her black dress with a pretty lace collar, and on her knee a beautiful child in starched white cotton.

'How did that skinny thing produce that doll?' he sneered.

'Oh, don't be mean. Her husband had gypsy blood, she told me,' Celeste replied.

'He must have been deaf, dumb *and* blind to marry that thing,' came his reply as he returned to his cigar. May's letters were never of any interest to Grover yet he seemed to resent them when they came. 'What's she on the scrounge for this time, this protégée of yours?'

Celeste ignored him.

Selwyn's Christmas card was illegible and Bertie managed a few lines about rowing on the Cam and trying for a Blue. It was May who was becoming quite the little writer now, keeping tabs on Father's health. Celeste kept May's letters in a special drawer in her bureau so she could reread them, hugging them to her chest. They were a life line, a last link with her family home.

Ever since joining the Women's Relief Committee, Celeste had felt a new purpose in her life, a new energy and sense of being useful. She was no longer sitting around like a dressed-up doll waiting to be picked up and played with by a petulant child. She had dates in her diary that weren't just shopping trips or dinner parties or church fêtes.

She looked across at her husband, now slumped in the chair.

Grover was a spoiled bully, and the more they lived together the more she hated her life with him. It was getting harder to hide their arguments from Roddy. He was at the kindergarten during the day but at night she had to make sure he was asleep before she dared answer back.

Christmas had been spoiled by Grover's worries at work. Her husband was now a bigwig with the Diamond Rubber Company. The chairman, Frederick Barber, had retired to his mansion after some boardroom squabble. There'd been lots of games played to find his natural successor and Grover hadn't got that top post and was in a sulk.

'Let's get some fresh air,' she offered. 'It'll give us all an appetite and Roddy some exercise. He can wear his new mittens. He can take his new bat and ball too.'

'You go, I've work to do.'

'But it's Christmas Day,' she protested. 'A family day. Your parents will be here soon. Oh, do make the effort.' As soon as the words left her mouth she realized her mistake.

'An effort! What do you think I do all day? Those letters from England are turning your head. That woman is currying favour with you, that's all. All you think about is that blessed *Titanic* business. Don't you think it's time you stopped all this scribbling?'

'Nonsense, May's lonely. I'm lonely; she reminds me of home.'

'This is your home. How can you be lonely, you're never at home? How many trips have you made this year? It's costing me a fortune in hotel bills. You'd better cut them back.'

'I take your mother with me. She enjoys a change of air.'

'A change of shops, more like. Pa is complaining too.'

'Let's not quarrel, it upsets Roddy. We mustn't spoil his day.'

'You spoil him all the time. He follows you round like a lapdog.'

'He's only little and they grow so fast, Grover. You're always welcome to come.'

'Someone has to pay for your extravagances,' he said, eyeing the sapphire and pearl antique bracelet he had bought her, now circling her wrist.

Christmas Day was turning out to be just as joyless as every other day. If it wasn't for the tree festooned with baubles, the greenery over the mantelpiece and the cards placed around the room for all to see, it could be any other day.

How did I fall for Grover's apparent charm and his handsome face on that visit to London? No one warned me to look behind the façade to what lay beneath? She had been too young and inexperienced not to be swept off her feet by his promises. Her parents had been equally charmed by Grover's American confidence and good looks. Now his eyes were glassy and cold, his drinking had thickened his waist and his skin was florid but he held all the power. He paid the bills and kept the purse.

In his world women were just decorative objects. It was the men of industry who ruled, backed up by armies of servants to wait on them. If she ever left she'd have nothing: no child, no money, nothing but her pride. Recently she felt that might be the better option. Then she looked at little Roddy and knew it would be impossible to abandon him to the Parkes regime. She thought of the Committee members who were raising funds. How many of them woke in the morning battered and bruised and humiliated? Sometimes she wondered if it might have been better to have drowned on that terrible night, but her thoughts always came back to Roddy. He was her reason to live, to stay strong. Somehow there had to be a way forward. There had to be more to life than this existence.

'Come on, Roddy, we'll wrap up and go to meet Grandma and Grandpa down the drive and leave your daddy to his work in peace.'

37

The March streets were crowded with spectators waiting for the grand procession. It was the big St Patrick's Day Parade in New York City – one of the biggest of the New York festivals. The parade was being held early on the 15th because St Patrick's Day itself was in Holy Week. Families were out on the sidewalks in their green costumes. There were bands and dancers swirling in the dusty streets. Angelo stood watching for a few moments, sniffing the aromas of roasting chestnuts and popcorn.

Salvi and Anna had wrapped their bambino in a green scarf. They were happy with the extra trade the celebrations brought to them but he was feeling miserable.

Another letter had arrived from Maria's family on paper edged with black. They begged Angelo to return home to the *paese*. But how could he – a man who'd unwittingly led his wife and baby to their deaths – face them?

There wasn't a note of reproach in the letter. Whoever had written in such careful script had measured their words with compassion.

He who leaves the old way for the new knows what he loses, but never knows what he may find. God has chosen to take Maria and Alessia to his heart. Who are we to ask why? Father Alberto says we will find out only in eternity.

He hadn't told them about the shoe with the Tuscan lace. It seemed cruel to raise their hopes or his own any further. After months of enquiry no one had come forward, just a woman who thought she had seen the pair of them on the *Titanic* in the saloon, dancing to an Irish jig, but she couldn't be entirely sure. The scene haunted him. Maria always loved to dance, her feet hardly touching the floor as she twirled around laughing.

They should be here enjoying the spectacle together, the baby on his shoulders, Maria standing by his side in her white dress with the lace edging she was so proud of. Her skills would have been in demand. She had been bringing all her equipment: her cushion and tombola, her fusilli and some of her master's designs. She'd planned to teach lace making, to sell her work. He thought again of the shoe that sat on the shrine he'd created with their portrait and the statue of the Madonna del Carmina. What if she'd sold those shoes on board and some baby here was wearing his daughter's clothes? He couldn't bear the thought.

He watched the spectators crossing themselves in fervour as the Madonna's statue bobbed past on the shoulders of burly Irish navvies. Across the street a group of Irish shop workers giggled and waved at the procession. One girl hung back, wrapping herself in a shawl, a straw boater perched on her head, her eyes cast down until she glanced at him staring at her and smiled. He glanced away, shaken by his response.

Oh no you don't, making eyes at a colleen and your wife not gone a year. But the instinct to find comfort was strong. He turned away ashamed as the procession of bands in their green uniforms blew out their tunes into the fetid air. It was stifling in the crowd and he badly needed a drink. He always needed a drink these days. A bottle was his solace and faithful companion. It helped him sleep. 'Work hard, work always and you'll never know hunger,' his papa had always said.

He'd worked hard, and for what? What was the point? Salvi was always nagging him to wash and comb his black curls.

'You're a handsome *boia* ... go find a *ragazza* to give you comfort.'

He'd wanted to hit him but couldn't be disrespectful to his elders. How could he look at another woman? How could he forget his Maria just like that, like turning off a faucet?

There were graves far away in Canada where the recovered bodies had been buried. He should have sought her there but they said there was no record of Maria or Alessia being found. Anna and Salvi had written to the Welfare Relief on his behalf and had heard there was compensation on offer but it only covered Maria's property. Angelo could claim for a bundle of lost lacework. But how do you compensate for the loss of your wife and child?

The priest at Old St Patrick's was on his side but had told him to be patient in his grief. It would ease, given time, but Angelo didn't want it to pass. The pain was his punishment, but to work he must sleep and to sleep, he must drink. He was in danger of losing his grip. Would it matter if one morning up in the gantry he slipped? Would it matter if he ended it all?

Only the thought of his mother's shame and pain stopped him. That and the little shoe. What if Alessia was somewhere out there? The torment of such a yearning must be blotted out.

Angelo turned his back on the parade. He'd seen enough happy families for one day. He needed a stiff drink, a cheap bar and a few hours of oblivion in the back alleys of Mulberry Bend.

Later he woke on the stinking floor of some dosshouse. His pockets had been picked clean. He smelled of booze and worse. Where was he? As he stood up the room began to spin. Stepping over drunken bodies snoring off their hangovers, he heard the bells calling the faithful to Palm Sunday Mass.

He couldn't recall how he'd landed in this den but his head was swimming with a thumping headache. Had he been at the poteen with some Paddy mates celebrating? Did it matter? Nothing mattered now he'd lost his pay, or rather what was left of it. He needed a change of clothes before he faced Salvi and Anna, who'd tear a strip off him, shamed by the sight of this tramp, the man he'd become.

But what the eye doesn't see and all that ... 'Don't miss the Holy Saint's Day, he will always help you out,' His mother's voice was in his ear, but would St Patrick hear his pleas? What would he care about one more drunken Italian?

Angelo was confused, hung over and desperate. He must find somewhere to clean up and honour this day.

He smiled, thinking of his mamma wagging her finger. 'Show me your friends, Angelo, and I'll tell you who you are.'

He stared down at the prostrate drunks, ruffians, pickpockets and assorted low life. *I'm not one of them, am I? Holy Mary, have I come to this? ... Help me! Why, oh why, Maria, did you have to leave me? What'll become of me without you? Why did you get on that doomed ship?* The tears wouldn't stop as he staggered out into the spring sunshine, the light stabbing at his eyes. He held onto the doorframe to get his bearings and, putting an unsteady boot on the sidewalk, he aimed towards the sound of the bells.

38

April 1913

Their letters had clearly crossed in the post. May sat in the park to read hers through over and over again before she posted it.

Dear Celeste

This will be a short note. I can't believe it is a year since our first fateful meeting. I can hardly bear to think of the days to come when the word *Titanic* will be once again on everyone's lips and in the papers. There are to be big memorial services across England. It breaks my heart that I have no place to lay flowers for Joe, and when I think of the family life snatched from us so cruelly I still find it hard to bear.

Your father has put the flowers for you on your mother's resting place. He misses her company, especially in the evenings. It's a time when couples eat and talk by the fireside, isn't it, a time of closeness and comfort denied to widows and those who mourn?

It's funny how you have taught me to talk on paper. I like to think we're sitting over a cup of tea and just having a chat. I miss the mill girls for that. The women in the college are a bit clannish and there's one I don't like, called Florrie Jessup, who is a right nosy parker, like a ferret. I keep clear of her if I can.

Your father has asked us to tea on the 15th, for which I am grateful. Only he really knows how terrible that date will be for the rest of my life. I will take some éclairs, which I know he likes.

I can never thank you enough for giving me this chance of life away from pitying eyes. As long as I live I will be in your debt and if there is anything I can do in return to help you, you only have to ask. We may have come from opposite ends but somehow I feel in our letters we are becoming the best of friends. I do hope you feel the same.

God bless you,

May and Ella

'Is there nothing for me in the post, Minnie?' Celeste was puzzled. There had not been a word from May in weeks, which was unusual, especially as the fateful anniversary was looming. For the umpteenth time, she checked the silver salver in the hall where letters were laid.

'Sorry, madam, nothing I've seen,' Minnie bobbed in reply, avoiding her eye, which was not like her.

Celeste sighed. 'I was hoping for a letter from England.'

'From your *Titanic* friend?' Minnie said. The servants all knew about her correspondence with May and steamed off the stamps for Roddy's little collection. 'There's a big memorial in town for all the drowned souls and a Mass in the Catholic church.'

Celeste was hoping to join the big memorials in New York but it was getting harder to get Grover's permission. But she did have an idea that might work if she put it to him carefully. They must take Roddy. He was getting quite clingy and Susan said he was wetting the bed again.

'We won't trouble Mr Parkes with this. He's got so much on his mind,' Celeste had said. Why did she always feel she must make excuses for him? She knew he might punish Roddy and make things worse. A trip to New York would be good for all of them; time together as a family might make Roddy a little more secure. Why did she feel so torn between home and her other work? Perhaps if she wrote to May it would clear her mind. At least on paper she could be more honest with herself.

I think our letters must have crossed again. Funny, how we keep writing at the same time. A year has gone by but I can still hear those screams of stricken passengers in the water. I try to fill my time making sure those *Titanic* voices will never be drowned out or fall on deaf ears.

If I'm honest some of the Survivors' Committee meetings are boring. Women can fight their corner as good as any men and there are some strident voices who want their way of doing things above others . . .

She wrote on, lost in all her news, trying not to sound too important.

Sometimes I sit in the Church Sewing Bee listening to the tittle-tattle around me until I could scream. Then I spout forth about all I hear in New York about voting rights for women and my mother-in-law looks across in horror. 'If this is what you get up to with those suffragette types, I don't think Grover will want you mixing with them.'

I tried to explain why men can't appreciate our best strengths as being as important as theirs on the world stage. Oh dear, I'm sounding like a pamphleteer. I get torn between my duties as mother and wife, and those of being a good citizen. I'm wondering what's left of the girl I used to be, the one with all those dreams. If I were back with you would I be chaining myself to railings and marching with Mrs Pankhurst? I do hope so.

How terrible to be complaining to you in this month of all months when we must think of those poor souls who will never have a voice again. Forgive me for being so thoughtless. I

do look forward to your letters but it seems weeks since I last
heard from you. I hope you find a quiet place to mourn your
dear husband. Don't leave it so long before you write again.

Yours in agitation and remembrance,

Celeste

She looked for a stamp but there was nothing in her letter case.
Grover wouldn't mind her taking one of his. She needn't tell
him it was for a letter to May. She made for his study, hesitating
briefly outside, recalling the last time she'd ventured in there
and the blows that followed.

She checked his silver rack on the desk. Nothing there either.
She never dared look in his drawers, but anyway, they were
usually locked.

As she bent down to check she noticed an envelope with a
British stamp and familiar handwriting in the trash basket. An
opened letter from May, read and then discarded. The room spun
for a second as she took in the fact that it was one she'd never
seen and which, according to the postmark, must have arrived
only a few days ago. Of course May had not forgotten her friend
on the first anniversary of the sinking.

Celeste sat down in Grover's mahogany chair and read the
letter through carefully. It was all she could do to breathe, such
was the rage burning inside her. She wanted to scream with
frustration at this treachery.

Am I not even to have privacy or friends of my own? How
dare he? This was too much to bear. She sobbed as she read it
again and placed the letter back exactly as she had found it. Her
anger bubbled up again. Two could play this game, she thought,
unsealing her own letter to add a postscript.

PS. Your letter has just arrived. Please disregard my silly
rebuke, but since you offer to help me out, I do have a request,
a funny one but I'll explain later. From now on please address

your letters to Mrs Parkes c/o The Post Office at Akron and
not here.

It was the best she could do on the spur of the moment. If
Grover thought their friendship was on the wane, he'd relax
his guard. Little did he know what he'd just achieved. Weak as
she might be, he'd touched a nerve, stiffened her resolve. No
one was going to stop her writing home, or to anyone she
chose. If this was war then she'd won the first skirmish. But she
sensed there would be worse battles ahead before victory was
hers.

May read Celeste's strange letter three times, trying to get the
gist of it. The middle bit was all about Votes for Women and a
woman called Alice Paul, who'd been in England on hunger
strike and now was fighting for the suffragette cause in the States.

I've joined the Congressional Union for Women's Suffrage. I
have to do something to help women's rights here. Why should
half the human population have no say in its affairs? Twenty
million women are denied the vote here. Alice says each one of
our efforts counts like the hymn 'You in your small corner and
I in mine'.

She read on, confused, especially about the change of address.
    She'd seen suffrage campaigners handing out leaflets in the
marketplace in Lichfield and pictures of them in the newspapers
picketing outside Parliament.
    'Grover thinks I am doing *Titanic* Survivors' Committee
work, which is sort of true. I have to do something ...' Her
handwriting was scrawled over the page as though Celeste had
been in a hurry. What *was* going on?
    It wasn't that May didn't believe in votes for women herself.
They'd been very hot on that in Bolton in the cotton mills, and

she'd signed up with the Union years ago for Universal Suffrage. There'd been a riot when Mr Winston Churchill passed through the town and she knew many of her fellow mill workers were still active in the north. Joe believed in the socialist cause but it had all gone a bit haywire, what with Mrs Pankhurst and her scuffles with the police. The burning of Lord Leverhulme's bungalow in Rivington recently had shocked her but she'd let it all pass over her head since her arrival in Lichfield. It all seemed so far away from her life now.

What would Canon Forester think about his daughter gallivanting over the country with banners? Her husband must be very understanding to let her make such an exhibition of herself. But women like Celeste didn't need to work, May sighed. They could pursue their hobbies and not worry about the cost. But something was up, she could sense it, and she was worried. Celeste didn't sound herself.

May reread the pages about Celeste's busy life and felt ashamed of her own quiet existence. She did her chores at home, her domestic work. There was Ella to mind and she collected her pension with gratitude. She sat quietly in the back pew of the old parish church in Netherstowe every Sunday trying to settle her restless mind, which continued to torment her with dreams. It was hard living a lie in her letters, covering her true feelings about Ella and what she had done, but Ella was so much a part of her now she'd never let her go.

Funny, how they were both hinting about their worries but never spelling them out. Hers were too terrible ever to be committed to paper.

To make matters worse she'd had a set-to with Florrie Jessup, who'd caught her coming out of the Provincial Bank one afternoon.

'It's not often we see one of us with a savings book,' Florrie smiled, eyeing the bank book in May's basket with interest.

May felt obliged to say something. 'My husband died at sea

and this is a pension,' she offered, wanting to scuttle off in the opposite direction from this large nosy woman.

'Is it now? We wondered how you manage to keep you and the kiddie so well turned out on the pittance we get from up there,' she sneered, pointing in the direction of Cathedral Close and then looking back at May's smart black coat.

May didn't like the sound of the 'we'. She hoped she and Ella weren't the subject of local gossip. 'Ella gets parcels from America,' she tried to explain.

'So you've got relatives there? Is that how you got this job? You do extra for the canon now, and I heard Letty Fagan wasn't right pleased when he let her go in favour of you. Word of advice, love, this is not how you go about getting jobs round here. People think Letty didn't do a good job for him.'

May flushed. 'Well, his house was in a bit of a state when I called the first time. I thought he didn't have help.'

'What were the likes of you doing calling on the likes of him in the first place?' Florrie was dug into the pavement now, barring her path.

'I met his daughter once . . .' Big mistake.

'But she's in America, wed to some bigwig. She was on the *Titanic*. How come you know her?'

'Oh, friends from the church, it's a long story.' She made to push the pram away but Florrie stood firm.

'I'm surprised you bother to turn up to work at all, what with such posh connections and a private pension.'

The gloves were off now. How could May defend her corner? 'It's not like that at all. I like my work. There's just the two of us, I have to work.' May turned to go again but Florrie grabbed her arm.

'Not so fast. That's not what I heard. You turned down an invitation to join the Cooperative Guild.'

'Who told you that?' May was impatient to run from all these accusations. 'I need the baby minding every time I leave the house. It costs money or favours,' she snapped back.

'Listen, Mrs Smith, if that's what your name *really* is, let me give you a bit of advice for free. There's town and gown in this city: Cathedral Close or Market Square, and it doesn't do to mix or try keeping one foot in each camp. You are one of us or one of them, see?'

'I'm not from here. I'm from Lancashire and I don't take sides.' May's hackles were rising now.

Quick as a flash Florrie dived in. 'So? What brings a north erner all this way then?'

'I was widowed,' May said under her breath. 'Can't a woman have a change of scene?'

Florrie prickled at the reply, showing not an ounce of sympathy as she stood aside. 'Pardon me for breathing but we wondered if you weren't exactly a *regular* widow, you know.'

'What do you mean?' May looked Florrie full in the eye, catching her off guard for a second.

'Well, we wondered if someone's set you up, like ... out of the way with you and the kiddie not exactly short of a bob or two and no visitors.' There was a blush on her cheek as she spoke.

'How dare you suggest such a thing? Joseph was my husband, my childhood sweetheart. It's only a year since his death.' Tears filled her eyes.

'Hold yer hair on! I didn't mean any offence but you do keep yourself to yourself. People are bound to ask questions, now, aren't they?'

'What is it to you who I am?' May snapped back. 'Now, if you don't mind, I've still got some shopping to do.'

'There's something about you I don't understand; a bit of a mystery, by my reckoning. But not to worry, I'll ferret around until I know the truth of it. Pension indeed ...'

Florrie stormed off laughing and May felt sick. So much for peace and quiet. Tittle-tattle by the college staff was the last thing she needed. *Damn you, Florrie, for stirring things up just as I was settling.* Thank goodness Ella had slept through the whole episode. Let them think what they liked, they'd get nothing else from her. Perhaps it was time to find another job. Why couldn't they leave her alone? She didn't have to answer to an interfering busybody like Florrie, but she must be more on her guard from now on.

It was true she didn't mix much, but with all her jobs and the little one there was no time and she was so tired; she still slept badly at night.

Her only friend was across the ocean and even she was acting queer. Was it a proper friendship where you never met but just the once in such extraordinary circumstances? Yet somehow that bond was a comfort and strength, her letters were a chance to pour out her feelings and speak her mind. A woman like Celeste wouldn't keep writing if she didn't want to.

If only she could dare tell the real truth about Ella. Maybe she'd sleep then. But that was too much for any friend to take on board. I am a liar and a thief and a dissembler, she sighed, but what I did seemed so right at the time.

All that mattered was Ella's welfare. She was saving every penny so the little one could have the best she could afford: good shoes, dancing lessons, a proper schooling. When the time came Ella would take her place one day not at the bottom or the top but in the middle, with chances and opportunities in life. If others thought them both standoffish, then tough. Ella was worth all of them put together.

In her own mind, Captain Smith had put his trust in her to do her utmost to give the baby a proper life. Not in some orphanage like herself and Joe had been but with the freedom to choose her own path. May had jumped at school learning, even as a half-day scholar at the mill. She loved a good book to read. She was interested in the cathedral and its history and liked listening to organ music and the choirboys singing. In fact, she was beginning to like this ancient city, even though it was flat with no hills around, so unlike the moors at Edgeworth.

If she'd been born higher up the ladder, maybe she'd be like Celeste, all fired up about women's votes. Perhaps she should join the Guild and show willing. She might learn a few tips and make friends outside her work. But friends asked questions and poked around in your life. There was safety in distance. Better simply to stick to things as they were and not go rootling for trouble.

Ella was all that mattered now. She must succeed and have her chances so that the theft of her true identity could be justified. Only when that happened would May find some peace.

39

It was here, the day Angelo was dreading. He rose early for work, glancing with sadness at the little shrine in the corner with its shoe and photograph. He was sharing a room with Salvi's boys. They insisted he live with them now that he'd lost his apartment, after complaints to the landlord about his rowdy all-night carousing with drunken friends and falling behind with his rent.

'No Bartolini sleeps on the street while I am alive. My brother would kill me,' said his uncle. 'But you find a job and pull up your boot strings or else.'

Slowly Angelo had sobered up enough to hold down a job again. It was a chilly clear spring morning, and from the rooftop in Manhattan he sat staring out over the city skyline, over the skyscrapers to the bridges and the river stretching out into the harbour, recalling that terrible night a year ago. How had he survived such loss, such pain and emptiness?

He turned up to work each day and climbed onto cranes and up scaffolding, perching high above the building sites. Work was key, work was comfort and he built up his reputation once more as a stevedore who was reliable and trustworthy enough to be sought out and chosen above other more experienced local men.

Today he would finish early, put on his best shirt and jacket, and head to Mulberry Street and Old St Patrick's for the special Mass. There, he would light a candle for Maria and their little one alongside other grieving relatives.

He knew many of the Irish by sight now, the old women and young girls, the red-haired navvies who kneeled alongside him. St Pat's was like a lighthouse in the darkness, somewhere to sit and smell the incense and feel safe in this loud brash city.

Angelo liked the old cathedral better than the big new one. It reminded him of home. The stonework was cool to his touch. Father Bernardo had seen them all through such a difficult time like a true shepherd, but this was a Mass that brought back such memories of that night in the rain last April.

The girl in the plaid shawl sat in front of him again, her coppery curls caught up in a bunch that fell down her back. He'd seen her in the street at the parade. She was weeping so hard one of the sisters touched her arm.

'Now, Kathleen, they're all with the angels now ... I know it's hard but they wouldn't want you to take on so.'

Angelo struggled to stay in control of his own tears. He knew only too well what she was feeling right now. When the service was over he got up to leave but the sisters were directing them into the parish room. 'What you're needing now is a strong cup of tea. It's laid on in the back. Come on, Angelo, you as well. After a hard day's work you must be thirsty.'

He would rather have downed a barrel of whiskey but he smiled and made his way with the others. They all sat around awkwardly, strangers connected by this terrible chain of events. He nearly choked on the sweet milky tea. The girl in the shawl looked across at him and smiled. She had the greenest eyes he'd ever seen, like polished marble. He smiled back and her cheeks flushed.

'My sister, Mary Louise, got on the ship at Queenstown,' she whispered. 'And you?'

'My wife,' he replied. 'Maria and our *bambina* from Italy at Cherbourg.'

'You poor man.' She shook her head in sympathy. 'It never goes away, does it?'

Suddenly he was glad he'd changed his shirt and trimmed the wildness out of his black hair; relieved that Anna insisted he shake off the dust of the building site before he came to Mass.

Everyone was sitting, drinking, making polite conversation in their own languages. In a few moments they'd all go their separate ways for another year.

On the steps of the cathedral, the Irish girl hesitated, wrapping her shawl around her shoulders, giving him a chance to catch up with her. It was not yet dark and he felt himself drawn to her side. 'It's a *bella notte,* a good night for a walk around the block, a *passeggiata,* in my country,' he offered, towering over her tiny frame.

'Yes, to be sure, it's too nice to be indoors,' she replied. They both looked at each other shyly, and then turned away.

'I'm Kathleen O'Leary. And you are . . . ?' She paused. 'I can't walk with a stranger.'

Angelo bowed, lifting his cap. 'Angelo Bartolini,' he replied as they took a few steps towards the sidewalk and the bustle of Manhattan at night.

They didn't see Father Bernardo smiling a benediction on their meeting as he watched Kathleen take Angelo's arm, nor hear the kindly priest muttering to himself, 'The Lord works in mysterious ways his wonders to perform.'

40

I am sorry for the delay in writing but I've heard some strange news. There's been a public subscription raised to build some memorial to Captain Smith. I thought you'd like to know. I am not sure where yet, somewhere in Staffordshire where he was born or maybe even here. It is to be a full likeness, a statue, I think. There was a piece in the *Lichfield Mercury* that caught my eye. I am glad they are doing something. When we are all long gone, those memorials will be there to remind people of the gallant men and women who gave their lives for our safety.

Just the mention of our captain's name makes me break out into a sweat. There have been so many reports blaming him for the disaster, saying he went too fast in the night, but I don't want to think ill of that poor man or indeed about any of it. That night will haunt me for the rest of my life without my casting blame left and right. I thought once the anniversary was over I'd feel better, but I don't. I just don't want any more reminders, do you?

I am so glad I have you to share these feelings with. Only someone who's seen what we have can understand the terror of recalling it all.

There's been a lot of talk in the paper about building up the navy and army to face the Kaiser, should he turn his guns on us some day. There's even a shooting range in a farmer's field where Selwyn goes to practise his aim. If ever you were thinking of coming across on a visit, say, for Christmas, I'd do it soon, my dear friend, just in case. Let's hope it's all a false alarm. It would be grand to see you and your family, though.

Celeste locked this latest letter in her bureau, unsettled by May's news. Perhaps it was time to cajole Grover into a family trip. It was worth a try. An English Christmas would do them all good.

She chose her moment carefully. Dinner had been perfect, with every attention to detail he liked: his favourite chicken pot pie followed by canned peaches and cream. Roddy was in his nursery and all was well.

'I'd like to visit Papa and my brothers for Christmas. We could all go together,' she smiled at Grover as they sat opposite each other. 'There's talk of war in Europe. Papa's not been in good health and he'd love to see little Roderick. It's been such a hard year here with those terrible floods in March, the Ohio and Eyrie canal destroyed and those poor Akron folk drowned. I've been so busy with the Relief Committee. The doctor suggests perhaps a change of scene will do me good.'

There was a silence as Grover slowly put down his linen napkin and gave her a hard glare.

'You get plenty of that with your trips south. I would think you were sick of trains, and boats, for that matter. Your place is here at home at Christmas.'

'I know that, but my father would love us to go over.'

'Your brothers are quite capable of keeping him company.'

'He misses me, and Roddy would love to see the old country and his grandpa.'

'You're not taking my boy across the Atlantic, not now, not ever, and certainly not to that godforsaken little island full of fog and rain. I'm too busy to accompany you. Let him make the journey over here for a change ...' Grover dismissed her plea and reached for the cigar box.

'Oh, but it's so special in the cathedral. Please think about it. Roddy must meet his grandfather.'

'He's got all the grandparents he needs here. You go if you want to – at your own expense. The boy stays with Susan like he did last time.'

'But May says in her letter—' The words were out before she could bite them back.

'May! I'm sick of that name. Why you've picked up this snivelling little scrap to play Lady Bountiful with beats me. Don't think I don't know that you still send her extravagant parcels. Mother says you are in and out of the linen shops spending your allowance on girl's dresses,' he snapped.

'Perhaps if I had a girl of my own ...' She paused, seeing his eyebrow rise at this defiance. There would be trouble bringing up this subject again. Grover never made love to her without making the point of putting on those dreadful rubbers.

'Here we go again. All you think about is babies. We've got our son and heir. He's out of diapers now and becoming more like a human being every day. I am not having you growing fat and ugly again and drooling over cribs like some ignorant peasant. It's not as if you even enjoy making babies, is it? You're a cold English spinster at heart. I should never have married you.'

Stay calm, don't respond, Celeste urged herself, but the anger flared up like a wild horse on the rampage, and the words were out of her mouth before she could rein them in.

'And you are a cruel bully who shows no mercy in getting what he wants when he wants it, no matter how tired or ill I feel. You know I've always wanted a larger family. How can you deny me another child?'

Grover was up out of his chair in a second and he grabbed her by the hair, pulling out the padding and the combs. 'You go too far, madam. Don't think I don't know what you've been reading in secret: women's suffrage and women's rights pamphlets. I'm not having that garbage in this house! I let you squander your time with the *Titanic* Committee because at least you meet the right people there. Contacts like them with husbands in power will help our company. The other mob are just a bunch of blue stockings. I don't want you going near them. They are man haters, the lot of them. There's only one place for a woman like that and it's on a bed with her legs in the air. They need to know their place and so must you.' He pulled her from her seat, out into the hall and across to the stairs.

'No, please, not now, you'll wake Roddy. Just calm down. We have to talk this through . . .'

She was not going to say she was sorry for speaking her mind. She pulled back but he pushed her forward, grabbing her again by the hair. 'Get up there and shut up! You should know by now, you do not argue with me. Move it!'

'No, I will not!' she shouted, not caring who heard her. He slapped her hard across the cheek, dragged her the last few yards to the bedroom, punching her in the stomach as he threw her on the bed.

'You, madam, are my wife and I will fuck you when and where I please.'

Celeste struggled to free herself from his determined grasp. 'This isn't right. What did I say to make you do this? I won't submit to this degradation any more . . .'

'Oh, yes, you will!' She saw the hatred in his eyes but a moment's hesitation too. This was her chance.

'Why do you hate me, Grover? What have I ever done that makes you do these things to me? There has to be a better way than this,' she pleaded, trying to reason with him. When she turned her face she saw his eyes glinting as if he was in another place, looking at her as if she was the scrapings off his shoe.

'There you go again with your fancy airs and graces, all prim and proper. I should've known better than to take on a parson's daughter. You've never been a real woman to me. You're so flat-chested and skinny, you look down your nose at my family as if they are nothing.'

'I've never ever done that, and worry has stripped the flesh off me,' she protested. His reply was a punch to her jaw and she felt her remaining strength crumble.

'Don't argue with me! Shut up or there'll be more where that came from. I am your husband. You owe me everything, bed and board. You are *nothing* without me. Women like you are nothing but simpering ninnies.'

'I bet you don't say that about the girls at Lily's Place downtown,' she whispered. 'Is that where you have most of your fun?'

'What of it? Those girls know how to please a man, not like you, you frigid bitch. You think you're so special . . . a survivor of the *Titanic*. Let me tell you, I wish you were at the bottom of the ocean . . . It's always Roddy first and foremost, or Margaret Brown and her fancy cronies. I'm sick of you looking down your nose at me. I didn't pick you out of the crowd to make a fool of me.'

'That's not fair and it's not true. Are you saying you're jealous of our son or my other life? It doesn't have to be this way. I thought you'd be proud that I'm helping others. Why are you so angry? Please, you're hurting me . . . We can talk this over,' she gasped, but it was a mistake.

'I'll show you just what hurt is!' he said, throwing her onto her stomach, pulling up her skirt, ripping her underwear and pulling her legs apart.

'No, no, please. Not that again,' she moaned. But there was no arguing. She had no strength left to fight him. She felt her supper gagging in her throat. There was nothing left but to bury her face in the counterpane and submit to the agony. But she would not cry out, or move or show him how much he was hurting her. Even as she gasped for breath and tasted the silk of the bedding on her swollen mouth, she vowed he would never do this to her again. She would kill him first.

Never had she felt so alone, yet a fire inside was burning. I hate you, she repeated like a prayer over and over again until his pumping ceased. *I will find a way out. I didn't survive the* Titanic *to end up like this.*

Afterwards she lay on the bed, exhausted but defiant. *If my brothers knew what Grover was really like . . . But how can I ever tell of such dirty shaming? How can I explain such a terrible mistake made in all innocence? How easy it is to believe what is on the surface is the real Grover inside.* Did he only see her as a prize and trophy or an obedient pet? How could she let Roddy grow up with such an example of what it meant to be a man?

It was then she turned to see Roddy's sleepy face staring at her. He was holding his special teddy bear.

'Why are you are lying like that? Are you sick, Mama?' he asked as she tried to raise herself.

'Yes, but back to bed now, darling.'

'You woke me up. I heard shouting. Is Daddy angry again?'

'No, no, just tired. He works so hard. He likes us to be quiet,' she offered. *Why am I defending him? Only so that Roddy doesn't know the truth.*

'What have you done to your face?'

Celeste winced as he touched her bleeding mouth. 'Silly Mummy fell and banged her face,' she said. This was new, a concerning development. Grover had never hit her on the face before. 'Back to bed now.' She tried to stand up but the room swam before her. With every ounce of strength she guided him back to the nursery.

No one else must see her like this. Her cheek was bruised, her lip busted and she looked a mess. Oh Lord, how was she going to explain this away?

If only there was someone she could trust here, someone who would give her the courage to tell the truth. But Grover had discouraged close friendships. He said the wives they knew were only out to get a promotion for their husbands.

Harriet and her husband might call tomorrow so she must stay in bed and claim a cold or something.

She must seek help. Someone somewhere would tell her what to do or point the way out of this living hell. But who? There were mature ladies in the Episcopalian church where she taught in the Sunday school. But since Grover's promotion onto the board of the Diamond Match Company, they'd set themselves apart from her, no matter how many friendly overtures she made. And how could she attend Matins looking like this? She considered wearing a thick veil, but she was now out of formal mourning.

There was only one woman in the country she trusted, whose shoulders were broad enough to carry her and her face showed she'd lived some and a lot more. Margaret Tobin Brown. She was living apart from her husband, so she must've seen life in all its shades of grey. Yet to talk behind Grover's back was such a betrayal. For better or for worse; she'd made the marriage vow in all sincerity.

Grover had given her a new world, a comfortable life and a lovely son. In exchange for what? The appalling indignity she'd just endured? How did this battering tie in with the love of marriage; that two shall become one flesh? It was making her head spin with confusion.

Love was the only thing that mattered – not wealth or status, love – and there was precious little of that left on either side. She disappointed him and he disgusted her. There had to be an end to this and soon.

In the morning a bunch of cream and red roses appeared outside her bedroom door with no note. Was this an apology or a warning? Whatever it was, she was trapped in this gilded cage unless she could set herself free.

41

Angelo paced up and down the sidewalk in the snow waiting for the linen shop to close. He wouldn't dare to go in, not with all those female clothes hanging in the window. For over six months now he'd been walking out with Kathleen O'Leary. He'd kept her a secret at first but now he wanted to take her to meet Uncle Salvi and Aunt Anna for supper.

Sometimes he felt it was too soon to be seeing another girl. He tried to explain that Maria would always be his wife and he wasn't looking for anything other than friendship.

Kathleen had speared him with those green eyes of hers. 'And what makes you think I'd be after anything more myself?' she retorted. 'If and when I marry, it'll be one of my own kind, full of Irish blarney.' That had felt like a slap in the face until he saw the twinkle in her eyes.

The Irish and Italians might live and work cheek by jowl but the Irish had been over here longer, with their own customs, festivals and language. Even their Catholic devotions were more intense.

Angelo's family were suspicious of the friendship at first but suggested he must bring Kathleen round for a look over. He hadn't dared to subject her to the inquisition, not until he was sure that she was the one for him. Kathleen was a city girl, a shop girl living in a hostel with a family from Dublin. She'd been in service and come over to the States for the opportunity of a new life. She was as proud as she was pretty, with a mouth on her once she got over her initial shyness.

They'd been drifting along, going nowhere, sitting in cafés, walking in the park, going to the Moviedrome. It was time to firm up where they were heading. They hardly even held hands, and Angelo was confused.

He hugged his jacket round him against the chill of the evening. She was late. Had she stood him up?

Then there she was, scurrying out of the door, her hand clinging to her green beret, her hair tumbling around her face as usual. She wore a long jacket with a hobble skirt and neat boots: a smart city girl.

'Where's it tonight? It's too cold to hang about,' she said, linking her arm in his and making him feel ten feet tall.

'Would you mind if we went to my uncle and aunt's for supper? They like to meet my intended,' he blurted out, and knew by the look on her face he'd not got his English right.

'Is that your idea of a proposal? Is that how you did it first time around?'

Angelo shook his head confused. 'We were in Italy. There are customs, meetings, arrangements, you know?'

'No, I don't know. I'm Irish and when a guy asks a girl to be his wife, he goes down on his knee and makes a meal of it. I'm not second-best. Good night!' She spun round and made in the opposite direction, trying not to slide on the sidewalk ice.

'*Per favore, Katerina*, what I do wrong?'

'Everything.' She stopped and sighed. 'You walk the soles off my shoes for six months and not a word of this, and now you want to parade me around strangers, with no warning, no chance to change my clothes. This is not Italy or Dublin. This is New York and we *both* have a say in making a marriage. If I'm only allowed to do this once, I'll do it right. If you want to marry me, you will court me properly. You've got to persuade me to spend the rest of my life with you.' She was walking back to him now.

'So what do we do now?'

'We'll make it up as we go along. In America we can make everything different, if we choose.'

'But I promised Anna I would bring you. She's in America but it is still Italy too. She never met Maria. Please come.'

'We'll call there later. It's still early, take me somewhere special to mark our engagement,' she smiled.

'We could go to Battery Park?' he offered.

'In this weather? I thought Italian men were romancers?'

'I don't have much dollars, I have to pay my rent.' How could he explain how every bit of his wages went on paying back his old debts.

'That's another rule. We share the tab, we go halves. I got my wage. Let's find a hot dog stall and go wild.'

Angelo was shocked. 'But it's Friday, fish only.'

'Forget that. We may be good Catholics but we're not that holy. It's not every night a girl gets herself engaged.' When Kathleen laughed she lit up the street. 'Come on, Romeo, show a girl a good time.'

His heart lifted. Kathleen would never be Maria. She was a fiery Irish girl with wild eyes and hair. But she would suit him well, and she was right. It was time to start anew. They were in America now.

42

March 1914

'I'm not going back in that church again.' May was spitting fumes as she banged the crockery down on Canon Forester's sink. 'Have you seen what the vicar wrote in the *Lichfield Mercury* about Captain Smith's statue being unveiled in Museum Gardens? He says that the officers received a warning that there was ice in their path and yet the speed of the ship was not reduced.' She paused. 'Is this true? It wasn't like that, I'm sure. Mr Fuller says we shouldn't honour this captain above others. I don't understand. We've *all* contributed to this statue. He did his duty and he saved my child.'

'Then write to the paper and tell them, Mrs Smith. That will silence them. You can bear witness to his brave act,' the canon replied.

'Oh, I can't, I've never written a letter to a paper before, not me . . .' she hesitated. 'It's Ella that should be writing . . . not me.'

'Then write on her behalf. Tell them your story. Celeste has written about what he did that night but she wasn't sure if it really was Captain Smith in the water.'

'Would you write on our behalf?' she asked, but the canon shook his head.

'I don't think I ought to get involved in this argument.

Feelings are running high about what really happened. There are those who say the captain was careless and improvident.'

'Never!' May put down her washing-up brush, all hot and bothered. 'He came to the side of the boat and handed over the baby from the sea. They offered him a place onboard but he refused it . . . Celeste told me so . . . I didn't actually see him but one of the crew did.'

'It's all hearsay, my dear, but you must write on his behalf if you feel so strongly.' His words gave her courage. She loved this kind old man; he never made her feel small or stupid.

'I will, but you'll have to check over the spellings, sir. I don't want to make a fool of myself or sign my name in public.'

Over the next weeks the arguments piled up in the paper for and against the statue being placed in Lichfield. May bought notepaper and a new pen. She drafted letter after letter, evening after evening, saying nothing in church. To tell the vicar to his face he was wrong, that wouldn't be proper coming from the likes of her. She started to attend the cathedral services instead.

Then came an anonymous letter in the paper, which drew her fury.

> It would be a pity to allow our garden to become a dump-
> ing ground for monuments of men who have no connection
> with the city and are unknown to fame. We must face facts and
> I believe it is a fact (and I say this at the risk of being labelled
> uncharitable) that the late Commander of the *Titanic* was
> unknown to fame before he committed the error of judgement
> which . . . led to one of the greatest catastrophes of modern
> times . . .

The gloves were off now. May tried to read the rest but her eyes steamed up with fury and exhaustion. This wasn't fair. The dead couldn't defend themselves. It wasn't like that. He didn't design the ship or put too few lifeboats on it. He didn't ignore the warning shots and pass by like the Pharisees who let people drown. Everyone knew it was the *Californian*, the mystery ship on the horizon, that was to blame for not answering the distress call when it was nearby. Others said there was some other ship so close they could see its lights but it passed by on the other side too.

It wasn't the captain who had roped off Third Class and put guards on the steps to the upper decks. There were so many conflicting stories in the papers. Which one did you believe?

If only Celeste were here, she'd write a proper letter. Perhaps May could write and ask her to send a wire to the papers to defend the captain. No use writing; it would take too long for a reply.

May wanted to tell the paper what she thought of them all but she felt unsettled enough, what with talk of war far away and troops in the garrison at Whittington on full alert. The college kitchens were awash with rumours. Florrie Jessup said there were spies round every corner but still this debate about the unveiling in the local paper dragged on, and still May couldn't bring herself to write. What if she drew attention to herself and Ella? Since Florrie's outburst, she'd been nowhere but the shops, the church and the Foresters' house in Streethay. She couldn't take the risk of exposure.

At least other folk cleverer than her had sprung to the captain's defence. But there was talk of a local petition against honouring him. She was disgusted.

One night, unable to sleep, she peered from her bedroom window where she could see the outline of the cathedral spires silhouetted against the dawn sky. The thought came to her that it was finally time to put pen to paper.

As one who was there on that terrible night, as one who felt the chill of the icy waters and watched my husband and child lost to the frozen sea, I *know* that Captain Smith was a good and brave man. As one who was rescued from the deep in despair, saved above others, I thought I had lost all, but into my hands was delivered the very child who is my heart's delight. Captain Smith swam out with her in his arms and refused to be rescued himself. I have witnesses to this act of mercy. Lichfield should be proud to have such a memorable reminder of that truth: greater love hath no man than this, that he lays down his life for others.

Only them who were there can tell you what really happened. This petition is a disgrace to the city.

Yours sincerely

(Name Withheld)

The ink was barely dry as May sealed the envelope and rushed out into the dark to post it in the box at the end of the street. It must be done before she lost her courage.

May searched through the *Lichfield Mercury* the following week to see her letter in print, but there was nothing. It was as if they had ignored her story as something fanciful. She should have signed her name, but she knew that that would bring people to her door: curious, nosy neighbours and staff asking more questions.

A week later disturbing news of war accompanied the announcement of the local unveiling ceremony. She and Ella would certainly make sure they paid their respects to Captain Smith. She was on her way to enquire about the ceremony when she called into the general post office for a stamp. It was then she found the one in her purse that should've been put on the envelope addressed to the newspaper.

So that was that then. The letter must never have been delivered. Her defence had gone unread. She felt such relief. She'd nearly given herself away in her fury. She would not be drawing attention to them both again. Her guard was back up.

43

Harriet came unannounced into Celeste's bedroom wanting to know why she'd not been at church on Sunday. Celeste tried to hide her scars with her hand but she was too late.

'Oh dear, has Grover been losing his temper again?'

'Is that what you call this? I'd call it assault and battery,' Celeste replied. She was ice cold.

Harriet had the decency to blush. 'I'm sorry but you have to understand the stresses men are placed under at work. There's a great amalgamation going on in the rubber works. Grover's company are making big changes. We have to make allowances. He's like his father. They don't mean to do these things . . . You have to understand.'

'Is that what you do?' Celeste said, seeing the blush spread on her mother-in-law's face.

'What do you mean?' Harriet bristled.

'You know what I mean. He wasn't born a bully. Someone showed him it's acceptable to knock your wife into submitting to—'

'Look, my dear, you must admit, lately you've provoked him with all your suffrage talk. You're never at home, you neglect the boy . . .'

'That's not true. I've never neglected Roddy! Just because I take a day out a month to attend meetings in Cleveland . . .'

'Men must be masters in their own homes. It stands to reason, otherwise they are belittled.' Harriet walked around her room, nervously fingering trinkets and clothes.

'I was taught all of us are equal in the eyes of God.'

'There you go again on your high horse. Man was made in the image of God and we came out of his rib so we are, of course, lesser beings.'

'That's nonsense. Humans come from their mothers' bodies,' Celeste laughed.

'You must learn to keep such heresies to yourself if you are to stay married to my son. Be submissive, it is the only way with strong-willed husbands.'

'I was not brought up to act like that.'

'You are so English, dear.'

'Yes, and proud of it. We don't like to be browbeaten. We fight for what we feel is right, no matter how hopeless the cause.'

'Then I pity you,' said Harriet, picking up an antique silver hairbrush that had belonged to Celeste's mother. 'Though you do have exquisite taste in furnishings.'

'Is that all? Will you be repeating what I've just said?'

Harriet shook her head. 'You've changed, Celestine, and Grover is confused.'

'I have the *Titanic* to thank for that. How can I endure this treatment after what I witnessed on the ship? He couldn't even be bothered to meet me off the rescue ship and I've discovered he hides my mail.'

Harriet paused at the door. 'I see. I'm glad we've had this chat, Celestine. Good day. I'll tell everyone you're indisposed.'

Celeste sensed they would never talk of this again. Harriet had been shamed, her own secret humiliation discovered. If only they could join forces, there might be hope of reconciliation. What am I thinking of? Celeste sighed. Nothing I can say will change Grover. But my actions just might make him think again.

44

It was a struggle for May to find a vantage point. The Lichfield crowds were out to see the Mayoral procession wending its way down Bird Street from the Guildhall to Museum Gardens for the unveiling of the statue.

The town crier was in his top hat, his mace and sword glinting in the July sunlight, and a motley crew of the Court of Array in medieval costumes slowly filed past the curious crowds. Next came the Mayor and Sheriff, sweltering in their scarlet and fur and tricorn hats heading up the dignitaries and guests dressed as befitted such a civic occasion, some in sombre blacks, others in muted silks, their skirts rustling with braided hems to brush away the dust.

A fanfare of scarlet-coated buglers heralded their arrival, striking a grand note as the parade filed into Museum Gardens where naval officers stood guard over the shrouded statue. There was a shuffling into appointed positions before the proceedings began.

May hid herself from view. She couldn't hear most of what was said, and Ella was squirming in her pushchair, more interested in the ice-cream vendor on the corner, who was doing a roaring trade amongst the crowd who'd gathered to see what was going on.

She noted with pride how white the clergymen's robes were that she'd helped launder, starch and iron that very morning. They were ranked in order of importance around the bishops, in their gold stoles and mitres. It was a theatrical pageant perfect for a cathedral city.

'Who's being done?' said a man in a cloth cap, dripping ice cream from his cornet down his whiskers.

'It's the unveiling of the captain's statue, Captain Smith,' May offered.

'Oh, him, the one who sank the *Titanic*! What do we want a statue of him for?'

'He was a brave man, a very brave man ...' she snapped, unable to contain her vexation.

'What do you know?' he argued, eyeing her up and down. There wasn't much of her to attract attention, she reckoned; just a young woman in a grey loose dress, pinched in the face, hair the colour of wet sand scraped into a bun under a straw boater. With one cutting word about being a *Titanic* survivor she could've shut him up but she bit her tongue and edged away. She wanted to hear what the Duchess of Sutherland had to say but she caught only snippets of her speech as a woman pointed out another young lady in a grey flowing dress.

'That's Lady Scott ... widow of Captain Scott, the great explorer ... she made the statue,' whispered the lady standing next to her. 'Now there's someone who deserves a bronze likeness. A hero among men, he was.'

It was evident Captain Smith was not among friends here. May wondered why they'd even bothered to turn up. It was the talk of the city that no one wanted this statue in Lichfield; a petition with seventy signatures had been sent to the Council in protest at having it erected.

If only she could speak out on his behalf. Then she caught the duchess's final words.

'Don't, my friends, grieve ... because Captain Smith lies in the sea ... the sea has swallowed silently and fearfully many of the great and many of those we love ...'

You can say that again, May sighed under her breath, not wanting to listen any more. There were too many memories rising to the surface with those words.

Now there was talk of war and men taking up arms again. How many of them were also destined for the deep?

May's eyes were drawn to the slender figure of a girl in a white dress and picture hat, her dark hair falling down to her waist. The captain's only daughter, Helen Melville Smith, who was going to unveil her father's likeness. Her mother was seated close by, anxious as the girl tugged on the sheet to reveal the broad-shouldered figure of a naval officer, his arms folded as he looked far, far across the assembled crowd, far beyond the three spires of the cathedral and the museum dome, and out into the distance. The crowd clapped without enthusiasm.

Here he was, stuck on a post as far from the sea as it was possible to be, landlocked in a lukewarm Lichfield, deaf to all the speeches from the great and good of the county. It had been the talk of Cathedral Close for weeks who would be attending this show: Lady Diana Manners and her sister, the Marchioness of Anglesey, Sir Charles Beresford, the MP, and more. Everyone had wanted to make speeches but there were rumblings of dismay, especially when the vicar of St Chad's stirred up the protest in the newspaper. Many worthies had stayed away, making lame excuses not to attend.

May tried to view the seated guests. Among their ranks were the captain's relatives from the Potteries and officials from the White Star Line, as well as survivors like herself. She'd like to have given them her public support but she knew she had to watch from a safe distance.

It was a great turnout, despite all the fuss, and a comfort to his family, she hoped. Her eyes were fixed on his widow, Eleanor, as she placed a wreath of red and white roses at the foot of the plinth. How she'd borne her cross with dignity over these past two years. What must she be thinking now?

The sun was in May's eyes. They were hot and crushed, and Ella was fractious. 'Ducks . . . feed the ducks,' she demanded. May hoped to get a closer view of the statue when the crowd dispersed. She pushed her back towards the shade of Minster Pool so they could feed the ducks as she'd promised.

The procession receded, the cadets and naval reserves fell out of line, people shuffled past the cordon to take a closer look and read the plaque.

'Ducks . . . feed the ducks,' Ella insisted.

What a hoo-ha there'd been about this inscription! She'd heard the canons arguing over their port and the students in the college debating it over their cocoa before compline, and she was curious to see for herself what had been chosen.

Now the show was over, the seats emptied and the crowds strolled into the park, crowding into pubs and tearooms to cool off. Only then did May wheel the pushchair towards the statue for a closer inspection. No one here had a clue about her connection to this famous man, and reading the plaque she could have wept. There was just his name, rank and dates with a nondescript flowery epitaph:

> BEQUEATHING TO HIS COUNTRYMEN
> THE MEMORY AND EXAMPLE
> OF A GREAT HEART.
> A BRAVE LIFE AND A HEROIC DEATH.
> BE BRITISH.

How dare they not mention that he was the captain of the *Titanic*. Canon Forester had been right when he said the aldermen would 'fudge the issue and damn the man with faint praise'.

May hadn't wanted this reminder on her doorstep but now she felt she must stick up for its presence. Here in the pram was living proof of his valour. If Helen Smith was his real daughter, then in a strange way Ella was the captain's daughter too, born of the sea.

If only Celeste were here. She must write again, telling her all about this ceremony and sending the local paper to furnish her with all the details.

May looked up at those stern features, the sadness in those faraway eyes. The sculptor had caught something of the man, she was sure. She sighed as she turned, shaking her head. Captain Smith was not the only one to lose his life or his reputation on that fateful night.

Later, in the sultry heat of her bedroom, she dreamed the same dream again, thrashing in that black endless sea, crying out when the fickle frozen water, swayed by moon, wind and tide, sucked down all she loved into the deep. Sometimes she woke with relief thinking it all a nightmare until she looked at the wooden cot, saw Ella's curly head and knew it for real. Who was this stolen child?

Was the price of the comfort she was giving to her an eternity of secrets and silence? What else should she have done? *You survived. She survived. That is all that matters now. Did I do right? Oh, please, give me a sign that I did right . . .*

45

Dearest May

Thank you for your description of the unveiling ceremony. I wish I could've been there but my mind has been occupied. I have done a terrible thing, or it will be terrible if my husband ever finds out. You know how much the *Titanic* Survivors' Committee work means to me. Well, I made an important decision to sell off a few bits and pieces of jewellery Grover has given me over the years, stuff I never wear. I call them blood gifts.

I went to Cleveland in secret and got a good price for them. It felt so liberating to have real money of my own and to be able to give a decent donation to our cause. For months now I've found it increasingly difficult to live in useless splendour, and selling these trinkets felt good. I have a little money left to me by my mother which I call my 'rainy day money'.

I can't believe I'm writing this but there is no one else to trust with my decision.

As you may have guessed from my silence on the subject of my marriage, it has not been a happy one. I can no longer bear what must borne. I know I promised under God to honour my vows but I fear there is no marriage left to honour.

I am sorry to burden you with this knowledge. I hope it explains why my letters of late have been full of frantic busy-ness. When I am busy, I do not think. Please don't be shocked.

You have had to work so hard for everything while I can sit sewing in comfort. You have lost your life's companion while I am wishing to shed mine. How strange and unfair life can be.

Don't worry about us. I am making plans of which I can say nothing yet. It is imperative you tell no one at home about my troubles. Please send your next letter to the post office. I shall wire to you later. As you will have guessed, Grover did not approve of our correspondence so we must go behind his back.

You may not hear from me for a while. It is not neglect on my part but because I am trying to alter our sorry situation with plans of my own.

Yours in desperation,

Celeste and Roddy

Celeste waited until Grover was out before she found the key to his walnut bureau where all their documents were held. All she wanted was her birth certificate, and Roddy's. She had been priming him for weeks that it was time to take Roddy and Susan for a trip to the coast, to sail his boat and get some fresh sea air. They would spend a few days in a hotel and travel by rail car to see the Great Lakes on the way home. She'd bought a new sailor suit for Roddy, a fresh straw boater for Susan's uniform and some pretty silk dresses for herself.

For the first time in months, she felt alive with anticipation. Susan would have to come with them or she might raise the alarm. She was trustworthy up to a point but she had her own family to support in Akron. It might not be wise to persuade her to cross the border into Canada. According to the New York papers, things were increasingly serious in Europe after the assassination of Archduke Franz Ferdinand in Sarajevo. There was talk of war with Germany. She must get out now before borders were closed.

If Margaret Brown and Alice Paul had taught her anything, it was not to sit around being passive, waiting to be rescued but to seize the day and take her future in her own hands. She must go north into British territory, claim her birthright and take Roddy across the sea where Grover could never reach them.

It was time she saw her own family. If there was a war, her brothers would want to fight and Father would be bereft. It was her duty to see them and introduce her son, before he forgot he was ever half English himself.

The excitement was hard to contain. But then one night Grover came home saying he'd be joining them for a week in August, and her heart sank with disappointment. These plans must be delayed for a few days more. He'd be coming to check that they were where they said they were, up the coast in Maine, as close to the Canadian border as she dared.

She'd hinted she'd like to pay her respects to the *Titanic* victims buried in Fair Lawn Cemetery in Halifax, and for once he'd not protested. He was still being nice to her after the latest beating. He must have known his mother had seen her bruises.

Now Celeste prayed everything would go smoothly. She made a false lining in the bottom of the trunk in which she hid her dollars and papers. She must appear calm and submissive in his presence but the enormity of this deception sent her heart racing. The thought of the ocean voyage was terrifying. Surely lightning couldn't strike twice?

It would be high summer in England. She had scoured the papers for lists of transatlantic crossings, finding Halifax, Nova Scotia was as good as any. It would be a last-minute fleeing from Halifax and she would take any passage across the Atlantic she could find.

At night she lay awake terrified of what she was planning. The escape must be foolproof. She would send Susan back on some pretext so the poor girl would not be subject to Grover's wrath when he found out he'd been duped.

If she escaped there'd be no more insults and violence, and no one could separate her from her son. The thought of seeing her family once more – May and Ella, too, rekindling old friendships back home – gave her the courage to stay calm and composed. Soon she would see them all but until then no one must even suspect any of these plans.

When May's letter arrived with news of the unveiling, it was a relief to Celeste to break her silence and prepare her for what was to come. She smiled to herself, thinking how soon she would be seeing them in the flesh.

Roll on August vacations, she smiled. We're coming home!

7 August 1914

Angelo stood in the small side chapel of the cathedral waiting for his bride to arrive. There was just the priest with a smile a mile wide, some girls from the linen shop and a line of Bartolinis in their best finery. How different from the simple wedding in Tuscany with Maria, a lifetime ago. He hoped she didn't mind this desertion so soon after her loss.

'You do well to start again. Kathleen is a good girl. She will give you back a home and family,' said Father Bernardo. 'You were sent to each other.'

'What do you want to marry Irish for?' his gaffer had said at work. 'She will take the pants off you.'

'I like her,' said Anna, the first night he brought her home. 'You will have beautiful babies.'

He thought of Alessia and the feeling that never went away that she was out there somewhere ... He'd kept the shoe in the hope that one day he'd find her, but as the years went by he sensed it was a lost cause.

There was a stir and the congregation rose. Kathleen was coming. He turned and through his tears saw a vision in a lacy cream dress floating in his direction. Don't look back, look forward, his heart whispered. Ghosts will not warm your bed at night but here's someone who will.

There was a section of Fairview Lawn Cemetery in Halifax, Nova Scotia, set aside for the *Titanic* victims whose bodies had been collected from the sea. Over a hundred small granite cubes lay side by side, tended with flowers. Already some had names and the numbers of when they were gathered up by the salvage boats: a terrible harvest for the sailors who'd brought them in. Perhaps May's husband lay unclaimed, unrecognisable amongst them? Celeste sighed, clutching a bunch of violets as she strolled along the paths while Roddy skipped ahead.

It was a peaceful resting place. She searched out the little stone plinth dedicated to an unknown child, which had caused so much concern in the newspapers that a subscription was raised to bury him with all due dignity. Celeste shuddered, knowing this might have been Roddy if she'd taken him with her. He was so full of life among the dead. How could she be thinking of risking another ocean crossing? But what choice did she have?

There was a ship leaving tonight, according to the newspaper listings.

She'd wait and give Susan her fare home, make some excuse about finding out about May's husband and then make for the dock and book her passage.

She'd done a secret recce around the port, where she'd seen a bustle of marching soldiers embarking on a troopship. The talk of war in Europe was on every billboard but she hadn't wanted to think about that yet. Time enough when they were safely on board.

Her heart was pounding with the enormity of her actions but it was now or never. It was time to buy their tickets. The money was burning a hole in her secret pocket. They were to travel Second Class so as not to draw attention to themselves. She'd make sure their departure was not easy to discover.

An idea had grown from the scandal on the *Titanic*, when it was discovered that many passengers had travelled under false names. She thought of that French family aboard the ship, a Mr Hoffman, who had stolen his sons in France to bring them to New York. It wasn't exactly false, but she would modify her own name. Her maiden name, Forester, was close to Forest and another name for 'forest' was 'wood'. Celestine was too unusual, but why not use her second name, Rose? Rose Wood might help cover her trail.

She took leave of the cemetery with a heavy heart. How many lost hopes and dreams lay under that soil? Now it was her turn to be strong and resolute. She'd been given life and strength to do what was right for Roddy. There was no going back.

First she must let Susan go. She was standing watching the tall sailing ships on the harbour. It was hard to look calm. They were watching the soldiers lining up to embark and Roddy was jumping up and down pointing at them. 'Soldiers, look!'

'It's time for you to catch your train,' Celeste smiled, pointing to the station.

They walked Susan back in that direction but suddenly she was reluctant to leave.

'I ought to stay, ma'am. Mr Parkes said we were to stay together at all times.'

'I know, but here's a letter explaining everything. I did tell him I wanted to pay respects in Halifax and see how they are

trying to identify victims. We'll be following on in a few days …'
She tried to sound casual and not raise Susan's suspicions further.

'But, ma'am …' There was a look in her eye of genuine
concern. She must know what went on in their house. Did she
guess that this was a farewell?

'Now off you go and enjoy the train journey. I'll get a porter
to see to the luggage … And thank you,' she added. How could
she leave that unsaid?

'What for, ma'am? For doing my duty?' Susan was looking up
at her curiously. She must know what was going on now as
Celeste shoved the letter in her purse and some money.

'A little extra for your comfort; you've been a good nurse to
Roddy.' Celeste held her hand. 'Give Susan a kiss.'

'Susan's coming too.' Roddy held her hand tightly.

'No, not today. Susan has to go home,' Celeste smiled. 'Don't
you?'

'I want Susan, I want Susan …' Roddy was steaming up for a
paddy.

'You'd better go before he has a tantrum.'

'I can't leave you … let me stay on, ma'am. Where are you
going? I know things have been difficult. I can help. Please take
me with you. I don't want to leave Roddy.'

'I wish it could be otherwise but you must go. You've been so
loyal and so discreet.'

'Where will I find you, ma'am?'

Celeste shook her head. Trying not to cry, she reached out her
hands, gripping her maid's tightly. 'You must go and tell my
husband I sent you packing, refused to let you continue with us,
forced you onto the train.'

'They shoot the messengers, don't they?' Susan answered
anxiously.

'Only in stories. Here's a letter of reference. It will help you
find another position. I wish you every happiness in the world.
Take care.'

'It's been a privilege to serve you, madam. You are a good mother. I know what you are doing is for Roddy as well as yourself. I wish you the best luck in the world.'

'We'll need it, Susan. Now go before we make fools of ourselves.'

Roddy was crying, sensing the emotion. Susan was weeping into her hanky and Celeste tried to choke back her tears. The platform was bustling with folk pulling their baggage from the incoming train, so many passengers hurrying to the port.

'I expect they're all trying to get home,' Susan said. 'What with the war starting . . .'

Celeste dismissed this with a wave of her hand. 'Oh, that's not going to happen yet. What's England got to do with Austria and Germany's squabbles?' She hadn't time to let such terrible news sink in. She almost shoved Susan onto the train and waved her off with a forced smile. Roddy was too young to know he'd never see her again, she sighed as they made their way to the ticket office. The queues were long and impatient, full of anxious women flapping tickets in the officer's face.

'Ticket holders to the left, others to the right!' he shouted. There was a murmur of protest among the crowd. 'I've not got two pairs of hands. Be patient.'

'Mama, I want to pee pee,' Roddy said, tugging at her skirt.

'Can't you wait?' she cajoled, not wanting to lose her place in the queue.

'I'll mind it for you,' offered a woman with a kindly face. 'There's a gentleman's convenience over there.' She pointed.

It was warm now and Celeste removed her coat.

'Would you hold this too?' she asked, not wanting to let go of the rest of her luggage.

Roddy headed for the little urinal but Celeste made him come with her to the ladies' comfort room. She daren't let him out of sight in this crush.

When they got back to the queue she searched for her place

but the woman had gone and so had her coat. She asked round in a panic, but everyone shrugged their shoulders.

'There's always a few chancers, madam, waiting for an opportunity. She jumped up the minute you'd gone.'

Celeste was too angry and tired now to protest that the man could have stopped her. It was back to the end of the queue, despite dusk falling around them.

'Next!'

'Two tickets to Liverpool, please.'

'Sorry, madam, nothing to be had until Saturday now. Can I see your passport?'

'My what?' she asked, handing over her and Roddy's birth certificates instead. 'I'm still a British citizen.'

'That's as may be but no one will take you on board without documents of passage.'

'Since when?' she snapped, cross and scared. 'I crossed over on the *Titanic*. No one asked me for anything then.'

'Sorry, madam ... new regulations since April. All passengers crossing to another country must show their identity documents.'

'But here are our birth certificates,' she argued.

'Sorry, madam, you will have to apply for the correct papers ... Next!'

Celeste was not going to budge. She'd come too far. 'But how long will that take?'

'I'm not at liberty to say. There's a war on, you know.'

'Since when?' Her temper was rising, flushing her cheeks.

'Since ten o'clock this morning, madam. Have you not seen the papers? Look around you at the troops. England and Germany are at war, Canada is sending troops and they have priority over civilians. Step aside, please ... Next!'

Roddy sensed her desperation. 'Are we going on the big ship, Mama?'

'No, not today,' she croaked. Celeste wanted to sit down on

the dock and howl with frustration. Where now? Time was of the essence. She must get back before Susan took the letter to Grover. They must find a night train south. What a stupid ignorant fool she'd been to think she could escape so easily.

Now they were trapped until this war ended or until she could procure a genuine passport home. All her bravado instantly evaporated. If they didn't arrive with Susan, Grover would be waiting. There was nothing for it but to find a rest room and sit out this panic that was descending like thick fog, blocking out all other thoughts. Until she heard a familiar voice like a foghorn in her head piercing the gloom.

What the devil are you going back for: more of the same, honey, more black eyes? You've made your break, gal. Just vamoosh . . .

'But I can't,' she heard herself cry out.

Why ever not? Who will be looking for Rose Wood when the world's in turmoil? Make a run for it while you can and don't look back. You're like me, one of the unsinkable sisters. You'll be fine on your own.

Celeste stood up expecting to see Margaret Brown at her shoulder but there was no one. Could she do it? Could she make a run for it, get on a train and go anywhere she pleased? She had the dollars. She had her most precious possession holding her hand. Anything was possible if you wanted it badly enough.

So she couldn't make it across the ocean but that didn't stop her getting as far away from Grover Parkes as she could. Mother and child stood invisible among the thronging crowd, Celeste smiling for the first time with relief as she made for the station.

Go hide in a crowd, Rose Wood. No one will find you there.

Part 2

1914–1921

48

Washington, DC, November 1914

Dear May

You may be wondering where I am since I last wrote. We are living in the capital city of America, lodging with friends until I find something permanent.

Before all post across the Atlantic goes haywire, please will you do me the most enormous favour and readdress any letters arriving for me, especially from my husband, back to me here and post these letters to him with a Lichfield postmark? Enclosed is a money order. You must not be out of pocket because of my deception.

It is vital that Grover thinks I am back home and not likely to return. To compound things even further I shall be writing to Father as if we were still in Akron. It's best if he knows nothing of this. If you can offer to post Papa's own letters for him and readdress them here, I would be forever in your debt. I apologize for burdening you with all this. I did plan to come home but I was not well enough prepared and had to change plans at the last minute.

I am trying to build Roddy and myself a new life here. I am now Mrs Rose Wood for the time being. It is important to stay incognito just in case ... 'O what a tangled web we weave ...'

Life here is interesting. I am helping in the office of the

Congressional Union for Women's Suffrage at the moment. Roddy is in first grade and getting used to his new life. We follow what is going on in France with fear and concern for my two impetuous brothers, who joined up in haste so as not to miss the show.

How our lives have changed in the last months – England at war, and us, fugitives – but I have no regrets. If the *Titanic* taught me anything it was that our lives on earth are precious and to be savoured, not endured.

Keep safe in these troubled times.

Best love,

Celeste (a.k.a. Mrs Rose Wood)

May sat on the park bench rereading this epistle and shaking her head. Who'd have thought Celeste would make a run for it? How on earth could she be part of these mad schemes? Her husband would be on the next ship, demanding her return. What would poor Canon Forester make of it all? How could she, May, deceive him? But she must if Celeste was in danger. She owed Celeste her life.

Lichfield was all of aflutter organizing homes for Belgian refugees and putting up posters warning of spies. There were guards on the railway lines and troops on the march. She couldn't cross the streets for convoys of lorries and wagons. The whole world was going mad and now Selwyn was off on training exercises and his brother Bertram was already overseas.

May pushed the baby up the hill towards the cathedral. It was a good place to cool off and just think. It had stood through many wars and troubled times; the tattered banners hanging from the ceilings of the side chapels spoke of conflicts. What should she do?

They paused by the marble effigy of *The Sleeping Children* tucked at the back of the Lady Chapel. The Robinson sisters were buried together. Eliza Jane's nightdress had caught fire and she had died of her burns, while Marianne had caught a chill and had died soon after. How their parents must have grieved, as she grieved for Ellen; such a beautiful memorial glossing over such awful deaths. If only she had a place to mourn her lost loves. No one was ever alone with their troubles. Everyone had them, and now Celeste was having hers. You don't walk past someone in trouble, she reasoned, especially a friend. Celeste had been a good friend to her when she had been more alone in the world than ever. She must now grant her friendship in return, no matter the cost. She must do what she could to help.

49

'Do I have to stay?' Roddy argued. Celeste knew he didn't like Thursday afternoons. All the boys in his class were allowed to run home and play ball or ride on their bicycles round the Washington streets, but he had to change into his best knickerbocker suit, comb his hair and open the door to their guests. He hated standing there as a troop of girls, towering above him, flounced in one by one to be announced at the drawing-room door.

'Good afternoon, Mrs Wood, how are you today? Good afternoon, Roderick.' One by one they curtsied and bobbed in pretty dresses with ringlets in their hair, smelling of rosewater and lavender. He helped serve tea in china cups on a lacy tray and hand round sandwiches and then pass the cake stand on which sat dainty cakes, iced fancies, to be eaten with cake forks.

Each of the girls had rehearsed a poem to recite and Celeste helped them when they stumbled. He had to clap and look pleased.

'Why do we have to do this?' he asked time and time again.

'This is how I earn my living now, teaching girls to refine their accents and learn deportment,' she replied, 'teaching girls to be ladies.'

'But why do I have to stay and watch?'

'Because you are such a help to me, Roddy. This is something we can do together and when the young ladies are here I still need to be keeping an eye on you.'

'But Pa should do that,' he argued.

'Not Pa, Father . . . I told you before, we don't live with Father any more, and won't for a very long time.'

In truth, Roddy could hardly recall his father's face. It was over a year since they'd fled south. At first they had lived in a room crammed with other women, sleeping on a camp bed on the floor until Celeste found them a little house to rent in D Street at the back of Capitol Hill close to Eastern Market. Roddy had to go to the public school down the road, coming home with bruises until one of her friends taught him some self-defence moves which had proved useful to her when they were cornered on suffrage marches.

They attended rallies but Celeste made sure they stood at the back and melted into the crowd when it got noisy or there were photographers taking snaps. Roddy liked walking down the Mall and standing outside the White House gates, crushed up with other kids. While the mothers were huddled together, they got to play ball or sneak off while all the shouting was going on.

But Thursdays were his bugbear, when she earned extra, taking girls through their paces so they walked and talked like little ladies, not the noisy cackling hens who jumped down the porch steps when they closed the door after the two hours of refinement they must endure.

It was through contacts at St John's Episcopal Church that Celeste had had the idea of this class. Sometimes the President and his family came to worship. Newly married officers' wives came in the evening to learn how to set the table with forks and knives, or how to greet people. Others came for elocution lessons, wanting to copy her accent. They liked the way the English spoke in a slow, quiet, deliberate manner, and everybody who came wanted to be seen as refined.

Had she done right to rob Roddy of a normal family life? They were poor now. She counted out the dollars and put some in the special tin: 'For when we go home.'

'Where's home?'

'It's across the ocean in a city called Lichfield.'

Home was where her brothers lived, she sighed, not smiling in their smart uniforms from her mantlepiece. Sometimes she'd pull out an atlas and point to the pink bits belonging to England. 'One day we'll go home, where we'll be safe, Roddy, one day soon,' she whispered.

Sometimes Celeste wept with tiredness. It was hard keeping up appearances. Eastern Market was smart, full of naval families living in elegant, expensive houses. She felt she was split in two, pretending to be a colonial widow fallen on hard times and a modern office worker with bobbed hair and shortened skirts. It had taken such an effort to escape from Akron, and Grover's clutches, and then having to reinvent herself here, hide her true identity and live a life of lies, was so difficult. But it was so much easier to bear than her life with Grover.

How glad she was to have sent the letter to England from Halifax, the letter to Grover ending her marriage. She could still recall every word she'd said, sitting in the train station with a writing pad on her lap, crying as she poured out her feelings.

I have no reason to return to the life of misery and humiliation I've endured at your hands and I have no intention of letting my son grow up with such a vile example.

You may wonder where I found the nerve to defy you in this way but believe me, when I saw the bravery of those wonderful men who stepped aside so women and children might be saved on that fateful night two years ago, I couldn't recognize you as being one of them.

Sitting in that lifeboat, I knew in my heart you would have made every excuse to wheedle your way onto those lifeboats to save yourself, as did so many of the First Class men . . . How I wished you gone from my life before then but, unlike those poor souls who never got to say farewell to their beloved spouses, I am giving you the courtesy of ending our marriage with some explanation.

By the time you read this, I will be far away, back with my own countrymen, in a place where I do not have to fear saying one wrong word in case my arms are bruised and my spirit beaten. Look to your conscience as to what makes you behave in such a sick and offensive manner, like a child who cannot get its way without tantrums.

How you fooled me into thinking you so charming and courteous when we were courting. How kind you were at first, but then it was as if once I was securely yours, separated from all who loved me, some devil sprang into your soul and made you cruel, cold and angry when all I wanted was to give you love and affection, to bear your children and be a good wife.

It took a near drowning to make me realize you will never change unless you look deep into your cold heart and get rid of such a demon. Until that time I will not be subjected to such a monstrous regime as was our marriage, nor must my child ever have to bear witness to your cruelty. The risk to him if he ever defies you does not bear thinking about.

Did no one ever tell you that we catch more flies with honey than vinegar? A kind word goes a long way, a loving gesture can work miracles in a woman's heart. I fear you are sick and need the Great Physician who can cure all ailments of the soul. I don't want to hear or see you again in this life. I have not kidnapped our child but released him into a more loving and caring family.

Celestine

It was a harsh letter for any man to receive but she would not alter one word of it. Once it was in the post, she felt as if a great burden had been lifted from her heart. There were no regrets, only sadness that the two of them had been so ill suited from the start and that her innocence and naivety had ensured his behaviour had gone unchecked for so long.

May had done her part to throw Grover off the trail, sending Celeste's letters as if from England. There were letters in his handwriting, from their lawyers, from Harriet, but they were gathering unopened until she could face them. He would not follow her during the war but when peace came, perhaps he might search them out. She must remain careful.

When they first arrived in Washington, DC, Celeste had turned up at the offices of the suffrage society in desperation. There'd been a spate of arrests and force feedings, and a safe house was set up where women could recuperate from their ordeals out of the public eye. She'd offered her services as a dogsbody, anything to get a bed for them both. The condition in which some of her friends arrived shocked her. It was much worse than anything she'd endured because it was chosen and borne for their cause: emaciated bodies, swollen throats, eyes filled with fear and anguish from the treatments – how could her heart not go out to them? Having Roddy around gave some of the older suffragettes a source of amusement, helping them to forget their suffering for an hour or two.

Working part time in the office, Celeste found herself alongside brave single women who broke every convention. They were militants, loud and courageous in their fight to get the vote and rights for female employees. She wondered if any of them would have been subjected to the humiliation she'd allowed for so long. They had borne imprisonment and public derision for the cause, sustained by friendship. She'd been starved of women's company for such a long time.

'When you put your hand to the plough you can't put it down until you get it to the end of the row,' their leader, Alice Paul, used to say.

Celeste had put her hand to it the night she'd fled from Halifax, taken the long train south to Washington and sought out Margaret Tobin Brown's advice by letter. They'd met in the lobby of the Willard Hotel, amidst the grandeur of marbled pillars and a floor that gleamed. Her words had given Celeste the courage to forge a new life.

So far Grover hadn't sought her out but she was always wary. It was Roddy he would snatch, not her. She assumed he'd hire private investigators to find her in England but where better to hide in the States than in the capital, amongst the crowds. She was free to work and was learning to live on her wits.

Only May knew the truth and she did her best to glean news of the family as best she could while not pushing her for answers. Now Celeste must stick it out and stay her hand to the plough with this new life for her son's sake. His future had been sacrificed for her bid for freedom. She couldn't afford to send him to private school. He was growing coarser, tougher and more defiant, and, at times, she saw a flash of Grover's petulance in his eyes.

What else could she do? She earned more on a Thursday and in the evening than from the humble office work she did all week. It kept them in decent clothes and in a reasonable property in a safe district. May had parcelled up a few pieces of precious china, which somehow arrived intact, much admired by her students. They still had the smell of home on them, mementoes she'd have to sell if times got tough.

She steered clear of the few young English wives that she came across in church. They were all excited about building the new cathedral and busy raising funds. She had neither the money nor the interest in its erection, magnificent though it was going to be. She yearned for the ancient quietude of Lichfield. Their English voices reminded her of home and she wouldn't relax until she and Roddy had made the journey back to England. This time she'd applied for the right documents to get an entry back home but the passport rules were stricter now and Roddy would have to go on hers. She claimed his father was dead and she was a widow. What else could she do? Every penny she could save went on tickets and preparations for this homecoming.

How they'd live once they were there was no matter. One thing Celeste had learned over the past year was to survive on little, to exaggerate the truth where necessary and to take one day at a time. She hardly recognized who she'd become in a year: older, more suspicious of folk, careful with every dime and not so easily impressed by outward show.

Why was she surprised? A woman who had defied the ocean and survived the *Titanic* sinking knew how precious life was. A woman who'd endured physical humiliation at the hands of a brutal husband valued the shutting of her own front door without fear. She may now be a woman who lived hand to mouth from month to month but she managed their meagre budget as if it was that of the State Treasury Department.

One thing was certain: her aching hand was welded to this damned ploughshare and she was not turning back when the end of the row was almost in sight. No one was going to stop her and her son returning to where she belonged.

50

Lichfield
June 1915

Dear Friend,

I beg you read the enclosed letter before you read my own. I don't know what to say other than you have my deepest sympathy on your loss. Bertram was killed in action close to a place called Neuve Chapelle. Like so many students he was so eager to enlist. He came to say goodbye in his smart officer's uniform. Now he has paid the ultimate sacrifice, as the papers say. They have a way of making death seem so clean and peaceful and dignified. We know otherwise.

I know you will feel so helpless not being here to help your father but he has such good friends around him, many of them losing sons and grandsons too.

Everyone is trying to be brave and keep cheerful with fundraising concerts and sewing bees for the troops. I am not one for those sorts of gatherings but I have a little job serving tea at the station to passing convoys of troops. How many of them will ever return home? Hearts are sad, money is tight and the winter was long, but the Lichfield blossoms don't know there is a war on and cheer us no end.

Ella continues to bloom and chatter. I have got her a place in Meriden House School, in the nursery, where she can play with other children. She loves to be in company but I am such a hermit, it's not fair to hide her away. She is a comfort to your father, who spoils her with sweets I fear she will choke on. She is a constant worry and delight.

I wish I could hold your hand at this sad time. War must end soon and you will be reunited once more with all you love. God protect you and comfort you in his loving arms,

May

PS. I have just read a terrible account of the sinking of the Cunarder *Lusitania* off the coast of Ireland. 1200 souls perished. Only we know how it must have been for those struggling in the water. I have not been able to sleep for the memories it brings back. There were Americans on board with children. The Hun will pay for this cruel act.

51

Dear May,

I hope the Christmas parcel arrived safely. You hear rumours of things going missing at the port. It was a good idea to number our letters so we can know the gaps. I hope the preserves and cans of butter and meat were useful. I hear things are pretty tight over there and I know my father has a sweet tooth.

We are well enough. The news of Selwyn's wounds in the Somme offensive brought me low but your assurance that he was on the mend in hospital gives me hope of a full recovery. I will write but Father hinted to me he was not ready yet for corresponding. I still can't believe I will never see Bertie again in this life.

Your new lodgings near Stowe Pool sound good with a fine view of the cathedral spires. One day I hope I will see those Three Ladies of the Vale for myself again.

There is a chance of work in government offices if America comes into the war. I will have to expand the truth a bit. They won't accept married women but a widow might just get an interview. I'm still doing the refinement classes. Friends of friends seem to like what I organize for them. I suggested we all read the same novel and discuss it together, which they thought hilarious at first. I'm sure some of my clients usually never read anything other than fashion journals, but it was a lively session.

If America enters the conflict in Europe, surely this wretched war will come to an end. The might of this country has to be seen to be believed; millions of young men on the march will end the stalemate.

Can I ask you in all honesty, does my father suspect anything? I ought to tell him our true position but I don't want to burden him further with bad news. He has enough to worry about at the moment.

My parents' marriage was all you could ask for in love, friendship and trust. He will be so disappointed in me for not sticking to my vows. You are my ears and eyes, as always, and words can't tell you what a relief it is to have someone who knows the truth.

I hope the blouse fitted you, and little Ella will grow into the dress. They were clothes discarded by one of the rich wives in my class. Little does she know I wear some of them myself. Did Papa like our portrait? Roddy looked so smart in his sailor suit, don't you think?

I look forward to your next epistle. For someone who said they couldn't write a letter, you put me to shame.

Your dear friend,

Celeste Rose

Celeste didn't know how badly Selwyn was injured, not so much in the body but the mind, May sighed. His father had visited the asylum where they treated wounded officers for something they called shell shock. He didn't speak or listen. He just stared out of the window in another world, the canon had told her in confidence. She didn't know what to say.

'I am glad that one of my children is safe away from all this mayhem,' the canon told May. 'I couldn't bear for anything else to happen to them.'

It was then that May offered to go and see to Red House herself. They were billeting soldiers there and Mrs Allen, the daily help, was none too happy with the state of their rooms. The garden was dug over for vegetables and Ella liked to play there and chase the rabbits. May was glad to get away from the college. Florrie Jessup never let up, mocking May's accent, hiding her dusters and brushes, trying to goad her into a row. One of these days May would give her one she'd not forget. You don't grow up in an orphanage without learning to defend yourself.

When they were in the kitchen garden, she could forget college bullies and tidy it all up. Outdoor chores they may be, but keeping busy was the best tonic. She would watch Ella prancing around trying to be helpful. 'Who is this dark child with the deep sparkling eyes? Where was she born? Who does she look like? Why is she happiest with pencils and paper in her hand, drawing pictures? How could I have snatched her for my own?' she asked herself.

The burden of this secret crept up on her more and more over the years. Did I do a wrong thing for a right reason or a wicked thing for my own selfish needs? Always at the back of her mind was the dreadful thought that someone somewhere might be mourning the loss of their child. Was it fate that brought them together? Was it fate that the *Titanic* should sink? These thoughts tore at her mind so that she feared that if she gave into them it would make her mad.

Then she saw Ella digging up plants, making mischief in the borders. 'Just stop that, young lady, put them back this minute!' Ella was here and she was here, and nothing could change this now.

52

Boston, October 1917

Private Angelo Bartolini woke to find himself in a hospital ward sweating, not knowing how he came to be prostrate. His throat was burning and there was a stone slab on his chest.

'Welcome back to the land of the living, son. You're one of the lucky few who cheated death.' A man in a white coat was standing over him, feeling for his pulse.

Angelo couldn't reply. His brain couldn't translate. It hurt to think as he stared up at the ceiling. One minute he was in the yard outside the barrack huts playing baseball, waiting for transport onto the ship for Europe. Where was he now? Everything was a blur of pain, heat and strange dreams. He'd seen Maria with outstretched arms waving him to her side, smiling, and he'd felt himself floating towards her and then ... nothing.

'You've had the flu, boy, a very bad dose, but you'll live.'

'*Dove sono?*' he said. He'd been drafted in the first wave posted for infantry training, ready for the big push in France.

'Speak English ...'

He could recall Kathleen waving him off at the station, little Frankie howling at the sight of him with cropped hair and in a strange uniform. Jacko was still a babe in arms. Angelo could have tried for exemption but he was a patriot, proud to serve.

His family would look after their own. There was a medical, an inspection, then weeks of training to toughen up the new recruits for combat duty. They were all squashed in barrack huts with no air in the summer heat. There were colds and coughs aplenty but nothing like this. He remembered standing in a train to the port, feeling queasy and shivery, his limbs stiff and aching. By the time they stood down he'd crumpled to the floor, the stone flags came up to meet him and he'd flaked out. How long had he been here?

'They gave you the last rites but you're a tough son of a bitch. Still stateside.'

Angelo couldn't understand half of what the doctor was saying. His head was fuzzy. 'When do I go?'

'Not so fast. You stay here until we tell you to go. First you must eat and get some flesh on those bones.'

He tried to rise up again but his head was spinning. Where were his buddies, Ben and Pavlo, all the guys he'd trained with for weeks? Now he could hardly breathe, as if there was a hole in his chest and air was in short supply. It took the nurses days to get him walking on those stick-like legs. What had happened to his tree trunks? Angelo felt only shame not to be with the other men. He was stuck in this terrible place with sick soldiers arriving every day, trading places with those wheeled out at night on the death trolleys. What the hell was going on?

His only comfort was Kathleen's letters. This sickness was all over the eastern seaboard but particularly bad in Philadelphia and the ports where the soldiers were gathered. She was gargling with some concoction Salvi swore would cure all, and so far they were clear. Some hero he was turning out to be. Then came the final blow to his pride when the doctor examined him.

'Discharge for you,' he said, pointing to Angelo's heart. 'You've done some damage there. Still, better a clock with a slow ticker than getting your head blown off over the pond. You're gonna have to take it easy, build up your muscles.'

'How can I support my kids like this?' Angelo cried. 'I'm useless.'

'Give it time, nature heals,' the doctor replied. 'You're young and tough enough to survive when thousands haven't.'

That wasn't what he wanted to hear. How could he hold his head up when he had never fired a shot in anger? He'd prove them wrong.

It was as much as he could do to change into a suit, pick up his kit and head for New York. He felt like an old man, sitting on the train wheezing, people staring at him as if he were a deserter.

Kathleen was waiting at Grand Central station to greet him. She immediately smothered him in her arms. 'I've been so worried. The flu is everywhere. I didn't bring our babies. They told me you might die,' she sobbed.

'I'll never make a soldier now.'

'That doesn't matter. I've got you back in one piece, that's more than some folks in our block. Come on, let me give you a hand. You look done in.'

Angelo felt limp and lifeless. She mustn't know yet about his heart and its weakness. It would worry her too much. He needed time to heal or how could he ever be a man again?

53

Lichfield
Christmas 1918

Dear Celeste,

Your parcel arrived safely and unopened this time. What treats there were. Thank you from all of us.

Our first Christmas of peace at long last. How we've all prayed to be released from the terrible mess this war has become. After those first days of celebration and excitement at the Armistice, there was a horrible dampening of spirits. No one who has lost boys and girls has the heart for any festivities. We remember those who won't pull the crackers, who won't eat plum pudding, nor sing carols round their family tree. Our food shortages still go on but I saved enough coupons for a few treats for Ella. She will have her stocking, some sweets and home-made toys, thanks to your brother's kindness.

Selwyn is back at Red House. His face is scarred. He shuts himself in the coach house and mucks about with things that need mending. I go up with your father and tidy the garden. He doesn't speak much to me so it was a surprise when I found a toy cot in the hall. He'd knocked it together out of scraps and smoothed it down and oiled it to a sheen. It looks brand new. Father Christmas will be sending it down the chimney on Christmas Eve for Ella's dolls. Ella is such a one for dollies and lines them up as if she was the teacher.

Now for my big news. I did it. I gave Florrie Jessup what for and saw her off. She went too far. I was telling one of the cooks about Selwyn's kind gift and Florrie overheard and started mouthing off about how I had earned the toy on my back. How I was always nipping off to the house to give the soldier his comforts and such like.

Did I see red? I certainly did. I gave her a right-side winder round the ear. She had it coming but the housekeeper saw the whole thing and sacked us both on the spot so that was me out of work with a child to support, just when they have the students rolling back to college. Some of them are in such a sorry state.

I was all for packing my bags but to my surprise some of the girls stood up and told Matron how things had been for years and how I had put up with rude remarks, so in the end it was Florrie who got her marching orders, not me, which is a relief.

I told your father a little of the hoo-ha. Word gets round like wildfire in the Close. He suggested I might like a change of employment, helping Mrs Allen at Red House and doing for a few of the other clergymen, which was so kind. I will think about it. I'm not sure Selwyn will want two women round his ankles. He has black moods some days.

It felt as if I'd found a bit of spark in myself I thought I'd lost and perhaps I'm not such an offcomer in the city after all.

Let us hope 1919 brings hope and relief to all of us.

Your loving friend,

M

53

New York, Summer 1919

Kathleen was keeping their apartment off Broome Street spotless. Not a speck of dust was allowed to settle, even in this hot summer. There were lace nets at the window to catch any flies daring to enter, but there weren't many six floors up in the tenement. The family had three rooms and a living room with water on tap, and a parlour with a box bed for the little ones, Jack and Frankie. Now there was another on the way. She was praying for a little girl.

It had been almost two years since Angelo returned to them. He complained of a bad back and so she helped out in the fruit store as best she could. Kathleen showed she was no slouch, but a hard worker willing to serve behind the counter and mind their ever-growing troupe of wee ones.

It was Angelo she'd married, not Salvi's tribe of dark-eyed, wild-haired Latinos, who raged and stormed at each other. Together the couple had raised themselves from one room to three, but the thought of another mouth to feed was daunting. Sometimes she wondered if it was right to have stayed on in New York after the sickness. Her own family pleaded with them to return back home, but to what? Picking potatoes on her uncle's farm or in service on some English estate? And there were troubles back home too.

Here was life and hope, and now she had these darling toddlers. Her drowned sister wouldn't begrudge her this new life. Angelo still clung to strange theories about his wife and child. He never talked about Maria and Alessia, whose little picture hung on the recess wall of their bedroom, nailed high over the shelf containing a little altar he'd made, decorated with cuttings, candles, letters and the baby's lace shoe. He was still convinced it was his daughter's. When it had drawn near to the anniversary, even seven years on, he had gone quiet and worshipped at this shrine, even lighted a candle as if they were ever-present ghosts watching over them by the bedstead. If she'd argued with him he would walk away not looking at her tears.

'You have to let them rest in peace, Angelo,' she said. '*We're* your family now. Little Jackie, Frankie, they're your heirs. I can't bear to see you stare at them and not at us . . . Don't you love us?' Her temper flared up when he turned his back on her.

'Let a man say his prayers in peace, woman!'

'It's not healthy,' she confessed one day to Father Bernardo. 'He worships them as if they are still alive. What can I do? I can't compete with the ghost of a beautiful wife and mother, who'll never grow old or sick or fat, who doesn't get angry when the kids make a mess.'

'Where there's mess there's life, Kathleen. Never forget that's a sign that you're living, changing and growing in a way they'll never do. In his heart Angelo knows they aren't real any longer but he's still blaming himself for their deaths. "If onlys" are a devil to throw off.'

'But that little shoe, it torments him. He thinks I don't know he searches out all the lace shops with Italian imports and trimmings, just in case anyone knows if the shoe is from his region. He's convinced it's from his district. It makes me feel as if we're not enough for him.'

'Give him time, Kathleen. Time will ease his pain.'

'But it's seven years now, Father. I don't want these things staring at me every day when I dust. There's so much dust if I open the window and the children trail so much into our rooms from the streets. Then there's all the postcards and cuttings, anything to do with the *Titanic* gets pinned up – newspaper cuttings, pictures. Why can't he just let it rest? They're gone and we're here.'

'Oh, if only it were that simple, my dear. Everyone has to live with their past. You have your babies. He has time to dwell on things he can never change.'

'What can I do? I have to say something now there's this wee one on the way,' she sighed, patting her belly. 'If it's a girl he says she must be named for his Alessia.'

'Alice is a good saint's name,' the priest smiled.

'Pardon me, Father, but it's just another reminder. This bairn must have her own name, not one for his dead child.'

'Are you really jealous of these poor souls?'

'Yes, Father, and I can't help it,' she said, bowing her head in shame.

'Then pray and the answer will come to you, child. Go in peace now and no more fussing.'

As the summer grew hotter and her baby bigger Kathleen ignored the little shrine, never dusting round it. Sometimes she felt as if eyes were staring into her back until she got so hot and bothered one morning she threw her brush at the corner of the room and Maria's picture slipped off the wall, the glass shattering.

'Now look what you've gone and done!' she screamed in panic. The frame must be repaired or Angelo would fret. Pulling out the sepia photograph, she shoved it into her private drawer and the tiny shoe into tissue paper in the fancy nightdress case made from Irish linen that she never used.

Yous can all wait, she thought. As for all this mess, you've done it now so shift the wash stand, clear the shelf and give the corner a fright.

Kathleen set to with gusto, clearing the clutter, scraping off the wax from the wood, polishing the surround and scrubbing the wooden floor. She took the yellowed cuttings off the wall with care. They had left white marks. She dragged over the crib and tucked it into the recess close to the fireplace. It fitted snugly. Nothing like shifting furniture to make a tiny room look fresh and new. She covered over the gaps in the faded wallpaper with her own sacred pictures. Now the corner was ready for the new baby.

As if waiting for this cue, that night she went into labour with a mercifully short delivery at dawn. The baby was all she could hope for, with a mass of flaming curls.

Angelo was kept out of the room but his eyes lit up when he saw the little girl swaddled in her crib.

'A girl, Angelo, one of Mary's angels. Father Bernardo says I'm to have the naming of her. A new girl for a new country, so she's to have an American name: Patricia Mary. What do you think?' To her surprise he didn't protest nor did he notice the changes to the room until much later.

'Don't worry, all your things are safe,' she smiled, pointing to the drawer. 'You can look at them any time. The picture just fell off of its own accord,' she added, knowing she'd have to confess on Sunday for this lie. Angelo said nothing, he wasn't even listening, too engrossed in the beauty of his new daughter. '*Bellissima Patrizia,*' he cooed.

'Thank you.' Kathleen raised her eyes to the little Madonna on the shelf. 'Now we can really start our new life.'

Angelo smiled over the crib. He knew the score. Kathleen's face told a picture of blushing half-truths. He could read her like a book. But for once she was right. He was blessed three times over for his loss now. Not that that would stop him thinking about his first wife for the rest of his life, but the little shrine must be hidden in his heart, not on show for Kathleen to worry over. Baby Patricia was a gift of love. Two sons to educate and a dowry to save for, now that would take some hard work and saving up. They must come first.

When Father Bernardo sought him out after Mass one morning he'd given him a gentle warning. 'You'll go mad, son, if you don't let go of your grief. It's an insult to the living, and the dead are at peace now and know no more. Be thankful for what you've been given ...'

But no one could quench that little flame of hope he still felt in his heart. He'd told no one, but when he thought he was dying it was Maria who had come to him, and she'd been alone. Her arms had been empty. Somewhere someone knew something more. That was the thing that tormented him most, and no priest in this world could make him snuff out his hope.

55

Lichfield, July 1919

May hurried across Cathedral Close. It was the Friday of the National Peace celebrations and she'd meant to pick up a few bits for Canon Forester from the market: fresh bread, vegetables and cheese. She liked to make him a pot of soup to last the weekend. She'd forgotten the square was closed off with scaffolding, ready for the big parades. The bell ringers of the cathedral and St Mary's were practising for the next day's peals. There was going to be such a party for the children in their schools this afternoon. Ella was as high as a kite.

As she turned into the little cobbled courtyard, a tall man in a smart suit was standing looking around at the red-brick Tudor houses with their exposed beams. May was used to seeing tourists looking at these ancient buildings. He stared down at her and her basket. 'Which one's the canon's home?' he asked, his grey eyes flashing. May heard his American twang and automatically stiffened.

'Which one would you be looking for, sir?' She tried to smile though her heart was hammering in her chest.

'I wish'd they'd stop that din,' the man yelled, pointing to the spires. 'Can't hear yourself think . . . Forester, Canon Forester.'

'Step along with me, I'll be delivering these to him shortly,' she replied, wanting to delay the knock on the door. Her heart was still thudding. She'd recognized this man from the wedding portrait Celeste's father treasured, one she'd polished a hundred times. Here was Grover Parkes in person, come to find his wife. She prayed the canon would be in the cathedral or visiting the sick.

She had a key but that was for her to know. The stranger had not a clue who she was. Dare she take him to the wrong door, to the one where the cleric was on holiday? That might turn him away for long enough to make sure no one was at home when he called again.

'Who else lives in these quaint little boxes? I guess there's not enough room to swing a cat,' he joked, looking around the cobbled courtyard, but May wasn't fooled by his apparent friendliness.

'Retired clergy mostly, or their wives.'

'You live here?' He gave a hard stare at her shabby jacket.

'No, sir, I oblige for some of them . . . I work in the college. I think the canon will be out now, sir,' she added, praying he was. 'It's the Peace weekend . . . The whole country is going to celebrate. You've seen the flags?'

'You can't move in London for the darned things. What is it with all this fuss? The war's been over for nearly a year . . . I'm here on business in Silvertown in London. I couldn't get anywhere for ladders and decorations. The whole country's at a standstill . . . and as for the trains . . .'

'We've waited a long time . . . out of respect for our dead soldiers,' she argued. How dare he criticize this celebration? 'I'm sure the canon will be out.'

'I've not come hundreds of miles not to go and check . . . Show me the door.'

'I'd better come too. He's a little confused and hard of hearing these days.'

Parkes beat on the door with impatience and, to her horror, it opened and the canon smiled out. 'Oh, May, dear . . . two visitors at once, that's nice.' He looked up at the man and stared. 'Do I know you?'

'You sure as hell do, I'm your son-in-law . . . Where is she?'

'I'm sorry, where's who?'

'Where's my wife and my boy?' he shouted.

'I'm sorry, young man . . . come inside, please. May, put the kettle on; there's some confusion here. Grover, the last time I saw you was at your wedding. Now when was that . . . ?'

'Quit the flannel. I want to see my wife and my son. Where are they?'

'Aren't they with you?' The old man was scratching his head. 'I don't understand. May, have you any idea what this is all about?'

She stood there trying not to blush, shaking before fleeing into the kitchen recess. This man was here on a mission; she must not let slip a word.

'I don't understand. I write to her. She's in Akron. You post the letters, don't you?' He was staring at May, now cowering in the doorway with the tray.

'I haven't received any letters . . . not since—' Grover broke off. 'What's going on here? Who's being paid to shut their mouth.' He stared at May. 'Is this who I think it is?'

'Mrs Smith is my housekeeper, a loyal friend to our family. Please address her with courtesy, young man. Now sit down and tell me what this is all about. Are you here on business?'

Grover turned to May, ignoring the question. 'Did my wife pay you to deceive me?'

'That's enough,' the canon interrupted, for once his hearing sharp. 'Please explain yourself. This is my home. There's obviously some terrible misunderstanding here.'

'Then let me enlighten you, Reverend, dear father-in-law. Your daughter, my wife, has stolen my only son and brought him to this wretched place, and she's not going to get away with it.'

'Get away with what?'

'Kidnapping what's mine.'

'There must be some mistake. Celestine's not here. Besides, surely a mother can't kidnap her own son? Even if that were the case, a child is not a possession to be owned. Roderick belongs to no one but himself.' He was staring up at his portrait on the mantelpiece, winded by the news.

'Oh, quit your sermons,' Grover snapped. 'Where is she?'

'I haven't the faintest idea. I've been under the impression that she was with you. Her letters have said nothing to make me think otherwise.'

'I don't believe you! You know something, or she does . . . Look at her, quaking in her shoes . . . Well? I'm all ears.' Grover turned to May, towering over her.

May started to explain but the words wouldn't come. The canon did his best to defend her.

'If this is your attitude, kindly leave this house until you've calmed down . . . I can't have you upsetting my housekeeper.'

'I'm not finished with you yet.' Grover stood tall in his smart suit, every inch the prosperous businessman, wagging his finger at them both. 'You tell my wife, wherever the hell she is, if she thinks she can run away from me she has another think coming. I'll find her. She has something that belongs to me. As for this woman, I know now who you are. You and your kind put the idea in her head, you and those man-hating banner wavers. Votes for Women! You've turned her mind!' He glared at May, willing her to break down. 'Do you know where she is?'

He was just like old Cartwright, the bullying overseer in the Bolton cotton mill, who'd tried to browbeat his girls with taunts and threats of dismissal. The one who demanded favours when no one was looking. They'd all clubbed together and complained, and it was he who had got the sack. May knew his sort and was having none of him.

'No, sir, and if I did, it's not my place to break a confidence.'

'So she told you then . . .'

'No, I know nothing.'

'Ah, but you've told me everything. Cunning vixen. She never left the States, did she? Thank you.'

'But I don't know anything . . .' May protested.

'It's what you don't say that's given the game away.' He was staring at the mantelpiece. 'And here's the proof, a neat little photo for Grandpa . . . My, how's he's grown. I've not seen him for five years. How do you think that makes me feel?' For the first time May recognized pain on his face, and longing. He examined the photo closely and then put it back with a smile. 'I bid you both good day. Thank you for putting my mind at rest. Your daughter can go to hell but don't let her think I'd let her take my son. My lawyers will see to that.'

With that he turned, bowed his head under the doorway and slammed the door shut.

Canon Forester lay back on his sofa, white-faced and breathless. 'What an unpleasant young man! I don't recall Celeste's husband being anything other than charm itself. What on earth was all that about? Do you know?'

'I'm afraid I do. I promised I would help Celeste when she wrote but she never explained fully.'

'Why didn't you tell me? Does my son know too?'

May bent her head, not wanting to look him in the eye. 'It wasn't my place.'

'Oh, but it is now, my dear. You're her friend and I'm her father. You must warn her wherever she is to come home, and soon. I take it you've been posting my letters to her? You don't think he'll find her, do you?'

'I didn't until he picked up Roderick's portrait, the one I wanted you to put in a frame. Have you seen the stamp on the back? I've dusted round it often enough . . . It's from a photographer's studio, Cohen's in Washington. He saw it too. We have to warn her.'

'Send her a telegram. Go to the post office and send it immediately. What on earth has gone wrong? I don't think Grover
will take a no for an answer, not by the look of him. He wasn't
like this when they married . . . Poor Celeste, she must have had
good reason to leave but I wish I'd known . . . If only her mother
were here . . . they were so close. You must tell me everything
you know.'

May rushed to the post office, unsettled by the encounter.
The thought that Mr Parkes was in Lichfield was a worry, but it
was bound to have happened sooner or later. Would he follow
her home and try to make her reveal more?

Grover Parkes was handsome and successful but there was a
sneer to his lips and an icy coolness in those grey eyes. What had
happened to make Celeste run away? She would write her own
letter to follow the telegram. Celeste was in danger. That was for
certain. He would try to rob her of her son and that must never
happen. May knew only too well how precious one's child was.
Few words were needed to convey the urgency of her appeal.

'PARKES IS HERE. LETTER TO FOLLOW. KNOWS
ABOUT DC. COME HOME NOW. MS.'

56

Washington

Ten days later Celeste was busy choosing vegetables in Eastern Market, having rushed from her office back home in time for Roddy. Since that telegram had arrived from Lichfield, warning her about Grover's visit, she'd been frantically making plans. No one must know of their imminent departure. Today she must prepare for the girls' refinement class, baking English scones – or muffins, as they called them – with the last of the wineberry jam. If she hurried there'd be time to lay out the parlour ready for the usual line-up of polite introductions: how to sit down and when to stand, how to put guests at their ease and keep conversations from flagging.

It was all so ridiculous in this modern age. Her pupils were spirited girls who must aspire to more than just marriage and the social round. How easily she'd been sucked onto that carousel and how hard it was to jump off. Sure, she missed some of the trappings of comfort and money but such luxury came at a price. To be free was all that mattered.

After May's letter telling her of the encounter in the Close, the first thing she'd done was bob her hair and darken it with strong tea. Red hair was so noticeable. She was glad to have shed all those ringlets. All the women she worked with had bobbed their hair. It made her feel shorn of her girlhood at first, but neat cloche hats and berets covered her giveaway colour. The fashion for hobbled skirts was giving way to shorter ones but she hadn't the money to follow the latest fads. A black two-piece suit served her well enough, and it was sufficiently dowdy to help her blend into the bustling crowds and shoppers.

Suddenly some instinct made her turn round as she sensed someone at her side, close enough to be staring at her before turning to their purchase with a half-smile of recognition. It was a middle-aged man in a homburg and mackintosh who stank of cheap cigar smoke. Celeste felt a stab of fear. Had she seen him before, somewhere on the tramcar? Was he following her? Her heart was floundering in panic. If he was, that could only mean . . . She dropped her bag of carrots and made for the exit, not looking back, knowing the side streets around Eastern Market, and making a detour towards the Naval Hospital, where she had to cross Pennsylvania Avenue. She hoped she'd given him the slip. The sidewalks were crowded and she tried not to run but when she came to a line of shops close to South Carolina Avenue, she found herself darting into a shop, breathless and sweating with fear.

'Can I help?' A woman, also in black, stepped forward.

'There's a man following me,' Celeste blurted. 'A man in a black homburg, He's been following me.' She could hardly spit out the words.

'Come with me,' said the woman kindly. 'There's a back entrance out of the store. If he comes in here, he'll wish he hadn't. Where're you heading?'

'D Street . . . South. Thank you.'

'You're not American?'

'English,' she smiled. 'Which is the quickest route from here to D Street?'

'Make for 12th or 13th and keep heading down towards Kentucky Avenue. There are plenty of back alleys for cover. You just leave him to me, honey. Out the yard and down the passage. Good luck.'

'I can't thank you enough,' Celeste stammered.

'We widows must stick together. They think we're easy pickings without a man.'

Celeste didn't contradict her. All she could think of was getting back to Roddy. What if Grover had sent this man to snatch him? What if he had him already? May had told her about the photo and the studio address on the back. It didn't take Sherlock Holmes to make enquiries about obtaining a copy. He didn't know her new name but perhaps the assistant would ferret out their appointment date or something? What if this man had been following her routine and she hadn't noticed until now? She ran until her lungs were bursting, not daring to see if he was in sight. It was such a relief to see Roddy, waiting on the step for her return, oblivious to her panic.

'Come inside!' she yelled, her hands shaking as she tried to turn the lock.

'Aw . . . Mom!'

'Come inside now!' she screamed, dragging him out of sight of the street, bolting the door behind them. 'Has anyone been here asking for me?'

Roddy looked up, shaking his head. 'Do I have to get changed?'

'Not today. I want you to pack all your favourite things in the carpetbag, the one under the stairs, and some books – just special ones, though. I'm going to pack our case.'

'We're going on a vacation?'

'Sort of . . . a trip north.'

'But you've got the tea party. It's Thursday,' he said.

'Not today. I'll leave a note on the door. Hurry, there's not a moment to lose. This is going to be a big adventure.'

'Yippee,' Roddy yelled. At least someone was happy.

Her mind was whirling. How were they going to get across Washington to Union Station? Take a tram? Or risk walking in the open? Or stay here until dark? If Grover's gumshoe was watching the house, it could be dangerous. What if Grover was lurking around, ready to pounce on his son himself? Perhaps she'd imagined the whole thing but the look of triumph on that man's face remained imprinted in her mind.

Calm down! The moment you've been dreading has come but you knew it would. Everything is ready enough for your flight.

It was then she had a crazy idea to put the man off her scent. It was dangerous but worth a try. They must leave; she couldn't risk another failure. No one would be taking her son, not now, not ever.

Calm down, think it through. If he's out there with Grover, he'll be expecting you to dash out now. Wait, there's another way not so obvious that might just work, but you'll have to act fast.

Later Celeste tried to stop her hands shaking as she rattled the teacups and passed the cakes around.

'Now, girls, we're going to play a game today, a sort of dressing-up and changing clothes game to know how it feels to be different. A lady must judge people not by outerwear, plain clothes or being in servants' uniforms but by the kindness of someone's actions. I want you to see how it feels for me to put on one of your uniforms and remember how it felt when I was fourteen. We'll take a walk in the street together and pretend.'

'Like charades?' said Mabel, one of the girls from church.

'Not quite,' Celeste replied, sensing their confusion. 'Let's have some fun walking around outside, seeing how it feels going shopping in someone else's clothes, perhaps. You all know how to take tea politely now. I think it's time for us to learn how to walk in each other's shoes for a change.'

She could sense they were intrigued and up for a diversion from the usual polite regime. It was risky, but worth a try. Trying to persuade Roddy to put on a girl's frock was another matter.

'Oh, Mom! I'm not playing this stupid game.'

'Please. Do as I say,' she whispered. 'IT IS IMPORTANT! It

won't be for long, I promise.' His disguise was the key to their escape. 'And you must wear a hat too.'

The smallest girl swapped her dress and petticoats to squeeze into his sailor suit. They plonked his boater on her head with her pigtails stuffed inside. Everyone laughed. Roddy sulked. Celeste slipped on Mabel's school uniform, and everybody laughed again. She was so slim she could fit into it easily. She covered her hair with a beret and made for the door, trying to look as if this was just a silly game and not a deadly serious attempt to avoid detection.

She looked back with regret at what she was leaving behind. It had been a safe haven until now, four rooms they could call their own. This was not time for sentimentality, though; there was no room for anything but essentials and documents. She was prepared for this journey, and she was not making the same mistake again.

'Round the block, just for fun, and look out to see how it feels,' she ordered.

There was a lot of giggling as they made for the front door and down the steps to the sidewalk, all dressed in each other's clothes and hats. She waved back to the empty window as they left the house, her eyes darting to the street corner. And yes, the same man was slouching there, pretending to read a paper, trying to ignore the gaggle of noisy schoolgirls as they walked past on the opposite side of the street and turned round the block. Would it only be a matter of time before Grover arrived too?

The man was still waiting when they turned the corner and made for 16th Street. Celeste stopped them. 'This is where we must part company. I'm sorry to deceive you all with this charade but we must go,' she whispered, and she darted to the back yard where the bags were tucked out of sight behind the door. The girls all changed back, puzzled and silent. Roddy threw off the dress, watching as she said goodbye to each girl in turn, kissing each on the forehead.

'Tell your parents that I'm taking a sudden vacation and I'll let them know when we return by letter. Thank you for being such sports but I have one favour to ask. Mabel, can I keep this uniform on for a few more hours? I'll leave it at the left luggage in the station.'

'What's happening, Mrs Wood?'

Celeste didn't answer. How could she explain the bizarre behaviour of these last precious minutes? There was no time. She and Roddy needed to get downtown before the investigator rumbled their deception. 'Let me just say, girls, thanks for going along with this. It may seem silly to you but you'll never know how much we appreciate your playing this little game today. Remember, never be afraid to step out of line for what you believe in. Make sure you choose your path carefully, not drift into what others want you to do and you'll do just fine.'

Two of the girls picked up the travel bag between them and the other was taken up too. 'We'll walk you to the bus, if you like.'

'No,' said Mabel Whiteley. 'I've got a better idea, let's go to my house and Bluett can drive you there.'

Celeste could have broken down right there with gratitude but she smiled and merely said, 'Thank you, how kind.'

It was hard to leave but they had no choice. Grover knew where they lived and what they looked like, and there would be photographs. But with the minimum of fuss and disguise she'd bought some time. This time they had the right papers and the passage fare. This time she was going home.

All the way to Union Station, Celeste was sweating, peering out of the window in case they were being followed, certain Grover would not be far behind them now. The traffic suddenly slowed and the limousine drew to a halt. She wanted to run the rest of the way but knew it was better to sink down into the leather seats and relax, plan their exit, and calm her nerves. No one would expect them to be driving there in style.

Had her husband put a watch on the station? They should hide in the ladies' rest room after they had their railroad tickets to New York. Once on board, she was sure they'd be safe enough, though the thought of boarding a transatlantic liner again filled her with dread.

Pull yourself together. May did it in worse conditions than yours. Show some true grit.

57

Lichfield

One afternoon, unaware of Celeste's dramas, May was summoned after school to see Miss Parry. What was wrong? Was Ella ill? But she was sitting outside the office reading a book, looking surprised by her mother's flustered arrival. May was ushered in and the door closed behind her.

'There's just a little confusion I need to clear up, Mrs Smith. Don't look so worried but Ella has been telling her class that her father was lost with Captain Scott. We were doing a topic on brave men and I was telling them to write about snow and ice. Ella prefers to draw, as you know. She said her father sailed in the captain's ship and fell in the water.'

May felt herself go hot and cold. Miss Parry continued, not looking at her but fingering the papers on her desk.

'It's not the first time, Mrs Smith, that we've had pupils who are not quite sure of their parentage, who are perhaps not the result of a legitimate union. We're very understanding on these matters, of course, but it is not wise for a child to know of such affairs.'

'I'm sorry,' May spluttered, 'but she's got it all mixed up. Yes, it's true, my husband died at sea, Joseph Smith. He was going out to America to prepare a home for us. It was a terrible accident. Ella doesn't know the real circumstances. I saw no reason to tell her much. She's that fanciful, she's made this up. We have no grave to visit, you see. I'm sorry, I didn't think. How can she say such things?'

'I understand how difficult that must be, of course,' said the teacher. 'You know she's a very bright girl with a big imagination, and her drawing is well advanced for her age. Bright girls tend to romance and daydream. We hope she'll take a Minor scholarship in due course to the High School . . . not that we'd want to lose her but I am aware of your circumstances.' She coughed. 'Was your husband artistic?'

'He was good with his hands,' May offered. 'I don't know what to say. I'll make sure it doesn't happen again. She'll get her backside tanned for this.'

'No, please, Mrs Smith, this is a simple misunderstanding. She's just a little girl and like so many now she has no daddy to pin her dreams on. The war has torn so many families apart. She's too young to understand what she was saying. It's hard to work and raise a child on your own. She is a credit to you.'

May bowed her head. 'I want Ella to have the chances me and Joe never got. My husband and I were both orphans up north, we planned to start a new life in America. His loss was a terrible blow.' She felt herself welling up and ferreted for her hanky, sniffing. 'And now this.'

'Forget the whole matter. I'm so glad you told me. It will stay within these walls, I can assure you.'

'I don't like to think about it or care to remember the past. What shall I do about Ella then?'

'Nothing, just tell her the truth and make sure she knows who her real father is. Paint a mental picture so she can draw him and imagine him. Tell her his story and then she won't need to pretend.'

May left the study shaking. 'Come on, you have caused enough trouble for one day.' How could she be cross with Ella? But she was, for dredging up all their business and reminding her again of what she had lost and how she was lying to everyone around her. For many nights afterwards she lay awake mulling over Miss Parry's sensible advice.

How can I tell her the truth about her dad? I don't know who he was or is . . . or her mother, either. I have taken a child from her parents, dead or alive. How can I tell even more lies to cover this up? What do I do now?

Dear Celeste

Where are you now? Are you safe? I've not been able to sleep since the business with Mr Parkes. How silly of me to leave Roddy's picture on view.

I don't know what's wrong with me lately, but my nerves are all jangled. Ella's been playing up at school, telling fibs about her father being one of the explorer Captain Scott's crew. How his ship froze in the Antarctic and her father fell out into the ice. How can she think up such things at her age? Miss Parry said she may be pining for her daddy but she never knew him. I've told her what she needs to know, but not about the *Titanic*. She's too young for all that.

Sometimes it is so hard to keep up with her questions. I try to keep her busy. She goes to Miss Francetti's dancing class on Saturday mornings and to an art class after school. She has Sunday school and there is something called Brownies I have heard about in the paper. I take her to the picture house but that only makes her fancies worse. I hope she doesn't get teased at school for having such an ordinary background. Sometimes she clings and says her tummy hurts and that she doesn't want to go to school.

My mind has been going over and over the sinking and I keep hearing those voices crying for help from the waves. My appetite isn't what it was. You'd find me a poor wreck if you saw me just when I thought I was getting some spark back. I find everything an effort. I don't know what's happening to me. If only I could sleep better, but I lie awake going over things in my head, then I've no patience in the morning. Tell me to pull myself together. There are others far worse off than me. Please help me clear my head.

Yours, restless in the night,
May

In the morning she read over what she'd written and tore it up. No one wanted to hear such nonsense.

58

SS Saxonia, August 1919

Roddy looked up at the huge ship in the dock. 'Are we going on this?'

Celeste nodded, gripping his hand. 'All the way to England to see your grandfather and Uncle Selwyn.'

'But what about school?'

'I've written to the principal and to the parents of my etiquette classes. Now all the soldiers are back from war, they no longer want ladies in the government offices. You'll be going to a new school in the fall ... which we call autumn, by the way.'

'But why did we have to go away so quickly?'

It had been a long trek from the echoing noisy station to the docks, and the journey overnight to New York had left them tired. Celeste had paced up and down all night in case they were being watched. She couldn't believe they'd got here without trouble.

'Roderick, remember there was a nasty man following us. Well, he can't find us here.'

'Why was he nasty?'

'It's a grown-up story, darling. One day when you're a bit older I'll explain, but when anyone asks you about your papa you must say very politely that you haven't got one. He died in the war.'

Leah Fleming

'Did he?' Roddy asked puzzled.

'You just say you have no father now and people won't ask any more questions. You're not to tell anyone our business, not on board ship or when we get home. Do you understand? It's really important.'

He nodded, not really understanding any of it.

'Oh, and one more thing . . . you must keep this spare life preserver on at all times, no matter what anyone says.'

'I'm not wearing that thing. It's silly!' he said, pushing the child's yachting vest back at her.

'Make sure you keep it in sight when we set sail. There's a good reason why I'm asking you,' she pleaded. 'Things happen out of the blue.' She straightened her short wavy hair and grey tweed suit with the fur collar. In her rush she'd come without a decent hat and felt underdressed.

'Like what?'

Celeste looked up at the lifeboats, automatically counting them. 'If you hear a buzzer, run to the lifeboats and get in, no matter what they tell you. Promise me . . .'

'Yeah, Mom, but where'll we live? Why are we in such a hurry?'

'I told you, we're going home to Lichfield to see your grandfather and we'll stay with Uncle Selwyn until I can find work. He'll take us in. You'll meet my friend May and her little girl, Ella. She'll be there to play with.'

'Do I have to? I hate playing with girls. I'm not dressing up again.'

'That was just a game. That nasty man was watching our house and we had to get out without him following us.'

'Have we run away to sea?' Roddy looked up at her and she smiled.

'I suppose we have, Roddy. I'd never thought about it like that, but yes, I think we have.'

'Great! That's OK then,' he smiled, staring up at the ship. 'Nobody else in my class will be doing this, will they?'

Celeste was relieved to see his excitement. 'Come on, Jim Hawkins, the adventure begins.'

On the second day into the voyage, Celeste leaned over the railings, rain beating on her face, as the *Saxonia* glided through the choppy grey waters. They were out in the Atlantic, far from the haven of New York Harbour. How different from the last time. The surge of relief to be homeward bound was tinged with a shiver of fear that she was putting her trust in the ocean again. She'd tried not to think about her nightmares: screaming passengers, floating bodies, the sight of the mighty ship on its end, sliding down into the watery depths.

In some strange way, Grover's investigator had diluted her dread of coming aboard. They had to get away, but she felt sad to be telling Roddy a pack of lies, to be depriving him of his heritage. There was so much about the country she still loved and respected.

But the *Titanic* experience had changed her view of life for ever, as it must have done for so many of the survivors who had been left to come to terms with what they had seen and heard.

She'd even heard whispers of some of the society women divorcing their husbands for the very fact of them getting on the lifeboats in the first place. This was when, after the inquiry, everyone realized how few of the steerage women and children had survived. There were rumours that Bruce Ismay, the White Star Line chairman who jumped ship into the lifeboat, had had a breakdown.

Even after all these years the sight of the tall red funnel looming above her and the smell of salt water and steam, the hanging lifeboats on the great liner, made her shake with fear. But this time she was facing east and heading for Liverpool, and Roddy was by her side as they had walked up the gangway, Celeste trying not to look down or remember . . .

There was no luxurious First Class cabin this time, just a

modest room, little more than a cubbyhole compared to her accommodation on the *Titanic*. The ship was roomy enough, basic, battered from being used as a troopship but now refurbished. But the smell of fresh paint brought back memories and she felt sick.

Roddy was darting all over the place, exploring the decks and corridors, playing hide and seek with some of the other boys on board. She didn't want to let him out of her sight, but he was too quick and she realized she was in danger of nagging him into defiance. So she followed behind him discreetly, just in case. She'd not brought him all this way just to see him lost overboard. He was playing tag with a group of other boys and as usual not looking where he was going when he tripped over a cable and knocked down a man in a long tweed coat and trilby who'd been heading in his direction, limping with a stick. They concertinaed into each other, both collapsing in a heap and Roddy cried out with pain. The man in the trilby staggered, dazed, before scrambling to Roddy's aid.

'Hey, old chap, are you OK?'

She saw Roddy looking up, trying not to cry and grasping his ankle. 'It hurts.'

'Let me look at it,' the man continued, pointing to the ankle.

Celeste was at Roddy's side in a second, seeing the man about to reach for his stick for balance, looking shaken himself. 'I'm his mother. Roderick, you weren't looking where you were going . . . I'm so sorry.' She turned to face a young man with a grey face, who smiled and raised his hat with a smile.

'Another case of wrong place, wrong time, young man,' he replied. 'Let's have a look at that ankle.'

'Are you a doctor?' Celeste asked as the man bent to unloosen the boot.

'No, ma'am, but I did a fair bit of patching-up in the war,' he replied, not looking at her, more intent on examining Roddy's swollen foot. 'Can you wiggle your toes?'

Roddy nodded, whimpering. 'But it still hurts.'

'It doesn't look broken to me, but we'll have to let the ship's doctor see it just to be sure. You looked as though you were having fun,' he added, then turned to Celeste with a smile. 'Shall we carry him between us?' He was gesturing to his stick. 'Bit of a nuisance but it keeps this ship from listing port side.'

Celeste had to smile as she helped him to his feet. 'The war?' She looked at his stick.

'The war,' he shrugged. 'Battered and bowed but still afloat ... Archie McAdam, late of His Majesty's Royal Navy. And this young man?'

'This is my son, Roderick Wood. Stay put and I'll find another deckhand to lift him,' Celeste offered, looking round only to find they were alone now. Together they helped Roddy to his feet and he limped down the stairs to get his ankle strapped up.

'Thank you, Mr McAdam.' Celeste appraised the man with care. He was English, broad shouldered, with a weatherbeaten naval face with a beard. His hair was silvered at the sides. Celeste was homeward bound and in no hurry to dash away, but when Roddy appeared strapped up and he offered to take them to tea, she shook her head. 'It's Roderick who should be taking *you* to tea,' she protested.

'No, I insist. It will be good to give the stick a rest and you can both tell me what you two are doing on this old rust bucket. On vacation?'

'I'm going to see my grandpa. I've never seen him before and Mom says—' Roddy said but Celeste was quick to step in.

'I'm sure Mr McAdam doesn't want to know all our history,' she laughed, seeing how eagerly the man was observing them. Roddy mustn't get too familiar with strangers.

'But I do, and it's time for afternoon tea,' McAdam insisted. 'I'm starving, aren't you? You know, I was just looking around thinking as we set sail that everyone on this ship is on a journey, bound for the familiar or unfamiliar, and all the passengers have a story to tell. Then wham, I'm on the floor and the stories begin. So when I've found a table for three, ordered teacakes, fancies, whatever you like, young man, I shall tell you why I'm here. I bet you didn't think I'm travelling over the Atlantic just to go back to school?'

'Grown-ups don't go to school. Do they?' Roddy was curious.

'We call it university but it's still a school.'

'I've got to go to a new school in England. My other school was in Washington.'

'Well, there you go, you have a story to tell already. Come on then, us two old crocks will mount the stairs together.'

Roddy put his hand in Mr McAdam's and climbed, leaving Celeste staring up after them.

'Everyone's got a story, indeed. Well, Mr McAdam, you're not going to hear mine,' she muttered, following in their wake, not sure if she was intrigued or afraid of such a sudden encounter with this Englishman who was charming her son like the Pied Piper of Hamelin.

Roddy was confined to quarters later to rest his swollen foot. He would have been bored, but Mr McAdam called, bringing him some peppermints, a game of draughts and some *Boy's Own Paper*s with pictures of ships in them. He even loaned Roddy a reading book he'd bought for his nephew.

Somehow they kept meeting in the dining room, and when the band played Celeste reluctantly allowed herself to be persuaded to have one dance, but Mr McAdam, who struggled with his stiff leg, was glad to sit down again. He'd been visiting friends in New York for his vacation and had taken the opportunity to see a special surgeon to see if he could get his legs straightened out. He said he was keen on tennis, rugby and cricket, and collected cigarette cards and stamps from his journeys. He even promised to teach Roddy to play chess. He was easy to talk to and good with her bored young son. He had a deep throaty laugh that made people turn round and smile. Celeste was on guard, though, sitting up very straight and giving little away, so that he never got beyond calling her Mrs Wood all the time.

She could sense Roddy was dying to tell him all about their own adventures, about running away to sea, but she kept giving him icy stares, reminding him about their secret and how no one must ever know their business.

'You worked in Washington? It's a great city. Were you a teacher?'

She shook her head but Roddy butted in, 'Yes you were. We had classes in our house. They were *so* boring.'

'Roddy, it's rude to interrupt ...' She explained about the Women's Party and their successful Votes for Women campaign.

'We still haven't got the full vote in England yet, but it's coming. I think it's a disgrace that half the human race don't get a say in national matters. My wife used to say—' he broke off, then smiled. 'If men had the babies there'd soon be a change.'

'So you're going back to see your wife and children?' she asked, relieved at this news.

'I wish I were, but they were caught in a Zeppelin raid over London: wrong place wrong time.' He suddenly went quiet.

'I'm sorry,' was all she could muster.

'And you two? Your husband works in England?' He looked up. Roddy was waiting to see how she would reply.

'I have no husband now,' she said. 'Roddy's my man of the house, aren't you? We're going back to my home town to start again, aren't we?'

'Where's that?'

'Lichfield ... Grandpa lives in the cathedral,' Roddy jumped in.

'Roddy, we don't tell strangers our business.'

She saw Mr McAdam blush and felt mean to be so secretive. He wasn't a stranger now, just a rather pleasant young man going back to an empty house.

'You can write to us,' Roddy piped up, smiling. 'You can write to us from your new school, can't he?' he added, biting on his sticky bun, grinning with mischief.

'Of course, if Mr McAdam so chooses, but I expect he'll be very busy.'

He smiled at Roddy and winked. 'I think I might find time to put pen to paper now and again to give you my school report.'

Celeste couldn't sleep that last night aboard *Saxonia*, and for once it wasn't for fear of an iceberg or Grover's henchman: it was all Archie McAdam's fault. Why did Roddy have to bump into him? She steered clear of drawing unwanted attentions but Roddy's little accident brought this stranger into her path. He should have been discouraged, shaken off and dismissed.

There was something disturbing about the past few days in the company of this widower, sailor, scholar and educated man of her own class. He was the sort of man Papa would welcome at the door, but as Archie had said: 'Wrong place, wrong time.' Why couldn't she just be honest with him, tell her story, such as it was. That would soon put him off. But Roddy thought him a hero, and couldn't get enough of his sea dog stories, which she sensed were tailored and censored so as not to upset the sensitivities of a young boy. He was a man's man with the limp to prove it, and she was keeping him firmly at arm's length. He made them laugh and it was so refreshing to hear the fun in his voice instead of the fear Grover had instilled in her with his.

Ought she to let him write to them from Oxford? It wasn't that far from Lichfield on the train. Was she keeping the door open until such times . . . ? She had to admit an attraction to his bright eyes and deep voice. If only she were free. All the lies she'd built around their life to protect them over the years were like a hard shell, one she couldn't risk cracking.

Better to say nothing, to seem remote and disinterested, than to give false hope. She longed to tell him why she was so nervous, that any jolt in the ship's engine sent her straight back to that night on the *Titanic*. Then there was the business of making Roddy carry his yachting vest, pointing out where every lifeboat was situated and the route up onto deck in case of an emergency. What did he make of all her fussing?

They'd had the smoothest of voyages so far, uneventful but not boring, not now she'd met Archie McAdam. Something in his no-nonsense honesty and humour attracted her to him. It was a good job they would be docking in Liverpool tomorrow.

These five days had changed her life in so many ways, with the disruption of her carefully constructed peace of mind. She thought of the night she'd met Grover in London: those intense candlelight suppers, the corsage of flowers, her silk dress, the scents of the dining room, their rush to be married and away. She'd not been a good judge back then. This man was charming but he might be a charlatan, a sailor with a girl in every port, but she sensed his heart was of a different mettle. He showed such genuine interest in them. She could see him delight in Roddy's enthusiasms, his polite deference when she refused to relax and open up to him. It must be hurtful not to have her relax in his arms when she was dancing, her awkwardness and stiffness deliberate and off-putting. He must be puzzled, sensing her discomfort, thinking her disinterested in him, perhaps, because he looked older than his years and had a limp. What was holding her back?

Many things: fear of getting it wrong, fear of getting involved when she wasn't free, fear of jumping into some onboard romance. How could she ever trust another man after her past experience?

Though she had trusted him with one thing. They'd walked on deck when Roddy was settled for the night and she talked a little about going home, about having no means of support now, and she had confessed her nervousness at returning after so many years abroad. She admitted her father needed her and her brother was unwell.

'This war has broken so many lives,' Archie agreed, looking out to sea. 'None of us can be the same because of it. Thank God young Roddy will never have to face such grimness, Mrs Wood . . .'

She heard the sadness in his words and relented. 'Please call me . . . my name is . . .' They were almost in England now. Time to shed the disguise. 'People call me Celeste,' she said. 'Celestine Forester.'

He turned and smiled, reaching out to shake her hand formally. 'Thank you, Celeste. What a beautiful name for a lovely young woman. Would you mind if I wrote to you both sometime?'

She withdrew from his grasp, afraid of the feelings building between them even in this simple act. 'If you think it would help.' She paused, knowing she should reveal something else to show her trust but the words dried up in her throat. Then he said something extraordinary as he held her eyes with such intensity.

'I hope, in good time, you will tell me what or whoever in the past has given you such fear. Forgive me for being impertinent, but I sense your reserve and it goes against your nature. Don't worry,' he smiled. 'I have no intentions of prying. Wrong place, wrong time yet again, I fear . . .'

'Let's leave it at that then,' she interrupted, pulling away from the magnetic force drawing them closer. 'Good night, Archie. Mr McAdam . . .'

'Good night but not goodbye, Celeste.' He backed away, leaving her alone to fathom out his meaning amongst the moon-light and the stars.

59

On the last Saturday of August fifty excited children poured out of the station at Colwyn Bay in North Wales carrying bats and balls, bags of bathing suits, and waving their straw hats in the sunshine. May thought they looked like a flurry of white butterflies scattering over the beach with excitement. She was so tired from all her sewing, from not sleeping, from worrying if she should come here at all. But she wanted to keep an eye on Ella, just in case she blurted out any more tall tales.

'I want no more nonsense about Captain Scott or any telling fibs,' she had warned her. 'Your father was Joseph Smith, a carpenter from Edgeworth.'

'Like Joseph of Nazareth,' Ella said.

'There you go again. Don't be smart with me, listen to what I'm saying.'

'You won't wear your black crow dress, will you? You promised,' Ella added. 'My friend Hazel's mum has a new dress. Wear your new skirt.'

It was a shock to think a girl as young as Ella noticed and compared one woman to another. May had met Mrs Perrings at the school gate several times. Hazel was Ella's best friend at school. They seemed sensible sorts.

Dolly Perrings knitted for the duration of the train journey, chatting about this and that, and her new-found friend, George, a soldier from Whittington Barracks, who was always smartly turned out with clean fingernails and a moustache. Mrs Perrings was wearing a bright pink and white summer dress, her hair bobbed and feathered around her face. No wonder Ella thought May was a plain Jane of a mother.

Those words had hurt deeper than the child could ever know. She thought of jackdaws, black like crows. They stole bright things, and what was she if not a thief? Perhaps she deserved that name. She felt so wound up, like a coiled spring inside, tired, listless, as if perched on the edge of a steep cliff. One puff of wind and she'd be over the side. The confidence she'd been feeling since that episode with Florrie had vanished into tiredness. Everything was such an effort, even on this bright summer's day. When she smelled the seaweed, the salty breeze, she gagged, feeling sick. The sea. How had she been persuaded to come to the seaside of all places? This was madness.

She hung back from the other helpers. 'Come on, Mrs Smith . . . May. Let's see if we can get some tea and a walk on the promenade, take the air while Miss Parry and the teachers take the girls on their nature walk. It's still lesson time for them but not for us.'

May felt as if her feet weren't attached to her body. She drifted along with the flow and they found a little tearoom, but she could only taste warm water in her mouth. She felt faint at the sight of the rolling sea.

'What a lovely view,' said Mrs Perrings. 'We can watch the tide coming in from here. It's like a silver lake out there, so smooth and silky . . . just look . . . like a mill pond.' She chattered on, oblivious to the fact that May sat with her back to the water.

'The sea has another face, a cruel face,' she suddenly muttered. 'It can lull you into a false safety and spew you out in its roaring waters.'

'Ah yes, I'm sorry, dear, Hazel told me that your husband died at sea. It's a terrible thing to be widowed so young. When I got the telegram that Philip had been killed in Gallipoli, well, I don't know how I'd have managed without the little one for comfort. Hazel is my little helper and Ella looks the same to me. At least we have a bit of our husbands to remind us.'

May looked at the woman as if she'd never seen her before, got up and went off down towards where the children were walking in a crocodile, pausing to pick shells and stamp footprints in the sand.

The sea might rise up and drown them all, its waves crashing over their heads, and she heard again the cries of the dying in the water, those agonizing cries to God and to their mothers for rescue. *Help me!* She put her hands to her ears to drown out those terrible voices, the thrashing of frozen limbs, the lapping of the oars on the water rowing away from all who needed help.

Then she saw some of the girls paddling, their skirts rolled up into their knickers, and far out a man swimming, his head bobbing on the surface of the water just as Joe's had done. He was too far out for safety. The man was drowning like Joe, and in her mind she was there again trying to catch him up.

'Turn back, turn back! Look, we must help him!' she yelled. 'He's drowning!' She felt her limbs thrashing after Joe, their precious bundle floating away. She screamed, 'Bring him back, the sea will have him . . . Bring them on board. Ellen . . . Joe . . . Wait for me! Come back!'

Suddenly an arm was around her. 'Mrs Smith, Mrs Smith, you're unwell. The man is quite safe and the tide is coming in.'

May threw off the comforting arm. 'No . . . I want my Ellen . . . I can't see her any more.'

'Ella is fine, Mrs Smith. You must calm down, you're frightening the girls. Stop this at once.' The voice was sterner now, a schoolmarm voice pulling her back from the shore. 'Come along with me. You need something to calm your nerves.'

May lashed out at her comforter's restraining hand. She could still see them both.

'Ellen, come back to me . . . Joe, come back to me. Wait for me, I'm coming.' She ran into the water, splashing, oblivious to the chill of the Irish Sea. She was wading in deeper, ignoring the voices calling her back. She must find them, calling out to her in the darkness of that awful night. She belonged with her family, not with strangers here.

There were stronger arms now dragging her back to the shore. She fought them all the way as if they were the arms on the lifeboat dragging her back, away from her baby and Joe. Someone was slapping her face.

'Pull yourself together, woman! Ella is safe. Look, here she is, Mrs Smith. Calm yourself, no harm will come to her. We're all safe on this beautiful summer day. Ella will help you.'

May stared at the darkling child looking up at her with horror. 'I don't want her. She's not my daughter . . . Ellen lies at the bottom of the sea.'

'Mrs Smith,' a man's voice shouted, 'enough of this nonsense. Your daughter is safe by your side. This has to stop.'

'This is not my daughter,' she insisted, her wild eyes examining those dark lashes and chocolate-button eyes, shaking her head, suddenly so very weary. 'This is not my baby. My baby is dead.' Then something was stabbed into her arm and she knew nothing more.

Ella had watched her mother's eyes rolling wildly, listened to her screams and thrashings, had seen her new skirt soaked with salt water, her hair unpinned, dripping in rat's tails. She'd looked like a witch, a scary witch from a picture book. When she had turned on them so angrily, denying her own daughter, Ella had run as fast as she could from the crowd of horrified girls, open-mouthed at what they had just witnessed. She was so full of fear and shame and fury, all rolled up into one tight ball inside her, drawing her tummy so tight she wanted to howl. What had she done? What was wrong? Why was Mum so angry and making such a scene?

The seaside day trip was ruined for everyone now, and she felt so angry and embarrassed that it was her mother's fault.

They bundled Mum into an ambulance with a locked door like a Black Maria. Everyone was staring and gawping, and Ella wanted to disappear into the sea and hide under the water.

It was Miss Parry who came to comfort her. 'I'm afraid your mother is unwell. I think there has been much strain, and she'll have to be looked after for a while. Don't worry, she'll get better, given time. Now we have to think about you and who will be looking after you. Mrs Perrings says she can have you for a few days. I shall inform the College . . . I'm very sorry this has happened, Ella.'

'What did I do wrong?' she asked in a faraway voice.

'Nothing at all. As I said, she's unwell and when people are sick in their mind, they say unspeakable things. It's the nature of brain fever. Put such thoughts out of your head. Don't worry, she won't remember any of this, I promise you.'

But I will, thought Ella miserably. 'She said I wasn't her daughter,' she cried out.

'That's the fever talking nonsense. Of course you are her daughter. Don't take heed of that. Come, we're all going for tea before we return to the station. Hazel will sit with you and you can be with the teachers in the quiet compartment on the journey home. I'm sure you're very tired now.'

Ella stared back at the rolling sea, hearing the gulls wheeling overhead. The salt spray and the seaweed stung her nose. As long as she lived she'd never forget the sight of her mother running into the waves as if she meant to drown herself. Who will look after me now? she sobbed as silently as she could.

She turned to look at the water stretching out to the grey horizon. Clouds were gathering, dark storm clouds. The sun was hidden and the sea was choppy and noisy in her ears. Somehow her mother's fever was all the fault of waves and water and shore.

I never want to see you again . . . I hate you . . . I never want to see the sea ever again.

60

Celeste stood on City station. They'd come straight from Liverpool a long enough route that she had had time to adjust to hearing those Midlands voices shouting down the platforms. The platform air was stiff with hops from the nearby brewery, iron filings and soot, and a stiff easterly tugged at her coat.

'Look,' she pointed out to Roddy. 'The cathedral spires.'

'They're not very tall,' was his only comment.

'Let's give Grandpa a surprise,' she said, then saw him looking puzzled.

'Grandpa's not here, he's in America.' His tiredness was making him confused.

'You are a lucky boy to have two grandpas. Come on, we'll put all our things in a taxi.'

Roddy wasn't impressed by the vehicle. 'This is only a horse-drawn one – where are the automobiles?'

They had travelled light with just their hand baggage. Not a lot to show for ten years abroad, Celeste reflected, but none of that mattered now. She wanted to track every inch of their journey. What shops did she recognize? There was the old theatre, now a picture-drome, the clock tower, the Swan Hotel, the museum and library buildings and Minster Pool, just as she'd left them. They turned into the Close through the ancient wall and alighted. She couldn't stop smiling. What a surprise she was going to give them.

Half dragging her son through the little tunnel into Vicar's Close, she felt like a child again, ringing the door pull of number four, desperately hoping her father would be inside.

An old man with a stoop stared up at her, amazed. 'Oh my goodness, come in, come in. May thought you'd not be long in coming home again, but this ... and this young man must be Roderick. I've heard so much about you.'

Celeste stepped inside the tiny cottage. It was a muddle of books and papers. A smell of tobacco smoke and burned dinner greeted her nostrils. 'I see May's not seen to you for a few days,' she laughed.

Her father paused. 'Oh, you won't know, will you? Poor May's in hospital.'

'How?' Celeste replied, shocked. This was not how it should be. 'I didn't know she'd been ill.'

'That young May is full of secret sorrows, I fear. We had no idea either. Selwyn was most upset. How wonderful to have you back with us after all your ... your difficulties. Your timing is perfect. So much has happened. But sit down, let me fill the teapot. It's around here somewhere.'

Celeste jumped up. 'I see we're going to have to roll up our sleeves and sort you out. Oh, Papa, you've no idea how long I've been waiting for this return.' She stopped, seeing her father peering over his half-moon glasses at her son.

'He's so like Bertie, isn't he?' he said, looking at the silver-framed picture of Bertram in his uniform. 'I still can't believe he won't be coming home to us. I'm glad your mother didn't have to know this ... but now, how wonderful to see you both. Wait till Selwyn hears. I must warn you, though, Selwyn isn't quite as you will recall him. He's been very ill but he'll mend given time, like May.'

'What *is* wrong with May?'

'Didn't I say? She's in St Matthew's.'

'The asylum?' Celeste was shocked. 'How?'

'She's not herself. They can help her there.'

Celeste took another deep breath at this bad news, knowing her return was not a minute too soon. Here she was needed and here she was welcome. They were home at last.

61

May awoke, not knowing where she was at first. Her eyes blurred as she tried to focus on the room. It was a ward with high ceilings, iron beds along the walls and the smell of Lysol in the air. She felt she'd been asleep for a long time: her limbs were stiff and heavy, her tongue thick and her mouth dry. Her hands fingered the thin nightdress that had ridden up, barely covering her. Her head was throbbing as she tried to lift her head off the pillow. What was she doing here?

Panic flooded her body and she sank back. I don't care where I am I'm so tired, she thought. Her head was as fluffy as cotton wool. At first she had no recollection of how she came to be here, nothing except sleep and heaviness with glimpses of a long journey somewhere at the back of her befuddled mind. Her throat was sore and parched. Where was she?

There were other women shuffling up and down the room, eyeing her with interest, but they soon moved away when a nurse in a stiff white cap marched in. At the sight of her movement she smiled. 'Ah, Mrs Smith, you are with us once more.'

'Where am I?'

'You are in St Matthew's Hospital, my dear. Here for a long rest and a good long sleep.'

May couldn't take in her words at first. What was she doing in an asylum, a lunatic asylum? 'Where am I?' she asked again.

'I told you ... in hospital.'

'But where?' Bits of memory were jolting back into place. She'd been on the train and there were crowds and the sea. Oh my God, the sea!

'Where's Ella? My daughter?' She sat up to get out of bed but the room spun round and she almost collapsed.

'Now, just get back into bed, Mrs Smith. Your daughter is being well cared for, don't get upset.'

'We were at Colwyn Bay . . . I know we went on a train. Am I in Wales?' Why did her lips not move when she tried to speak? Every word had to be forced out of her mouth.

'Now do I sound Welsh? You're in St Matthew's, Burntwood. You've been here over a week now. Don't go getting upset. We need to keep you calm. I don't want you upsetting the other patients. I'll tell Dr Spence you're awake. He'll want to speak with you.'

What did I do to be put in here? May's mind was searching for those shards of broken memory – the icy stabs as she was thrashing in the water and the screaming. What had she done? Where was Ella? She wanted to feel anxious but everything was numb.

'I've got to go home. I shouldn't be here. I have a job. I must go home and see to things.'

'If you don't calm down we'll have to put you to sleep again,' the nurse insisted as she bent over her, straightening the bedding. 'You need to rest your mind, not stir it up. You've been very run down.'

'When can I see Ella?'

'We don't have children visiting, but your friends have come. They will give her news of you.'

'What friends?'

'The lady from the cathedral has been asking about you. She's called in twice with flowers. See, over there? The beautiful gladioli.' The nurse pointed to a glass vase full of coloured spears that were out of focus.

Had the wife of the college principal been visiting? How kind of her. 'I'm sorry to be a trouble, but I must go home.'

'Now that won't be possible, dear, just yet, not until you're better. You tried to drown yourself.'

'I did what?' May shrank under the covers.

'You ran into the sea and had to be restrained. You scared people with your antics. Now we can't have that, can we?'

May's head was spinning at her words. If only she could remember, but everything was fuzzy and blurred, just pictures that fell into pieces when she tried to stare at them. There was the sea, yes, like a silver mirror glinting, reflecting her wickedness back at herself. She had wanted to smash that mirror. It stirred things up in her head she'd never wanted to see again. How the waves had crashed over their heads . . . how the ship had slid under the surface of the cruel ocean. She felt tears, but none came; her eyes were dry and sore. *Why am I here? What did I do wrong? And where's the captain's little girl now?*

She turned her face from the nurse in shame, wanting to sink back into the mist of forgetfulness, to disappear into the autumn fog drifting over Stowe Pool early in the morning.

In the days that followed everything around her seemed bleached and colourless. She felt like a stranger in threadbare laundered linen wandering around in a daze of confusion. The food in the dining hall was tasteless, like over-blanched vegetables, and her drugged limbs were heavy as she dragged herself into the exercise yard and later around the corridors to the day rooms.

There was a smell of bonfires drifting through the open windows, and when she shuffled round the grounds of the hospital, the leaves scrunched under her boots like crushed glass. Her fingers were stiff and swollen as she sat in the workroom watching others struggling with basketwork. She couldn't concentrate on stuffing toys or knitting. A nurse tried to persuade her to do something. 'I can't,' she complained. 'My fingers don't work.'

It was as if everything here was in slow motion. She watched a woman making lace with pins and bobbins bent over her cushion slowly twisting threads, ignoring her, deep in concentration. If only she could lose herself in something like that.

She fingered the bone bobbins wrapped with cotton and saw herself young with all the hope in front of her, the clack of the machines, the chatter of the girls mouthing their gossip over the noise. She was back in the mill, so full of life and love and expectation. Who was that girl? Where had she gone? Who was this drab sorrow-burdened old woman?

'Would you like to try this, Mrs Smith?' asked the nurse, guiding her to a seat to watch how the lace was woven from pin to pin. The cotton threads followed the pattern of the pins, the lace grew so gradually, so delicate but so slow, and her eyes were soothed by the flicking of the bobbins, the rhythm of the twisting threads. She thought of spider webs, loops and links with gaps in between. Her mind was like a piece of lace, full of holes and spaces, and gaps with threads of worry twisting round the pins. Joe and Ellen. Ella, the ocean and that terrible night. Would the nightmares ever end?

How could she make sense of any of it now? She was too tired and fearful, but she could twist threads and make something grow. She sat down and watched and wondered at the delicate bobbins, like tiny fingers dancing over the cushion. This was something she could try.

Later, as she paced around the outer building, she sensed St Matthew's was not the workhouse of her fears. It rose majestically like a brick castle out of the mist, and she was overawed by the size. She had heard about this place but had never seen it. Here she didn't have to think or prepare meals but just sit in the vast dining hall and be served. She was given menial jobs to do but there was time to sit with the bobbins and lose herself in the threading, learning a new skill that was loosening her stiff fingers.

Life here wasn't real, none of this was real. She'd been taken out of the real world into this mansion for a rest, but across the valley there was the child to consider.

Ella didn't deserve what was happening to her. She was just a child, confused and frightened, now orphaned in effect. Who was looking after her? If only she wasn't so tired and heavy. Perhaps Ella was better off without her? Who would want a mother like her?

During the weeks that followed the terrible trip to the seaside everyone at school was kind to Ella. She felt people were tiptoeing around her as if she was wearing a label round her neck that said: 'Her mother is locked away. She's got no one to look after her so don't keep staring.' But that wasn't true. Hazel was kind and her mother was letting her stay with them, on a camp bed in Hazel's room. She didn't understand why Mum had to be taken away with her arms tied up or why she wasn't allowed to visit her in St Matthew's. Mrs Perrings tried to explain.

'She needs rest, love. She's been under a lot of strain. Seeing the water, well, it reminded her of your father and how he drowned. The doctors will take care of her. She'd want you to get on with your schooling. I've been to see Canon Forester and the College, and they will visit her and she'll get what she is entitled to . . . Don't worry. We'll collect her post and get a few things for you.'

Ella had just one question: 'How long will she be in there?'

'Until the doctors think she's well enough to come home, but don't fret, you can stay here for a while until we see how things unfold.'

It was good walking with Hazel to school, and Miss Parry kept her busy if she looked sad. She missed Lombard Gardens and the view from her own room over Stowe Pool. She didn't have time to go to the cathedral as the Perringses were Methodists and she had to go with them on a Sunday to their Tamworth Street church.

No one there knew about her mother being sent away, and soon, as the days turned into a week, she began to get used to living with this new sister and her mother and meeting Uncle George the soldier.

On the first Saturday together they played alongside the brook at Netherstowe and Ella remembered the little shrine to St Chad that had been their wishing well, covered over with an ivy roof. When Hazel was at her piano lesson she took herself down the road to the well and said a long prayer to the saint, telling him to hurry up and make her mum better. Why had Mum not come home? Did she not want to see her again? Was it right that she wasn't her real daughter? She had to know the truth. It was then that she had her big idea.

62

'We've come to see Mrs Smith,' Celeste announced, clutching some pink dahlias as she and her father stood in the grand entrance of St Matthew's, watching the clock ticking round to three and listening for the visitor's bell.

'She's not having a very good day,' the nurse warned. 'Very weepy ... She has these spells. Still, your visit might brighten her mood.' It was Celeste's third visit but so far she'd not seen the patient. This time she was determined to see for herself what had happened to May. She eyed the hospital with a certain admiration. Of its kind it was clean and functional and on a grand scale.

They followed slowly behind the nurse, the canon faltering to catch his breath, stumbling with his stick. It was not one of his good days either, but he was determined to accompany her.

The nurse pointed to a woman slouched over a table, working her fingers at something. She didn't look up when the nurse announced, 'You've got visitors again, Mrs Smith.'

'May?' enquired Canon Forester. 'How are you today?'

There was no response. She seemed lost in her lace weaving. 'I've brought someone to see you. Look, do you recognize who it is?' The canon touched her shoulder, smiling. Celeste stepped forward trying not to look shocked at how pale and thin and aged May had become. She could have passed this woman in the street and not recognized her. Gone was the feisty May who, from her father's account, had taken no nonsense from Grover on his visit and stood her ground against a bully.

'May ... it's me, your friend, Celeste, back home from America for good.'

May turned her head, staring, not recognizing her at first and then when she had, she covered her eyes with her hands. 'I'm sorry, who are you?'

'I'm Celeste, your pen pal from the States, your friend.'

'My daughter turned up on my doorstep without a word of warning. It's so lovely after all these years. Doesn't she look well? And I have a grandson, so high.' Canon Forester lifted his hand to indicate Roddy's height but Celeste could see May was not listening.

There was a strange blankness to her features, deep furrowed lines on her brow. How could this be the same woman who had written such lively letters, who'd boxed Florrie Jessup's ears? What had gone so very wrong for her?

She was staring at them, still trying to focus on their faces. 'It was a long time ago. I forget so. I'm sorry you've had a wasted journey,' she replied, turning back to her bobbins and cottons as if her visitors' presence was not her concern.

'Of course, I should come to say thanks to you for all you did.' Celeste sat down, forcing herself on her friend again. 'You redirected my letters, cheered me up when I was low. Now I'm here to help you get better. We've so much to catch up on.'

'I'm not good company, ma'am. I don't deserve to get better.' She turned her back on them again, but Celeste was not going to give up easily.

'Then let's help you get better. Is there anything you'd like us to bring? Don't worry about your daughter. She's being looked after. I saw her myself only yesterday. She's a credit to you. We're going to take her out for a day to meet my son, Roddy. He's longing to meet her.'

'She's not my daughter.'

'Of course she is. What put that idea in your head?'

'I'm not her true mother. I'm not fit to be her mother.' May started weeping and a nurse stepped forward.

'I'm afraid I did warn you ... not a good day. She gets these ideas in her head. The doctors are doing what they can.'

'But it's all poppycock. I saw the baby in her arms in the life-boat ... We were shipwrecked together. That's how we met. I owe her so much. She's an excellent mother. This is terrible ... what can we do?' Celeste wanted to weep at the sight of the broken woman. She reminded her of some of the force-fed victims in the suffrage campaign, broken by the torture and sense of failure that they'd felt in swallowing food to survive.

'Time will heal her, Celeste. She needs rest now.' Her father touched her shoulder. 'The mind is a mystery. Some of our college students are much changed after the war, some have lost faith, others have had to go into retreat away from alcohol and substances. War is much more than buildings and machinery and bodies destroyed. I'm sure May will heal. She's in my prayers every night. We'd better go now. I think we're upsetting her.'

Celeste was not so ready to leave. 'Has she seen her daughter yet?' she asked. 'That might shake her out of this dream world she's in and bring her back into real life.'

'Children don't visit. It's not advisable. It only upsets the patient more, in my experience,' the nurse replied briskly.

As they walked down the long tiled corridor Celeste shivered at the sight of so many shuffling people lost in their own worlds. She'd heard about these places and this was better than most, being bright, airy, clean and spacious, but it was also cold and clinical, so vast in size, without any feeling of home. How could May get better in such a place, cut off from everyday life? Not to see her child, to deny she was her mother was madness indeed. What had put that idea into her head? She looked so muddled, so distant, lost in her own fantasy. Her eyes were like those of a dead fish on a slab, glazed, blank, her hair stringy and greasy. Her dress hung off her shoulders. How did she come to be so hopeless and lifeless, like an empty shell?

Had May survived their ordeal on the *Titanic* just to end up this shadow of her former self, making her daughter an orphan? There must be something she could do to bring her back to life, give her something to live for.

She recalled what Archie McAdam had said, how he'd survived that torpedoed ship, clinging to the lifebuoy, knowing they had only hours to live. How he'd made everyone sing songs and hymns, telling the men stories and jokes and making them picture all their families at home, telling them how they must get back there and keep awake. 'I just refused to give up,' he'd said, smiling that grizzled grin, his eyes brimful of life. They'd received a letter already with his new address and as soon as she'd opened it, Celeste knew she'd reply.

Life goes forward not backwards. She didn't want to think about her Akron days now. Would she have ended up in one of these places if she'd not escaped from Grover?

She'd kept going forward, relieved to be home amongst the familiar once more. May must be helped to move forward out of this terrible pit of gloom. What was it all about? She was going to have to find out more.

Now they were settled back with Selwyn at Red House near Streethay, camping in the rambling old place, crammed full of family furniture and clutter. His temporary housekeeper had given notice, saying the work was too much for her, leaving Mrs Allen, the daily help, to cope alone, and Celeste could make herself useful there for the moment. It was a ridiculous red-brick three-storey house with eight bedrooms. An old farmhouse off the old road to Burton on Trent, it was in need of repair. It looked like a doll's house in shape but needed a good cleaning from top to bottom and was far too big for a single man.

Selwyn accepted Celeste and Roddy needed a roof over their

heads, and he'd not asked too many questions or pried into what went wrong with her marriage. That was some relief. She was too ashamed to tell anyone her business, not even her father, who she caught staring at her with concern.

'Are you all right, child? I'm afraid May is really quite sick, much worse than I thought,' he sighed. 'Such a shame, and that poor girl, all alone in the world.'

For all her father was frail and forgetful he was a good judge of his children. He'd refused to come and live with them in Selwyn's barn of a house. He realized they needed their space. Now he sighed as he surveyed the gardens of the asylum from a bench. 'I'm afraid I've landed you right in this. I'm sorry.'

'What for? May stood by me for years. I'm not letting her rot in here,' Celeste replied. 'She will get better, won't she?'

'That's in Greater Hands than ours. We'll do what we can and trust to providence.'

'I wish I had your faith, Papa . . .'

'I'm old and I can look back and see patterns in life, turning points, roads not taken. You've had a hard struggle but one bad mistake needn't ruin the rest of your life, child. You need time to heal too, and where better than with your own kind?'

'May has no one . . .'

'She has Ella, she has friends and she has you. She's thrice blessed,' he whispered.

Celeste stared out at the pristine lawns where a man was gathering up fallen leaves into a wheelbarrow and another patient was clipping hedges. Life was so complicated. Her return hadn't quite turned out as she'd imagined. Had she struggled all this time to untangle one strand of her life only to find herself picking up the threads here? She was in danger of making even more knots.

63

Ella told Mrs Perrings she was going into town, but caught the bus to Burntwood at the Market Square. She'd got enough pennies for the fare and in her shopping bag were the drawings she'd done for a present. She asked around enough to know just how to find the hospital, but when she got off the bus and walked the last bit of the country lane, the sight of such an enormous building made her gulp. How would she find her mum in there? It was like a castle with a tower and windows with bars across them.

There were signs everywhere: 'Main Entrance' was what she was looking for as she scurried past the lodge and the gates, and down the tree-lined drive. There were lawns and a park. It was like visiting a great mansion. She tried to look inconspicuous, but it wasn't long before a man stopped her path.

'You can't go in there! No kiddies allowed,' he said.

'But I want to see my mum,' Ella replied, holding out her bag.

'I'm sure you do but it's not a place for children.'

'I want to see my mum,' she began to cry. 'I haven't seen her for two weeks and I've written to her. And I know she wants to see me.' The sight of a child in tears had the desired effect.

'Now, love, don't cry ... I'm sure she understands, but rules is rules.'

'But I've brought her some pictures.' Ella was beginning to panic. Why was he stopping her? The groundsman turned her round, pointing her in the direction of the road. Ella began to howl so loudly that people passing stopped and wondered what was happening. An old man in black moved forward to ask but through her tears she didn't recognize him.

'Ella ... Ella Smith? Oh, my dear, what're you doing here?' He turned to the red-haired lady from America, who'd called after school with a lovely musical box.

The lady smiled. 'Oh my goodness! Ella, how did you get here on your own?' She stepped forward to comfort her but Ella was having none of it.

'I want my mum. She's in there,' she cried, pointing to the hospital.

The groundsman gripped her hand. 'Now stop this fuss, you'll get me into trouble! You know this kid? Tell her she can't go in.'

'She's come all this way on her own. Surely something can be done ... It's cruel not to let her see her own mother. Mrs Smith needs to know she is safe.' Her mum's friend was trying to help. 'Father, we'll have to go back. Just stay here.' The lady darted back up the drive while the canon found a hanky for Ella to blow her nose on.

'They're being very kind to her here. She's having a long rest and needs to be kept quiet, but don't worry ... she's safe.'

Ella had always liked Canon Forester. He fished in his pocket and brought out a wrapped sweet. 'It's only a cough drop. My daughter will see what she can do ... If anyone can bend the rules she'll find a way.'

Ella blinked back tears, nodding. 'She brought me a present yesterday.'

'That sounds like Celeste; I still can't believe she's come back to us ... Look, she's waving us to come up and see ... I told you, Celeste can work miracles, so dry your eyes and give me your hand. Slowly, don't rush.'

Ella was dying to push ahead, hoping to see her mother at the doorstep, but there was only the young lady with the short skirts smiling and pointing to a window at the side. 'Look, Ella, over there, in the day room window.'

Mum was standing looking at her, not smiling but staring hard. Ella put her hand in the shopping bag and held up the pictures she'd done of the cathedral spires. 'I did them for you!' she shouted, waving them in the air. Her mother nodded. She looked so faded and pale; the sides of her hair were all sticking out and grey. Ella reached out her hand and touched the glass of the window to feel her mother's hand in hers.

For a second Mum turned away and then stopped and put out her own hand on the window, her fingers splayed out, covering her daughter's small hand.

'Are you getting better?' Ella shouted. 'I've been to St Chad's Well. You will get better soon. I want you to come home.' Mum nodded and then her lips turned into a little smile and she patted the window again. The attendant led her away and she faded back into the room and out of sight.

When Ella turned round the lady was wiping her eyes. 'It will do your mother more good than all the tablets in the world to know you are here. We'll hand in your beautiful pictures for her to keep by her bed. I'm sure she'll love to have them. You're a very clever girl to be able to draw like that.'

Ella walked back down the drive holding the lady's hand tightly. Mrs Perrings would be wondering where she was by now. How strange her life was with no one around to call her own. She looked down at the three spires of the cathedral, which came into view as they drove down Pipe Hill. At least she now knew Mum was safe in the castle, but still she felt very lost.

'So, young lady, what are we going to do about you? When I take Papa back to Vicar's Close, I think you should come too and I'll make tea. Then I'll take you back to your lodgings, pack your bags and you can come home with me to Streethay for a few days. I want you to meet Roddy. And we can get to know you better. I saw you once as a tiny baby but you are so grown up now. Such a pretty girl. I want to know all about you and who taught you to draw like that.'

'Thank you, miss, but Mrs Perrings looks after me now.' She didn't want to stay with strangers.

'And I'm sure she's done a sterling job but now it's my turn to oblige. Wait until you see Selwyn's old house. There's enough room to billet an army in there. There's three enormous conker trees and the conkers are ripening. Roddy needs someone to play with. You'll love it. You can call me Aunt Celeste. Your mother's been like a sister to me in the past.'

Ella looked into those bright blue eyes and at the red-gold hair tucked under a pretty beret. Perhaps her mum wouldn't mind her changing digs for a few days. This lady looked fun and she'd given her the chance to see that her mum was safe. So she sat back in the bus, staring out of the window with a flutter of excitement and curiosity. The tight band round her chest didn't hurt so much now. She could breathe again, and for the first time in weeks she felt things were turning out better. Perhaps St Chad had heard her prayer after all.

64

New York, 1920

No one on the block was happy about the new prohibition laws, least of all Salvi and Angelo Bartolini, who'd been stowing away wine for months before the ban came into place. 'Wine is part of our way of life like whiskey is to the Irish. I just don't understand,' Salvi moaned, and Angelo agreed.

'How do we celebrate baptisms, marriages and wakes without something to liven things up? Who wants tea or fruit juice?'

They knew there were gangs already importing whiskey from Canada, shipping booze across the Great Lakes in secret, hiding rum at the ports disguised in anything that would hold liquor. Now everyone was finding hidy-holes, from hot-water bottles to petrol cans and hip flasks in which to store their booze. The law didn't forbid the drinking of the stuff, only the selling of it in public, and there would be ways round this.

'We'll make it ourselves,' Orlando suggested. Salvi's son was never short of bright ideas. He'd bought in blocks of pressed wine pulp that looked like bricks. All they needed was to add sugar and water and let it ferment and they should have themselves some decent wine.

'Better yet, let's make ourselves a still, like in the old days, fine grappa on tap,' added Angelo.

'Over my dead body!' Kathleen shouted. 'I'm not having

hooch in my house. The last time my uncle made it, it blew out the windows of the farmhouse and killed a cow.'

But Salvi and Angelo were not to be deterred and they set up all the tubes and glass jars and heat necessary for the job so that it was easy to dismantle if the law came to call, each piece with its own special hiding place.

Orlando suggested they made sure the local cop got his full share, with a few dollars to turn a blind eye. That was happening all over town. The cellar of their fruit store was the perfect place. There were old barrels to be cleaned out, buckets, plenty of space for home brewing.

'We'll start simple: fruit skins, pulp, extract the juice and put it through the tubes,' Angelo ordered. He'd seen his family do it so many times when he was a boy.

Salvi decided he was the front man, knowing nothing about this business. Angelo also added the syrup to the wine blocks and shoved them into the barrels to ferment, hoping the miracle of turning water into wine would work like it did in the Bible.

The results of the grappa experiment were encouraging and Orlando had the big idea of scooping out the insides of water melons and filling them with their brew to sell out, sealing the top with wax so customers could carry out their fruit with a clear conscience. Word went round that the Bartolini watermelons were worth a sample so far and wide that one day a guy in a black fedora marched in and pulled out a gun, threatening Salvi. 'You pay up or we drop a hint to the cops just what you're doing. No one sets up without our permission, *capisce*?'

'So the mob know about the hooch but not the wine. No one knows about that,' Angelo murmured, proud of his venture.

'You don't go behind the backs of these guys. They have all the protection rackets sewn up round here. How do you think we stay in business? We pay, we stay. We refuse and we are cinders.'

It wasn't fair but that was the score on the Lower Eastside. No one breathed without the Rizzi gang knowing. They were the 'family' connected to even bigger 'families'.

The Bartolinis were small beer, easily disposed of if they stepped out of line. But it worked two ways. They would be a source of decent liquor supply, the real McCoy, not watered-down rubbish. Better to pay up and get what was going before some store round the block got their share. Didn't those folk who were running the country realize that by setting up these stupid laws, they made bootlegged booze into liquid gold for the gangs of New York?

The raid came one evening when they were shutting the store, about to set out on some deliveries. The shop was crawling with blue uniforms searching for bottles while Salvi carefully crated up his melon balls in straw. 'Please feel free to look around, but don't bruise my fruit here.' He winked.

Two officers were pulling apart the cellar, bypassing the tubes hidden with bits of junk in separate sacks looking like innocent items of rubbish waiting for the garbage cart.

'What's in the casks?' smiled one of the cops, knowing he'd found gold.

'Just fruit vinegar,' Angelo replied, sensing the game was up. 'We brew it for the *insalata* dressing.'

'Sure don't smell like vinegar to me,' said the cop. 'Open it up.'

Angelo's heart sank. They were caught red-handed so he passed over a tin mug and turned the tap. All his work would be poured down the drain.

The officer sipped the liquid and spat it out. 'Hell fire, that's strong stuff. You weren't having me on. How you folks can stomach such stuff on your tomatoes is beyond me. It's not fit for humans, but each to his own.' He threw down the tin and climbed the stairs, leaving Angelo staring down at his failure. What would Salvi say? All this wine now vinegar and fit only for the drain. Still, he reasoned, even Rome wasn't built in a day.

65

May sensed she'd slumped to the bottom of the pit and slowly, after that first sighting of Ella through the window, was beginning to climb out of her deep depression. She found her way to the work room each morning, where she was getting the hang of simple threadwork. The drugs trolley still appeared and she opened her mouth like a child, receiving a dose of brimstone and treacle. If she took the pills, maybe it would speed her out of this place. Sometimes, as she fingered the bobbins and focused on the little line of pins and patterns, she found she enjoyed watching her simple lacework grow. Sometimes when she walked around the gardens her feet were not so heavy and fresh air stung her cheeks. She began to feel again, and with the small pleasures came the pain of her losses, that ache in her heart that would never ease. Joe and Ellen were gone, but concern for the child in the window who gave her pictures, who'd made her own way to see her, fuelled her progress. She realized one night that she must have done something right to earn such love, even if she was a false mother.

Colours were coming into focus again, the fresh greens of new leaves and buds, the red brick shining in the sunlight. That cloud of confusion and weariness no longer pressed on her forehead and she knew there was hope, but she must guard her tongue if she was ever to find her way home.

'Why do you keep saying Ella is not your child?' Dr Spence

asked, searching her face to see if she could give an explanation. It was hard to hold back the truth but she knew enough to know that what she'd done on the lifeboat was a criminal act, and that would mean prison. What happened to her was of no matter, but Ella must not be abandoned now. Better to eat her words, choke back the truth, swallow them no matter what the cost to herself.

'I look at her and don't recognize myself in her,' she answered carefully. 'I didn't know what I was saying.'

'Can you say more?' Dr Spence persisted, leaning forward.

'When I see her, I see her father and how he drowned. I see him. I couldn't keep close enough. It was so cold, the water, ice, the debris . . . We were on the ship on our way to a new life, the three of us. The child and I were rescued. Joe was never found . . . It was so cold.'

There was a silence. 'Is this true?'

She looked at him. 'It's the *Titanic* Relief Fund that's paying for my treatment here.'

'You are a *Titanic* survivor? Goodness me, why didn't you tell us before?'

'It's not something to shout about, watching your husband disappear under the water,' May said, twisting her hanky into a ball in an effort to stay calm. She had the doctor's full attention now. She wasn't just poor Mrs Smith, she was a *Titanic* survivor, one of the special ones with a story to tell. Only she wasn't going to tell the real truth of it all, never.

'Are you saying Ella reminds you of your lost husband?'

She nodded. 'He was dark. I think of him and I wish it was him who was saved. He was a good man; he didn't deserve such a death. That's a terrible thought, I know. I didn't want to lose him. I can't forget what I saw. I didn't want to go on without him. I wished we were all dead.'

'But, Mrs Smith, you have survived and made a home and a new life. You should be proud of yourself. But any change under such terrible circumstances is stressful. What you suffered was an extraordinary event. No wonder it's taken such a toll on your mental strength. Why has it taken months for us to get this out of you?'

'The child needs me. I've been away too long as it is. I need to go home.'

'I gather you've made adequate arrangements for her, so our welfare visitor tells me?'

'She's staying with a fellow survivor. We've become friends over the years. Her family found me work and now they've got Ella until I'm well enough to work again.'

Dr Spence shook his head and smiled. 'Ah, the formidable Celeste Forester and her father, the canon: two firebrands. They've been loyal and very persistent on your behalf but we mustn't rush things, Mrs Smith. An attack like yours takes years to build up. It won't disappear in a day or a week, but the fact you want to leave is a good sign. You've been very run down and it's taken a toll on your general health. Your body is under-nourished. So you will have to look after yourself and eat well and find new employment if you must, but don't rush to be too independent. Take any offer of help you can. A survivor of the *Titanic* indeed . . . We've not heard mention of that terrible disaster for years, what with the war. I'm so glad you told me. Now we have an underlying cause for your earlier derange-ment, an explanation for your distress. We must see if a home visit will help you along, if we can entrust you to the care of relatives, or friends, even. Perhaps we can look towards a refer-ral back into the community. You will have to attend a meeting of the panel to assess your suitability for discharge but what you've told me will go a long way towards gaining their approval.'

May had thrown him crumbs of truth, but not the whole slice. She would have to stomach this awful secret for the rest of her life. It was the price she must pay for her crime. It might eat her away, given time, but that didn't matter. She wanted to be with Ella and start again. The child must be given every chance to succeed, and a mother in a mental asylum was not a good recommendation. The sooner she got out of here the better.

66

When Celeste called again, she found a different woman sitting with her lacework, smiling at her arrival.

'They're letting me come home for a visit, just for the day. After all these months, I don't know how I'll manage. Is Ella all right, her school work? Oh, Celeste, you've been such a friend. I'm sorry I've been so bad. What must you think of me?'

Celeste grabbed May's hand, smiling back. 'Think of all the letters we shared, the secrets and the kindness you did to me. You're getting better. I can see it in your face. We all want to see you back home with us. You and Ella can go for lots of walks. Don't worry, she's fine. She and Roddy are getting used to each other. Selwyn will bring you out. He's been very concerned for you. It's so good to see the light back in your eyes. We've so much to catch up on, haven't we?'

Celeste hopped into Selwyn's car, stopping to pause by a country lane to admire the view. He'd been trying to teach her to drive but she was better on her own when he couldn't shout at her if she crashed the gear stick. Now she was getting the hang of the winding roads and making hand signals. Suddenly she felt as if all the different strands of her life were coming together at last.

Ella would be so excited that her mother was coming to stay at Red House until she was stronger. Celeste brought her round to their rooms in Lombard Gardens to pack up their belongings to put into storage. The rooms were to be relet and the owners were anxious to have the place cleared out.

What have I taken on here? she had kept asking herself since her return to Lichfield. A whole new life had evolved, one she could never have planned. Father was still refusing to move. Roddy was in the Choir School. Selwyn needed a woman's firm hand to keep his hearth and home from disappearing into a fog of smoke and dust, and Ella was so much part of her life now. Celeste insisted that she had extra art lessons at the local art college in Dam Street. A talent like hers needed nurturing. There was hope of a scholarship to the Girls' High School, too. She hoped May would not find her plans too ambitious.

Sometimes Celeste felt she was like Captain Smith, steering all these makeshift family members through troubled waters – but not into a submerged iceberg, she prayed. Ella had insisted she go to see his statue in Museum Gardens. It was indeed a true likeness.

'It was he who saved your life,' she said, and Ella looked at her askance.

'Your mother and I were in the lifeboat together. That's where we met, did she not tell you?'

Again, Ella looked puzzled. 'No, my daddy drowned in a ship going to America. I know about that.' She skipped off, uninterested in this news.

So Ella didn't know anything. Celeste knew it was not her place to say more. Why did May have to make such a secret of their rescue? What was wrong in telling the girl how she came to survive such a famous disaster? But who was she to judge? She hadn't exactly opened up to Roddy either. For her it was all tied up with going back to Akron and Grover.

Roddy had started to ask questions about his father. He'd seized their wedding portrait from her father's cupboard and pored over it with interest.

'We ought to let him know that we're here. You make me tell

lies that I've got no pa and I have ... He's not dead, is he? If you don't tell, I will, and Uncle Selwyn will give me the address.' There was a glint of anger and determination she recognized only too well.

She stormed into Selwyn's garage, all guns blazing. 'What have you been telling Roddy about Grover?'

'All this cloak-and-dagger stuff, changing surnames ... the boy is confused enough. He has a right to know about Grover. I can't understand why you left a perfectly good billet and dragged him halfway across the world from everything he knows,' Selwyn snapped.

'Oh, you don't, do you? Let me tell you then that that "perfectly good billet" was a marriage from hell. If your sister was late she was beaten and knocked about. If your sister wanted to sleep, she was forced to submit to the sort of assaults you read about in the newspapers. On many a hot summer's day I was forced into long sleeves to hide the bruises up my arms. Do you think I wanted my son to see that and think that was how men treated their wives? You have no idea what I have been through, so don't say another word.'

She rushed out in tears and he raced after her, white with rage. 'If I ever get my hands on Grover Parkes ... I'm so sorry, Sis, I'd no idea. Please forgive me.'

'You can see why I don't want him in our lives again. But this is all between you, me and the gatepost ... please.'

Her disclosure sent her brother into his silent shell once more, shutting himself off from them in his garage, banging at his repairs as if his life depended on it. Celeste couldn't believe the change in Selwyn. The scars on his face from the burns were superficial though the scars of war had gone deeper than she could ever fathom. But this row cleared the air and there was no more talk of giving Roddy the address when Christmas came around.

Now she was busy clearing out Ella's home. May had so few

possessions, Celeste felt ashamed of all the family clutter in Red House: the writing bureaux, cabinets, chairs, clocks, the pictures, the linen. The Foresters were great hoarders; the Smiths had lost everything.

Ella was being helpful, gathering up all her toys into a box and packing her mother's clothes neatly into a case. At the bottom of their pine chest, stuffed under winter clothes, there was a carpet-bag that smelled of mothballs.

Ella opened the bag and out spilled a pile of baby linen that Celeste recognized immediately. 'Look, your lovely baby clothes!' Inside the bonnet tucked into the bottom was a cloth bootee with a tiny leather sole, edged with a fine lace cuff. 'You were so tiny. Look at the lace on your nightie, such beautiful edging. Your mother must have kept them as a memento.'

Ella was barely interested. 'They look like old dollies' clothes to me.'

'You must take them to show your mother. They're very special.' It brought back such memories just to finger them: rushing with them to the laundry, trying to keep May and her baby warm, dry and comforted. How could May have not told her daughter about the *Titanic*?

'Will it make her upset again?' Ella's eyes were wary. She'd seen too much for her young age, things that she didn't understand, things that she shouldn't have to understand. 'Better put them away.'

'She'll be fine, but if they upset you, I'll keep them safe. Your mother must explain your story, not me. I've said too much already.'

'About what?'

'Run along and check everything.' Celeste knew she was in choppy waters again.

As they closed the door to the house for the last time she saw Ella looking at the view.

'I like this house, I like being close to town,' she said with a sigh, but being wise beyond her years she saw Celeste's look and added, 'But I like Red House too, and having my very own room up in the attic. I like going on the bus and Uncle Selwyn's car makes such big bangs everyone jumps when it explodes.'

The girl was going to be a beauty with her dark hair and gorgeous eyes, Celeste thought. She knew nothing but this city now, nothing of her background, nothing of the *Titanic*. It was about time both their children knew just what had happened on that night, but she didn't want to set May back again. She must have her reasons for not telling Ella the truth, just as she was reluctant to talk about Grover to Roddy.

They were two of a pair for holding things back. Was this the fault of what they had gone through on the *Titanic*? No one who was there ever talked about it much. There was so much anger inside over all the belated information about the doomed ship. The public inquiry all those years ago had revealed so many scandalous breaches in safety rules. At least now every ship had to carry enough lifeboats and practise an escape drill. What else had been covered up or glossed over? No one cared now, not since the war. It was just a piece of forgotten history.

Had the horror of such an experience claimed the minds of other survivors like May? No wonder secrets were so hard to bring to the surface when so much hope and innocence had sunk with the ship that night. It was all too deep to fathom and now was not the time. All that mattered now was making a home for the Smiths and putting a smile back on the face of this child.

67

They drove down the winding Cross in Hand Lane.

'I like this route down to the city, it's peaceful. Are you looking forward to your visit?' Selwyn asked, looking straight ahead as May gathered her thoughts, clutching her handbag for comfort.

'It's been months; I'm not sure. I gather we're going back to your place. I wonder what Ella will make of it all. I feel so ashamed, being so weak-minded.'

'Don't talk rubbish, woman, you were ill. The mind's no different from the body when it's sick. Look at me when I came home. I'll tell you one thing, though: you'll have to find something to get up for each day, something to occupy your mind. Celeste will help you.'

'I'm not one for company at the moment. I just want to see Ella's all right. I have to make it up to her for being away for so long.'

'This is just a day visit to test the water. Don't expect too much and you won't be disappointed. Take it from one who knows. You don't want to spend any more time in hospital than you have to, but it is its own little world and not easy to shift its routines. You'll be fine.'

If only she could be so sure. How could she admit to being terrified of seeing her child again after what she had said? How could she have been so cruel, telling her she wasn't hers? Would Ella want to see her again? She seemed settled with the Foresters, from what they said. She suddenly felt sick.

Ella was waiting at the door of Red House. 'You're back! Oh, you're back. Come and see, we've made scones with jam and I've set the table in the dining room. Come and see . . .'

A boy was standing down the hall, hanging back, looking every inch the schoolboy in his uniform. 'This is Roddy.' Ella pushed her forward to meet him. He was staring at her, not sure what to do but eventually he held out his hand.

'Pleased to meet you,' May whispered, wishing everyone would go away and leave her alone with Ella. Celeste was reading her mind and whisked the others away. 'We'll put the kettle on and let May and Ella have some peace in the drawing room.'

May had never sat in the big room before. It felt formal and chilly, and neither of them fitted in. 'I'd like some fresh air,' she said. 'Let's go down the tow path of the canal like old times. And I wouldn't mind a root around in the garden. How's it doing?'

'It's our den now. No one does anything in it much. I can show you where there's a blackbird's nest,' Ella offered, holding out her hand. May took it with relief, trying not to grip too hard to steady her nerves.

'You weren't kidding, were you? It's a right mess. Don't they have a gardener any more?' Then she recalled the old man had died and his son had been killed in the war.

It was a summer afternoon and the blue sky lifted her spirits as Ella chatted about school and Hazel, how Roddy and she kept falling out over who would ride Selwyn's old horses, Bentley and Whiston. How he came out of the barn and shooed them off, saying the horses were retired and no one must ride them now.

She chattered on and May drank in her news with such relief. *She is still my Ella and I am still her mother.*

But then some of Ella's news jolted her back. 'There's someone in our rooms now. I had to pack everything up. It's all here upstairs. Where will we live?'

Had Celeste warned her about this flitting? She must have said something to her but her memory was like a sieve. She felt a stab of panic as they headed back for tea.

Eating wasn't easy. She couldn't taste much but she did her best to look grateful. Ella had her chair pulled up to the table, chattering away whilst shoving cakes on her plate. Selwyn was keeping out of their way. She watched the clock moving to the time she must leave but to her surprise she was reluctant to make for her coat and hat.

'What do you think of the garden?' asked Celeste. 'I never was one for planting and harvesting. I keep nagging Selwyn but he's worse than me.'

'You'll have to advertise for a gardener then,' May offered. 'It's a big plot.'

'I thought if you gave me a hand and showed me how to do things . . .'

'I'm not rightly sure. I'll have to be finding myself work when I get out of . . .' She trailed off.

'That's what I meant, May. There's enough room for all of us here. Ella is settled. Would you consider coming to live in, help me in the house and garden?'

May felt herself prickle. 'You've done enough, you don't want me hanging round your neck like the albatross in the poem. It's a kind thought but I ought to stand on my own feet.'

'Why? What's wrong with living here and finding your feet on paths you already know? We think it's a good idea, don't we, Ella?'

'So you've cooked this up behind my back? Don't I have a say in how I bring up my daughter? I can see she's made herself at home.' May rose to leave. 'It's time to be going.'

'May, I didn't mean to offend you. I just thought it would be good for all of us to spend some time together, let the children have company. Please don't get upset.'

May could see Celeste was struggling and shaken by her harsh words. She ushered Ella out into the hall and closed the door on her.

'Just because I've been in the madhouse, doesn't mean I have no pride,' she said toi Celeste.

'Just because you've been ill, doesn't mean you can throw out my offer without giving it some serious consideration. You told me once you were a hermit. I know how you struggled with Florrie and the others at the college. We know a lot about each other. I know Ella doesn't know she was on the *Titanic*, though why that is such a secret, you alone know.'

'You know all about me but I know nothing about you except that you've run away from your husband. Sharing with friends has to work both ways.'

'Then perhaps it's time I told you what I told Selwyn. I ran away because he was a bully. The night I returned from New York, five days late, he beat me black and blue, and worse. We all have our troubles, May. Not everyone has a happy marriage as you did with Joe, short as it was. You are not the only one with secrets.'

They stared at each other and then both found they were crying, holding onto each other for dear life. 'You helped me escape. I will be beholden to you for the rest of my life. So climb down off your high horse and meet me halfway. Come on, I'll drive you back and we can thrash this thing out once and for all.'

Ella clung to her as she left, wanting to go with them, but Selwyn held her back. 'Your mum and my sister have a lot of catching-up to do. Don't worry, she'll be home soon for good. Let's enjoy the peace while we can.'

68

New York

If Angelo heard one more word about Frankie's First Communion, he swore he wouldn't go. Kathleen was determined to make a splash and kit her son out in only the best.

'What's wrong with a second-hand suit?' he argued.

'What's *right* with it?' she snapped. 'Do you want your family shamed before the Fathers? He needs boots and stockings and a white collar. The others must look presentable, and you too.'

'Have you robbed a bank? Where will we get such stuff?' he said. 'I'm not made of money.'

'No, but you drink plenty of it away. I've been putting bits by for the feast and the favours. I want to show the family we can do things proper, not skimp round the edges. It is his special day.'

Why did women like all that kneeling in the old cathedral with the incense wafting, the white lace vestments, the candles flickering in the dark recesses and the statues? The sound of Latin in his ears left him cold. It wasn't real Italian, loud and passionate and full of life, piercing the walls as neighbours rowed, shaking the Holy pictures off their hooks.

He looked at his two sons: Frankie, neat and quiet, could read billboards in the street before he went to school, and Jackie, his little brother, was a roaring child, tearing round the streets, while Patti pranced around in her second-hand tap shoes, driving them crazy with her antics while he was trying to listen to Caruso singing on the ancient wind-up gramophone they'd acquired for a debt in the shop.

There'd been such a barney about that. 'Where did it really come from, Angelo? We can't afford such things. There's Frankie's Communion suit to pay for.'

'You could run him up a shirt and trousers. It's only for one day. I don't want my son spending hours in that church. It's not right. A boy needs air and street fights. You'll make a sissy of him. Once those Irish Fathers get their hands on his soul . . .'

'What's wrong with Father Reagan?'

'What's right with him . . . wanting him to sing in the choir at his age . . . Time was when all we Italians were fit for was to worship in the basement of Old St Patrick's and now you are wanting my son upstairs with the Irish.'

'He's half Irish!' When Kathleen got mad she lashed him with her tongue and he stormed out, uttering oaths under his breath until he calmed down. Their rows could be thunder and lightning one minute and hot and steamy the next.

Angelo made a little extra from their secret brewery in the fruit store but somehow he would find his feet drifting towards a smoky hall to play cards and to drink, and there was hell to pay when he rolled home and emptied his pockets. If they were full of winnings it was a good night; if they were empty then Kathleen went silent on him.

On Sunday she took the children to the Irish congregation for Mass. Now they must all make a show of unity for this big passing-out parade and exhibit some enthusiasm for the fancy clothes and new rosaries for which most of the families would be in debt for the rest of the year.

Angelo never came to church unless it was Easter or Christmas, even though old Father Bernardo always asked after him with a sigh. He did still honour the 15th April and told his kids all about the *Titanic*. He and Kathleen had taken them to see the

Lighthouse Tower, on top of which there was a time ball that rose and fell, dropping to its base each midday to show the time the *Titanic* departed. The children knew about Maria and the baby and Ma's sister, Lou, all of whom had drowned in the sea for want of lifeboats.

Each year he'd bring out the little shoe with its lacy frill that he believed was the baby's own. Each year it got harder to believe the baby could be still alive, though he'd shed a tear and that made Kathleen cross.

Sometimes he found he was breathless and tired. Lifting boxes in the store made him sweat and his back ached. He would often need a stiff drink to ease the pain. Now they were scrimping and saving for Frankie's big day, living off *zuppa*. Kathleen was the Soup Queen of Lower Manhattan, he'd joke. No one could stretch a bowl of broth better than she could, but he feared his kids went to bed hungry.

Sometimes they'd all walk down to Battery Park to watch the great liners sailing out of New York Harbour past the Statue of Liberty.

'You are Americanos now,' Angelo would say, wagging his finger at them. 'You make this big country work for you . . . Take no notice if they call you names . . . You are born Americano boys. Baseball, football, do anything you choose but stay away from the Irish Fathers . . . Church is a *cosa femminile*. Do you hear me, Francisco? . . . a woman's thing.'

Frankie was up at four in the morning on the day of his First Communion. He'd been told to fast from midnight and not touch anything until the holy sacrament touched his lips. Angelo was furious. The boy was too keen, too young not to have water.

'It's my special day. I can't wait for it to come. Will I feel the Lord when he comes to my turn?' He had laid out all his clothes so neatly. Angelo felt ashamed of his own lack of faith. 'You'll look like a prince in all that finery. What's this?' He picked up a long lace collar in the finest lacework. 'Where did this come from?'

'From Italy. Aunt Anna had kept it for her boys. It was Uncle Salvi's when he was little. Mamma has washed it and pinned it out.'

Angelo fingered it, examining the stitches, the fine thread, the pattern. He'd had something similar himself when he was a boy but it wasn't that thought making him weep, it was the pattern, so similar to that of his little baby shoe. They were the same, from their region without a doubt. Just when he was coming to forget his grief there was this reminder. Perhaps it was a sign.

69

May was dog tired. It was a warm day, the marketplace was bustling and Selwyn was in one of his difficult moods. He'd been fettling up one of his motor bikes in the kitchen.

'Get that oily rag off the table, Mr Forester, this is not a garage,' she'd blasted in anger, seeing the mess on the floor.

'Stop fussing, woman!' he'd said. 'It's like Piccadilly Circus most days. Give me some peace.'

It was going to be one of his bad days. She could read him like a book. Once he'd had a pint or three in the Earl of Lichfield he'd start to spout rubbish about the government: the lack of homes for heroes, the state of the country. The more he drank the more angry and argumentative he became. It took courage for her to walk into that public house on her own to tell him it was time to shift his bum off the stool. She hated the smell of those sawdust and spittoon places, the stench of tobacco smoke and stale beer, and she hated that glazed look in his sad eyes.

She wasn't cross with him inside, sensing his grief and pain and something of the world he'd lost. He'd never gone back into the lawyer's office in Birmingham. She often caught him staring into the field, watching his old horses grazing.

'I've been put out to grass like them, useless old bugger,' he'd mutter.

'What do you make of that McAdam chappie who came for luncheon on Sunday?' he'd asked May that hot morning. 'Looks sound enough to me. He seems pretty keen on my sister. Not sure she's a good judge of men, though.'

May liked Archie McAdam. He had a way with the children, and Roddy hung on his every word. Roddy was now a weekly boarder at Denstone College. Celeste wrote to this young man and had told May how they'd met on the ship home.

'You never risked going down the aisle then?' May had asked, knowing a man like Selwyn would be hell to live with in his moods though he was handsome in his own way, especially now the burns on his face had finally healed over

'Who'd have me? I can't even hold down a job. Why would I want to bring children into this lousy world?'

'That's me told then,' she'd replied, folding her arms. He'd looked down at her and laughed.

'That's what I like about you, lots of northern fury. Roddy and Ella are fine specimens; you can be proud of your daughter. You're not a bad looker yourself if you like feisty argumentative types.'

'Is that supposed to be a compliment, sir?' she'd mocked.

'Please yourself, but kindly leave me to my sulks in peace.'

They had a repartee, a banter, a funny sort of friendship that unsettled her sometimes and left her wanting more.

It was over a year since her return to Red House and she couldn't fathom him. He was distant one minute, talkative the next, as if he trusted her to keep his confidences. The war had done damage to so many lives. If Joe had stayed in England he'd have been among the first to enlist. Perhaps he'd just be some name on a brass plaque on a war memorial by now.

Selwyn had survived and a part of him wished he hadn't. He never said as much – how could he? But she recognized his feelings only too well and it gave her the patience and courage to storm into the pub and demand her due when she'd done the shopping. He always obliged, raising his hat like the gentleman he was and staggering towards her, three sheets to the wind.

'Here she comes, on the warpath, my aide-de-camp ... what would I do without her ... ?'

May tried not to smile but when he came out with his quips she wished she could shoot him down with one of her own. He was clever with words, educated, and she couldn't compete.

He didn't drive back home, he sort of aimed the car up the Greenhill, then left towards the Burton Road and down towards Streethay village, and she prayed that there were no carts or strays on the road. He always carried her shopping into the kitchen while she made him a strong cup of Camp coffee, and sometimes that was the sum total of their conversation until the following week.

She took her own tray into her sitting room, once a breakfast room, sunny in the morning and cosy at night, where she could leave her tatting and lacework, knowing it would be undisturbed.

Celeste was away chasing a new position. 'Now Roddy is settled, it's time for me to find work outside the home. I can leave the house and garden in your capable hands with Mrs Allen to do the rough work. I must do my bit to keep this ship afloat.' It was all very mysterious.

May had to admit she liked being in charge. She'd pulled the garden into shape, reinstated the flower borders and made a shady hidy-hole for herself to read in when it was hot. Her breakdown seemed like a long time ago but there were still nights when she couldn't sleep and those panicky feelings rose up.

Ella was growing fast, with a mane of glossy black hair and fine features. She had friends in school, joined in anything she was invited to and now had a shed full of her models and art work. Where did this artistic streak come from? That's something they'd never know, but it troubled May in the small hours of the night.

How can I go on lying to her, fobbing her off with half-truths?

Because you must. Just calm down and go to sleep. You don't want to end up in St Matthew's again. Stop harping on about things you can't change. The time for speaking out's long gone. Who would believe your story now?

70

The summer garden party on the lawns of the Theological College was an annual event and a highlight of Cathedral Close. This year Celeste brought out her new cream cotton dress with lace cuffs and hem. It was too lovely an afternoon not to dress up and show off the new shorter style.

She was here to escort Father, who would enjoy the afternoon tea, watch the tennis contest and skittles, and pass time on a bench with some of the other retired clergy.

She smiled, thinking of how many of these events she'd had to endure as a youngster. How English it all was, how familiar, as if there hadn't been a terrible war. So many college student faces were no longer present, just names on the memorial plaque.

But today was about celebrating and relaxing in the sunshine with parasols and large hats to keep the ladies' faces pale or stop her own freckles from darkening.

Roddy refused to come, preferring to stay with May and Ella, or pester Selwyn, who never ventured into anything but a public house. Selwyn never attended the cathedral services, much to his father's sadness, but he had his reasons. The war had destroyed his faith as it had enhanced other's.

It was nearly two years since her flight home, and Celeste couldn't believe how quickly the time had passed. She still dreaded anything with an American stamp on it. There had been no enquiries from Grover's lawyers but that didn't mean he wouldn't appear out of the blue one day. She didn't want to think what might happen then.

Part of her was restless to take up the causes she'd fought for with the Women's suffrage movement. There was a partial vote here now but you had to own property and be over thirty-five to qualify. The steam had gone out of the suffragette campaign. Many women were charting their own courses, going to university or taking up careers, but that was not an option for her. If truth were told she'd been at a loose end at home now May and Mrs Allen, the daily help from the village, were taking over the reins of Red House.

She'd seen an advertisement in *The Times* that had intrigued her enough to make an application, but she was sure nothing would come of it and promptly forgot to post it. Her restless spirit had been channelled into escaping from Grover's brutal regime and keeping Roddy safe by her side. Now he was away at school all week but still only a drive from home. She'd wanted to keep him close in Lichfield but all the Forester men had gone to prep school in Denstone. They insisted it would give him the best education and help him settle. She was not so sure. He'd had so many changes.

Celeste felt the warm sun on her body, the cool cotton crispness of the lace on her skin, the smells of roses in the college garden, which sloped down to Minster Pool, where the sunlight refracted into shards of sparkling mirrors. She was coming alive again, alive to the world around her, alive to smells and tastes and the sound of glasses tinkling, hearty laughter and cheers as someone won his tennis match. Her eyes feasted on the starched linen tablecloths groaning with sandwiches and cakes and scones, the teacups with crimson and gilt rims. Deep in her heart she felt safe for the first time in years, safe from the fear of having to hide her words, safe from the constant fear of disapproval and criticism.

They knew her only as the canon's widowed daughter, and as

she turned to make for the tea awning, there was a man staring at her, a broad-shouldered young man in a blazer, grinning from ear to ear. Her heart skipped a beat. Surely not? Not here on the college lawn: Archie McAdam?

He raised his boater in a mock bow. 'There you are, Mrs Forester. I thought I might find you here.'

She stood, her mouth agape, feeling the heat of the flush on her cheeks. 'What on earth are you doing here?'

'I came up with a friend, Tim Beswick, just to look round . . .'

'But we've taken you round the cathedral many times.'

'When I've called on you before, I've never really looked around Lichfield.'

Just at that moment, Father strolled up with the principal, Lawrence Phillips. 'This is the young man I was telling you about, Bertram . . . McAdam is an ex-naval officer, Oxford man, now bit of a classics scholar. He's coming to join us. I told you the numbers are going up. We need new staff.'

There was silence for a second as Celeste took in his words. 'I see you two have got acquainted already,' said Prebendary Phillips with a twinkle in his eye.

'Mr McAdam and I first met on board the ship home. He's been teaching Roderick chess . . . by post,' Celeste said with a stiffness in her voice that belied her confusion.

'Is that so? Well, don't let us interrupt your reunion,' the principal said, pulling her father along to greet the guests as his wife was circulating in the opposite direction.

'Say something, Celeste. You don't exactly look pleased at my news.'

'It's a bit drastic to enrol as a student,' she snapped.

He burst out laughing. 'I've not taken holy orders. I've come to top up their Greek and Latin, that's all.'

'I didn't really have you down as a classics scholar,' she muttered.

'Well, there you go, something else you don't know about me.

I've just been on a refresher course. I always intended to go back to teaching.'

'Oh, you were a teacher before the war?'

He nodded. 'Don't be surprised. I'm a man of many parts, but the fact that I was a Cricket and Tennis Blue might have helped in their decision. I'll be joining the staff in the Michaelmas term. We'll practically be neighbours.'

He was so sure of himself and she wanted to wipe that smile off his face before he got any ideas. 'No we won't. I hope to find a post soon,' she said off the top of her head.

His crestfallen look lasted all of five seconds. 'You'll not go far away, not with your father and the boy, but don't worry, I've no intention of raining on your parade without an invitation. I know when I'm not wanted.'

'It's not that . . . It was just a shock to see you standing there. I thought I was seeing things . . .' How could she disguise the turmoil of seeing him again? 'You've been so kind writing to Roddy at school.'

'I know how lonely it can be for a boy in his first year in a new school. He seems to have settled. I haven't had a letter for weeks now but he's on his holidays. I'd hoped you'd be pleased to see me too.'

'It is always pleasant to see a familiar face in a crowd.'

'A very diplomatic avoidance of the question indeed. I'd like us to get to know each other better. This opportunity came up and I took it . . . entirely coincidental.' He paused. 'Well, not quite . . .'

'I need time to think about this. It's all so complicated, you see.' Now was the time to tell him she was still married and not widowed, put him straight once and for all.

'What's so complicated? Man meets mother and child on board a ship, they correspond for months, man visits. What's so wrong with that?'

'Oh, look, the principal's wife is beckoning me,' Celeste squeaked, making to flee from this encounter.

'Coward!' Archie raised his boater. 'We'll meet again soon.'

Not if I can help it. Damnation!

Celeste sped to Mrs Phillips's side on some silly pretext. She had to get away from him, his grinning confidence, his physical presence, those green-grey eyes and the flutter inside her stomach when she'd recognized him. She'd just got everybody settled and organized and he turned up on her doorstep demanding entry into her life.

In her heart Celeste sensed Archie was the sort of chap capable of twisting her life into a whole new tangle of knots. There was nothing for it now. She must search out that job application and get it in the post quick. She had to get away.

71

Roddy kept the letters in his tuck box out of sight. There were eight of them now and the last one had been the best of all. His father was coming to London and wanted to see him. He was so excited to think he would be meeting him in secret. He'd wangled an invitation to stay with Charlie Potter, the son of a vicar with a parish near Wimbledon. They were going to see the city sights: the Crown Jewels, the museums, the Changing of the Guard. He would be down there for two whole weeks while his father was sailing into Southampton and coming by train to their London factory in Silvertown for important meetings.

He couldn't believe he'd had the nerve to write. Getting the address was easy when Grandpa had told him that Pa worked for the Diamond Rubber Company in Akron. He had an important job there and was bound to get letters. He'd written in evening prep, putting his School House address at the top in his very best handwriting, and with his dictionary by his side. The first letter was the hardest because he didn't know if his dad would be cross with him.

Dear Diamond Rubber Company,

I am writing to ask for information about my father, Mr Grover Parkes of Akron. I am his son, Roderick Grover Forester, presently in school at Denstone College, Staffordshire.

Should he wish to make my acquaintance, please tell him to write to me at the above address.

Yours sincerely

Roderick (aged 12)

It was like writing to a stranger at first but when that first reply came back with the photo of his own pa, he was so excited.

Dear Son

I knew one day you would be curious to know about your American family. I applaud your initiative in finding my workplace. Your grandma, Harriet, and I are delighted to know you are safe and well in England. It is not what I wanted for you, of course, but it will do for now. Please tell me all about yourself and your life.

I, for my part, have no desire to acquaint your mother with our correspondence. I don't think she would permit us to continue.

Needless to say, I am overjoyed to have you back in my life once more. It was never my intention for us to be parted for so many years.

Perhaps when I am next on business in London we will have the opportunity to meet again. I look forward to this reunion. Please send me a photograph if you can.

Your loving father,

Grover Parkes

Roddy had written every week after that but worried about how to continue in the summer holidays. It was Pa who came up with the idea of meeting in London in August, and now Roddy couldn't wait. He was to go on the train unaccompanied. The Potters would meet him at Euston and take him back with them. Somehow he must make an excuse and ask to go home early so they'd take him back to the station and he'd say goodbye and meet up there with his father for a few days. It was like one of his *Boy's Own Paper* adventure stories coming true.

It was hard keeping such a big secret. If it came out his mother would be upset and angry that he'd gone behind her back, but it was silly pretending he had no living relatives in America. It was a lie, and the chaplain at school was always going on about how little lies became bigger ones. If his own mother could lie about being widowed why shouldn't he do the same? Only it wasn't a lie, it was true. He had a pa who cared about him, who'd missed him and had tried to find him. He'd had important lawyers tracing them. He knew they were in Lichfield. He knew everything about their journey from Washington but he had told Roddy that he knew they'd see sense in the end and come to some arrangement between them so his father could be part of his life again.

Father told him he had a big house in the country with horses, and that Grandma Parkes was longing to see him too. He wondered if he'd bring her over with him. He couldn't wait.

He'd begged Mama to buy him a smart new suit for London with long trousers, but she said you didn't wear long trousers in summer until you were at least sixteen and she chose some shirts, a pullover and white flannels for him instead, just in case he was going to play tennis with Charlie.

Ella was miffed because she wasn't going to London. She went on outings to Birmingham Art Gallery and still played with Hazel Perrings, but she wanted to see the National Gallery and other stuff that Roddy considered boring.

There was a hairy moment when Mother said they'd all go on a day trip and meet up with the Potters in town but everyone was busy on the day she was free. He knew she wouldn't mind when he told her after the visit. It would be too late then for her to protest. It was all so silly, living apart in separate countries when you were supposed to be married. He didn't understand why she'd left such a kind man.

Here they were, living in a muddle with the Smiths, who were no relation, and Uncle Sel, who was always moody and who cared more for his horses than he did real people. He was sent off to school with a load of strangers because that was what happened to boys like him at a certain age when all the time he had a pa far away who cared for him and never saw him. None of it made sense so why shouldn't he keep this all a big secret? They didn't deserve to know.

He thought about telling Mr McAdam all about his plans but now he was coming to work in Lichfield, it wasn't a good idea, and Mother had gone into a tizzy for some reason and was busy applying for a job helping people. She was quite happy living here with the Smiths. Sometimes he felt all mixed up, living in this house of women. He felt as if he didn't count any more. Other times he liked being part of this big funny family where he was left in peace to roam around the canal watching the barges on the tow path and fishing.

Now he was buzzing. Would his pa like him? Would they recognize each other? Would he look like him? He couldn't sleep for excitement. As he packed his suitcase, he wondered how he'd feel when he returned to this room after their meeting. Another flutter of both fear and daring made his heart thump. He'd done this off his own bat. It was his big secret and he hoped it would all turn out just as great as he was imagining. What a story he'd have to tell the other boys in the dorm when he returned.

72

Ella was finding the long school holidays boring. The house was so quiet now Roddy had gone to London. All he thought about was sightseeing, while she was itching to go to the palaces and places she could only read about in books. It was market day and they'd gone into town as usual; shopping, changing library books, a cup of tea in the Minster café while waiting for Uncle Selwyn. She was in a sulk.

Hazel had gone to Prestatyn with her family for a week. Everyone she knew was away. There was no chance Mum would ever go back to the seaside again. Even Ella's little studio at the top of the garden was full of flies buzzing around, annoying her.

'You've got a face on you like a wet wakes week. Be thankful you've got a holiday. When I was your age I was going half time at the mill, young lady,' Mum chided her. 'If you want to make yourself useful, take this washing soda and dolly blue up to the canon's house. His nets are getting grubby again. I want to give the place a bottom out while he's away next week. I'm going to the shops on the way, so I'll see you there. Run along and smile. No one wants to see a sulky face on such a sunny day.'

Mum was never happier than when she was cleaning, tidying up Selwyn's mess, grumbling over how cluttered the house was. At least she was cheerier, and Ella didn't have to keep watching and worrying in case she became ill again. Aunt Celeste was hoping to get some special work from a company in London, and they were attacking the garden again, pruning back bushes and planting fancy tubs full of flowers, just in case she was called away.

Ella dawdled through the archway into Vicar's Close to admire the higgledy-piggledy cottages. She could let herself in with the key under the brick, if the canon was out on his morning walk.

She knocked but there was no reply. Turning the handle, she found the door unlocked and shouted, 'Only me, sir!' He'd gone out and left the door open in his usual forgetful way so she left the shopping on the kitchen table top and turned to leave. She didn't know what made her look up the little stairwell but her eye caught a boot hanging at an odd angle. In the boot was a foot. She tiptoed up slowly, feeling sick. It was too quiet and too still up there and she was scared.

Ella fled out of the yard and back down into the town, tears rolling down her face.

She made straight for the Earl of Lichfield and to the bar stool where Selwyn was supping his beer. 'Come quick ... It's your father. There's been an accident ... Please come quick.'

It was as if the day went into slow motion after that. They'd picked up her mother and rushed back to the cottage. Ella had stayed at the bottom of the stairs, not wanting to see what was happening. Mum came down grey in the face. 'The poor man, taken so sudden like that.' She'd been helping Selwyn get him on the bed.

'He's dead?'

'Yes, love, sometime last night before he went to bed. Dropped where he fell ... He wouldn't have known about it. Such a kind man. He took us in all those years ago, gave me a job, a real Christian gent.' They both started to cry and Selwyn came down.

'I've put him on his bed. I'll call the dean. They'll want to say prayers but first we must tell Celeste.'

They drove slowly for once, silent, shocked and saddened, each lost in his or her own memories of the man. Celeste was in the garden just where they'd left her, beavering away, her foxy red hair awry, dirty handprints on her garden apron.

She looked up, smiling. 'You're early.'

Then she caught the look on their faces. 'What's happened?'

Her brother stepped forward and walked her up the garden.

The next day was taken over with the whole business of funerals and service planning, visitors calling with flowers and letters of condolence. The drawing room was like a florist's shop.

'Roddy must come back for the funeral. I want him home with us,' Celeste announced. 'I'm going to telegram the Potters and ask them to break the news and put Roddy on the next train to Lichfield. Selwyn will see to Papa's affairs and the under-taker. The College have offered to prepare the funeral tea, isn't that kind?'

The grown-ups were all wearing black but Celeste insisted Ella wore her summer clothes. 'Papa hated black on children. He used to say our children are the hope for our future. Come with me to Trent Valley to meet the afternoon train, Ella. Roddy's going to be very upset.'

The morning sped by and there was so much to do, helping Mrs Allen and Mum prepare the rooms and try to keep Celeste's spirits up. Ella had never seen death at close hand before. It was an awful lot of hard work and she felt important to have been the one to alert the family to the accident.

They stood on the station platform waiting for the London train to arrive. For once it was on time, and as the crowds poured out they searched up the platform for Roddy.

'The blighter, he's missed the train!' Celeste tutted. 'Still there's one at six o'clock. Selwyn can come to meet that.'

Home they went and on the hall's silver tray was a telegram. Celeste tore it open.

'I don't understand. It's from the Reverend Mr Potter. He says he put Roderick on the train at his request two days ago . . . I don't understand.'

Selwyn snatched it out of her hands and read it again. 'What's he playing at? Where else would he go in London? Pack me a sandwich, Sis . . . I'll drive down there myself. There must be some mistake . . .'

Aunt Celeste sat at the foot of the stairs shaking. 'How could he play silly games at a time like this? Where is he? Why didn't they let us know he was coming back early? It's not like him. I think we should call the police. He's only a child . . . Surely he hasn't run away?'

Ella's mum made cups of tea and supper but no one could eat anything. They went back to the station just in case, but Roddy wasn't on the platform. Ella felt fear inside. Aunt Celeste collapsed in a chair shaking and crying and Mum made her go to bed with a brandy. Uncle Selwyn had such a worried look on his face as he rang the police station to ask for advice. Something was terribly wrong but no one knew just what it was. A mist of gloom, fear and panic swirled around Red House and Ella didn't know what to do to help. Boys had no idea; they were useless specimens. She was glad she'd soon be going to a girls' school.

73

Roddy was having a wonderful time with his new father. The plan had gone swimmingly. He'd waved off the Potters on the platform, sat in the compartment for five minutes until they were out of sight, jumped out and ran to the barrier where a tall man in a smart blazer and slacks was waving. He was so handsome and jolly and he'd bought him an ice cream. They went to one of the finest hotels for luncheon and he'd scoffed everything they'd put in front of him.

'I'm glad you've still gotten an American appetite, young man. You look just like me at your age. I would have recognized you anywhere. Has your mom found herself a new beau yet?'

Roddy shook his head. 'She's too busy looking after us all for anything like that. There was a kind man we met on the ship home. He's taught me to play chess ... Mr McAdam, but she doesn't like him very much.'

'I shall teach you to ride a horse and play baseball. You'll love Akron. So many people are dying to meet you back there. I've got such plans for us but first we'll make a little trip to the American Embassy.'

'I'd have to ask Mom first,' Roddy said, feeling swamped by this information.

'Plenty of time for that, son ... We're going to have such a good time. I've finished my business early so we can get to know each other good and proper. I want to know all about your life and what you do at that school of yours. Do you play sport?'

'I'm in the second eleven for Rugby and first for Junior Cricket . . .'

'Those are English games. We've gotten the best pro American football team in Akron. We can go see them play, if you like.'

Roddy didn't know how to explain he'd have to go home soon, that term would be starting again. There was no time left to take a trip to America. 'Thank you for the meal, sir,' he said.

'I thought we'd go see a show in the West End and Madame Tussauds, but first we'll call in at the embassy. I have a bit of business there.'

They took a cab to a grand mansion house with marble stairs and the great Stars and Stripes flag hanging over the door. 'We have to answer questions when we visit here. It's a piece of home right here in London so whatever the man asks you, you must give a straight answer . . . understand?'

It was a funny meeting. They went into a room where the man behind the desk asked Roddy his name and his date of birth and where he was born and was this his true father and who was his mother and where did she live. The man passed his father pieces of paper and smiled at Roddy. 'Enjoy your trip.'

'Thank you, sir,' he replied. 'I am.'

All the touring and excitement made him very tired and hungry. He bought some postcards as souvenirs to send to Ella and Mom. He always had stamps in his leather school wallet. They went to see a musical, which was all singing and a bit sloppy. He could hardly keep his eyes open and fell asleep in the taxi on the way back to the hotel. His father was so concerned he gave him a warm drink to help him settle for the night and he went into a deep slumber.

When he woke in the morning he found himself in a railway carriage rattling along the coast with no idea how they'd got from the hotel onto the train.

'Hi there, sleepy head,' Pa smiled. 'Welcome aboard.'

'Where am I?' Roddy asked, staring out half awake.

'On your way home, son, to the U S of A . . . We're almost at Southampton water. You and I are going on the trip of a lifetime. Back to where you belong on the White Star Liner, *Olympic*, no less, sister ship of the *Titanic* . . . what do you know?'

Roddy felt the panic rising. 'But I have to go home. Mom will be worried.'

'Don't you fret about that . . . it's all sorted. Your mom doesn't mind. She always knew I wanted you to be educated in the States. She knows it's for the best.'

'But I haven't any books. All my stuff . . .'

'You've enough for the journey and when we get across the pond, I'll be kitting you out in some decent clothes. Don't you just love the idea of living back there again?'

Roddy didn't know what to think. His head was fuzzy and his mouth dry, and he wanted to pee. *Had* his mother given permission? Was this a big surprise they'd thought up together? He didn't think so. 'Can I ring her on the ship . . . we have a phone.'

'Sure, if you can get a line free. Why not send her one of these postcards. She'll like that.' He handed him a picture postcard of an ocean liner.

The train slowed down at the dock and a huge ship with four huge funnels rose up over his head. They were escorted up the gangway to a First Class apartment with twin beds, its own bathroom and sitting room looking out onto a balcony. He'd never seen anything so grand. Roddy bounced on the bed, excited but scared to be doing this without saying goodbye to his family and friends.

How could he get off the ship without hurting his father's feelings when he'd gone to so much trouble to secure this passage for them together? They'd been apart for so long, perhaps he owed him this time with him. He could always come home at a later date. He sensed this man might get angry if he said he didn't want to sail. Roddy was torn.

He sat down and wrote three of the ship's postcards, one to Mom, one to Ella and one to Grandpa, telling them he was safe and with his father, and going to sea again on a vacation. He walked down the corridor to find a steward and asked him to post them before the ship left the dock. The young man saluted him and put them in his pocket, which made Roddy feel very important.

Later, Roddy stood on deck watching the liner slowly edge its way from the dock. He saw the passengers waving to friends, waving hankies, and he wished he could have his own family waving back to him. That was when he felt sick. Had he done the right thing? A flutter of panic rose into a wave and washed over him, making him tremble. Now everything was out of his control. He'd set this meeting up in the first place. His father had taken it as a sign that he was important in his life again. There was no turning back. From now on, he guessed, his life was never going to be his own again.

74

May was rushing round trying to keep the household running, taking broth up to Celeste, who lay prostrate, under sedation from their doctor. Red House was plunged into a black house of mourning. Everyone was tiptoeing around on the morning of the canon's funeral, pinning on brave faces. May needed time to get Celeste dressed. She was so weak and exhausted, sitting on the edge of the bed shaking, holding the letter that had broken her heart.

'He's taken my son. They met in London and he says Roddy wanted to come back to America with him. I don't believe it! Roddy was settled. How could he go behind my back like this? What have I done, letting him go unescorted to London? He doesn't know what he's doing. I have to go after him now.'

'Not today you can't. It's your father's funeral and you have to bury him as he would wish. That's enough for today. Things will be clearer tomorrow. Let's find your dress. It's a beautiful day outside but it will be cool in the cathedral.'

Selwyn was interviewing policemen and phoning round to his former office in Birmingham to get advice. In fact, he was taking charge like it was a military operation, ordering them about. May had never seen him so bossy, but someone needed to steer this rudderless ship and she was glad of his knowledge of how to go about things.

Roddy had claimed his American citizenship. The police said

they could not interfere in this domestic dispute. He'd gone of his own free will and would now be in international waters, out of their reach, in the care of his legal father.

One silly postcard had shattered his mother. On it was a picture of the *Olympic*, the identical sister ship of the *Titanic*. One look at it and Celeste had fainted clean away in the hall. May had stood firm at the sight of those funnels and bow. She never wanted to see that image again and pushed it out of sight. Then came the letter from Mr Parkes, claiming his right to Roddy as if he was a lost parcel in left luggage, and all this the day before the canon's funeral.

'Of all the ships in the world, he takes him back on that one! He will ruin my son, teach him to be a bully. His mother will spoil him. I have to have him back with me.'

Celeste was beyond reason but May sat with her until she fell into an unnatural sleep.

May's next job was to be the gatekeeper, ushering out visitors if she thought they were lingering too long with their condolences. How were they going to explain Roddy's absence?

The locals thought Celeste a widow, not a runaway wife. This news would be a nine-day wonder in the Close once it was known, so the longer they kept this situation secret the better. Who better than May Smith at keeping secrets? Selwyn would say nothing and Ella must be ordered not to spread any gossip.

Celeste was glad of the thick crepe veil covering her face as she stood to receive her father's coffin. The cathedral organ boomed out, the congregation stood in respect as they followed behind it, and she remembered the day of her mother's funeral and all that had happened since.

She couldn't believe Roddy had deserted her like that, her only son walking out of her life as if she was nothing. Anger and sorrow burned in her throat. To mourn her father was natural but the thought of losing Roddy was unbearable. He must have been bribed, bemused by Grover's attentions. She felt sick knowing how her husband had charmed her so easily. Roddy was an innocent; how would he survive back in Akron without her? How would he go from one world to another? He didn't even know his grandpa was dead, and he was still little more than a child, and a devious one to hide all this from her.

She had so few rights in the matter. Selwyn explained that legally she was still a married woman. A custody battle would be useless at this stage. She was so full of hatred of Grover, so angry that Roddy had put her in such an impossible position. She'd worked so hard to bring them back to England and this was how he'd repaid her. The boy had no idea who he was dealing with. Grover wanted him as a trophy, a son he could control. He'd pay her back by making him into a miniature of himself. Roddy wasn't used to that sort of discipline. How would he cope with Grover's outbursts if he were to be disobedient?

As they were walking down the aisle she caught a glimpse of Archie McAdam staring at her with concern. He knew everything now. He'd turned up on the day of the postcard to offer condolences for her loss and had found himself in the middle of a maelstrom of confusion and tears. There had been no point in disguising from him what was going on.

'My husband's lured my son back to America,' Celeste said, showing him the postcard of the *Olympic*. 'Better you know the facts. I left him years ago, brought up my son alone and now this . . .' She'd not been able to continue or look him in the face.

'I'm so sorry,' was all he said. 'Is there anything I can do?'

She shook her head wearily. 'Selwyn says we can only wait and plead our case, try to get access and custodial rights. I'll have to go back to the States. I won't lose my son, I can't. He's the only thing that matters to me.'

'I don't think you will ever lose him. He's just temporarily mislaid,' Archie offered, but she was in no mood for joking. 'That's not funny,' she snapped.

'Forgive me, but it wasn't intended to be. He's mislaid, misguided, a young boy on an exciting adventure. Children don't think of the consequences of their actions. Why should he? He's been well brought up, loved and cosseted. He trusts people. He may be a little confused right now, but you have to trust that all you've taught him won't be lost. I know a little of young people and Roderick will come through this. Chasing after him will only tighten the noose your husband has thrown around his neck. Selwyn has told me a little of his nature . . . I'm sorry.' He reached out to her hand but she pushed it away.

'He had no right to tell you about my private affairs.' Celeste couldn't believe her brother had been so indiscreet. 'You don't understand any of this!'

'Sadly I know only too well what it is to lose a child, but I also know love given freely is never lost. Roddy knows you care. He will find his way back to you in time.'

Celeste stormed off, not wanting Archie's advice. She wanted Roddy now, not tomorrow. But somehow, now, the warmth of this man reached out to her as she clung onto her brother down the aisle. She felt Archie's strength. She sensed his concern and his kindness. They were going to need all the friends they could muster to live with this sorrow. Every word of Grover's letter was burning into her heart.

You didn't think I'd let you get away with stealing my son, did you? He is mine, by rights, and I have seen to it that he will be brought up a true son of his country, not some mollycoddled English schoolboy at the behest of females.

Don't come chasing after him. He will write to you when I permit in the holidays and on other occasions. He must be left alone to develop the strength he gets from his father, which will take him far in this new world. He will have only the best money can buy.

You've had your turn, now it is mine to form his character and make my heir. You've done your part. You stole his early years, now I will have his grown-up ones.

There will be no divorcing until I say so. It may be prudent to find a more suitable wife to offset your influence, but until such times, my own mother will suffice.

We could have been spared all this business, if only you'd learned obedience. But you English never learn, do you? You are a cussed obstinate race on the whole. I thought I could train you up, but you were a disappointment. Roderick will not make the same mistake. I shall break him in slowly to our way of doing things. He'll soon learn what is best for him.

I hope you are suffering as I suffered when you stole him all those years ago. So you can go to hell in a hand cart.

Grover Parkes

How will I live with this? How can I survive knowing he's so far away from me? Who will take this pain from my heart? Why ever did I let him go to London on his own? And why did he hide his father's letters from me? How could I have been so stupid not to know that Grover wouldn't try to take him back? Oh, my son, my poor silly boy, you don't know what you've done.

There was nothing to hope for, nothing to do but count the days until she would hold him in her arms again. Her life from now on would be an existence. She stared up at the great West Door opened in honour of her father. *As God and the saints are my very witness, I'll not sink without a struggle.* She saw again the giant ship plunging into the waters on that terrible night. There must be no giving up now. She was unsinkable. She had survived certain death. There must be a way back to him somehow. There just had to be.

Part 3

BROKEN THREADS

1922–1928

75

For months after Roddy left, Celeste was inconsolable, unable to function, lost in her own despair. May began to wonder if she would end up in hospital, as May herself had done. Their whole world had been turned upside down and now May was in charge of running the household, making all the mundane decisions, writing lists and giving orders, while Celeste drifted along as if in a bubble, interested in nothing but news from Akron, news that had been filtered out through Roddy's grandmother, news that was not helpful at all.

Roddy is fine. He's settled in school, he has a bicycle and his own horse to ride, and he loves hiking around the country with his friends, so don't go pestering him with pleas to return. He doesn't want to. The attorney's letters are not helping your case with Grover. He throws them in the trash. Do not waste your money paying their fees. Roderick is here to stay. He will write you in due course.

   You brought this on yourself when you ran from all your duties here. Everything has its price, my dear. Everything has its price . . .

'How can they keep my son from me? They've turned him against me. I have to go there right now and make him see sense,' Celeste wailed, kneading her hands in anguish.

Selwyn tried to calm her down. 'Not yet . . . it's too soon.'

'I shall go mad waiting here,' she cried.

'Then go out and find yourself something to get out of bed for,' he offered, just as he had spoken those words to May all those years ago. Now he too was back in harness, back practising law in Birmingham again, fighting cases for war veterans who desperately needed homes and medical treatment. Roddy's drama had shaken Selwyn out of the lethargy that had plagued him and May felt that for the first time in years he was back in charge of himself. Even his drinking sprees had diminished. Now he came home only to potter around in his barn. Sometimes May took out a drink and sat down on the bench watching him tinkering about. They didn't need to talk to feel comfortable with each other. The silence was comforting.

In stark contrast, Celeste was hard work, flitting from one idea to the next. Thank goodness her friend Mr McAdam called in so often to take her for a walk, bringing her back a little more settled. May wished she had a friend like that, one who'd look out for her and cherish her. Joe had always been attentive and generous with his compliments. Sometimes she wondered if Selwyn would ever notice how she spruced herself up and made an effort around him. But if it was not metal, rusty or in need of repair, it barely received a glance.

Much as May loved her friend, she was beginning to trip over her in the house and garden. She left her stuff everywhere and then promptly forgot where it was. An untidy daughter was enough, two people making a mess everywhere was shredding her nerves. Then one morning as May was clearing away their copy of *The Times*, she noticed that Celeste had ringed round an advertisement for a domestic agency in London. It was a start. May felt a flicker of hope for the first time in months. She cut the advert out and placed it on Celeste's writing bureau.

* * *

May seized the moment while Celeste was sitting slumped over her cocoa.

'Here, why don't you reply?' she demanded, shoving the notice under her nose. 'It can't do any harm finding out what they do, can it? You've too much time to brood and that's a highway to nowhere, as I well know.'

Celeste looked up and smiled, shaking her head. 'I've seen this before. It does look interesting, in fact ... where did I put my application ...? The Good Lord knew what he was doing the day he brought you into my life and no mistake.'

'Get away with you! What are friends for but to hold each other up when the going gets rough? I'm only doing what you've done for me in the past. Remember what you used to say: "If I'm busy, I don't think." It'll come right, I promise, but in the meantime why not try something new? It just might help.'

76

Akron

Roddy stood on the Portage Path trail. He'd gone to see the Indian statue, and was looking out westwards to where the old boundary between Indian country and the United States began. He paused, gazing out over the wooded ridges, trying to imagine how it must have been in the olden days, but his heart wasn't in this hike. He was feeling homesick for the flat Trent Valley, for his old brick school and the cathedral city, for the rough and tumble of life in Red House. But most of all for his mother.

Since the letter came telling him Grandpa Forester had died on the very day he'd set sail for New York months ago, he had felt awful, wishing he could have gone back to pay his respects and comfort his mother. How she must have despaired losing her father and son on the same day.

He looked around at the tall trees leading down towards the deep ravine of the Cuyahoga River, which snaked along the edge of town. Houses now dotted the Portage Path. The country club encroached on Injun territory, pushing them ever backwards and out of sight.

This place was where he had been born but it didn't feel it was where he belonged. It had all been a big mistake to walk away from his old family. But what was done was done, and he couldn't see a way back.

His thoughts roamed to Ella's accusatory letter telling him he was a traitor and an ungrateful pig. How on earth could he reply? She didn't mince her words, she let him know exactly how distressed his mother was, how ill she'd been since he had left.

'She blames herself for not going to London with you, and she cries when no one is looking, so come home and make her smile again.'

Roddy had pored over her letter, feeling wretched. He hadn't written home much since he'd been here, just a letter of condolence to his mother and Uncle Selwyn, and a brief account of his new school. He'd added some snippets of information about Granny Harriet, but not mentioned the fact that his father had a constant companion called Miss Louella Lamont, who sometimes sat with them in St John's Church, and came for tea. She was pretty enough in her fancy clothes but she had a voice like a foghorn.

The house was high up in the West Hill district, ornate with coloured bricks, statutes in the garden and a paddock and orchards. It was not nearly as big as the Seiberling mansion, or Elm Court, where the Marks family lived, but he'd never seen anything so big in Lichfield.

He had his own suite of rooms, as did Granny Harriet at the far end of the house. His father seemed to work day and night these days and when he came home late he was always snappy. The promises he'd made on board the *Olympic*, all those things that they would do together as father and son, were long forgotten and never discussed.

Nothing here was quite as he had expected but he'd made friends at school with a boy called Will Morgan. None of the others had lived abroad and weren't interested in his life before coming to Akron. All they were interested in was the progress of the Akron Pros in the National Football League. They were studying hard for good grades that would lead to most of them heading to the coast to Harvard or Yale. Roddy couldn't think that far ahead. He'd had too many changes in his young life already.

He just knew he'd done a terrible thing in trusting his father and he still couldn't quite understand how he had got from the London theatre to the *Olympic* in Southampton. It was all a blur. But he was here now and his presence was a matter of great pride to his father, even if he wasn't around very much to take him out.

Not that his days were empty. There were riding lessons, driving lessons from the chauffeur in the new automobile that sat on the drive, extra tuition in science and chemistry so that he might join the Diamond Rubber Company in due course. It was as if his whole life was being mapped out for him and he was just sleepwalking through it.

Standing by the lone statue of the Indian with a canoe on his back, he thought of their lonely treks on foot from the Cuyahoga to the Tuscarawas River, when all around them were woods. He felt sometimes as if he too were tracking with a big weight on his back, bending him low.

His grandma kept telling him to straighten up and stop slouching or he'd grow a hunchback. She was a stickler for what people thought. The Parkes family were society. They mixed with the wealthy rubber barons and their families, and he had been absurdly glad of Mom's old refinement classes when they were entertaining and he had to talk politely to a line of old biddies. 'Remember, always ask a question. Show interest in your guest, put them at their ease.' His mom's words rang in his ears, words from his Washington days, which made him sad. At least on these occasions he wouldn't let her down. He tried to hold on to his English accent but that annoyed his father no end. 'You're a Yankie boy, get rid of those vowels!'

But others loved his accent, especially the girls at church and old ladies. They asked him to repeat phrases over and over until he felt like a performing monkey.

Everything he could possibly want was spread out before him: a beautiful home, a horse and buggy, a fine education, beautiful scenery to explore. So why was he so miserable? There was something missing amongst all these trappings of wealth and success, something important, and Roddy couldn't quite work out what it was.

Whatever the answer, it sure was leaving a big hole inside.

77

'Mrs Forester, can you take on the Stratford clients?' enquired Safara Fort on the telephone.

'Of course, I'd be delighted,' Celeste replied to the doyenne of the Universal Aunts Agency. 'These Americans are from where?' she added, hoping that they might be from Ohio. Celeste sat at the foot of the stairs, clutching the earpiece and smiling. Applying to be a 'Universal Aunt' had been a lifesaver. It was a new organization based in London, which offered chaperonage, home furnishing services, care of children, research work and responding to all sorts of unusual queries. It was a haphazard sort of career. Sometimes the task was mundane, taking a wealthy lady's pet to the veterinary surgeon to have its claws clipped, for instance, or helping a newly married wife choose furnishings from Rackhams or Beatties stores. Escorting tourists to Stratford and Anne Hathaway's cottage was a regular feature of the season. There were splendid Tudor coaching inns with four-poster beds and oak beams that the American visitors loved, along with the hearty English fare.

'They're from the Great Lakes somewhere ... Ann Arbor ... very keen on Mr Shakespeare so they want the full tour, a good hotel, a tour guide – the usual – but only for two or three days. They also want to do Edinburgh and York Minster. Then Paris, of course, and what with your living in America in the past ...'

'Leave it all to me, Miss Fort,' Celeste replied. 'I'll book everything ahead by wire and plan an itinerary to suit their budgets.'

'There's no budget; only the best for the Stimpsons. He is big in cereals, I gather. I'm so glad we have you up north to see to things, Celestine. You're proving to be quite a find. When I interviewed you, I sensed you'd be versatile. You're a gem. Many are called but few are chosen, my dear. You've no idea how many applications for Universal Aunts are so unsuitable. We are very particular about who we take on, but so far your assignments have been impeccable and reports say the children are now asking especially for you.'

'Thank you, Miss Fort,' Celeste beamed. She loved the work. It kept her busy and prevented her from wondering too much how Roddy was faring with his father. Not that her son was ever far from her thoughts.

'Mustn't keep you from your planning. I look forward to your report.'

Celeste had turned up at the Universal Aunts offices near Sloane Square in her best tweed suit. They'd asked her questions about her life and professional experience, but when she told them she was a survivor of *Titanic*, a friend of Margaret Brown, and on the Women's Relief Committee, the interview had come to an abrupt halt.

'We'd be honoured to have someone like you work for us.'

So far she'd escorted dozens of nervous children from Birmingham, Wolverhampton or Stafford to their new boarding schools in the country, and vice versa. She'd done it all before with Roddy, making sure their tuck boxes were full, that they had plenty of travelling games and snacks, comics and magazines handy for the journey, which she hoped would take their minds off their final destinations.

She had had to pay a quarterly booking fee of half a crown to have her name on the Universal register, but it was money well spent. It got her out of the house and mixing with strangers who didn't know her circumstances. In every child she met, though, she saw something of her own son.

She couldn't believe it was nearly a year since that terrible day when Roddy had left, a year of stilted correspondence, of polite, careful enquiry to Harriet. She would never write directly to Grover again, not after what he had done. She couldn't trust herself not to let rip in a way that might make things even worse.

Roddy's letters were short and muted. She sensed he was struggling to readjust to American life, but the photographs he enclosed showed her how fast he was growing up. He was now out of short trousers and his legs were sprouting. She ached to visit him but knew that would only unsettle the uneasy truce she'd made with Grover. She must tread carefully, bide her time and keep Grover sweet. She felt such a failure as a mother. Her son must have found her wanting indeed to choose the very person she'd shielded him from all those years ago, or did he have any choice in the matter once he was in his father's clutches? If only she'd not let him go unescorted.

Through all these months, May was there, quietly standing by, a shoulder to cry on. And so was Archie, but their relationship must remain a secret.

Archie was a single man in a theological college, where standards were high, and she was still a married woman, if separated. He was presented as Selwyn's friend, not hers, so his continued presence at Red House would not be commented upon, but everyone knew he was in love with her. There was always that look of admiration in his eyes that gave her the courage to keep going when the pain of Roddy's absence stung too deep.

He always sensed her distress, gently touching her hand for reassurance. He'd lost his wife and had known terrible suffering in the Great War. He was her 'Rock of Ages', as the hymn went. Yet there was no future for them, not unless Grover released her or she tried to petition for divorce herself. She couldn't risk losing contact with her son; her own happiness depended on that. One day he'd come back to her. One day this nightmare would be over.

Until then she'd go on helping other families whose children were in transit. No child would ever go missing on her watch. What she couldn't do for Roddy she would do for her young clients. Besides, there was always the hope that one day Miss Fort would be looking for someone to escort a client over the ocean to the United States. That would be her chance, but until then she was making the best of what was on offer.

78

Ella loved watching the stonemasons at work. In Quonians Yard the Bridgeman & Sons restored masonry and carvings, and re-created broken tracery for the roofs of churches and cathedrals. They'd restored the front of the cathedral, with its fine statues and carvings. She sensed the skill and craftsmanship of generations coming from that workshop as she examined the beauty of the pieces standing in the yard waiting to be packed and shipped across the country and abroad.

Sometimes she would dawdle with her shopping just to catch glimpses of how they dressed the stone, how they prepared it using ancient tools. She longed to be able to do something so physical herself.

The girls at the High School teased her about her collection of photographs in her scrapbooks, pictures she'd cut out of posters, magazines and newspapers. Now she had a little Brownie box camera she could take pictures of anything that took her fancy. She'd visited the churches in town, bought postcards from Birmingham Art Gallery where she was studying women in the art world, including the Victorian stonemason who'd helped carve the statues in the front of the cathedral west wall. She'd written about Kathleen Scott and Captain Smith's statue until Hazel got sick of standing in front of it.

Hazel was still her best friend. They'd gone up to the High School together, although Hazel was into science and biology, and couldn't see the point of art. She stared at Ella, eyeing her figure. 'You'll get arms like a boxer doing sculpture,' she warned.

'I don't care,' Ella said. She'd become a sculptor if it was the last thing she did. First, though, she must find out about the great masters, learn about artists of the past and how they worked, as well as the new ones who sometimes exhibited in the art galleries. There were anatomy lessons to master, reading skulls and musculature. It was all a big mystery but one that filled her with increasing excitement. Would she ever make it to Rome or Florence, or Paris to see Rodin's work?

Ella was impatient to be out of school and into the real world, where people lived their art and had the freedom to experiment. Her own feeble efforts in the shed at the bottom of the garden were stupid, inferior models of faces that she wanted to smash up in frustration. But materials were expensive and her mother hated waste.

She loved faces: the power and the magic of worn faces, cheekbones, crooked noses – all those distinctive features that changed a face from plain to majestic. She marvelled at how a lump of plaster could be turned into something that would last for ever.

She loved paintings too, but it was the portraits of faces that she loved the most. She asked for a skull for her birthday but had to make do with a sheep's one. It was important to feel the bones and the shapes inside a head, to build from the inside out.

It was scary how desperate she was to have the chance to study art and make things for herself. Would she have the physical strength to help cast bronzes and bigger pieces? She was wiry and slender but not very tall, and probably more suited to be a dancer than a sculptor or a stone carver.

More than anything she wanted to leave school and go to art college, but her mother was having none of it.

'You must stay on and get your certificates after all the fees and education you've gone through. You must have a good

profession behind you in case we fall on hard times . . . a school-
teacher, a secretary or comptometeress working an adding
machine.'

'But I don't want to work in an office.'

'Well, maybe a nurse then . . .'

'I don't want to be a nurse. I'd kill all the patients.'

'Don't be funny with me. You'll do as you're told, my lady.
There's been enough people in this house who never knew
when they were well off,' Mum sniffed, looking at the portrait
on the mantelpiece.

Roddy was never mentioned by name. He was the silent
ghost in the corner of the room ever present but never spoken
of. He'd been disobedient and broken his mother's heart. The
warning was implicit: she must not do the same to hers.

Mum and Uncle Selwyn ruled Red House now, an odd alli-
ance, if ever there was one. Aunt Celeste was always off on one
of her trips, leaving them bickering or sitting down for supper
like an old married couple. Uncle Selwyn had come out of his
shell a bit but he still liked to do his soldering in the barn. It had
been on one such occasion that Ella had had the bright idea of
making pictures out of odd bits of metal. If only she could solder
metal into shapes.

Selwyn had said no at first when she asked him to show her
how to do it but finally, after a lot of pestering, she persuaded
him to show her the basics. He'd insisted she watched from
behind a protective visor, standing well back as the sparks flew. It
was hot, gruelling work, but good practice for working molten
metal into moulds if she ever wanted to do proper busts or larger
work.

Then her mother had come in with a mug of tea and seen
them both working and flown into a rage with him. He'd sworn
at her for interrupting.

'For God's sake, woman, can't you see the kid's got spark and
imagination? She's got some big ideas. What's a few burns on

her hands . . . ? Let her learn anything worth making costs blood, sweat and tears. Don't be stupid and limit her dreams.'

'Don't you call me stupid, Selwyn Forester! I know she's got brains and beauty and talent for the two of us put together. You've no right putting her in danger. That's not a girl's work.'

'It was in the war, or have you forgotten the steel makers and munition workers we all depended on then?'

Ella left them slugging it out in the garage. She hated it when they argued over her. Roddy would have marched her up the garden to cool off and made her laugh. She missed him.

Storming off to her shed she found her last piece of clean paper and drew from the white-hot heat of fury a picture that was in her mind: Selwyn's broken face bent over the soldering iron, her face aglow watching from behind the shield. In her mind's eye she saw a strange shape emerging. Two figures with arms raised in despair while the third squashed in the middle of them was forcing them apart. Her hand flew over the paper until she was spent.

If she was going to college they would want to see her work. She had to start somewhere, so what was wrong with right now?

Ella felt her head was bursting with ideas and, at the same time, her body was changing too, filling out, softening and curving. As part of the crocodile of High School girls marching along the pavements each morning, Ella passed boys on their bikes on their way to King Edward's Grammar School, who winked and whistled at her. She blushed, knowing they were admiring her shape, and her black hair woven into a plait to prevent it from springing into curls.

Hazel would stare back at them and giggle. 'He likes you.'

'Stop it,' Ella snapped, trying not to look pleased, though Lichfield schoolboys were so ordinary, all legs and pimples with sticking-up hair, not a bit like Michelangelo's beautiful creatures or Burne-Jones's portraits of the Knights of the Round Table.

She stuck her nose in the air, pretending not to notice their whistling.

'You only make them worse,' Hazel moaned, nudging her. 'I wish Ben Garratt looked at me like he looks at you.'

'I haven't time for complications in my life. I'm going to be an artist. We must pour our feelings into our work not waste them on spotty sixth formers,' she sneered.

'Listen to you, Ella Smith! From what I've read, artists have very complicated love lives. Look at that Miss Garman, the one who gave us that talk. My mum says she lives with a married man in London now, a right scandal.' Hazel looked so funny when she was trying to be sniffy, Ella thought; her nose twitched like a rabbit's.

'Oh, you mean Jacob Epstein, the sculptor, her lover.'

'And she's had his baby . . .'

'So? Artists do things differently.'

'I think his portraits are so weird and ugly. You don't want to be like him, do you?' Hazel looked shocked.

'I don't know what my style will be,' Ella confessed.

'You'll have to watch saying things like that or you'll have Miss Hodge on your tail.'

'No fear, my mum would skin me alive if she heard us now,' Ella laughed. 'I want to start my career now, not be stuck at these boring books.'

'You can never have too much education, my stepdad says.' Hazel's mother had just married George, the soldier.

'But learning to be an artist is an education too. I want to do it all the time, not just for two periods a week.'

'Then go to art college. Cynthia's brother goes there,' she sighed. 'He's so good looking.'

'Where? I can't leave home.' Hazel was voicing one of Ella's own thoughts.

'There's Walsall, Birmingham, loads of places. You could go by train.'

'But college costs money and things have always been a bit tight at home, though it's easier now we live at Red House. I suppose there's the ship money.'

'What ship money?' Hazel asked, intrigued.

'The cheque from the Welfare for my dad. I saw it once and it has a ship in the corner. I would ask Mum but I don't like reminding her about my dad. I was only a baby and we don't talk about it at home. Mum gets upset. It was ages ago, and what with the war and everything ... You don't get anything for your dad, do you?'

'There was a widow's pension, an allowance, but I think it stopped when Mum married George. I'd miss you if you left.' Hazel grabbed her arm as though to stop her from going.

'Oh, we'll always be friends. We can catch up at weekends. I'm not sure I'd be allowed to leave school, though. The Welfare lady will have to know. She keeps her eye on our affairs, checking whether we are still entitled. But you've given me an idea.'

'Oh, I'm not doing it for you,' Hazel grinned. 'If you leave Lichfield, then it leaves the pitch clear for me to work on Ben Garratt. Like I said before, it's never too soon to get an education.'

79

Celeste was pacing the floor with excitement. 'I've got an assignment ... you'll never guess where ... There's a family in Boston with a young girl who's been staying in Birmingham with some relations of the Cadbury family. She's homesick and she's returning home but the Elias family want her to be chaperoned. They want someone who's travelled to America before to escort her. Can you believe it? I can get across to the States for free! Who's to stop me seeing Roddy now? I can easily get a train from Boston to Cleveland. When Miss Fort told them I was a *Titanic* survivor and more than up to this task, it was all settled. They're very protective of Miss Elias ... Phoebe ... I love her already. I'm going to write to Harriet Parkes and demand to see my son.'

'Better to ask her nicely, don't you think?' May offered, concerned. She knew how much Celeste missed Roddy and was worried that her friend's hopes would be cruelly dashed. From what she'd seen of Grover, he wasn't someone who would acquiesce to this request lightly.

'You're right, of course. Softly, softly, catchee monkey ...' Celeste laughed, already looking brighter than she'd done for months. 'The Elias family will pay my return fare and I've got some of Father's money left ...'

'You're not expecting to return with Roddy?' This was the big question no one dared ask but May felt she must.

Celeste shook her head. 'I've resigned myself to losing him until he's old enough to choose for himself. But to see him after all these years . . . I just can't wait. And who knows . . .'

There was a spring in her step as she flew out of the room, leaving May shaking her head. Life in Red House seemed to be full of comings and goings these days.

She'd been rattled by Ella pestering and fussing about going to college, a summons to the school for an explanation as to why she was being withdrawn, getting approval for her grant. Now Ella was going on the bus to Walsall College of Art without a backward glance at the opportunities lost at the High School for Girls.

Miss Hodge had tried to persuade Ella to stay on, but when the minx got that flash of hard coal in her eye there was no gain-saying her. May had given in, knowing if all else failed at least Ella could resort to teaching art in a good school. Part of her was proud that her portfolio had been deemed good enough. How could she refuse Ella anything?

It was funny, not having her tearing home from school all legs and cardigans, flinging off her hat with relief, kicking off her school 'coal barges' and racing up the stairs two at a time. Red House was quiet now, too quiet until Ella returned home, usually late and covered in plaster of Paris or paint, her face all aglow. May sighed. It was all Selwyn's doing.

One morning, he'd shoved Ella's drawings under her face as she ate breakfast. 'These are damn good for a girl of her age. She's got original ideas and a style of her own. You can't teach this stuff. It's innate. Her talent shouldn't be left to rot under the weight of academia.'

He'd talk such big words, losing her at times, but there was no getting away from Ella's gift, one May knew didn't come from her family. 'She deserves a chance, don't you think?'

Selwyn knew how to wheedle round her, to soften her frustrations. Celeste had taken his side too.

'I just wish I knew what Roddy's talents are now. Judging by his letters, all he seems to do is play football and go for hikes. You must write to the Welfare and ask for a grant. It's her due ...'

Her words made May feel so guilty. Here she was with a child who wasn't hers while poor Celeste was robbed of her true son. What a strange reversal of fortunes.

Their arguments wore down her resistance like a pumice stone on hard skin until Ella threw her uniform into the laundry basket for the last time and was kitted out in a serviceable dress, which lasted all of a day before she demanded to make a smock and wear old Land Army dungarees.

It was a lovely autumn afternoon a week after Celeste set sail for New York with her charge when May cycled into the city with her new shorter skirt on show. Selwyn was in Birmingham and she'd got time on her hands for a change. The bicycle gave her a sense of freedom to enjoy the fresh air. She'd packed her basket full of shopping, and headed back with the wind behind her, making her feel as though she was flying. It was a good feeling to be free. She was going to make a Lancashire hotpot for supper. As she considered whether she had enough potatoes for the topping, she took her eye off the road for a second too long, hit a stone and fell with a clatter, scraping the back of her leg on the kerb. Passers-by rushed to help her off the road. She sat shocked for a few moments, feeling foolish. The gash wasn't too bad, the skin bloodied and full of grit, so she patted the wound with hanky, remounted and pedalled home for a welcome cup of tea.

80

Akron

'I've had a letter from your mother, Roderick. She's on some visit to Boston and intends to visit with us. We must make preparations.' Grandma Harriet waved the letter in his face, unaware he knew already that his mother was coming. She'd sent a wire to the house and his father had not been in a good mood, stomping about. 'I told that woman she's not welcome here.'

'But she has to see the boy. It's only fair,' Grandma had argued later, but his pa had fobbed her off as if he were squatting a fly from his lapel.

'She's not coming to this house. What will people think?'

'She can stay in the hotel downtown. She'll want to spend as much time as she can with Roderick. It's not you she's coming to see,' Harriet snapped back, which was something for Gran, who usually crept around his father, sensing his bad moods and keeping out of his way.

'Did you know about this, boy?' Grover turned to Roddy, his eyes boring into his own. 'Is this all your doing?'

Roddy shook his head. 'But I would like to see her, sir.'

He could see his father weakening at his polite request. 'If you must, but don't go overboard with the welcome mat. I don't trust her motives. I don't want to see her. She stays in Mother's wing, and I don't want her to set foot anywhere else inside this house. I don't want Louella being upset.'

'Then you should divorce your wife and marry the girl. She's always hanging around here,' Harriet said.

'Hold your tongue, you old gossip. Divorce means courts, publicity and costs. Things will remain as they are for now. It looks better.'

Roddy stared at this man with despair. Once upon a time, he'd wanted desperately to be like him. So wanted to be his son. But not now he was beginning to realize just what sort of man he was. Nothing Roddy did was ever good enough in his eyes. How could he talk to his mother like that? He hoped he'd never answered his mother the way Grover grunted at Granny Harriet. He sensed that he was a disappointment to his father; his grades were average, his sporting prowess good enough but not spectacular. His father never praised his achievements or good reports; in fact, he never praised anyone. It was a shock to Roddy to realize that he didn't like this man much at all. He was mean and hard to the servants, bullied the dogs, and Louella too when he drank too much.

It was best to keep a low profile when that mood was on him. True, he worked hard and times were tough for the Diamond Rubber Company. They were battling with competitors in the town. There were boardroom arguments; he'd overheard heated debates on the telephone and the thought of having to join that shark pool one day was not appealing. But it was what his father expected him to do. And so he'd have no choice but to do it.

Roddy craved the outdoor life. Increasingly his tracking and hiking was a release and enabled him to escape from the cold atmosphere at home. What would his mother think of him? Did she forgive him for leaving her? The young boy who'd set sail on the *Olympic* seemed so far from who he was now. That silly schoolboy who wanted to be the apple of his father's eye was long gone. He sensed one of these days he was going to have to stand up for himself. But Grover was a big man with big fists. Roddy had already received a cuff round the ear once or twice when he'd stepped out of line.

It was after that last beating he'd discovered what was missing here, something that he'd taken for granted at Red House. It was love, tolerance and a feeling of safety. It was the difference between a house and a home. Selwyn, with his courage and quiet ways; Archie McAdam, with his interest in education – these men had compassion. His mother loved him simply for who he was, not for what he might become.

His father didn't love anyone but himself and Roddy wasn't sure he even knew what love really was. He showered Louella with brooches and bracelets and took her to fancy restaurants, but that wasn't love either. It was about possessing something beautiful.

All he hoped for now was that in returning with his father to the States, he hadn't sacrificed his mother's love and compassion. She had once said that love was like an ever-flowing cup that refilled itself over and over again and never ran dry. He hoped that was true. This visit would prove it one way or the other.

81

The wound on May's leg just wouldn't heal. It itched like mad and she kept scratching it open. She tried the old bread poultice treatment to draw out the infection and then smeared it with goose grease to seal it but it grew hot and swollen, making her leg stiff. She tried to ignore it but when Selwyn saw her limping he insisted on driving her to Dr Howman's surgery. The doctor took one look and said he didn't like the look of it.

'How long has it been swollen and fiery?'

'Two or three weeks, I think,' she replied.

'Doesn't it itch like blazes?' He gently pressed it, feeling the heat of it.

'A bit,' May confessed. 'I shouldn't have kept scratching at it, should I?'

'No, you shouldn't. You must be a saint to put up with that for so long. I want you in the hospital. Now. We need to get that infection down.'

'But it's only a scratch,' she protested.

'I'll be the judge of that, Mrs Smith. It's creeping up your leg. You should have come sooner. I'll give you a letter to take with you. The sooner you get down to Sandford Street clinic, the sooner we can start treatment.'

May was bemused by all the fuss. Yes, she did feel a bit feverish but not enough to justify a hospital bed.

There was so much to do with Celeste away. Selwyn and Ella

would have to fend for themselves. The injury to her leg was such a nuisance but it wasn't getting better of its own accord, she acknowledged. Perhaps it would be better to rest it. Perhaps there was still a little bit of grit in it. Now it looked like a great purple spider spreading out in all directions up her thigh and all because she'd fallen off her bike. She didn't understand how such a graze on her skin could make her feel so ill. The doctor was right, she should have gone to him earlier before it went septic, but once she was in the clinic they would soon sort it out so she could get on with her life again.

82

October 1926

Ella loved college. Every day was new and exciting, different from anything that she had experienced before. There were lessons in observing the shape and form of objects. They spent hours in sculpture class looking and thinking and trying to put what they saw down on paper. There was a chance to work with traditional implements, learning how to transfer ideas onto a block of stone, seeking out the shape within the stone.

She'd even attempted to sculpt a head from clay, making drawings from one of her classmates, looking at how each head was unique. But most of all there was the amazing work of other artists, teachers who were famous in their own right, whose work adorned the walls and distracted her from the worry of her mother in hospital.

She rushed back on the bus for visiting hours and found Uncle Selwyn standing outside the ward, looking worried. 'Your mother's got a fever and they're trying to get it down. She's rambling a bit. But don't look so worried, I'm sure it'll be over soon, once the fever breaks. They've put her in her own room off the corridor.'

Her lovely day suddenly fizzled away to be replaced with a sinking fear. Mum had been in hospital for a week and it seemed things were deteriorating rather than improving. 'Can I go in and see her?'

'She may not know you; fever befuddles the brain,' he warned.

Even so, Ella wasn't prepared for the change in May. She seemed to have swollen up more. The nurse smiled, ushering her to the bedside. 'Your mother's sleeping. We're keeping her cool.'

'Is she going to get better?'

'She's very poorly. The infection has got hold of her system, I'm afraid, but we're doing all we can to hold it at bay. You'll have to be a brave girl.'

Hearing voices her mother looked up with glazed, bleary eyes, staring at Ella as if she wasn't quite sure who she was.

'It's me. Mum, I'm here.'

May shook her head. 'You shouldn't be here, I'm not fit for company. Go home. Your tea's on the table and tell Celeste I want to see her. This isn't getting any better so tell Joe too. I want to see Joe . . . Where are Joe and Ellen?'

'It's the fever,' said the nurse, mopping May's brow.

'Uncle Selwyn did warn me,' Ella nodded, trying to be brave and stop herself from shivering. The words brought back memories of that day at the seaside all those years ago when Mum had had that episode and ended up in St Matthew's, but somehow this was worse. 'She will get better, won't she?' she asked again.

'We're doing everything we can. With God's help . . .'

Soon her mother fell asleep again and Ella crept out, but when she saw Selwyn she burst into tears. 'Who's Ellen?' she snivelled, hurt that May hadn't once asked for her. 'Mum asked for Joe and Ellen.'

'You are Ellen,' he said.

'But I'm Ella.'

'It's short for Ellen, didn't you know that?'

'She's never called me Ellen before. Is that really my name?' The name took her aback for a second. It was as if he was talking about another person.

'Don't ask me. It'll be on your birth certificate. I told you she's not really with us.'

'Is she going to die?' she asked, desperately hoping he'd reassure her.

There was a long pause and Selwyn gave her a kind look. 'The infection is in her bloodstream, and that's not a good thing. I saw it in the war in some of my men. But there is always hope. Her body can fight it off if it is strong enough. And your mother is nothing if not a strong woman.' That was not the answer she'd hoped for but Ella couldn't take in any more bad news. 'When is Celeste coming back? I wish she was here. Why did she have to go away now, why can't she come back?'

'I've sent her a wire. I'm sure she'll be back as soon as she can.'

How could Selwyn be so calm? Did he not care? Ella felt as if her whole world was falling apart, a million miles away from the grown-up she'd felt earlier. If Mum wasn't here, who would look after her?

83

New York

Angelo was finding it hard to breathe in their apartment. There was a fight going on next door; screams and shouts were coming from the open windows but not a breath of air. Patti had the wind-up gramophone at full volume and was trying to do her tap routine. She was in Mandelo's Tiny Troopers, dancing and singing wherever they could, showing off their frilly costumes that Kath sewed using remnants from the garment stores.

Jack was cheeking his mom again but Angelo hadn't the energy to cuff him. He was turning into a tough street boy and had fallen in with a gang of hoodlums who hung around the alleyways. Who knew what he got up to out of their sight? He feared the *Padrones*, who funded the secret speakeasies that littered the city, were ruthless in getting boys touting for business in exchange for dimes and nickels.

Angelo coughed again. He'd been ill for weeks, exhausted even by climbing the stairs. It was the same old problem and everyone knew about the weakness he tried to hide. Across the room Frankie was trying to study for his entrance exam with Patti's racket going on around his head. Angelo looked to the portrait of the Madonna for comfort. How could he sort them all out, cut Jacko down to size and shut Patti up? Now Kathleen had to go out to work in an Irish linen store and he was left to rein in these holy terrors.

He couldn't shift the nagging fear that his time was running out. He, who'd never darkened the door of the church for years, had started making his confessions to old Father Bernardo once more. The doctor said he'd suffered dust on his lungs from too much smoke and bad air, and the weakness from the flu would take him early to his grave unless he got some fresh air and proper rest.

Kathleen had been distraught, wanting them to go and live in the country; easier said than done. Now all the energy had gone out of her, and Jacko was taking advantage by skipping school to roam with his gang.

Frankie had offered to leave school and work in Uncle Salvi's store but Kath wouldn't hear of it. 'We came to this country for a better life, maybe not for ourselves but for our children. You won't be leaving school, Frankie, not when the Fathers of the Blessed Sacrament are so pleased with you. They say there will be a place for you at junior seminary. We'll survive. Jack will settle down and make us proud, and little Patti will have her name in lights on Broadway one day, so she tells me.' She smiled, eager to hide her fears from her beloved son.

Angelo had never felt so helpless. If only he could get some strength back to be a proper husband and father instead of watching life carry on without him. It was bad enough that Frankie's head was stuffed with Latin and Greek, with math and the liturgy. He loved music, too, chanting in the choir stalls, plainsong, carols, organ music. Frankie'd never wavered from his calling, even from his First Communion, no matter how many times Angelo had sneered at him. It was a never-ending argument with Kath and for once she was getting her way.

'If God is calling him for a priest who are you to say nay?'

'I'm his papa, I say no son of mine will join the Church.'

'Well, I'm his mamma and I say he will.'

Once the illness had struck hard, taking the wind out of all these arguments as he struggled for breath, there was no time to worry about any of it.

Angelo was stuck in a bed made from two leather armchairs, looking out over the street, watching the horses and carts, listening to the honking horns of automobiles, putting on a brave face while he waited for the priest to call for the last time. He sat staring at his little box of photographs of Maria and the baby he never got to meet. And of course that little shoe.

They all knew the story of the *scarpetta*, the one Angelo was convinced was his first daughter's bootee. 'She lives,' he smiled, waving towards the street. 'Out there ... my Alessia. I know it.' He would point to his heart and the tale of the *Titanic*'s sinking was repeated over and over again until the whole family knew every detail by heart. How he'd been on the building site when the news came, how he'd waited at the dockside but Maria and Alessia hadn't appeared, how he'd gone to the White Star offices every day and seen for himself their names on the list of missing passengers.

Kathleen would calm him when he started to cough and splutter, getting upset. 'If she's out there, one day she'll find you ... and if not, she's with the saints and waiting for you.'

One day the doctor called, accompanied by a colleague from the hospital, who pounded Angelo's chest and made him take deep breaths. 'What he needs is good sea air away from the city – mountain air,' was his verdict.

Angelo laughed. 'Have we won the lottery? There's a family here who needs feeding, or haven't you noticed?' he sneered at Gianni Falcone, a good man but not living in their world. 'I'm a goner. Just give it to me straight, how long?'

The man ignored his question. 'You lost your wife on the *Titanic*, every one knows. There is a fund still going, and a chance that you could qualify for some financial compensation. And you lost your health in the army, yes? Two cracks at the whip, Angelo.'

'I ain't no charity case.'

'No, listen,' Kathleen said, pleading, flashing those magnificent eyes. 'With that money we could get you away, give you a chance to heal. There are medicines we could buy.'

'You can't heal what I've got, they've already told me.'

'Not so fast before you order your shroud; things have moved on since the war.'

'Where could I go, out west?' he asked, suddenly feeling hope surging through his veins despite himself.

'Better than that, Angelo.' Kathleen waved a slip of paper into his face. 'How about Italy? The sea air, the mountain breezes of Tuscan hills, a chance to see your parents before they pass from us? I have sent off a form for a special grant. The doctor will sign it.'

'But the children, it's a long way . . .'

'They stay with me. This is your trip. It's you who needs the cure. I don't want to lose you. We love you.'

Angelo felt the tears coursing down his cheeks. 'You are a good woman.'

'I know, but I need you around for years to come. I've lots of work for you to do. Don't you think it's worth a try?'

He nodded, seeing how serious her face was, and after they'd gone, he sank back with relief at the thought of seeing his old country once more.

Akron

Celeste dressed with care for this most important visit of her life.

She was nervous, having sat for hours on the train dreading the thought of returning to a place where she had been both happy and sad. Only the thought of seeing Roddy again made her determined. She'd wired ahead, hoping someone would meet her because she didn't know where their new house was. It was a grey cloudy day, in keeping with her mood. What if this visit was a disaster?

As the train drew in, she caught a glimpse of factories and chimneys, wide roads busy with trucks, all the industry of the town. Akron was growing prosperous. It had left her behind almost fifteen years ago. She picked up her suitcase and parcels, trying not to shake. She was all fingers and thumbs today.

Then on the platform she saw him: her son, no longer a chubby boy in knickerbockers, but a lanky youth crowned with a flock of blond hair, wearing jacket and flannels. He had come himself; a good sign. She choked at the sight of him, so tall and handsome. 'Oh, Roddy! I've missed you so much.'

She wanted to hug him but sensed he would be embarrassed by any public show of emotion. She'd seen it so many times when parents left their boys in her care to escort them back to boarding school: the little ones clung, the older boys always swallowed and coughed and pretended it was all very easy.

'You look neat,' Roddy smiled politely holding out his hand to her. 'Have you had a good journey? Grandma has made tea for us. You'll love the house.' He carried her case and took her arm. She could have cried with the pain of being separated so long and this excruciating politeness. Who was this young man? Celeste suddenly felt afraid. *I've lost him. Things will never be the same again.* And another fear sprang to her mind. How was she going to survive after these precious days? But she was here now, a dream at last fulfilled, and nothing could or would spoil this reunion.

The house was ridiculous, an ostentatious facsimile of an Italian villa, all turrets and fancy stonework. It had a formal front drive and wide iron gates, which were flung open. Harriet stood at the door, a shadow of her former self, shrunken and wearing a deep grey long skirt and a fussy ruffled blouse of the old pre-war style. She was now quite white-haired and had to wear spectacles.

'So you've made it,' Harriet said with a coolness that couldn't be mistaken for manners.

'Yes, I'm here, I can't believe how Roddy has grown.'

'Grover is away on business. So we have the house to ourselves for a while. Roderick will show you to your room. Tea will be in the sun room at four. I'm sure you'd like to freshen up and rest for a while.'

This was going to be harder than Celeste had hoped, but she was relieved Grover was away. She looked up at the brightening sky. 'What I'd really like is a brisk walk; I've been sitting so long on the train. Roddy, could you recommend us somewhere to get fresh air?' She turned to her son. The chance to spend some time alone with him was uppermost in her mind.

'Cuyahoga Falls. The riverbed walk is good but not in those shoes,' he smiled, looking down at her. She couldn't stop marvelling at his height.

'Give me five minutes to unpack and change. I've got just the pair,' she said, forcing herself to sound casual yet bullish.

'Tea at five, then, Grandma?' said Roddy.

'If you must,' Harriet sighed, ringing the servants' bell. 'But don't be late.'

'When am I ever late?' Roddy joked and his face broke into a wide grin. Celeste felt herself relax. A spring of hope bubbled up inside her. If this visit worked it would be a springboard for others to come. And then maybe, just maybe, he'd come home.

Roddy couldn't believe his mother was here, striding out across the river path as if they'd never been apart. She filled him in on all the news: Uncle Selwyn's new mission to help war veterans, Ella's first term at college, Mr McAdam teaching class and playing cricket for the Theological College.

He created pictures in his mind of the tree-lined road to Red House, with the conker tree and the gate to the canal bridge at Streethay. He could see the cathedral lit with candles and the choirboys in their stalls. It felt so real but so far away. It was another world, a world he'd left behind all those years ago. Mom asked him about school and what his father had planned for him next: Harvard or Akron University in town? He didn't know why she was asking this. He'd once dreamed of going to Oxford, when Mr McAdam told him tales of river punting, boat races, the stone colleges and rugby games, but that was before he moved here.

There were so many questions he wanted to ask her about home, and so much he sensed she wanted to ask him. He was sure she'd want to know why he had deserted them but it was safer to stay on casual topics for now, idle chitchat. He took her in the direction of the Portage Path and the Indian statue.

'I used to walk here before you were born,' she smiled, staring out over the view. He'd forgotten how pretty she was and how her hair gleamed like gold in the sunshine.

'Why did we leave here?' He blurted out the question troubling him for years now.

'Because your father and I couldn't agree on lots of things.'

'You know he has a girlfriend called Louella? She's very pretty but she's not much older than me. Why does he hate you?' He saw her flinch at his bluntness.

'Because I defied him and refused to do everything his way, and he doesn't like being crossed.'

'Did he ever hit you?' Roddy asked.

She stopped and turned, shocked at his directness. 'Who told you that?'

'No one, but I saw him hit Grandma once. She was too slow with finding something so he pushed her and she fell. Why does he get so angry?'

'Has he ever hit you?' He heard the ice in her voice.

'Only when I cheeked him a long time ago. He doesn't like people very much, does he?' Why was he talking like this to her? He felt himself blushing.

His mother paused again, trying to read his face. 'Roddy, you mustn't stay in that house. I wish you'd told me before.'

'How could I tell you? I feel it's all my fault somehow, all of it . . . in leaving. I'm sorry I upset you all, what with Grandpa dying.'

'You were only a young boy. What did he say to make you leave us?'

Roddy shrugged, embarrassed. 'Nothing. He just assumed that that was what I had come to him for in London. We went to the embassy and the theatre. I fell asleep and when I woke up we were at Southampton docks. He'd booked it all in advance.'

She stroked his head, all thoughts of embarrassing him forgotten. 'Poor boy, you must have been so confused. No one has ever challenged him. I think he is sick.'

'Don't say that,' he protested. 'He's my father.' Roddy didn't want to hear her saying those things, even if they were true.

'A real man doesn't have to beat people into submission. Walk away from him or come back with me . . .' she offered tentatively.

'No! I'm fine. I like it here. I'm used to it now. Ohio is a great place for hiking and camping. I've made friends and Granny is kind to me. I wouldn't know anyone in Lichfield now.' He watched his mother stop to lean on a rock, winded by his words.

'I just want you to know I took you away when you were small because Grover's got a cruel streak. How else do you think he got you back, but by deceiving you and drugging you? He couldn't risk you saying no and coming back to me. I'm sorry, we've made your life so complicated. You're right, of course, having to choose isn't a good idea. I'll not ask that of you again. You must go your own gait, as May says. I just want you to be happy and fulfilled. I'm being selfish, I know. I've lost so much of you these past years but it's wrong of me to want you to choose between us. It's not fair. I see you are quite capable of making your own decisions when the time comes but don't get browbeaten into anything you don't want to do, promise me?'

Suddenly everything between them had become serious. He was in no mood for this lecture. Things were being said, awkward things he wasn't prepared to hear. He would be fine staying where he was in Akron. He wanted for nothing and there was a future in the factory if he wanted it. Right now he didn't want to go back to Lichfield but her words unsettled him. He didn't want to be part of their quarrel. It was nothing to do with him, and yet in a way it was. He just wanted to change the subject.

Why people married and then just fell apart over stuff, he couldn't understand. He wanted to be left alone and not have to worry about what was happening around him. True, he didn't like the way his father needled Granny Harriet. He felt responsible for her in a funny sort of way. His mother had managed without him. She had her brother, May and Archie.

He wanted his mother's visit to go well. It was a relief to know they were still friends. And yet part of them was estranged too. Seeing her again brought back longings and memories, but this was where he belonged now and this was where he was staying.

85

November 1926

May could sense a figure hovering over her bed but she could hardly open her eyes. What was happening to her? She was lying in bed, exhausted, and all she wanted to do was sleep. Every breath was a struggle. They were nursing her night and day when all she wanted was to be left alone to sleep.

Poor Ella was going to have to manage on her own. Celeste wouldn't desert her but she was so far away. How she longed to see her friend's kind face, to hold her hand for comfort. There were things she needed to get off her chest. Before it was too late.

She wasn't winning this battle. She didn't need any doctor to tell her that. But she wasn't sorry. Now she was going to join Joe and Ellen at long last. It wouldn't be long, she reckoned as she dipped in and out of sleep.

She'd lived a lie and she wasn't going to her Maker without making a confession to someone she trusted. The vicar or doctor wouldn't do. It had to be someone who'd help sort this out for her one way or another. There was only one person she could trust. Poor Selwyn visited every night with a concerned look on his face as if he really cared, but he wasn't the one.

He was a good man. If she'd been smarter she might have made a better play for him but he wasn't her class and it wouldn't have been a good match. Besides, she'd had her chance of happiness with Joe.

Oh, dear Joe. Sometimes she thought she caught a glimpse of him at the end of the bed in his shirtsleeves, just come from the mill, smelling of sawdust.

She was done with fighting the pain and sickness and the terrible headaches that made her feel like her brain was being squeezed in a vice. No point in hanging around. Ella was better off without her. She'd make a go of her life now. She'd only be holding her back with her rough, uneducated ways. Ella could mix in grander company, make a name for herself without having to worry about her, she sighed. That was the rub. The girl wasn't her Ellen, and though there'd been a bonding of sorts, was it enough to last a lifetime?

If only they could find out just who she was. It was time to tell the truth, if she could find enough breath to do so. She opened her eyes with difficulty. To her relief it was Selwyn leaning over her.

'You wanted to see me . . . You should be resting.'

'Plenty of time to rest where I'm going. Listen while I've still got the breath. I have to see Celeste. I'm hanging on for her to come home. Why isn't she here? Doesn't she know?'

'She'll be coming soon,' Selwyn reassured her, but May was impatient to continue.

'You will look after Ella, won't you?'

'Of course, now rest. We want you to get better . . . *I* want you to get better.' He reached out for her hand. 'We need you.'

'No, you don't, you'll all be fine. Promise me Ella will have a home with you.'

'Of course, always. Now rest.'

'Not till I see your sister. There are things that must be said.'

86

On the third day of Celeste's visit, Harriet stood in the hall rubbing her hands and looking anxious. 'Your father's come back early, Roderick. He's in the drawing room.'

'Good,' said Celeste defiantly. 'It's about time we caught up with each other.'

Harriet moved to accompany her but Celeste paused to bar the way. 'Thank you, but I'll go alone. What we have to say to each other is not for anyone else to hear.'

Despite her bravado, Celeste felt the colour drain from her cheeks as she straightened her skirt and braced herself for the meeting. *I am not the timid mouse I once was.* She urged her fighting spirit to the fore. *I am his equal, and more.*

'So the prodigal returns,' said Grover, standing by the fireplace with his hands in his waistcoat pockets, appraising her carefully.

'Grover,' Celeste said, ignoring the jibe, 'I'm glad we can talk at last. You've done a good job with Roddy. The school and Harriet have made him into a gentleman.'

'So you'll be going back to Lichfield knowing he's in the best place.' Why did he always have to sneer about her hometown?

'I wouldn't be so sure of that. Akron isn't exactly the great metropolis of the world, is it?'

'It's one of the most prosperous places in Ohio. The world watches all the developments here: automobiles, aeroplanes, rubber technology. There are lots of opportunities for Roderick here.'

'I'm not sure that's what he wants. He's got a wanderlust in his eyes,' she argued. 'I think he ought to travel.' She was looking up at her husband, hoping for a glimmer of agreement, but he stood stiff, unyielding. He'd aged, she noticed. His hair was tinged with grey, his cheeks were florid, and there were the unmistakable beginnings of a paunch around his belt. Grover was looking middle-aged. He bristled as if reading her thoughts.

'It's none of your business now, what he does. I have plans for his future.'

'I think Roddy might have plans of his own,' she offered.

'Stop calling him that baby name. His name is Roderick.'

'He'll always be Roddy to me.'

'Suit yourself. You came, you've seen him, now go . . .'

But Celeste stood her ground, no longer afraid to check his moves. He was all bluff and bluster. She couldn't believe she had ever thought him attractive in any way. What had she ever seen in him? 'I think there's another matter we need to discuss.'

'Is there now? Whatever can that be?' he mocked.

'Our marriage has been over for years, isn't it time we put it out of its misery? Divorce is not what I was taught to believe in, but why pretend we are anything other than strangers to each other now?'

'Is this so you can marry your fancy sailor beau. Don't bluff, Celestine. I know all about your Archie McAdam.'

'Archie is just a friend, whereas you have a pretty girlfriend, so Roddy tells me.'

'You keep Louella out of this. I can divorce you for desertion any time I wish, but I choose not to.' He smiled coldly.

'But Roddy is confused and we're not setting him a good example. His loyalties are being torn.'

'You should have thought of that all those years ago, when

you deserted your home.' He turned his back on her but she was not going to be thrown.

'You know why I left. I sincerely hope you treat your friend better than you treated me,' she snapped, and he spun round, his eyes raging.

'She knows her place. Unlike you. If you want a divorce go ahead, see how far you get. Roddy knows what's good for him too.'

'I hope you're right, for his sake. He's the one decent thing to come from our marriage. He must be allowed to choose his own path in life.'

'He couldn't wait to leave your clutches; his letters were full of boredom,' Grover sneered.

'I'm not so sure about that. What kind of father drugs his own son and ships him out like a smuggled parcel?'

At least he had the decency to flinch at her accusation.

'One that knows what's best for a boy if he is to become a man,' he replied, and Celeste knew from those cold words that what she feared had happened about Roddy's abduction was true.

'How can a young boy know his own mind? But he does now. I'd watch out if I were you, or one day he'll give you a shock.' Their voices had become raised in accusation and Celeste felt herself flaring up. 'I only ever came back from England on the *Titanic* for Roddy's sake. Sometimes I wished I'd drowned that night.'

'Pity you didn't. You'd have saved us all a lot of trouble. I think you've said enough. It's time for you to go.'

'I'll go when I'm good and ready!' she shouted. Being in the room with him made her feel sick with loathing yet strangely powerful.

'We'll see about that ... By the way, there's a cable here you might want to read, about your little lapdog friend.' He threw the telegram across the room. It was already opened. She read the contents and stared up at him with utter contempt, knowing he'd withheld the news just for this moment. 'You utter bastard!'

His mocking smile said it all. He watched the colour drain from her face as she reread the cable. She shook her head and stormed out of the room, slamming the door in fury.

'Call me a cab!' she yelled to Harriet, who was hovering by the door. 'It's time I went home.'

Later, with her suitcases packed, she stood on the platform waiting for the train for New York. The rain was lashing down.

Roddy had been shocked by the news of May's sudden illness and the fact his father had known the news for days since the wire had arrived at his office. 'I'll write to Ella, I promise. I wish you weren't going. What did Father say to upset you?'

'Nothing that hasn't been said before. But it's time I went. I know you'll do well, whatever you decide to do in life. I'm trusting you to do what is right and honourable when that time comes. Nothing will break the bond between us but I must go back. It sounds serious. May is like a sister to me. She and I may have come from different classes, but that experience on the lifeboat forged an unbreakable bond. I can't explain it. Perhaps one day you will have a similar experience. It's a special friendship like no other, forged in the fires of a terrible event. Sometimes I feel the *Titanic* will haunt me for the rest of my life, but it brought me May and for that I will always be grateful. She was there for my father and for me when he died and you . . . You do understand now why I have to get back for her?'

He nodded, realizing he'd never heard her speak of this special friendship before.

'Just be true to yourself, young man,' she continued. 'Don't stand for any nonsense. Your father is deeply unhappy. Please don't judge every marriage by the one you've had to live with.'

As the train chugged into the station Celeste felt a panic that this parting might be for ever. 'Keep in touch, won't you? Come and visit us one day,' she cried. 'It's so hard for me to leave you now.' Tears blinded her and she struggled to see where to put out her hand.

'It's OK, Mom, we'll be together one day. I'll write, I promise, and I'll think about all this stuff. You came; I always knew you would. You're the only mom I've got or would ever want.' He bent down and hugged her tight and she sobbed in a confusion of relief, agony and fear. 'Take care, son, take care . . .'

'Be seeing you,' he called as she boarded, peering out of the carriage window for a last glimpse of her darling boy. He walked down the platform right to the end, keeping pace with the train until it pulled her away from him.

Celeste turned to face the front, swallowing hard. It was so hard to part so abruptly but what else could she do? Now all that lay ahead was the long journey back home. But at least it would give her time to ponder all that had happened with Grover, and those walks and talks with Roddy.

But what was waiting for her in Lichfield? She must get back this time. Surely history wouldn't repeat itself? She never had a chance to say goodbye to her own mother. Please God she would be granted some precious moments with her friend.

Celeste went straight from the station to the hospital, praying that May was on the mend and sitting up in bed, chiding her for taking so long to return. She'd made plans on the ship to take her somewhere for a holiday – Wales perhaps, or even abroad if she could persuade her across the Channel.

The sight of her friend took the legs from under her and she almost fainted with shock. May was barely conscious, unable to breath without oxygen, shrunken and so ill, Celeste hardly recognized her. But those grey marble eyes were still aware as she turned to her.

'I'm here, May. I'm back and not going anywhere until you get better.'

May pushed away the mask to rasp, 'About time. I've been hanging on for you. I thought you'd not make it.' There was another gasp. 'I have to tell you . . . only you.'

'What is it, dear?' Celeste could hardly catch her words now, the sob in her throat was choking her.

'It's about Ella and that night on the *Titanic*. You must tell her,' she sighed. 'She's not mine. She never was.'

Oh, not that again, Celeste thought to herself. May was talking rot and she was suddenly so tired after her long voyage. 'Shush, May, I was there, remember? I saw her with you.' She leaned over to reassure her but May struggled away from her.

'They gave me the wrong baby and I never told anyone. I'm sorry, but as God is my witness, it is the truth.' May sank back exhausted by the effort of explaining.

'Are you sure?' Celeste felt numb. Was it true? Had May really taken someone else's child that terrible night?

'A mother knows her own bairn, especially one with blue eyes, not black . . .'

'Who else knows this?' Celeste whispered. 'Oh, May, after all this time . . .'

'I couldn't let her go, not when Ellen was dead. Dear Celeste, I'm so sorry I'm leaving this to you. Be a friend to me in this, I beg of you,' she whispered, her strength ebbing away, her eyes blurring, looking beyond the bed to something only she was seeing.

'I'll do my best,' was all Celeste could manage, her mind reeling.

'I had to tell someone.' May sank back onto the pillow with a deep sigh. There was one long rasp of air and then silence. Her journey was over. And now Celeste knew with a sickening certainty that hers was about to begin.

She found Selwyn staring out of the window in the corridor. She shook her head. 'She's gone. I don't understand. How can a simple scratch wreak such havoc on her body?'

'It was blood poisoning in her system, so simple, so deadly. I saw it many times in the war. Poor May, she didn't deserve that,' Selwyn sighed. 'My God, I shall miss her. We argued the toss over everything but she was one hell of a tough woman. She picked herself up from the floor and taught me a lesson or two. Shamed me, no end ... Life is so bloody unfair!'

Celeste saw her brother was close to tears, struggling for control of his feelings.

'I need a drink, a stiff one and I don't care who sees me having it.'

'The George?'

'Wherever, just get me out of here. You think you know your friends and then they ... Oh, Selwyn, we've got a problem on our hands, a big one.'

'Steady on, old girl, just calm down. I know it's a terrible shock but first we'd better find Ella. She's with Hazel and her family. She needs to be told.'

'Let her stay there a while longer. Besides, there's something you should know first. Something no amount of time is going to change.'

'The George it is, then?'

'Let's leave,' she said, suddenly weary beyond reason.

Oh, May, you know how to choose your moment, burdening me with this terrible knowledge. How could you carry such a secret for all these years? What are we going to do with this awful news?

She thought of Ella, safe with Hazel and her mother, unaware of what lay ahead. The poor girl. How could May keep such a thing from her? Celeste felt betrayed as if she'd never really known her friend. All those letters and kind acts ... Now she was in charge of an orphaned girl from goodness knew where. How on earth would they find out who Ella really was after all these years?

87

Ella sat by the canal bank staring down at the dank water and trying not to feel sick. How could her mother just leave her like that? She had looked so peaceful in her coffin with a soft smile on her face as if she was glad to be away from them all. Now she was buried by the healing well in Netherstowe, leaving her utterly alone.

It had been a simple funeral at St Mary's followed by a meal in a tearoom. Hazel and her family came, and Archie McAdam, and a few ladies from the college. Everyone was being kind to her but there was no one left for her now.

It wasn't the same at Red House without Mum there in the kitchen. Ella was glad to escape to college, where no one kept asking how she was feeling. Keeping busy stopped her hands from shaking. Sometimes she felt like a limp rag but she forced herself to make notes, to read, to study, anything to blot out the pain of returning home to the cold empty house.

There was a bit of stone she was working on which she was sure had a figure within it bursting to come out, but she couldn't bring it to the surface. Her tutor kept going on about art being an emotional response to the visual world. It was just words to her. Her emotions were all over the place and her hand kept slipping and spoiling her attempt to catch the spirit within the stone. More than once, she threw her tools across the room in frustration.

Her carving was in danger of looking like a statue in the local cemetery, sentimental and ordinary. This was a piece intended for the end-of-term exhibition, a chance to prove her skill. She was floundering in indecision, one minute wanting to do one thing and the next another.

At dinner that evening Archie asked about her day and she poured out her frustration, unable to eat. 'I can't do it, I can't think,' she moaned. 'It's hopeless.'

'Then don't think,' said Archie. 'Forget about it, do something to switch off and relax.' He was trying to be helpful but how did you relax when you'd just lost your mother? All she could think about was wandering around the city retracing the places where they'd walked together, a pilgrimage to comfort herself and remember all the little details of their life.

On Saturday morning she found herself walking from Lombard Gardens, where they'd roomed in the old house, to Dam Street, wandering up towards the cathedral as if she was going to see Canon Forester. Her feet took her to the West Front again, to the shelves of statues that were her old friends by now: the rows of saints, Old Testament prophets, Moses, and the small statues of the archangels Gabriel, Michael, Uriel and Raphael.

There were so many faces to examine inside, so many gargoyles, Francis Chantrey's wonderful *The Sleeping Children*.

Sitting in the corner of the cathedral, she knew her subject would be an ordinary face, a lived-in face with sorrowful lines. She thought of Captain Smith's stern sad face looking far out to sea, landlocked in Museum Gardens. How many times had her mother stood in front of him with tears in her eyes? Ella never knew why his presence there moved her so. When she had once asked her, she had brushed her off saying, 'One day ... when you are older, I'll explain.'

Now they would never talk again and so many questions in her head would remain unanswered. It was there, among the stone effigies, that she began to think that perhaps she could carve the one face that she'd known all her life. What subject better than her mother's face to find in the stone? She would scrap all those overelaborate ideas and carve the one she really knew.

She looked up at the arching ceiling. This was a good place to think. How many times had she sat here alone, waiting for Mum to come off her shift? How many times had they walked the aisles together?

Mr McAdam was right. You had to wait for things to rise up to the surface. Let them speak to you in their own good time. Was this what the tutor had meant by an emotional response to a subject? She'd no idea how it was going to turn out now, but it was worth a try. She couldn't wait for Monday now.

88

1927

Term was almost over and the long summer holidays were looming as Celeste sat savouring the late evening sunshine in the garden. Selwyn had gone into Lichfield for his usual night out with old comrades, and Ella and Hazel had gone to a dance and were staying at Netherstowe. Celeste turned to Archie, watching the rays of setting sun lighting up his craggy face. He looked relaxed, sated by a good roast and the first of their strawberries.

'Have you given any thought to what I told you the other night?' She'd blurted out May's confession to him after months of indecision. He sat sucking on his pipe listening but saying little. 'I have to find out if it's true,' she said, 'but where does one even start?'

'At the beginning,' he smiled. 'Go back to where May was born, find out if anyone there remembers them. It's not that long ago, there's bound to be a record of the baby's birth and a baptism. Ask friends still in the town.'

'All I know is that she came from an orphanage near Bolton where she met Joe and they worked in Horrocks's cotton mill. They gave her sheets when she left; she kept going on about losing those sheets on the *Titanic*. I don't want to stir up trouble but the more I think about it, May did seem defensive. She never went back to Bolton, which I thought strange at the time. Too many memories there, I thought, but what if her confession's true? I hate to think she'd deceived us all and took advantage of us.'

'Come on, that's not the May we knew. She was so loyal and protective of your friendship. The poor woman took a wrong turn and couldn't go back, I reckon. The lie just grew and grew until it was out of her control. We could take Selwyn's jalopy to Bolton and make a few discreet enquiries. Just to put your mind at rest.'

'We?' Celeste felt her heart beat faster. 'You'd come with me?'

'Of course, what else is a lecturer to do in his vacation but travel? Perhaps we could go onto the Lake District. I'd love to see Ullswater and Borrowdale again. Let's make a holiday of it, strictly legitimate . . . separate rooms . . .' he said in all earnestness.

'Oh,' she replied, feeling her face slump with disappointment. 'Of course.'

'I'm only thinking of your reputation,' he laughed.

'I'm not. In fact I'm fed up with the whole idea of sitting it out until Grover deigns to agree to a divorce. It's never going to happen.' She looked him straight in the face. 'But you and I, we've waited a long time, haven't we? Life can be so short and cruel. May and the *Titanic* taught me that. It's time we started living our own lives, don't you think?' She reached out his hand with a sigh. 'If only we'd met all those years ago.'

'It doesn't work like that. You can't turn the clock back. I was married then. There was a war and then Alice and Rupert died . . .' He paused, clutching her hand tightly. 'You're right, though. This is our time now, a second chance for happiness, darling girl, but I won't have your name dragged through the mud.'

'Who's to know if we go on holiday together? It's no one else's business,' she suggested.

'There's Ella. What sort of an example is it for her?' he replied.

'Believe me, that young lady is seeing it all at college. Only yesterday she told me that one of their lecturers arrives so drunk, they often put him to bed in a side room and one of the older students reads his notes until he sobers up. But there is your college post to think about.'

'How I conduct my private life is my business as long as I deliver a good syllabus and get them through the exams. But it's you I really worry about. This is a small city with some small minds ready to make your life a misery.'

'Archie, I love you for this concern. I don't know how I would have held up after Roddy left and Grover made things so difficult. And now May and all this mess about Ella.' She recalled that first chance meeting on board the *Saxonia*. Fate deals a hand once again, she mused. 'You've been my rock. When I think how I treated you when we first met.'

'Ah, the frosty Mrs Forester . . . I always knew you'd melt one day,' Archie smiled as he looked at his wristwatch. 'Look at the time, I ought to be shifting to my billet.'

'Why?'

'Because.' He got up to leave but she pulled him back down onto the chair.

'Stay, Archie. There's nothing to go back to your digs for, is there?' she blushed.

'Are you sure . . . ? What about Selwyn?'

'Leave Selwyn to me. He doesn't care a hoot about such things now. We've wasted enough time as it is. Your place is here from now on. People can think what they like, as far as I'm concerned. You can be our new lodger, whatever. I really don't care any more. I've spent years doing what I thought was my duty. Please stay tonight.'

'If I stay the night, I'll never want to leave.' He pulled her into his arms and kissed her.

'Good,' she replied. Slowly, she took his hand, closed the

veranda door and guided him up the stairs towards her bedroom. Why should they not steal some happiness for themselves while they were young enough to enjoy it? May wouldn't begrudge them this time together. If she was to take up the quest for Ella's identity, who better to share the burden with than Archie?

Carpe diem, seize the moment, she smiled, opening the door with a flourish. You're a long time dead.

89

Akron

All that his pa could talk about was the price of rubber falling
on the world markets and how the industry was having to lay off
men and cut wages to stop expansion programmes. Akron rubber
companies had raided Africa and the Far East for new supplies
of rubber to harvest, but prices were still tumbling. There was
talk of new tyre trials for long-distance trucks and farm tractors.
Every experiment took scientists and lots of dollars. Things were
changing in the industry and Pa was finding it hard to keep up
with the new men coming in who seemed to have the ear of the
big bosses. He was drinking harder and was crabby most of
the time, worried about his position, ranting at the staff for the
slightest delay. Some of them had already left to get better jobs
in the factories. Why should they keep on taking orders from a
bully?

Grandma Harriet kept herself out of the house, visiting, taking
sewing classes, lunching with old friends, so Roddy was left
alone to study. But his heart wasn't in his subjects.

In fact, since his mom had left Roddy had felt restless, unsettled, aware that all she'd said of Pa was true. He was a selfish user
of people, charming to strangers, but when the door closed on
their guests, he sat in his library, drinking bourbon until it came
out of his ears.

He'd dumped Louella for another girl, and then another one, each younger than the last, showering them with gifts. But they never stayed long. The last one had looked on Roddy with interest, which scared him. How could Grover prefer them to his own mother?

Her letters were full of Archie McAdam. He'd come to lodge in Red House to help Selwyn with the garden or some such excuse. They'd been to visit May's old home to notify her friends of her death, then gone on to the Lake District but it had been raining so hard they'd come home with relief. Ella had passed all her exams and been recommended for the Diploma course in Birmingham. She hoped to get a grant to travel with some of the other art students to France. He felt envious of their busy lives. Here he was, stuck in Rubber Town, going nowhere fast. Apart from playing baseball, soccer and tennis with friends he felt his life was aimless and without purpose.

One thing was definite: he did not want to go into the rubber industry. Those gargantuan factories with their acrid smells held no appeal, no matter how many times Pa suggested it.

What he did like was visiting the new truck depot where his buddy Will Morgan helped during his vacation. Motor Cargo had been started up to ferry tyres from the rubber factories across country to depots and garages. A few men had got together and bought one huge truck and then got licensed to transport across state borders into Pennsylvania, Virginia and beyond. They were building up fleets of contract transporters, drivers who could take any load anywhere. It sounded so simple, a brilliant idea.

Will had a head start learning how to drive these enormous trucks, and told tales of driving on the highways, testing out the new transport tyres for the rubber manufacturers. If one company could do it, why couldn't they follow this idea too? He suggested to his father one evening after dinner that they could do far worse than start their own haulage business.

'Whyever should I want to do that?' he sneered. 'It's no job for a gentleman.'

'Who's that then?' Roddy chipped in. 'I see no gentlemen.' The joke went down like a punctured tyre.

'I didn't pay out all those greenbacks to raise a truck driver.'

'But we could hire other men to do it for us,' Roddy continued. He knew he was onto something here.

'I brought you here to take my place one day,' Pa replied, ignoring his enthusiasm.

'It's only an idea,' Roddy said, feeling disappointed. It made common sense for them to set up their own business. If the worst came to the worst in the rubber industry there would always be other heavy goods needing shifting from one side of the state to another.

'Time you started at Akron University studying sciences. It'll stand you in good stead,' his father began.

'For what? I don't see myself as another Mr Marks.' Roddy referred to one of the most famous research scientists in the Akron laboratories.

'The way you're heading, son, with those grades you'll be lucky if I can pull strings to get you a place anywhere. When I was your age no one gave me a hand up.'

'But that's not true. Grandpa Parkes made money and sent you away to college.'

Just at that moment Grandma Harriet appeared in the hallway and Pa turned to her with a glare. 'What nonsense have you been putting in my son's head? If the Diamond Rubber Company is good enough for me it's good enough for him.'

'Why should I say anything against your work? I reckon Roderick's cut from a different cloth than you,' she replied, looking wary of where this conversation was going.

'What the hell do you mean by that?' Grover shouted, getting to his feet.

'Nothing, son. Roderick just wants to make his own way, that's only fair.'

'With his brains he'll need all the help he can get. I didn't bring him all this way to flunk his grades and not make college. Parkes men aren't losers.'

'It's not what I want,' Roddy protested.

'Who the hell cares what you want? You're my son and you do as I say.'

'Or else?' Roddy felt his heart beating with anger and frustration. 'Will you drug me, drag me through the factory gate? I'm not your servant!'

'Don't you cheek me, boy.'

'Or else?' Roddy squared up to his father, eyeball to eyeball. 'Or else you'll beat the shit outta me like you did my mother . . . and her?' He turned to point at his shocked grandmother, who had been quivering in the doorway and was now edging towards the stairs in horror at his outburst.

'What lies has that English whore been telling you?'

'Don't you call my mother that. You're not worthy to wipe her shoes. You're just a bully. I've got your measure.'

'How dare you?' Grover made to punch him in the jaw, but Roddy was braced for the blow, ducking to the side, raising his own hand to fend off the strike, lashing out at his father in fury. Years of pent-up frustration filled his limbs with iron and he felt himself rearing up, punching and throwing his father to the floor, beating him with his fists until the older man curled up against the blows, bleeding and defenceless.

'How does that feel?' he yelled as Grandma leaped in to drag him away.

'Roddy! Roderick, stop this. You'll kill him!' she screamed.

'Death's too good for him. I hate him. I hate him for what he's done to this family. You won't get the better of me, not now, not ever.'

Grover looked up at him with stunned eyes. He let out one final roar of fury. 'Get out ... get out of my sight!'

'With pleasure, but I'm taking Gran with me. You'll not touch a hair on her head ever again.' He turned to his grandma. 'Pack a bag, we're getting out of here. You can go to Effie Morgan's for the night.'

Harriet stayed put. 'No, I'm going nowhere. This is my home. I don't want tongues wagging.'

'I won't go without you,' Roddy shouted, but still she wouldn't move. 'I promised Mom ...'

Harriet stood firm, looking down at Grover. 'He is my son for better or worse. I never thought to see you, two stags rutting, drawing blood, but I guess it's been coming a long time. You'd better go. There'll be no more fighting in this house.' She pulled up her son, who still looked dazed. 'You've had this due for a long time, Grover Parkes. I'm glad Roderick isn't going to be a copy of you. What a mess you make of things. You've lost all that's good in your life and the pity of it is you don't even know it yet, but you will. One day you'll end up one lonely old man if you don't mend your ways. Burned bridges are awful hard to mend.'

Grover sat up, brushing himself down, not listening, before looking up at his son. 'Get that ungrateful pup out of here before I whip some sense into him.'

'Don't you ever learn? Your whipping days are over. Roderick will walk through this door and never come back if you don't apologize right now.'

'For what? Apologize for knowing what's best for my son?'

'You don't own him. You've had him on loan, that's all. That's all we can ever expect of our children . You've had your chance. I don't like to think I was totally responsible for how you've turned out. But I wonder ... Me and your pa must take the blame for letting you rule the roost too much. Look at you, who would ever want you for an offspring? I take back all I said about your wife. She knew what she was doing when she jumped ship. I reckon the *Titanic* taught her a thing or two. From one disaster to the next, she came. Say you're sorry before it's too late, please.'

There was a deafening silence as Roddy closed the door on his life at Oak Court. The moon was high, the bright stars torching his path as he made his way down the driveway clutching his carpetbag of clothes. Where would he go now?

All he knew was that he was free and it felt as if a lump of rock had dropped from his shoulders. Grandma was right: there was no turning back. He'd never go back again, but he was going to have to think up something pretty quick if he wasn't to starve or freeze to death in the night chill.

Heading down towards the city lights with a spring in his step, Roddy knew just where he was aiming for. He'd broken a cord, snapped those threads, and a new life was beginning. Scary as it was, he knew things would work out just fine.

90

It was nearly Christmas and Celeste was listing orders for the butcher, baker and grocery stores, determined to make the best of things in these grim times, trying to recall how May went about her preparations. How she was missed in the kitchen. This was going to be a poor season for many families when so many men were unemployed. She'd been serving in a special food distribution centre and clothing store. There was talk of a deep depression in the country.

She felt so privileged to have a loving home with people who cared for her, and Archie and Selwyn's steady incomes coming into Red House. They were the lucky ones and must share what they had with others. She wanted to make the festive season jolly for Ella, to lift their spirits after such a hard year. The tree was coming from Cannock Chase and they'd ordered a fine turkey from the local farm. She was making little stocking gifts for the children's comforts charity in the city.

Ella was nearing the end of her diploma year specializing in sculpture and portrait sculpture. She was helping in the junior department of Birmingham School of Art, travelling on the train each day, and she was in love.

She kept the object of her desire so secret that Celeste was afraid he was married and stringing her along. But Keir Walsh was a scruffy angular sort of chap of her own age, a socialist with strong views on the political situation and the rights of all working men. He tutored life drawing and he had no time for the Church, eyeing them all with suspicion at first. His parents were Birmingham Irish. He never talked about them – his conversation was limited to rallies and electioneering, and how the middle classes had no idea of conditions in the city. 'A rough diamond', her father would have said, but sincere enough.

She watched Ella's face light up when he lectured them at the table about the rise of fascism in Italy and Germany. The girl worshipped him, and he looked at her as if he couldn't quite believe such a beauty could be hanging on his every word.

'I'm not sure he's the right man for her ... she's so young,' Celeste whispered to Archie one evening. 'I was that age when Grover came into my life and what a mess that turned out to be.'

'But it's different now, the young ones have more freedom to be themselves. If they love each other, they'll find a way.'

'But his views are so extreme,' she continued, stuffing oranges and nuts into the stockings. 'He says Europe is warming up for another war. Germany is growing stronger, building roads and railways, making use of their unemployed. There can't be another war, surely? How can two young artists make a living to support a family in this climate?'

Archie laughed. 'It's early days. They've hardly known each other for five minutes. Keir looks like the sort of young man that'll not be settling down from a long time. Give them a chance.' Archie knew how to calm her fears.

Celeste had still not told Ella the full story of her identity or the real reason they'd made a detour to Bolton. Joe and May's story was confirmed but no one could say anything other than that there had been a baby girl. The vicar had baptized hundreds, he'd said, apologizing that one baby looked the same as the next to him. One of the mill girls did let slip that Joe was fair-headed and not dark, as May had insisted. How were they ever going to find out the true facts? She didn't want to speak to Ella until she had some tangible proof to offer her.

The trouble was there was never a right time to broach this subject, never a right time to open such a deep wound. Perhaps it would be better to let the issue slide, but Archie remained unconvinced.

'Ella ought to know what we suspect. She has a right to find out the truth. You must tell her about the *Titanic*. I can't believe she doesn't know even that.'

'I know, but now's not the right time. She's no ears for anything but Keir.'

This year their Christmas celebrations would be simple with the Christmas Eve midnight service at the cathedral being at the heart of them. Celeste had sent Roddy's parcel to his depot address outside Akron, which he was using as a base. She was not sorry he'd left Oak Court. He'd sent a long letter describing all the drama of his exit. She'd have loved to have seen Grover curled up in a ball, getting a dose of his own medicine. She was no longer in contact with her husband. When Ella knew how things stood and life settled down here again, she would be petitioning him for divorce, but first things first.

With his friend Will, Roddy was building up a fleet of trucks. They were crossing state lines, driving thousands of miles with freight deliveries, a team of drivers contracted out to run their lorries. He'd found a gap in the market and filled it.

Despite all his father's aggro he was making money, but he still sounded restless and dissatisfied. She could sense his frustration at how life had turned out for him. There was no mention of his returning to England and she no longer asked. Why should he ever come back now? But his continued absence was hard.

Much as Ella was like a daughter to her, it was Roddy who would always be first in her heart, her only son. There was enough of a family in this house now but it wasn't like the old days with just the five of them. She thought of Christmasses past, when there was May, Ella, Roddy and her father. Life seemed so uncomplicated then, with all those clergy to entertain, choir practices and choral evensongs, presents to buy, secrets to hide from the children, so many happy memories of this season.

Celeste smiled and sighed, knowing that the old life was built on the lies she'd made up about her return, the secrets May had kept too, and of course now they weren't exactly a regular family setup either.

Archie's presence was making such a difference. He'd helped Selwyn talk about the gap May had left in his home, helped him cut back his drinking and further pick up his career, helped him let go of some of the traumas of war. He could go where she could not, talk and share things only soldiers knew and she could only guess at. It was a secret society into which civilians had no admittance, just as she and May had shared that terrible experience on that dreadful April night at sea.

One morning while she was out putting the last-minute touches to her Christmas shopping, she made a diversion to Museum Gardens, thinking May would like her to visit Captain Smith's statue.

The captain was looking neglected, covered in bird droppings, almost hidden by shrubbery. He was a sorry sight. She recalled how proud he'd looked walking round the deck, his beady eye checking on the crewmen and passengers. What a sad end to his career this had been.

She looked up at his strong face and found herself talking to the man as if he could hear. 'What shall I do about the child, the one you saved? Who is she and where did you find her? How do I say what must be said without unsettling her? If only you could speak and tell me what you saw.'

Just seeing him brought so many memories flooding back of that terrible night and she shivered, feeling foolish to be standing in the chill wind talking to a piece of stone.

'I'm doing this for my friend May,' she said. 'We called ourselves "Sisters of the *Titanic*", bound for ever by its sinking.' She noticed for herself the fact that there was no mention of the name of the ship on his plaque; it was a name no one wanted to remember and he was a captain who no one wanted to honour for all his years of faithful service. Perhaps it was her duty to see he was spruced up with a bucket of water and a brush.

She noted the bold letters of K. Scott, the sculptor who had created such a fine likeness.

She recalled how May had once confessed how little Ella convinced herself she was a daughter of one of Captain Scott's crew. 'What a pickle she got me into and no mistake. I had to explain to her headmistress.'

Only you didn't come clean, did you? You told everyone what they expected to hear. No one challenged your word or your right to have this baby. I saw what I saw and assumed just like everyone else. I fought your corner and now I'm left holding the secret. Who is Ella? Is there someone out there who can tell us more?

91

Italy, 1927

Angelo kissed the ground when he arrived on the Italian shore. He couldn't believe he was back in the old country. It had been a slow journey from Marseilles but already he felt stronger from the bracing air, out on the deck, listening to the chatter of passengers, wrapped up in the warm new coat and hat Kathleen had insisted he buy before he left New York.

He would be going back not as a broken man but with a case full of presents, photographs and news.

The voyage was the easy bit, then came the train and the journey by horse and cart up the mule tracks to the farm. Everything seemed slower, smaller, in the golden Tuscan light than he remembered. He was a city man now, not a farmer's boy. He could scarcely understand the dialect he'd grown up with but he was so happy to be back in the scented hills.

His mother fell into his arms, so small, a far more shrivelled version of the strong woman who had waved him off nearly twenty years before, her fine features weathered by suffering. 'Angelo, my darling boy. Let me look at you ... so grey and skinny. I thank God I've lived to see you returned to us. Come in, come in.'

He felt like the honoured guest when he was given the room in the loft with the best mattress, a *vaso da notte* under his bed for his personal use in the night. The neighbours stood in awe of him as if he was a creature from another world, stroking his suit, his coat, beaming at him with toothless grins.

Onto the dining table came the *zuppa*, the pasta, the fine cheese, the country wine, the olive oil and wonderful *castagnaccio* chestnut bread, all with a fresh sharp flavour that came from the sun and the soil, and not from cans that had been shipped across the seas for months.

He was touched that all his letters and cards were pinned up on the wall above the shrine in the corner, treasured letters clearly read many times, and he wished with a pang that he'd written more often.

There was so much to tell, to explain. They thought he was a wealthy city slicker, not a man who was sick, out of work, only here because he'd been granted charitable funds. That wasn't what they wanted to hear. They wanted to know letting their young men go so far away was worth the sacrifice. He would not be disappointing them.

He had forgotten just how poor they were and why the farm couldn't sustain so many sons. By the fug of the *fornella a carbone*, he watched his little brother, Gianni, who he'd last seen in short pants, towering above him, looking anxious in case he was home for good and wanting his share.

'Come, eat.' His father pushed him to the table before anyone else.

'Only if everyone eats with me,' Angelo replied, knowing they would want him to have the biggest share. 'The doctor says I eat too much for my health,' he smiled, patting his stomach. 'So forgive me if I hold back. You have spoiled me.'

He could see the relief on the faces of some of the children as they pounced on the feast. How could he take the bread from their mouths? Angelo sat back wishing his own family was there to share this with him. They felt so very far away.

He sensed deep within him that this pilgrimage home would

do him good, along with the new tablets he must take each day. But first was another duty he must perform before any more festivity. He must make his way to Maria's family and pay his respects. There were things there he needed to know. He felt the little shoe in his pocket ... It had been there the whole journey. Would he find out the truth about its lace at long last?

92

Akron

Roddy was stuck in the depot making sure the deliveries went out on time, as the December weather closed in on the interstate roads. Everyone was in a festive mood, despite the wintry weather. Around him dangled a string of paper chains, which were not making his bleak office look any more cheerful.

The haulage business was brisk enough if he could make sure there was always a return load. They'd sorted out a deal with an insurance company so that every time they crossed a state border they had the right cover. Each state had different rules about loads, required different licences. Will was out on the road as once again Jimmy Malone had turned in sick, or so he said.

Jimmy was one of their most unreliable contractors who ran his own schedule if he wasn't kept in check. How could two greenhorn young bosses control men who had been on the roads for years, control wagon men who lived hard and slept rough to save time and expenses? Jimmy knew every trick in the book. Somehow they sensed when to come down hard and sack men who tried to make fools of them.

Freight Express was competing with the big boys now, businesses like Roadway and Cargo, but there was work for all of them. Roddy knew only too well that this business had to succeed. He'd cashed in Grandpa Parkes's legacy to buy a new truck and premises, but so far so good.

Roddy kept an eye on Grandma by turning up at church regularly enough. They dined in the Portage Country Club or in a hotel downtown, and she kept him abreast of his father's affairs.

'He's not so high and mighty now. The Diamond Rubber Company have been cutting back and have moved him sideways, tightening belts all round. He's lost a mint of money in unwise investments and he's got to sell Oak Court for a place in Talmadge. I'm not going with him. It's too far out at my age, so I'm going to stay with Effie Morgan. She's a widow and could do with some extra rent. Her place is big enough for the two of us and there's a bed for you any time you choose to come home.' Her eyes looked up without much hope of a response.

'I'm fine where I am, living on top of the job,' he said. Over the years he'd grown closer to Grandma Harriet. She'd softened with age. These meetings, away from his pa, meant she could relax and be herself, telling him stories of life in Akron when she was a girl, showing him her picture album with such pride. The years of being under Grover's thumb were coming to an end.

'In those days we Parkes could hold our heads up high, young man, so make sure you do the same when your success comes. Don't let it go to your head. But you're working too hard, and not even a girl on your arm yet?' She was always nosing around on that subject, pushing eligible girls in his direction.

'When do I have time to go courting, Grandma?'

'All work and no play, young man,' she smiled, patting his hand.

He smiled back, touched by her concern, but girls were not

in the picture right now. Not the churchy ones with their sickly sweet flirting. He was not going to make the same mistakes his parents had made.

He laughed at the thought that he would ever turn into his father in wanting an heir. This life suited him, driving down the eastern seaboard, across the mountains into Virginia, down south and out west, wherever he could deliver a load, then return with another. Tyres were not a problem, only rough roads and tiredness, but a flask of coffee was always ready. He ate in roadside diners and got to know other travellers and size up the competition.

Since that fateful night, when he'd turned up at Will's house begging a bed, he'd never looked back at what might have been. He was boss of his own life now, king of the road, a wandering star, one who could do every job he asked of his men if needed. He'd filled out; chunky was what his grandma said, eyeing him up with concern. He'd lost his private school manners. It was dog eat dog in this business. Christmas could come and go for all he cared. He'd be sure of a roast at Effie Morgan's place or at Will's parents. He'd parcelled presents for the Lichfield crowd. He'd even managed to find some fur-lined gloves for Ella and Mrs Allen.

It was on the wireless in a diner that he heard the plaintive sounds of a choir singing carols. For a second he felt sick with nostalgia for Lichfield Cathedral by candlelight, the table in the dining room groaning with ivy and holly decorations and May's plum pudding in which he used to search for the silver charms, pulling crackers with silly hats inside, playing charades and singing round the piano, and that brisk walk on Boxing Day across the Staffordshire fields.

It was another world away, and now he was a man doing man's work. If he was lonely, if the job was tough and tiring and unpredictable, it was what he had chosen and there was no going back.

Christmas Day was only a date on the calendar, just another workday. And yet, a part of him wished he could make the trip back home ... But how could it be home after all these years?

93

Frankie Bartolini loved the Christmas midnight Mass: the candles, the shuffle of the congregation round the adoration of the Magi on the Christmas crib. He felt important in his white robes as a high altar boy, set apart, holding the candles on poles as a priest solemnly intoned the Mass.

It was snowing outside, thick flakes, like a scene on a Christmas card. He could see his mother in her best hat, her red hair now tinged with silver at the sides. Patti was staring round trying to find her friends. Unsurprisingly, Jack was nowhere to be seen. He never came to church.

It was going to be their first Christmas without Papa. Everyone was putting on a brave face, trying to pretend his absence wasn't leaving a huge hole in their family life. He'd been so excited to go back to Italy and had sent postcards home, but he'd been away for over a month now and Mamma was missing him badly.

There was no money left over for treats this year. Work was tough and Mamma needed every penny, but soon there'd be one less mouth to feed. Frankie was going away to the seminary to study, to test his vocation. It felt like a desertion until he saw Mamma's proud face.

'You were put on this earth to be God's servant. Like Samuel, Hannah's boy, who heard the voice calling in the night. We'll manage fine. Patti's troupe show brings in a little and your papa will be home soon so don't you go having any ideas about packing in your new college. We start another year fresh over.

'It doesn't seem minutes since your papa and me met in the basement of St Patrick's Cathedral, brought together by sorrow and finding joy. Who knows what's ahead for any of us. To be sure, that's not for us to be worrying about now. It'll be a happy Christmas, Frankie, I know it will.'

'Can we go home and get cookies? You promised,' Patti whined. She was always hungry.

Frankie pulled up his vestment and fished in his pocket for two quarters. 'You can call in at the bakery and we'll have a feast.'

'Frankie,' his mother flushed, 'that's your choir money. You've been saving that.'

'So? It's Christmas. Everyone should have a treat.'

He'd taken so much from the family pot by not leaving school. This was only a token but it felt good to be giving it back. Jack would roll up in the small hours loaded up with wine, candy and treats. No one would ask where he'd gotten them from. He was a survivor, more man of the house than Frankie was already, an alley rat who'd not see his family starve. But that thought gave Frankie no satisfaction at all.

One day he'd have to prove that all their sacrifices on his behalf had not been in vain. One day when he took his vows he'd have to cut the ties that bound him to his family for good. His life would not be his own, but that was a long way off yet. Tonight it was Christmas and they must all have some fun.

94

There was a tension at the dinner table that the usual Boxing Day jollities didn't soften. It wasn't as if they hadn't played all the usual games, and dressed up for charades, but Ella still had such a pained look about her. She'd taken herself off to her freezing studio shed, wrapped in layers of woollies, and Selwyn had slipped back into his old drinking haunt, the pub next door. Celeste was beginning to feel she'd made all this annual fuss for nothing. Even Archie was lost in his own thoughts as she brought him a glass of sherry and sat down.

He looked up. 'I want to marry you. It's time we made a proper life together. I'm sick of being the secret lodger, the lover hidden in your cupboard.'

'But you're not,' Celeste protested.

'Hear me out for once,' he argued. 'This arrangement has gone on for so long, almost ten years. I think we should see a solicitor and get advice. If anything happened to me, I want to know you are provided for.'

'I am provided for ... well, sort of,' she replied.

'No, you're not ... you live in your brother's home, living off your father's legacy, which must have shrunk to nothing by now. I want you to live with me, share my name.'

'Aren't you happy here?' she asked, seeing the determination on his craggy face. What on earth had brought this on?

'Of course, anywhere you are, I'm happy, but what about you, living with all these stresses? It's not easy bringing up another woman's child. Ella's not exactly been easy to live with these past few months.'

'She's just young and confused. I think of Ella as my own. I know she's at that awkward stage but she needs a woman to guide her.'

'That young lady is quite capable of earning her own living. Before long a fellow will whisk her away from here, but not, I hope, before you tell her what she should know.'

'I can't, not yet. You've seen the state of her. I could shoot that Keir Walsh, playing with her feelings like that. He picks her up and drops her like a glove. We have to wait. You can see Ella's upset.'

'I can't wait, Celeste. I feel I've been patient long enough. It's time you made a life yourself. Selwyn's quite capable of living here on his own and Ella should know how things lie too.'

'So you've got it all sorted then, just like that. I won't have my life mapped out for me, not by you, not by anyone. Why is all this Ella business so urgent? She can wait.' Celeste felt herself flaming up with frustration. This was not a conversation to have at Christmas.

'I just want you to think about what I'm saying. I'm not a door mat. I have feelings too.'

'I know, it's just . . .' she sighed loudly.

'It's always just . . . with you, you put everyone before yourself. Why can't you take charge of your own decisions? Ella must know what we know. It doesn't feel fair for us to hold out on her.'

'What difference will it make to her to know?' she snapped back. 'Some secrets are best left undisturbed, like a wreck at the bottom of the sea. All women learn to keep secrets deep inside themselves. This one is best left buried.' Why was Archie being so stubborn?

'Because it's the honest thing to do. It's just as dishonest to keep May's secret as it is to pretend that I am just a lodger here. It's insulting to our friends' intelligence.'

'Don't keep going on about it.'

'Don't go on about what?' Ella had been standing in the doorway, watching them arguing. 'What have I done wrong now?'

'Nothing dear, just a difference of opinion.'

'I heard you keep mentioning my name. What's all the arguing about?'

'Archie wants me to ask for a divorce from Grover, so we can marry.' Celeste blushed at her cover-up.

'What's that got to do with me then?' Ella was standing with her arms folded defiantly. 'You were talking about me. I heard you.'

There was silence and Celeste looked for support from Archie, who just shrugged. 'I think Celeste has something to say to you.'

'Not now, dear, we're all a bit tired and fractious.'

Still Ella did not budge. 'What have I done wrong? I know you didn't like Keir, but I did.'

'Oh, it's not that.' Celeste felt herself shaking. 'It's got nothing to do with him. It's just . . .' she paused. 'Come here. Archie, can you fetch the sherry? Make yourself useful for once.'

He nodded and left the room, leaving her alone with Ella, cornered now into trying to deliver her news in the least upsetting fashion.

'Come upstairs with me,' she said, rising quickly before she lost her courage. She went to the linen cupboard on the landing and opened the door to pull out an old bag stuffed at the back. 'You remember this? We brought it from Lombard Gardens.'

Ella shrugged, disinterested. 'It's just a pile of baby clothes.'

'I told you then they were yours. Look at the pretty lace.'

'So? I haven't touched them, they smell,' Ella replied, wrinkling her nose. 'What's this got to do with anything?'

'Your mother never told you they came from the *Titanic*, did she?'

'No, why should she? I know you were on the ship. Roddy told me once.'

'And so were you and your mother ...' Celeste paused hoping for a reaction.

'Really? The famous ship that sunk? Is that where my father drowned? Why didn't she tell me? I don't understand.' She was fingering the clothes now, frowning.

'It's not quite as simple as that, you see ...'

'Wait till I tell Hazel. I was on the *Titanic*, in a lifeboat, saved from the sea. So *that's* how you met, then? Mum never said. I often wondered how you and her ... Why didn't she tell me?'

'There's no easy way to say this, Ella, but when your mother died, she told me something else, a secret concerning you. She said that the night she was rescued, the night her husband, Joe, was washed into the water clutching their baby, Ellen, she was rescued and put in my lifeboat. Then a baby was rescued, saved by Captain Smith, and the baby was given to her. *You* were that infant. Only when it was daylight did she realize you weren't Ellen but another baby. And by then she couldn't let you go.'

Ella stood staring at her, trying to take in this shocking news, shaking her head in disbelief.

'And you've known all this for months?' she said. 'She never told anyone but you? Don't believe her. She was mad ... She said I wasn't her daughter once before. It can't be true. She couldn't steal a baby.' Ella was running down the stairs now. 'I don't believe any of it. Why are you telling me this now?'

'Because Archie said I should have told you straight away, as soon as I knew. I'm sorry.'

'*You're* sorry? It's that woman who should be sorry. How could she steal a baby?'

'Don't say that! May always loved you as her own. You were

her baby from the moment she had you in her arms. No one claimed you on the *Carpathia*, the rescue ship, so she felt that she had been saved to give you a proper mother.'

'So who am I then?' There was a hardness in Ella's voice and a fierce anger. 'You tell me who am I. You've taken away one identity. So where do I find my real parents?'

'I don't know, somewhere within the *Titanic*'s passenger list perhaps. There has to be an answer. We could try to find out.'

'How can we? Not after all these years . . . who cares about the *Titanic* now? Anyway, it's not your place. You're no relation to me!' Ella snapped.

'I never was. But you're like a daughter to me nevertheless. I'm sorry. There was never going to be an easy time to tell you. I don't know why I'm saying this now but Christmas is a strange time for families with so many memories. We all get so nostalgic for past times,' Celeste offered, but Ella wasn't listening.

'You have a family. I have no one. You've just taken away everything I thought was mine. I hope you're satisfied.'

Archie came in at that moment with the silver tray, silently putting it on the table, looking up to see the two women glaring at each other. 'Please don't blame Celeste, Ella. This was my idea. It's just gone on too long, and I'm glad it's out in the open.'

'Well, I'm not. Keep your bloody sherry. I'm going out.' Ella stormed out and they heard the back door bang.

Celeste sat down, winded. 'Are you satisfied now, Archie McAdam, forcing me into a corner, confronting her like that? What a mess, an awful mess and all because you wanted answers because of your own insecurity. I hope you know what you've done.'

'Be patient, all shall be well,' he offered.

'Don't preach at me. It doesn't suit you. The jack is out of the box now and there's no shoving him back in. I'm off to bed . . . alone. You really can be the honest lodger for once. Good night.'

Celeste tossed and turned for what felt like hours. She ought to go to Ella and comfort her. She ought to put a hot-water bottle in Archie's cold spare bedroom, she thought. She ought . . . oh to hell with oughts. Tonight she'd think only of herself. She needed to sleep on all this but she was too tired and angry and frightened and uncertain about anything now. It would be a long night.

Ella took the lamp out to the shed. This was her little bolthole, with its paraffin stove and chair and all her unfinished artwork. She felt nothing but a raging disbelief at what she'd just heard, a roar of denials in her ears, and yet she knew it was true. Ellen was the name her mother had called out in the hospital. 'You're not my child,' she'd screamed at the seashore, all those years ago. It had to be true. Secrets and lies that had lain unspoken for years, making a mockery of all they'd done together. All that nonsense about Joe Smith the sailor lost at sea. Her mind was racing with incidents, conversations, half-broken sentences that had passed between them.

It was as if all the stitches of her life were unravelling back into twisted, broken threads. With those few words Celeste had destroyed her history. Who am I? Who was I? Where did I come from? Was there anyone left who even knew?

'You can't think about this,' she screamed out loud. 'You're a fake, a nobody, an impostor!' She found herself flinging her papers across the floor, scattering her tools, a chisel in her hand battering down on the face of a carving she'd been working on, the face in the stone that had somehow become her mother's face. 'I hate you all!' she yelled, hammering into the plaster. Months of work were destroyed in a fury that fuelled itself until she stood exhausted, weeping, looking round at the devastation she'd wreaked. 'I'm not staying here . . .'

'Oh yes you are, young lady. You'll clear up this mess. All this good work destroyed in a tantrum.' Uncle Selwyn walked in and focused his lamp over the chaos. 'What a bloody waste . . . Feel good, do you?'

'Go away!' she snapped.

'So you know the truth and you're angry. Quite right too . . . Everyone holding out on you . . . So you're not who you thought you were?'

'You don't understand, how could you?' Ella was feeling small and stupid now.

'Don't you tell me what I can or can't understand. I thought I was a gentleman and a lawyer, a fine upstanding man of the city, but when I stood on that trench ladder to go over the top, I found I was just another man: a beast, a killer, an unthinking automaton leading men into carnage, seeing them blown to shreds of bone and sinew. I am a man who bayoneted strangers in a fury of rage. The man who came back from no man's land to roll call was not the man who went over the top. I've spent years trying to find out who I am and more besides.

'So you were given life, given a home and love by a stranger? Did you ever consider her a stranger? Didn't May give you her last penny? She may not have been your blood mother but don't you dare say she didn't care for you . . . You've had a shock, a terrible shock, and it's changed a lot of things. You can't unlearn this knowledge. Sure, it's a reason to feel sorry for yourself, a reason to sulk and take it out on all of us for what we withheld. Or, Ella – and this is the hard bit – you can get on with what you are good at, knowing someone somewhere gave you a wonderful gift: the observing eye and hands of an artist.' Selwyn paced up and down, his eyes fixed on her. 'While you work with these gifts, they live on. Destroy them and they die too. Is that what you want? '

Ella had never heard Selwyn make such a long speech.

'But I want to know who I am. How can I not know who I am?'

Selwyn shrugged. 'Fair enough but not tonight. There's no

one who can tell you all that on Boxing Day, now is there? It's cold out here. Everyone's gone to bed. I'll make you some cocoa.'

'No,' she snapped. 'Thanks, I'll do it myself. You always scald the milk and I hate the skin.' She looked up, seeing him holding out his hands.

'We were never related but you've always been special to me, and May too. Time for bed . . . Things will look better in the morning for all of us.'

They picked their way down the frozen path by torchlight. Ella was feeling foolish, exhausted and empty. Selwyn was right. Finding who she really was would have to wait for another day. Yet shocked as she was, there was a tiny bit of her that had always known she was different in some way, that when she looked at her mother she'd wondered how she could have once belonged inside her body. It had made her feel so guilty and she'd learned to ignore that niggle in her head. Now she knew the truth and felt an odd sense of vindication.

She stopped to stare up at the winter sky and the moon. *Who am I? Where will I find out? Is there someone somewhere in the world who knows about me?*

95

Italy

Maria's mother was dressed in black from head to toe as she examined the baby shoe but her eyes were filmed over. 'I can't see. It is a pretty shoe but, I don't know, every baby has shoes like this. The lace is fine but do not pin your hopes on such things.'

'But Maria made such good lace,' Angelo argued. Her words were giving him no comfort.

'So do most of the girls in Anghiari and Sansepolcro. We have the Marcelli sisters to thank for that and their little *scuola di merletto*. Lace may only be thread and pins, but we've made so many beautiful pictures with it over the years: stars, animals, flowers, snowflakes. I remember how Maria used to sit with me at my cushion and watch how it was made. Now she is taken from us. It was God's will.'

This was not what he wanted to hear. 'I thought you would know these things,' he said, shoving his offering back into his pocket, embarrassed. It was never going to be an easy meeting. 'I wish we had not given her the ticket,' he sighed.

'You wouldn't have stopped her. She wanted to join you. For months she spent her spare hours making lace for the baby's clothes, and collars and cuffs, extra work that she could sell. Look, you can see the smile on her face in the picture, and the fine lace of Alessia's gown. She was so proud of her work, and the little one so dark like you.'

Angelo knew every grain of that precious photograph by now but he stared at it again as Maria's father filled his glass with rough wine. 'Get that down your throat, son. We bear you no grudge. You did not sink that ship. It was too big for the ocean and it swallowed it. She was on the wrong vessel.'

Angelo cried, 'But it's hard to live with this in my heart.'

'Then let it rest and live your life with your new family. We wish you all well. The son wants to be a priest? I should like to meet such a young man. But he is in America; that is good, for here he would be joining the young Blackshirts. Things are different here under Il Duce. Children are to be taught only what they want them to hear. The children of officials are pampered in leather and lace while others starve. It is not easy to speak your mind in the village in case someone complains to the mayor. They say it will be good for all of us to follow Il Duce. I think it's better to live free where you are.'

Angelo hugged them both. He knew he'd never see them again. As he walked through the village, people stared, thinking him a stranger. He felt like one. He smiled and waved but they went inside and shut the door to him. How quiet it was compared to the bustle of New York streets, the smell of garlic and frying onions, the barking of voices in the cafés and on the sidewalks selling fruit, the honking of the motors impatient to be on their way. New York was home now.

He made his way to a ridge high over the village where he could look down on the rooftops and across to the hills in the distance. It was here he'd kissed Maria for the first time, a lifetime ago. Now it was chilly, grey and misty, not green like in the spring, with new leaves and blossom and the scent of pine. Everything had its season, he sighed. Maria would always be springtime and he was now in the fall of his life. It was time to go home.

96

May 1928

Ella hung over the railings of the cross-channel ferry, breathing in the sharp air with relish. From Birmingham New Street to London, then to Dover and onwards to France – here was freedom at long last, after months of bickering and frustration with the Foresters. She knew she'd been a pain but what did they expect after holding out on all those secrets for months?

It was the archdeacon's wife who had come to the rescue, asking if Ella would be prepared to assist one of her friends in Paris as a mother's help for the summer.

Hazel had been green with envy as she packed her new pass-port, tickets and currency, feeling so grown up to be travelling alone; well, almost. Celeste had insisted she tagged on to a party of art students from Lichfield who were doing a tour of the museums. Little did they know she'd thrown them off at Waterloo.

This was her adventure, her chance to live a grown-up life without any interference from her guardians. She was being mean to them, she knew. Selwyn had bought her a beautiful leather case and Celeste had taken her into Birmingham for some summer clothes. Archie had found her some maps of Paris. 'You must see Rodin's work. I promise it won't disappoint.' As if she didn't know that.

They were nervous for her but the Reverend Mr Burgess was one of the chaplains at St George's Anglican Church on the Rue Auguste Vaquerie. She was to be in charge of his two little girls, and there was to be a new baby soon. There would be time off to go to art classes and she had no compunction now in asking the *Titanic* Relief Fund for a grant to attend as part of her education.

There had been a battle over this at first until Archie explained that no matter who she was, she had still suffered a great loss on the *Titanic*, as much as May. Poor Selwyn had gone to the trouble to seek out the original passenger list from the White Star Line, but she wasn't ready to look at it. It would mean confessing to the mistake May had made, besmirching her memory and making her own identity a false one. Better to stay Ellen Smith for the time being. She didn't want any more complications.

The seagulls screeched overhead and Ella's spirit lifted as she saw the French coast coming into view. No more bad memories, no more small-town gossip, she was on her way to a new country and new people, who knew nothing of her sadness. She couldn't wait for this new life to begin.

Part 4

LINKING THREADS

1928–1946

97

Postcards from Paris, 1928

Dear All

I have arrived safely. The chaplain and his wife were there to meet me at Gare du Nord. Hermione and Rosalind are being little angels so far. I can't believe I'm living here in the heart of the city. The vicarage is so central. I can walk to the Arc de Triomphe down the Champs-Elysées to the Jardin des Tuileries. Please thank Mrs Simons so much for recommending me.

Paris is the best tonic for the grumps. England seems so far away. It is everything I could wish for and more. The girls are coming with me to the parks and museums. I have to remember they are my charges and not let them run too wild. My French is improving every day and the shop windows are such a distraction – do not worry, Parisian life is far too expensive on my allowance! The classes are good and I am meeting lots of other foreign students. We are going down to the south of France for the summer holidays. I can't wait to see the Mediterranean.

Best love,

Ella

Dear Roddy

You don't deserve a letter as you hardly ever write to me but I wanted to show off my address in France and all the places I have visited. My sculpture class is mind-blowing. Everyone is tons better than I am. I have so much to learn.

I am collecting cathedrals: Notre-Dame. Rouen, Chartres, Tours, Orléans and Paris buildings are just one huge classroom.

Our visit to Cannes was such a surprise. It was so hot and I am so brown now that people come up to me and think I'm a native. It's funny how in the sunshine I feel like a lizard warming myself on stone walls. I will be sad when the autumn comes and I must return to more studies under grey skies. The little girls played on the plage and we swam in the sea every day. We have a new baby boy called Lionel, who has a nursemaid.

It has been good to be away from everyone, standing on my own two feet, having to cope with emergencies, how to deal with men who sit too close to me on the Metro and want to feel up my skirts. I kick their shins hard and make them wince with shame, I hope. I wish I were a boy who could wander freely everywhere without worrying if I am being followed.

I have become an expert at swearing in French under my breath when the art master criticizes my work. He has taught me to look at other work with a much more critical eye. There is just so much more to learn. I feel like a different person already.

I try not to think about my mother too much. It only upsets me that she died so young and needlessly for the want of a doctor's appointment. I'm sure she tried to treat herself to save a fee so money could be spent on me. I feel terrible how she went without to give me every advantage. She would never spend anything on herself. Now I am swanning around France like a debutante. I know it isn't fair but I also know she would be happy for me.

As I am sure you are aware, I now know all about the *Titanic* and how our mothers met. My mother had her reasons for not telling me. I sometimes think she was ashamed of being a survivor. All she claimed was her due pension so she could educate me.

It's all too late to understand things now. I suppose none of us understands our parents until we are parents ourselves. One day perhaps we'll feel as protective, fearful and hurt about our own kids. But I hope it's not for a long time.

No, there is no Rudolf Valentino in my life, just Leon and Friedrich, who sometimes take me out to the cafés by the Seine after class. There is no spark, though. I haven't time for romance. How about you, the big brother I never see?

I was sorry to hear your grandma died. I know you were fond of her. Forgive me for rattling on about myself. You work very hard and Celeste is proud of you. The divorce is going through at long last. It's long overdue but it will still cause a furore in the Close. Divorce is not as common in England as it is in your country and people don't understand that to spend a lifetime in a bad marriage is pure hell. Better none at all, I should think. Neither of us will rush into that state of affairs, I'm sure.

Do write back before I leave here.

Love, Ella

She hadn't told Roddy the entire truth about May and the *Titanic*. No one knew but her guardians, and that was how it was going to stay. Yet it was strange how at home she felt on the Continent, in the sunshine, listening to the chatter of languages. She was getting used to shopkeepers assuming she was local and jabbering at her in French so fast she could only nod and smile and shrug her shoulders.

Once on the beach at Cannes she heard a family laughing and screaming at their children and for a second she thought she knew what they were saying, as if some distant memory at the back of her mind recognized the words. She turned to hear more but they had passed on down the beach out of earshot. She didn't even know what nationality they were. It was unsettling for a minute until she was distracted by Hermione nearly burying poor Roz in the sand.

One thing she knew now was that this would not be her last trip abroad. She'd go to Spain, Italy, Switzerland . . . wherever she might find work or classes. If she was going to be a professional artist then she must learn her craft the hard way by training her eye to be critical and observant. Her work was amateur and conventional. She must learn from the classics, and that meant travelling. She must retain her identity and claim more funds. The *Titanic* had taken away so many lives, now it must pay for those it left behind, whoever they actually were.

98

June 1932

Celeste peered at her outline in the long mirror, pleased with the result. Aquamarine suited her colouring. Her wedding dress was cut on the bias with a flowing jacket and beaded trim. Her little silk hat clung to her waved hair, anchored by hatpins. It was a simple ensemble, ideal for a registry office wedding. She was glad her parents weren't alive to see her wed in such a cloak-and-dagger way. How different from last time, with all the pomp and ceremony of a cathedral service.

Grover had fought them all the way in the divorce. It had taken years of petty and ridiculous negotiations to make him sign. He'd finally left Akron for Cleveland after losing his position in some company dispute. Then Roddy had written saying he'd found a wealthy widow, and suddenly his signature on the divorce papers was secure.

She was hurt Roddy was not coming over for the occasion but he said he just couldn't leave Will and Freight Express. He'd sent them First Class tickets for their honeymoon passage to New York instead, and they would come on later to visit him. She couldn't help but feel it was a gesture borne of guilt but at least they would see each other.

Ella was back from Europe, bronzed, relaxed, full of her tour of Avignon, the Carmargue, and Perpignan to Madrid. Lichfield didn't hold her for very long these days. She'd turned the old barn into a studio base where she brought all her ideas into life. She was a free spirit, never settling too long before she was off on more travels.

They never talked about the past much when she was home. 'I am my own future,' she said. 'That's all that matters. I prefer to leave all that other stuff in the past where it belongs.' It was as if a drawbridge went up at any mention of searching for her real parents.

Today she was fussing round putting the final touches to the reception buffet in the dining room. The room stank of the ripe Brie she'd carted so carefully in her luggage across the Channel. Ella was determined to sophisticate them with French food and good wine.

She was looking a picture in a lavender voile floating dress with little capped sleeves and a corsage of cream and pink roses on her shoulder. If only May could be here to complete the picture. Celeste gulped back the tears that threatened to overwhelm her. She owed so much to her lost friend. Sometimes she felt her presence hovering, approving that at last she and Archie were about to become man and wife. She no longer felt burdened by her confession, just saddened that they had so little time to share it.

'It's time,' yelled Selwyn from the foot of the stairs. He'd cleaned the roadster and even put a white ribbon across the bonnet so they'd arrive in style. 'Don't keep the poor chap waiting. He's waited long enough for this day.'

The sun was shining but as Celeste looked up to those three majestic spires, she sighed. Only when they were blessed privately in the side chapel of the cathedral, which had been such a special place in her life, would she feel truly married.

Ella sat in the front seat clinging onto her spray of ferns and pink roses for dear life. 'Slow down, Selwyn, better late than never.'

'You know my sister, always late, so I'm making sure she gets there before the poor man gives up and goes home.'

They all laughed, the women holding onto their dresses as Selwyn shot down the road into the city whistling 'Here Comes the Bride'. Celeste's heart was thumping with excitement at the thought of the ceremony to come.

99

Akron

Roddy wanted everything to be perfect for the 'state visit' to his new house off Portage Road. His mom must see what a success he'd made of his life. His business was flourishing. Freight Express now had a team of freight transporters servicing thirty tyre companies across the States, from New York to Atlanta, from Wichita to Baltimore, and he was always busy. But not so busy that now and then he didn't jump into his flash roadster and check out some of his two hundred drivers to make sure they delivered on time. He wanted no time-wasters on his payroll.

It was a pity Grandma Harriet wasn't around to see his achievements but she had passed away peacefully in her armchair one morning after church. He'd faced his father at the funeral eyeball to eyeball. They didn't speak. They had nothing to say to each other until the afternoon he'd rolled up at Roddy's offices smelling of whiskey and demanding a job.

Roddy was dumbstruck for all of one second, thinking he might find him something until he recalled how he'd made his mother wait for a divorce for years, and that his father hadn't shown any interest in his new venture, ignoring him until he was successful.

He wrote him a cheque as a wedding present and told him there was nothing doing.

'Is that all you can say to your father after all these years?' Grover replied, greedily snatching the cheque.

'You told me to get out and I did. Best night's work I ever did, Pa. Now you have the cheek to roll up here and demand I hire you. To do what?' Roddy challenged. The man across the desk felt like a stranger.

'A man owes his father respect after all I did for you.'

'I owe you *nothing*. For Grandma's sake, though, I won't see you go away empty-handed. You have your wedding gift. Go make yourself a new life in Cleveland.'

His secretary discreetly showed Grover to the door.

'I hope you burn in hell!' yelled the drunken man for all to hear. Roddy knew he would never see him again. He was part of the old life. From now on he would be dependent on no one but himself.

If Roddy felt sad it had come to this, he also felt relief that now Archie and Mom had married at long last. For himself, he made sure he had no ties, no girlfriends, no hangers-on. It was good to be free to come and go wherever and whenever he fancied without having to account for his schedule. His home was his pride and joy, with its sleek leather sofas, glass doors opening onto a veranda, a fitted kitchen with refrigerator and built-in cooker. Sometimes he'd pinch himself at his success.

No one had handed him anything. He'd learned success meant hard work, long hours and determination. Freight Express was up there with Motor Cargo, Roadway Express, Yankee Lines and Morrisons.

He was thrilled his mother and Archie would see for themselves how he was prospering. They were sailing over to New York on their honeymoon. This way he got to see more of them than if he'd been able to go home for the wedding.

Ella would give him a piece of her mind in her letter about not coming over, though, no doubt. She was teaching art school and getting commissions for her portraits. He'd seen some of her work. Soon she would be off again through France to Italy. Like his, her work was her life and Mom worried that she shut herself off in the studio at the bottom of the garden too much. She sounded like a girl after his own heart. She had her priorities right, he reckoned.

Things were hotting up in Europe with Hitler, the leader of the National Socialist German Workers' Party, becoming an increasingly powerful figure. There was talk in the papers of trouble coming, something no one with relatives in Europe wanted to think about. He was going to try to persuade his parents to stay here for a while until it blew over.

Akron industry sensed the change in the wind and was busy building up supplies, air ships and balloons, special tyres for military vehicles. The airbase was busy expanding, and the years of depression seemed so far away now. He'd always meant to go back to Lichfield, but business came first and being away for a month was not on the cards. Things went slack if he wasn't at the helm. His business partner, Will, was more a family man at heart and a soft touch.

They didn't stay long in Akron. Celeste never felt comfortable there, worrying she might bump into Grover. Roddy assured her he was safely in Cleveland with his new wife but the place always brought back such sad memories. Archie was anxious to get back before term started at his new school near Stafford. It had been a wonderful trip, if exhausting. Roddy had been excited to prove to them his success, to show them off, to escort them to the most expensive restaurants like an eager puppy, and yet Celeste's heart was sad. He'd changed, grown a tougher skin. He was always on the telephone, focused on the latest crisis at the office, dashing off leaving them in his beautiful home until he reappeared hours later. His world was not their world. They'd grown apart over the years of enforced separation.

Besides, Roddy didn't think of England as his home now. He

was American through and through, proud of his town's great industrial prowess, proud of his haulage company and its hundreds of drivers carrying their freight name across the States. Celeste had her divorce and her new marriage and respectability with her beloved Archie but not her son. It felt like they had long ago gone their separate ways, she sighed.

She was sad that Roddy had no wife, no stable relationship. It was business first and foremost, just like his father. Celeste shuddered. Would he repeat the old pattern and turn to alcohol for comfort?

Harriet had done her best to keep him on track but she was gone now. Roddy had hinted they should stay and perhaps settle over here one day, which was tempting but impractical. Archie was desperate to return home and she owed him that. Her heart ached to hold her son, to be as they once were, but there was no turning back from the paths they had chosen.

The threats of conflicts abroad were bringing opportunities for his business, with an untold wealth of contracts to supply. It was going to be a great opportunity for growth and expansion.

His head was elsewhere, full of new plans as they said their farewells at the airport before flying back to New York. Celeste clung onto him with tears knowing she must keep all her emotions within her. There was so much she could say about 'the love of money being the root of all evil' and a false master. But it was no time for a mother's preaching. She must let the boy follow his own path, make his own mistakes. But she was halfway across the world if he needed her, and that meant their meeting again was unlikely for a long time.

'I wish you'd stay,' he pleaded, knowing full well that was impossible. 'Give my regards to all the folks back home.'

The folks back home were virtually strangers to him now: Ella, Selwyn, Mrs Allen and Lichfield itself. Celeste smiled and nodded. 'I sure will,' she replied in her best American accent.

Her heart was bursting with misery. *Why must it always be like this? Because I left here to escape from a dead marriage and Roddy's paid the price. He was torn between the two of us. He's made his choice so don't look back. He'll be fine and I'll manage . . . I always have. My parents must have felt like this when I left home. Letting go is never easy but I must . . . and there's always the chance that one day he'll return. But it will be in his own good time not mine.*

100

New York, 1935

The service seemed to go on for ever as each one of the ordinands stood before a line of bishops in their gold vestments. Angelo couldn't help smiling; it was a theatrical performance better than any of little Patricia's dancing displays. The music, the chanting, the organ, the incense and all the pomp and ceremony on this most important of days was like one long procession of tableaux, a feast for the eyes.

He and Kathleen were lined up with the other proud parents, women dressed to the nines in lace veils and the men in Sunday suits. How come all his kids liked to be the centre of some drama, he mused. Why couldn't they be ordinary guys like Salvi's boys, married with kids racing round their feet? Here was Frank, giving his life to his Church, lying prostrate before the altar with arms outstretched in total submission. For a second Angelo felt a stab of fear for his son and, if he were honest, a real sadness. There would be no wife or children for him. As America had taken Angelo from his family so the Church was taking his son, and he ached to understand why this sacrifice was so important. While Kathleen was bursting with pride, he felt only bereft.

Next to him stood Patti, at fifteen already a beauty, her life a procession of auditions, dance classes, appearances on the back row of some off-Broadway show, waiting for her big moment to arrive. She too had never wavered from her ambition. She could be in for a cruel disappointment ahead, he fretted.

Then there was Jacko, in and out of the State Penitentiary, always a worry, always in trouble, always promising to make amends, always being forgiven. His life was one trip to the courtroom or jailhouse, his parents never knowing where he'd end up next.

Kids were such a worry. What if Patti got in with the wrong crowd? What if Jacko went too far? At least Frankie was safe enough in the arms of the Church.

And now there was the Italian business. Mussolini had annexed Abyssinia and was making friends with Hitler. Angelo had seen enough of the changes to his old country to be fearful. He recalled Maria's father's words about the Blackshirts marching in the streets. There was talk of taking sides. What then?

He'd been spared to see his kids grow up but not to start fighting in wars, not after the last show. How could his own family ever be 'the enemy'? It was making his head spin as well as his legs ache from standing so long.

He looked at his pocket watch with relief. It would be over soon and there would be something to eat and drink, he prayed. Churches made him nervous, made him think of all the 'what ifs' and his mortal soul. Thank God, prohibition was long gone. On a day like this a man needed fortification.

101

1937

Ella entered the exhibition hall, trying not to shake, trying not to look at the corner where her work was being displayed in case there was no one there. She'd wanted to come alone, to get used to these strange surroundings before Archie and Celeste arrived with their friends to give her support.

If only someone had told her how terrifying it was to exhibit artwork in public. She'd been all over Europe staring at paintings and statues, examining student work as if there was nothing to it. Now she felt the humiliation of her work set up alongside others, ceramics of great delicacy and imagination, figurative metal sculptures, all twisted shapes and angles, and wonderful landscapes and portraits on the walls.

This was a Coronation year exhibition of the work of young Midland artists, a showcase for new talent, and some pieces were for sale. None of them could make a living from it, but to sell a piece, and the chance to be reviewed in the *Birmingham Post*, was a milestone on the path to public recognition.

She'd agonized for hours over what to put into it, borrowing back a bust of a child she'd done for one of the clergymen, a classical study of a hand and a new piece she'd been working on inspired by her recent study of churches in Venice and Florence.

She had been so taken with the Madonna and child images

in the Uffizi, especially the *Madonna of the Long Neck* by Parmigianino. She'd photographed the most famous ones and captured pictures of mothers and children at play in the streets.

It was from one of these snapshots on her return that she found her inspiration: a mother sitting open-legged, cradling a sleeping child on her folded skirt. There was something relaxed and yet poignant about how the shape echoed the future pietà of Christ in death in his mother's arms. She sensed the pride and sadness of motherhood, knowing it was tapping into her own unresolved conflict with the past. Somehow in creating these figures with affection, something new and more vibrant had come out in her work.

Now she was walking round, her hand gripping her wine glass, hoping it wasn't a mistake to have exposed her work alongside many famous artists. Still two hours to go before they could pack it all away into her borrowed van and disappear back to the comfort of Red House.

It was Selwyn who caught her arm from where she was lurking near the doorway trying to look casual. 'Well done, I see you've sold a piece already.'

'I have?' She tried to look unimpressed but he wasn't fooled. 'Stop hiding and come and see.'

To Ella's surprise there was a small crowd admiring her work. 'Here she is, the blushing wallflower.' Selwyn dragged her over to meet a tall man.

'This is Harold Ashley, our Head of Chambers in Temple Row. He's churchwarden of St James's and wants this or something like this for their Lady Chapel. I'll leave you two to talk terms,' he said, shooting away, leaving her stranded.

'You take commissions?' Mr Ashley asked, looking down at the little piece. 'She's lovely, tender and full of meaning. We would need one slightly bigger. I want to donate it in memory of my mother.'

'Thank you,' she croaked. 'I'm glad you like it.'

Then she noticed there was a sticker on the sculpted hand too. What was happening? Perhaps she had some talent after all. This called for a celebration. She made for the table and for another glass of wine. Two sales and a commission in one night, wow! Could this mean that her career was taking off at last?

102

How had it come to this? Celeste mused, trying to absorb all the latest air-raid rules and regulations. Many of Ella's students were disappearing into the forces and now there was talk of rationing and petrol coupons and restriction to supplies should war come. It was all very worrying. Would her art college close? Would her private clients dry up? How was she going to earn a living?

The billeting officer had already been round to inspect Red House with a view to placing evacuees or air force officers with them. The thought of having to share the family home with strangers was another disturbance. War. No one could talk about anything else. Lichfield had always been a military hub with its barracks and now a new airfield being built behind them at Fradley. The city was right in the middle of the great crossroads of the A38 and the A5, with convoys and equipment passing through at all hours. How could they have come to war again?

Archie knew teachers and students who were caught up in the Spanish Civil War, dying of wounds; all that talent coming to nothing in that terrible maelstrom. How many more young men would give their lives before this madness ended?

Suddenly old soldiers were digging out their uniforms. Selwyn signed up with the Territorials and Archie with the Royal Naval Volunteer Reserve, on standby to cover for regular soldiers. Their peaceful world was about to be turned upside down. All the women would be expected to make a contribution. Ella would have to enlist or find another way to serve, something that kept her in touch with her beloved career. It would be a pity for all her good work to dwindle into nothing.

They were taking the ancient stained-glass windows out of the cathedral. Artwork was disappearing from museums and galleries, parks and gardens being dug up for vegetable cultivation. It felt as if the whole country was going on hold and no one knew for how long.

Celeste heard the drone of aeroplanes circling over the city and shuddered at the thought of enemy aircraft destroying this beautiful place. It just couldn't be happening all over again, not within memory of the slaughter of the last war.

They were now living in one of the school cottages close to Stafford, where Archie was teaching classics. It was good to be alone, free from responsibility, and yet Ella had been such a presence in Celeste's life. They'd steered Ella through those hard stormy years after Celeste had revealed the truth about her parentage.

It had haunted them, becoming an obsession for a while, searching for facts about *Titanic* passengers as if finding her parents was their duty. Ella thought otherwise, calmly refusing to follow up any of their leads. Archie had read everything he could about the disaster, especially Lawrence Beesley's account, and they watched a dreadful film in the Palladium Picture house, which Celeste had had to leave when it came to the sinking. There *must* be other documents. She almost asked the *Titanic* Relief Fund but that would mean revealing May's deception, branding them both as fraudsters. She couldn't risk such scrutiny.

Selwyn advised her to leave well alone. 'It's up to Ella to sort this out when she's ready.' All there was to prove her identity was the little suitcase in which her baby clothes were pressed flat, a hand-stitched nightdress with the lace border upon it and the one shoe with its leather sole and upper made of lace over cotton. Celeste often fingered them as if one day they would reveal some hidden message to her. They were simple garments that could have come from anywhere in Europe and yet the lace border was so delicate and intricate. Whose hands had created them? Celeste closed the suitcase with a sigh, putting it back in the airing cupboard.

If only Ella could find some distractions other than work. She'd been bridesmaid to Hazel, who was now expecting a baby. Her husband had been stationed abroad. Hazel was her one true friend. If only she mixed with the young fry of Lichfield society. Her only follower was the faithful mongrel they'd rescued when she was found by the kerb, run over on the busy Burton Road, and that Ella had nursed back to health. Poppy gave Ella such companionship, guarding the studio door as she worked. Ella was totally wrapped up in her work and sometimes when Celeste called to chat, it was as if she was yet another interference.

There was one place where they both still gathered and that was in front of May's favourite statue. Poor Captain Smith stood hidden from view behind a screen of shrubs and overgrown greenery in Museum Gardens. No one had followed up her request to the Council for it to be cleaned up. They made it a pact every year on 15 April to go to his statue and place flowers on the plinth. It was a habit that was ingrained from Ella's childhood with May.

'Did he really pluck me out of the sea, or is that another lie?' she had once asked Celeste.

'I'm sure he did, though I didn't actually witness it.' How could she not answer truthfully, especially now that most of that night's events were a blur.

The captain's reputation had suffered over the years and he was at best forgotten, at worst reviled, blamed for the accident. Celeste often wondered about his own family and the daughter who'd had to unveil the statue all those years ago. How had her life turned out under such a cloud?

If war did its worst, damaging buildings and churches, there would be plenty of need for carvers and stonemasons and craftsmen to repair the stone. Perhaps Ella should offer her services there, use her own skills to mend what was broken.

There you go again, planning her life for her, just like a mother, Celeste thought. She's a big girl now, independent of all of us. Let her make her own way. Don't interfere. You've done your duty by May. Let it rest.

But how could anyone not worry for the youngsters with war on the horizon? At least Roddy was safely out of all of this in America.

103

October 1940

One morning in October Ella was chasing Poppy across the fields at the back of Red House when she heard the whirring of a small aeroplane coming in low with a cough and splutter. She watched it circling, aiming for the barely finished runway at Fradley, but it was losing height and clearly never going to make it.

'Poppy!' she shouted, ordering the dog back, but the mutt carried on blindly, scared by the noise.

Ella watched in horror as the plane prepared to land in an open field, sinking desperately and then skidding along in the wheat stubble, spinning before tipping on its side. With no time to think she raced across the field to help rescue the crew – that's if they had survived the terrible crash landing. There was smoke coming out of the fuselage and two men scrambled out, then dragged out a third out of the cockpit.

'Are you all right?' Ella shouted.

'Get out of the bloody way, it might go up,' yelled a voice from behind a leather helmet and goggles. They dragged her back away from the crash.

'You can use my telephone,' she offered, but they were still ignoring her.

'What did I just tell you? Get back! If this kite goes up we'll be toast,' yelled the man staring at her. 'Go on, shoo. Thanks for the offer, but we can hike back to the base over there.'

'Not with an injured man, you can't,' she snapped, looking at the navigator lying cut and dazed on the ground. It was her turn to give orders. 'I'll get Selwyn to give you a lift.'

'We've signalled ahead. They know where we are. The ambulance'll be here in jiffy thanks, Mrs . . . ?'

'*Miss* Smith,' she replied tartly. 'You were lucky to find flat ground and miss the canal.' She called out to Poppy but she didn't respond. 'Poppy! I'll have to go and find her. She's probably terrified.'

'Sorry for shouting,' the pilot replied. 'We'll help you. It's the least we can do. Where are we exactly?' He looked around, still in a daze.

'You're outside Lichfield,' she said, pointing to Fradley Airbase.

'Hell's bells, bit out of our way then. Engine cut out.'

'You were lucky . . . Poppy!' she yelled.

'No,' the other uninjured crewman smiled. 'Just another skilful manoeuvre from Tony here. Glad we found you, our rescuing angel!'

'I'm Miss Smith,' she repeated, distracted by no sign of the dog. 'Poppy, heel! Where are you?'

They found her minutes later, lying in the hedgerow, shaking, a piece of metal stuck in her leg. 'Oh, she's bleeding,' Ella cried as the pilot whipped off his silk scarf and fashioned a tourniquet around the leg.

'This is a job for the veterinary. I'm awfully sorry.' He picked the dog up, but then began to wobble himself. 'A bit shook up, head spinning like a bottle.' He promptly sat down and Ella lifted her dog from him gently. 'Don't move until the ambulance comes. I'll see to Poppy. She'll be fine.' She could already hear the bell of the vehicle as it raced up the farm track towards the stricken plane.

'What's up with Skipper?' said the second crewman.

'A bang on the head, I think,' Ella offered as they eyed her with interest.

'That guy's nuts enough without this. Trouble's brewing, we're off course, we've pranged a kite and we're out of leave. Trust Tony to lead us up the Swanee. How's your pooch?'

'Only a bit of metal, I hope. Must dash. Better luck next time,' she said, turning for home but pausing for one last glance at the scene.

'How'll he talk us out of this?' grumbled the navigator.

'If anyone can do it, Skipper will. He's a habit of landing on his feet and I'm not talking about the prang.' The man winked at her.

Ella rushed back, relieved that no one had been seriously injured. Now the most important thing was Poppy. She'd borrow the Austin and get her seen to in Lichfield.

Later, when she returned, there was a beautiful bunch of flowers in a vase in the hall.

'Some air force chappie left these for Poppy and a message for you somewhere in the middle of them,' Selwyn laughed. 'Watch out, I think you made a conquest.'

'Hardly. What did he look like?' She was curious though. Which one was it and how had he had managed to produce such lovely flowers when there was a war on?

The pilot arrived hours later, parking a little Morris tourer in the driveway. 'Pilot Officer Harcourt reporting for duty with a jalopy, only borrowed, I'm afraid,' he said, standing in the doorway with a grin a mile wide. Selwyn ushered him inside. 'How's the poor dog?'

'Limping, but she'll live,' Ella replied, glancing up at the stranger with surprise. He was as fair as she was dark, with a forelock of straw hair, and not what she was expecting behind the goggles. His cut-glass accent spoke of public school and privilege. Selwyn was clearly about to give him a grilling.

'How on earth did you manage to be off course, young man?'

The pilot pushed his hands through his hair and smiled. 'Bit of a long story, sir. Spot of mist over the Trent Valley and a navigator who needs better glasses and a refresher course. Lucky for us Lichfield aerodrome was on the map, though not fully operational yet. A bit of a dressing down at HQ is on the cards.'

Anthony Harcourt gave Selwyn a potted history of his own training from air cadet through flying school into Bomber Command. Now he was in an operational training unit forty miles east, preparing a crew for further missions. He'd come from the Yorkshire Wolds but his accent didn't. He kept glancing over to Ella and round the drawing room as if to find some common ground.

'I know it's an awful cheek but would you care to join me for dinner tonight? Might as well take in a bit of the local scenery while I'm here.'

'I've been called many things but not scenery before,' Ella laughed, wanting to cut this bumptious young man down to size. He must be younger than she was by a good few years.

'No, what I meant was, I've booked a table at the George.' Then he looked up at Selwyn. 'I'll make sure your daughter's back by lights out.'

'Miss Smith is not my daughter. She is quite capable of deciding when to turn in for the night. Don't you think you should ask her name before you whisk her off in your chariot?' Selwyn was trying and failing to keep a straight face.

'Oh Lord, I've made a hash of things again, haven't I, Miss Smith?' He had the grace to blush.

'Call me Ella,' she smiled, holding out her hand. 'I'd be delighted to join you,' she found herself replying, much to her own surprise. 'If only because it's fish pie tonight and I loathe it. Give me five minutes to change from my work clothes.' She pointed to her plastered smock.

'Ella is an artist. She's not normally so grubby but she's

working on something out in the studio. So what did you do before the war?' Selwyn continued his interrogation.

Ella smiled and raced upstairs. What could she wear? There was her church suit and her skirt and blouse. Her best frock was too chilly. Nothing seemed good enough. She wished she was in uniform to match his. There must be something at the back of her wardrobe. Everything was pretty drab. But when she opened the door, she smelled the camphor balls. No amount of her best perfume could mask that odour. If only she'd had warning to find a suitable dress. Then she found a peasant blouse, long-sleeved, embroidered on the collar and cuffs, something she'd picked up in Italy on her travels. It would dress up fine with her pleated skirt and jacket.

She tossed her hair out of the bun, tied it with a scarf to soften the effect, pinched her cheeks and put on her precious lipstick with care. Why were her hands shaking? Why was she so keen to make a good impression? Why had the sight of this handsome man suddenly made her nervous?

The day had begun so normally. She'd done her chores, been to her studio and walked the dog. And then suddenly out of the sky this young man had descended at her feet. How strange that he should just turn up expecting her to drop everything to amuse him for the evening. Yet she was doing just that.

How unlike her to dress up as if this was the most important night of her life when all they were doing was passing time until he went back to his base and out of her life.

When she glided downstairs, they were nowhere to be found until she saw Selwyn escorting Anthony out of her studio in the back garden. The place was a tip and she didn't like strangers visiting, but this was Selwyn up to his old tricks again, trying to ensure she was not to be toyed with by showing her escort her profession and its tools. No liberties should be taken with a woman who could wield a hammer and chisel with such deadly accuracy.

Anthony stared at her. 'You look lovely, and that bust in your studio, it ought to be in a gallery.'

'I'm still working on that. So what did you do before all this started?'

'University, Cambridge, Trinity College, I enlisted straightaway. You'd like to see the stuff we have at home. My father is a bit of a collector. Music's more my thing ... classical, jazz ...' He looked at his wristwatch. 'Better be off. I will take care of her, Mr Smith.'

'I'm Selwyn Forester. As I said, Ella is no relation to me, unfortunately, but that doesn't stop me vetting her guests,' he laughed. 'Have a good evening and don't worry about me eating Mrs Allen's fish pie, dear. Waste not want not. It can always be reheated for you tomorrow,' he called with relish from the porch.

They were shown to a table in the corner of the old coaching hotel's restaurant. The menu was restricted to two courses. Anthony ordered wine and offered her smokes from a gold cigarette case. 'This was my grandfather's, a bit of a talisman of mine.'

She declined; smoking held no appeal to her. *What am I doing here?* This was a big mistake. They'd nothing in common. He was still a boy, at least five years younger than she was, and yet she felt like a schoolgirl on her first day, nervous, edgy. What on earth were they going to talk about?

'Tell me about yourself,' she began, hoping to draw him out.

'Not a lot to say about Anthony Giles Claremont Harcourt,' he paused. 'I know, quite a moniker, isn't it? My parents live in an old pile of stones near Thirsk. I'm an only child and I'm adopted so I'm not sure who I am or where I came from.' He looked up, expecting her to take pity, but she shook her head in amazement.

'How strange, so am I. Well, sort of,' she replied, and for the first time she voiced aloud some of her own strange history, about May's voyage on the *Titanic* and her friendship with Celeste, leaving out the fact that no one knew who she really was.

'Why am I telling you all this?' she gasped, looking into those bright grey-green eyes. Funny how she wanted to cry as those words burst out of her.

'You know why,' he smiled, reaching out his hand. 'Because you have to. We're two of a kind. Why of all the fields in England should I have landed on yours? Why were you walking the dog just at the moment my plane conked out? Why do we share such a similar history? I've never asked about my parents. I could find out but I won't. Sybil and Tom are the only folks I know and I love them. I don't need to know anything else, but your story is different. A *Titanic* survivor – I've met one or two older ones. The son of our neighbour went down on that ship, their only son and heir.'

'You're the first person outside my family I've ever told. I don't understand,' she said, and she felt her face flushing.

'Look at me. Don't you feel this was all meant to be?'

'That's cheap novelette stuff. I don't believe in such silliness.' This was getting too personal, too serious, and yet she didn't want to pull her hand away from his.

Anthony was not fazed by her resistance. 'If war teaches us anything it's to seize the moment. I've seen too many good chaps buy it in training without ever really having a life. You grow up quickly in war. I take each day as it comes and today something extraordinary happened. My engine cut out on a routine flight. It could've been curtains for us but up pops a pancake of a field and I managed to save the show. Then, you appear looking like something straight off the silver screen from the Gainsborough Picture Company. We were meant to meet. It's in the stars. I'm Pisces, by the way, a water sign, or so they tell me.'

Somehow the tension between them eased as they lingered over dinner talking equally about her passions and his career.

They talked of the restrictions of the war, their hopes for the future, their families. She'd never talked so openly with a man before. Anthony might only be twenty-three but there was in him a weary look that aged him. Beside him she felt younger, untested, innocent and ashamed to have thought him shallow and brash. It was his defence against all that he was preparing for.

'Do you have to rush off tomorrow?' she asked.

'As long as we're back by 1600 hours, why?' he asked.

'I'd like to show you our cathedral. The services have choral singing and you could join us for lunch. I promise it won't be fish pie,' she giggled. 'You may never visit Lichfield again, after all.'

He stared back at her with a look that set her stomach in a spin. 'I'll be back. Don't play with me, Ella. Now I've found you, I'll not be so easy to shake off.'

They drove home under the full moonlit sky in silence. Ella sensed the tension in his hands and body as he kept glancing at her. She felt her heart thumping as if she were savouring every moment with him. The smell of leather upholstery and cigarette smoke mingled with her perfume and petrol fumes, a heady brew.

'Look, a bomber's moon,' he sighed, glancing up. 'Someone somewhere will be in trouble tonight.' He kissed her cheek and instinctively she offered her lips to him and was not disappointed. 'Good night, Anthony,' she whispered, tearing herself away, not sure if this was all a dream.

'Cinderella's pumpkin must be returned now, I'm afraid,' he shouted. 'It'll be Shanks's pony tomorrow.'

'Fine by me, we can walk across the fields into the city. Thanks for a lovely evening.' She was still standing there long after the roar of his engine had faded away, suddenly bereft by his absence. This was madness, a crazy *folie d'amour* but she'd never felt so alive, so wonderful in the presence of a man before. She wouldn't sleep. How could she waste such a feeling?

Shoving her nightdress into her dungarees and putting on a thick jumper, she took the hooded lantern down her path into her studio, drawing the blackout blinds. By the lamplight she began to sketch, capturing every feature of Anthony's handsome face, the way one side was slightly lopsided, the curl of his forelock, those full lips which had brushed hers, still flushed with the memory of his kisses. What was happening? How could one day change a whole life? But it had, and hers was never going to be the same again.

104

Celeste couldn't believe the transformation in Ella over the past weeks. It was as if she was walking with spring coils in her shoes. When she introduced her new beau one afternoon, Celeste saw that wondrous look of love in her eyes. He'd snatched a forty-eight-hour pass, roaring across the county on a borrowed motor bike to meet them, Ella clinging to the back, her dark hair stuffed into a black helmet.

Nothing could disguise the windswept glow of a couple in love. Ella's face was alive with excitement. It was as if this young man had turned her life upside down. Until then her only concern was war work and the row over women joining the Home Guard units. It was thought unseemly for women to pick up guns to defend their homes. Ella was furious so she had volunteered for fire watching duties. This meant she was alone in the dark on some rooftop all night, watching for incendiary bombs falling on factories and so dopey in the morning from lack of sleep. Now everything fitted around her time with Anthony. She would dash across to his base if there was a chance of some leave, and have to say farewell on draughty platforms, not knowing if she would ever see him again. How could two lovers survive in such a mad world? She was living for his letters, his precious leave, dreading news that he might be posted abroad. Only today Celeste had received a letter from her that changed everything.

★　　★　　★

Anthony's parents have welcomed me warmly. The house is overrun with evacuee children; he wasn't joking when he said Thorpe Cross was a pile of stones. There's a ruined abbey clinging to one side of the house. It is so cold at night I have to put on all my clothes at once before I dive onto the mattress.

Anthony is busy sawing logs with some of the bigger boys. They follow him round as if he was Biggles. I am giving some of the little ones rides on his old pony. The northern scenery is wonderful with stone walls and rolling hills in the distance, fields full of sheep and crops, and big skies but there's a bitter wind from the northeast.

The journey on the train was a nightmare, crushed in the corridor with a crowd of noisy soldiers. When I got off at York, I thought I'd been deserted and two of my travellers waited just in case they might get lucky. What a relief to see Anthony ambling down the platform. He'd been waiting outside the First Class compartments, as if I can afford such luxury. We do come from different worlds and I know I'm older than he is, but when we meet it is as if none of that matters.

We met just six weeks ago, but I realize he's someone I could spend the rest of my life getting to know; all my old prejudice against romance has evaporated. He took me to a dance at his base and waltzed me round, not stepping on my toes once. That's a first. The band were playing such a lovely tune, '*J'attendrais*'. I will wait. It's continually in my head. But we can't wait. If only life were normal and things could go at a normal pace. What a pity it has taken a war to bring us together.

Yesterday we took a picnic to Brimham Rocks, scrambling up to sit and stare at the countryside, so green and peaceful as if nothing has changed. Anthony turned to me and said, 'We are going to get married soon, aren't we?' as if he was saying, 'Pass the sugar, darling.' I turned to him and said, 'Of course.'

Please don't tell Selwyn yet. Anthony thinks he should ask

him for my hand as if he were my father. I think he would be
touched by such a gesture, don't you? Please be happy for us.
We want to live each moment of time we have together, as
close as we can. The future is not ours to know.

I'm going to ask Selwyn if I can join the Home Guard. I
don't see why women can't take up arms if the invader comes.
Anthony has been giving me shooting practice and I hit the
target twice. I just want to do more than teaching, important as
that is. When I think how he faces danger every day, how can I
not want to match his effort in some way?

When Ella returned from her next visit to Thirsk wearing an
antique ruby ring mounted in gold, there was no holding her
back. She was full of plans. What could Celeste say? These two
hardly knew each other but who was she to argue with the look
of excitement on their faces? Theirs was a hungry romance,
formed of snatched weekends and they seized every moment to
be together. She wished them well.

'Anthony knows a little place we can go to in the country for
our honeymoon. You are pleased for us, aren't you?' Ella's eyes
were wide with pleading.

Archie sucked on his pipe, eyeing them both, smiling. 'When
you know, you know. I recall bumping into a little chap on the
deck of the *Saxonia* and seeing his mother and thinking, I'm
going to marry her one day. It took a little longer than I thought,
though.' Everyone laughed a little too loudly. 'Congratulations!'

Anthony was a charming young man and devilishly good-
looking but Ella could match him in looks and Celeste thought
how handsome their children would be. They were so sure of
themselves, so caught up in that first flush of passion. She felt
afraid as well as anxious. Love like that wouldn't last unless it
evolved and mellowed into a deep contented friendship. Archie
was her companion, her solace at the end of the day. She badly
wanted that for them too, but war was dangerous work and the

heavy losses in Bomber Command were no secret.

Celeste felt a shiver of fear. 'We'll have to get going, if you want a wedding trousseau.'

'I'll get some extra coupons but we don't need anything too fancy,' said Ella, brushing aside the idea of a traditional wedding.

'I'm not letting you go down the aisle splattered with plaster of Paris. Indulge me, let me help you make the day special. We'll go into Birmingham together and see what we can find.'

'It'll be chilly and a new suit will fit the bill. A Christmas wedding would be so romantic, but it all depends on Anthony's leave.'

'She's right. It'll have to be a short notice affair, I'm afraid,' he agreed. 'I just hope my parents can get down. The trains are so unreliable for civilians these days.'

Somehow Celeste knew these two would make it all happen for themselves one way or another. It was hard to think that there was a war raging when they sat by the fire sipping tea and eating seed cake as if they hadn't a care in the world. But Celeste knew things had not gone well for the British troops this year, not after Dunkirk. The skies had been won by the RAF but not swept clear of enemy planes enough to stop the terrible night raids on the cities. They had seen the orange firelight over Birmingham and Coventry. How could those two make such promises of hope at such a dangerous time? Their wedding must be a wonderful spark of brightness in a dark, dark world; a defiance against the odds.

Ella deserved true happiness. It'd been a long time coming.

If only Celeste knew the same was happening for Roddy. She'd written to him to let him know the news.

Ella is getting married to an airman. Hardly known the chap two minutes but people seem to be rushing headlong into marriage judging by the number of notices in *The Times*.

I think danger is a great aphrodisiac, it fans the flames of love. I do wish them well but I worry.

To be honest I'd always hoped you'd return and sweep her off her feet yourself. Mothers have their dreams. But you will find your own partner in life one day. At least there is no beating of war drums over there to hasten your nuptials.

The raids have been terrible in the Midlands, as you may have heard. We are only told what it is thought best for us to know, but we have ears and eyes, and people talk. Parts of Birmingham have been flattened – Manchester, Liverpool too – but so far no invasion barges have crashed onto our shores, nor will they, thanks to chaps like Anthony Harcourt and his courageous crew who brave the barrages of fire over the Low Countries to give them a taste of their own medicine.

You feel so far away from us now.

105

February 1941

We've got a whole weekend in the country, Ella sighed, looking at Anthony sleeping so peacefully. It was a glorious February morning, perfect for a honeymoon walk in the woods. She smiled to see the sun creeping up behind the bare trees. How he'd wangled the extra twenty-four hours she'd never know. It gave them until Sunday night before they must part, simply ages.

They'd driven down in Selwyn's Austin with petrol begged and borrowed, down the leafy lanes of Oxfordshire to a little village called Leafield, where Anthony had borrowed a cottage from a friend of a friend, someone he'd known at school.

The cottage was perfect with its thatched roof and sloping ceilings. Someone in the village had lit a fire and aired the rooms and filled the downstairs with hyacinth bowls to mask any dampness: such a welcome gesture.

'That'll be Simon's mother. She has a place somewhere in the village.'

'Then we must go and thank her,' said Ella, sniffing the spring bulbs.

'Later,' Anthony smiled. First things first, he said, leading her up the rickety stairs. 'Let's go and christen the bed.'

Ella lay back reliving the moment when they had come together without fear of interruption or discomfort, lying together, holding each other, sampling the wonder of making love to each other. Now the bedroom was their sanctuary and she tried not to think about when Anthony would get leave again. There was no holding back the passion felt between them as they explored each other's bodies, finding new ways to give and receive pleasure. Now sated and sleepy, she recalled every moment of their wedding, squeezed in just before the start of Lent. She'd felt like a princess arriving at the West Door in a pony and trap, wrapped in a white fox fur stole lent to her by the dean's wife. She'd heard the organ playing their entrance twice before she got down the long aisle to the Lady Chapel. She loved the 'Trumpet Voluntary'; it was so jolly and British and hopeful. Poor Anthony was standing stiff with nerves in his dress uniform while she grasped Selwyn's arm to steady her excitement. All the people she loved were present wishing them well. Hazel, as matron of honour, walked behind her in a long burgundy evening gown she'd borrowed from a friend. Ella hoped her mother was there in spirit watching this most special of days.

It was worth it all to see the look on Anthony's face, so proud, so loving. She couldn't have asked for a more perfect wedding with a simple reception back at Red House, a crush of uniforms, cigarette smoke, speeches and toasts.

Celeste had insisted she wore her own mother's wedding dress cut down and reshaped to fit her figure and the Brussels lace veil that went with it. Ella had splashed out on a pretty suit and coat with new shoes to see her through the honeymoon and beyond. Mrs Allen had made her a slip and pants in the prettiest dyed parachute silk the colour of faded tea roses and edged with cream lace. She'd wanted to weep with gratitude at the gifts showered on them at such short notice. There was even a parcel of goodies from Roddy, including a saucepan to replace the ones they had given away for the Spitfire Fund in the first flush of patriotism, earlier in the year.

She'd have to stay on at Red House. The school were too short staffed to lose her just because she wore a wedding ring. Anthony's parents insisted she go and live with them but it was too far north from his base. She wanted to be as close as possible, and Lichfield was so central.

Every moment together must last an hour, time must be stretched out like elastic. Love in wartime was so unpredictable, so intense. For these precious hours there were no rules, no rationing; they owned the world. Ella shivered at the thought of Anthony's return to base. They knew the risks but nothing was going to spoil this wonderful honeymoon.

They took a trip into Oxford to gaze at the golden colleges and dreaming spires. They strolled along the Cherwell and ate dinner in an old inn before going to the pictures.

The film showing was *The Lion Has Wings*, with Ralph Richardson and Merle Oberon. It wasn't the happiest of films with its bombings revealing the reality of Anthony's life. Ella, finding the film's storyline much too close to reality for comfort, wanted to rush out into the fresh air. She wished they'd made another choice but Anthony was happy picking holes in the script and its inaccuracies, unaware of her fears. Be brave, she braced herself. Stop wasting time on what you can't alter.

They took a walk to the Rollright stones, such a magical place to stand and make a wish. They gave her hope, standing weatherbeaten against the elements. This war was just, a fight against tyranny, and she too must do her bit to offer her services where they were most needed. Perhaps she could join up now?

On Sunday afternoon they made their way to a lovely thatched cottage called Pratts to say thank you to Simon's mother for the welcome. A young girl answered the door and welcomed them in. 'Mother's in the garden,' she said. 'But do come through.' Mrs Russell-Cooke, a statuesque woman, was busy pruning in the vegetable plot. She looked up. 'Ah hah, the lovebirds have left their nest at last.'

Ella blushed, 'We just wanted to thank you for the cottage.'

'Simon told us all about you, and Anthony here was always a bit of a hero of his at school. I'm glad you made good use of it,' she winked. 'Come inside and have a sherry.'

They were escorted into a drawing room, beautiful artwork adorning the walls. Ella's eyes roamed over them with interest. 'What a lovely room,' she said, pausing at a familiar face framed in silver on the windowledge. 'I know that face!' she exclaimed. 'That's Captain Smith.'

Mrs Russell-Cooke nodded, surprised. 'Well spotted, young lady. He was my father.'

'You are Helen Smith? It was you who unveiled his statue in Lichfield?'

'Yes, but I generally use my middle name, Mel. How strange, you look far too young to have known him.'

'My mother worshipped him. I only knew his statue, the one by Kathleen Scott. I was just a baby but I was there at the unveiling in Lichfield.'

Mrs Russell-Cooke lifted the picture with a sigh. 'Yes, frightful business all round. I was too young to know about all the furore but my mother was very upset, as you can imagine. She never got over the slur on his reputation.'

Ella sat down, winded by the coincidence. 'I can't believe this. Did you know that your father saved my life? He put me in a lifeboat. I was just a baby. This is so strange. My mother was always convinced he was my rescuer.'

'Good Lord! I'd heard something like that had happened. There were rumours about a rescue story, but no one ever came forward as an official witness. Perhaps your mother could?' Mel Russell-Cooke looked up in hope.

Ella shook her head. 'Sadly she passed away a long time ago, but she was very angry at his treatment. It troubled her greatly that his statue was neglected.'

'Me too ...' Mrs Russell-Cooke paused. 'I'd have preferred

he should be looking out to sea at Blundell Sands near Liverpool, not landlocked in Lichfield, but I'm so glad someone cared for him there.'

'To meet the captain's daughter . . . I just can't believe it.'

'I think this calls for something stronger than sherry,' said the hostess. 'You've given me such comfort. What a coincidence, though I don't believe in coincidences. Perhaps this meeting was meant to be. My twins, Simon and Priscilla, were young when they lost their own father and I lost my mother the same year.' Ella watched Priscilla standing by the window looking at the photograph with fresh eyes, listening intently to this revelation.

'My father was always for the sea, but it was such fun when he returned home, laden with presents. Then he left one morning and never came back. Now, with a war on, we parents worry about our children. Mine have been such a gift and a consolation. Tell me more about your mother and the statue. It's absolutely intriguing.'

Ella didn't know where to begin. 'We visited him on the anniversary of the sinking every year. My mother lost her husband on the *Titanic* and returned to England. As for me, I spent so much time around statues and stone, living near the cathedral, that it gave me a love of sculpture. I want to make it my career.'

'Believe me, dear,' Mrs Russell-Cooke sighed, 'by the time this war is over, there'll be plenty of call for your services. We'll need monuments and plaques. I'm sorry,' she apologized. 'No morbid talk on your honeymoon. I wish you both all the joy in the world. You brave young things. Now I've met one of the youngest *Titanic* survivors. I keep meeting up with people from time to time. No one wants to talk much about their experiences of the sinking, and you won't even recall yours, being only a baby. But I feel you've given me a gift. How wonderful, I gave you a roof over your heads and you have repaid me tenfold. Thank you, and please call again. Do keep in touch. In fact, I know many sculptors of note. They may be helpful to you.'

'Sadly we must be going back tonight,' Anthony chipped in.

'If you meet up with Simon, keep an eye out for him,' said Mrs Russell-Cooke, holding out a firm hand and staring hard at him. 'He's the only son I've got and he's so very young.'

'I'll do my best,' Anthony replied. 'Come on, time to go and pack. And thank you again.'

Mother and daughter waved them off down the lane and Ella, still spinning from this unexpected encounter, clung onto Anthony's arm. 'I can't believe I've just met Captain Smith's daughter. How very strange.'

Ella couldn't get the coincidence out of her mind as they lay in the darkness that night, back at Red House. 'There's something else I never told you, darling, about that night on the *Titanic*,' she whispered. 'I didn't tell the captain's daughter the whole story this afternoon.'

'Hmm ... Go on, what dark secrets have you been keeping for all these years in the depths of that magnificent bosom of yours?' he asked.

Where should she begin? It was time to take in a deep breath before she revealed to her new husband what really happened on the lifeboat.

'After my mother died, Celeste told me ...'

She repeated everything she'd been told. 'So you see,' she finished, 'I really don't know who I am ... Anthony, what do you think?' She turned, waiting for his response but there was only the steady breathing of a man dead to the world.

106

December 1941

News of the attack on Pearl Harbor came to Roddy as it did to millions of other Americans on that Sunday afternoon in December. He was listening to a band show on the radio when suddenly a voice interrupted the music: 'We're getting reports that our fleet is being attacked by the Japanese. Ships are blazing.' He couldn't believe what he was hearing and hurriedly tuned to a news station. 'Planes have been hit on the ground ...' He kept switching channels, unable to take on board the full impact of this terrible news. 'Troops were machine-gunned as they ran for cover ...' The images burning in his head were too awful to contemplate. A few minutes ago there was peace. Now there was going to be war.

The phone rang, startling him. It was Will Morgan. 'Yes, yes, I heard it too. I'll meet you at the depot, I'm on my way.'

As he drove down into town still with his Sunday suit on, folk were clustered on the corners talking, neighbours standing in their yards stunned, looking to each other to confirm the news they'd been dreading. Roddy suddenly felt utterly alone. There was no one in his life to share this shock with, no Grandma, no Archie or Mom. No one but Will in the office.

He felt such rage about this invasion, such fury, utter disbelief that a nation could be so arrogant as to think it could attack another without impunity. It was Hitler's *blitzkrieg* all over again but this time it was on his doorstep. There was only one course of action for a decent man without ties.

'I'm going to enlist,' Roddy said, barging through the office door where Will was standing, surveying the maps on the wall. 'You can run things from here blindfold. It doesn't take the two of us.'

'But you're too old,' laughed Will. 'There's so much work for us. Besides, younger drivers will be enlisting so we'll need every able guy on the block to keep the trucks on the road. Here, have a drink and calm down,' he said, shoving a glass of Jack Daniel's in Roddy's hand.

'So we'll do what they did in the last war and draft in the women,' Roddy replied, thinking back to when his mother had worked for government in Washington.

'The drivers won't stand for that,' said Will, seating himself down on the desk.

'Reckon so? You wait, it'll be law in no time. I'm not too old to do my duty. One of us has to go and it makes sense if it's me. You're married with kids.'

'How come you've changed your tune? I've never reckoned on you becoming a soldier.'

Roddy sat down in the chair looking out of the window onto the truck yard, shaking his head as he thought of Uncle Selwyn's medals. 'My uncles were in the Great War, one was killed at the Somme and the other badly wounded.'

'But they were English. They had to fight.'

'You forget I'm half English. No one likes bullyboys taking over the show. It feels the right thing to do,' Roddy argued.

'And all the girls love a guy in uniform,' Will added with a wink.

Roddy ignored his partner's attempt to lighten the moment. 'It's not that. I can't believe what I just heard. I can't just sit here and let some guys pound us to pieces.' He flicked open the order book before shoving it across the desk. 'You can manage. I trust you. Maureen would never forgive me if I let you go off to war.'

'There'll be plenty of war work in Akron. You don't have to go seeking glory. We can guess how it will affect the business. It needs two heads.' Will shook his with a sigh.

'As I said, bring in the women. They'll want to do their bit too. I've made up my mind.' He stood up as if to leave.

'After just an hour listening to the news? Better to sleep on it. Have another drink.'

'No thanks, I don't need to sleep on this one. My mom and Archie and the folks in England have been going through hell these past years while we've had it soft. I've felt ashamed earning all this dough, and sending a few parcels isn't enough. We're all in it now. It's time I got off my ass and signed up before they put me out to grass. I've had it too easy.'

'I've never seen you so fired up. What's got into you?' Will looked puzzled, as if he'd seen a new side to Roddy.

'Pearl Harbor, that's what.' Roddy was on fire with indignation at what was happening. 'No one does that to us without getting the same back and more. I don't want a ringside seat in this. Those Japs don't know what they've just gone and done. We'll show them we're no sitting ducks.'

In the weeks that followed Roddy never doubted his decision. He enlisted at the recruiting office, was subjected to a medical, had his head shaved and pounded the barrack yard, sweating through long runs and aptitude tests. It was like boarding school all over again but this time there was a purpose. He never wavered from his decision to enlist just as his uncles had done all those years ago. It felt almost his family duty to get those Japs for the carnage and havoc they'd wreaked in the Philippines and Hawaii. So many innocent civilians had been lost in the bombings. It was as if he must sort them out personally. But it was a blow when they kitted him out in standard issue rather than tropical gear. He was embarking for Europe, not the Pacific. He would have to take his vengeance out on Hitler and his storm troopers. That was not in his plan at all and yet he felt guilty at the pleasurable thought that he might just see his family once more if he landed in England.

107

Father Frank Bartolini sat at his desk, staring out over the Harvard courtyard, listening to the lecturer drumming into them the important role of the Chaplains Corps in front line battle. They must be all things to all men and never let them down. They were God's representatives, a symbol of His loving care, always ready to counsel, pray, give comfort, console and rescue the wounded and dying, no matter the cost to themselves.

Frank had been given permission to leave St Rocco's Church, New Jersey to join the teams of chaplains of all denominations responding to the call to arms.

He'd been ordained for over six years now, working with the Italian immigrant community on Hunterton Street in a beautiful Italianate basilica-style church. It was the dream project of Father Umberto Donati who'd wanted to reproduce the church in his home town in Northern Italy.

Now, Frank was a second lieutenant who must take orders from the military. They were studying martial law, military customs and the discipline of army life, learning how to use equipment and work in close operation with other chaplains. They were treated as one group who must be willing to learn each other's liturgy and customs, even conducting services should it be necessary. He must learn the Seder service for the Jews and in turn they must learn the rosary and hear confessions.

The thought of being a universal minister taking care of the religious needs of men of all faiths was daunting as well as challenging. On top of this the chaplains were expected to drill themselves to physical fitness. As one of the younger priests he didn't find this such a problem but for some of the more mature men the hikes, physical jerks and route marches had taken their toll.

Now Frank was waiting for his placement, wondering where he would be sent. Like many others he'd listened to the radio broadcast on that fateful Sunday in December and wondered if he should volunteer. He asked Father Donati and he'd no hesitation in encouraging him to enlist.

'You go, son. We must fill our quota of priests. There are no atheists in foxholes and there's a job to be done. Those young men will need you by their side to teach them how to pray.'

Frankie felt proud of his uniform with the Cross insignia on its collar. His parents had bought him a purple silk stole, which he could fold up to use in field services. He was glad so many priests had volunteered, so many of them of Italian extraction like him. He still couldn't believe how Italy had been seduced into this war at Hitler's side. He no longer felt any connection to the old country, not like his papa, but his name was distinctive and he felt he must work extra hard to prove his loyalty.

Training was intense and many times he wondered if he would be up to the job when the moment came. Would he show a cool temperament when faced with shelling on the front line, or worse? How would he cope with the sight of terrible injuries, even though they'd prepared them with photographs of what to expect? Would the men respect him?

Frank knew he was no tough nut, not like his brother, Jackie. He would be unarmed, unproven, but the lecturer had said, 'Courage is only fear that has said its prayers. You must draw on your own faith to carry you through.' He only hoped that was true.

What he was dreading most was going to sea in one of the big troopships. His sea legs were hopeless. He felt sick even on a boat on a lake. How would his men feel seeing the priest with his head stuck in a bucket for the entire voyage across the Atlantic? He'd be a laughing stock before they even started.

On his embarkation leave he'd returned back home for a farewell meal with his family. He had devoured all his favourites dishes, *arrabiata*, dark and succulent, and a special cheesecake from Bellini's bakery. He'd sat at the table trying to capture every second of it in his mind. You'll have to feed off this in the months to come, he'd mused, as Patti chattered on and Mum smiled, pushing back the straggles of hair from her brow, while Jack glanced at his expensive wristwatch, anxious to be off to his haunts in the city.

His family were his rock, his flesh and blood, warts and all, as one of his new Protestant colleagues was always saying. He was going to miss their down-to-earth ways. He would have to work alongside men like Jack, tough, questioning, rough men, who thought priests a waste of space.

It was only when he was leaving that his papa shoved something into his hand for safekeeping. It was soft and oddly familiar. 'I want you to take this, Frankie, a keepsake from your papa. We're so proud of you.'

He looked down at the tiny shoe. 'I don't understand,' he said, wondering what this token was doing in his hand.

'I used to think it was my baby girl's shoe. Crazy, I know, but in my heart she never died. Whoever's shoe it was, son, it came from the *Titanic*. It survived that terrible disaster. I want you to keep it on you for good luck.'

'But that's just superstition,' he said, shaking his head, but his father once again pressed it on him.

'This little shoe stands for hope and love and survival against the odds. Plus, it's a small reminder of home, of your mamma and your papa, and all of us waiting here for your return. Please take it.'

What could Frankie do but agree and hold his father tight, slipping the package into his pocket. 'Perhaps it'll stop me being seasick,' he joked, trying to lighten the mood of the parting. 'Pray for me.'

'Every night,' Mamma croaked through her tears, her hands shaking as she picked up his plate. 'Take care, son, and Godspeed.'

Angelo watched his son leave trying not to give in to tears. He was so proud of both his sons: both enlisting, one in the infantry and one a front line padre. No one could say the Bartolinis were not patriots. He still couldn't believe his family back in Italy were now officially the enemy. There wasn't a mean bone in his father's body. But in their letters he sensed fear, confusion, silence and suspicion. He hadn't crossed the ocean and left his family to make enemies of them. He'd tried once to enlist, during the last war, but now he was too old, too weak in the chest, to do much but pray for their safety. Besides, someone had to guard the family honour. Patti was in danger of forgetting her Italian roots. She'd even changed her stage name to Patti Barr.

'What is wrong with Patricia Bartolini?' he'd demanded when he discovered this name on a theatre programme.

'It's too long. I need something modern, something short and snappy,' she'd argued, tossing her flame-red hair as if to remind him she was half Irish too. Children these days were showing less respect. He would never have dared cheek his father but one look from those green eyes and he was putty in her hands.

Besides, she had him over a barrel. 'I am doing a first-aid course,' she'd also announced. 'I might want to join up as a nurse.'

'Two sons in the army is enough for any family. There's no way I'll let all my children out of my sight,' he thundered.

'For once your papa is right. Hold your horses. Revues give everyone relief from their worries. Entertaining is just another form of service, after all,' Kathleen added, also petrified of losing her daughter to the battlefields. 'We want to see your name in lights one day.'

The dear woman knew just how to handle his daughter. He wondered how Maria would have coped with Alessia. She would be married by now in that life that never happened. This was real life, though, and he would concentrate on the family that needed him.

He felt foolish for giving Frankie the shoe, but for some reason it felt important. He would've given Jackie his watch if he didn't fear it would get thrown onto some poker table. What a world they lived in ... He sighed. And all he could do was sit on the sidelines and watch his precious children slug it out on the world stage.

108

It was turning out to be a hard labour. Ella felt she'd been trying to squeeze out her baby for days, not hours. It was snowing hard outside and getting dark. The midwife had called, gone, and called back hoping things were moving along apace. She examined Ella again and smiled.

'This little one is just too lazy and cosy in its nest to want to come into such a wintry afternoon, but there's no turning back now. You're fully dilated.'

Ella didn't want to know the details, she just wanted it over with. Anthony was flying somewhere over Germany, unaware that their baby was on its way. It had been the longest night of her life and yet, for all the pains, she was excited; a new life was coming with all the possibility it promised. She only wished her mother were here to share in the joy. May had been such a good mother, all the resentment and anger she'd once felt had long gone. If only she was by her side to guide her through the coming hours.

The nursery was already prepared. Celeste had returned to Red House, while Archie was on duty in Portsmouth. Selwyn was out guarding the railway lines from fifth columnists. Shortages were beginning to take their toll in shop windows. Cardboard cut-outs filled the empty spaces and knitting wool was scarce, as were cosmetics. Everyone was being extra careful to make their soap, their foodstuffs last, while trying to look bright and cheerful to keep up morale.

After several more hours, the midwife put her cone on Ella's stomach. 'I'm going to have to call the doctor if you don't get going.'

'Lying here doesn't help. Let me walk about for a bit,' Ella said, feeling trapped lying in bed waiting for each pain.

'That's not allowed. Mother should be on her side by now,' Nurse Taylor insisted.

'Then bring me an old birthing stool. They had the right idea in the olden days. If I walk about it might help things along.' She made for the rug, pacing the floor, willing the baby inside her to push its way down. 'Come on, come on!'

It was slow, agonizing, but in the end gravity did its work and the baby slid out purple, yelling and plump as a capon.

'It's a girl!' said the midwife, holding her up by her feet.

'Oh,' Ella gasped, a little shocked. 'I was sure it would be another Anthony. I never expected a little girl,' she smiled, examining her baby with care.

'Just you be thankful that she's a perfect specimen. You could always call her Antonia,' came the no-nonsense reply as the nurse bustled around her bed.

Ella sighed at the sight of this tiny mite with her mop of black hair and the darkest of blue eyes blinking up at her. A flood of love washed over her as she held her new daughter.

Celeste was allowed in to admire their new addition and Mrs Allen brought a knitted layette made from unravelled lambswool the colour of weak tea.

'I know it's a funny colour, but that's rationing for you. At least it'll be very warm. You must be so proud, Mrs Harcourt. Your mother would have loved to see her.'

Ella looked down at the infant nuzzling her breast, feeling confused by the flood of emotions rushing through her. Was this how my own mother felt, whoever she was; this overwhelming feeling of love and gratitude, pride and fear?

Later, Selwyn came in. 'Well done, old girl.' He seemed

pleased to see that the baby had finally arrived but gave her only a cursory glance, distracted by the latest wireless bulletin. 'I've just heard more news,' he muttered to Celeste, who was warming nappies by the fire rail in the bedroom. 'The American fleet has been attacked in Pearl Harbor by the Japanese. They're in the war now.'

Ella was too tired and sleepy for this terrible news. She sighed, shutting her eyes. 'No one will ever forget the date of your birthday, little one, but I'm not calling you Pearl. That's just too sad. We must send a telegram to your daddy and let him choose your name.'

And so Clare Antonia Mary was baptized on Christmas Eve in the cathedral wrapped in the lacy nightdress and bonnet from her mother's suitcase and a huge shawl; the very lace bonnet that had seen Ella onto the *Titanic*. Anthony was given short leave from his station in Lincolnshire. Celeste and Hazel acted as godmothers, with Selwyn as godfather. It was a chill biting winter, but nothing could dampen their spirits, even the letter from Roddy saying he'd enlisted and was in some military fort miles from anywhere.

They'd wired him news of Clare's arrival and he'd sent a pretty dress in a parcel marked as 'tinned goods', which somehow managed to get across the Atlantic and dodge the U-boats. The dress was much too big for her but at a time of rations and coupons it was precious.

Ella wept when Anthony's leave was over and he was due back to his station in Bomber Command. It was dangerous work and he was looking fatigued. He'd been waking each night, sweating and shouting orders in his sleep. They'd clung to each other for comfort but she'd discovered him early one morning staring down at his daughter in her crib as if she was too precious to hold.

'If anything should happen to me, at least I know there's a part of me in her somewhere, even though she looks exactly like you.' He paused, seeing the anxious look on her face.

'Don't talk like that,' Ella replied, anxious to stop his train of thought.

'No, listen, things have to be said. You know what I do, the risks. The odds are getting worse with each op. There's always a price for both sides and I may be one of the ones who pays it.'

'No, please . . .' She tried to steer him away from these gloomy thoughts. 'Let's go for a walk.'

He continued regardless. 'When I'm with you, I can live for a few hours as if there's no war. When I'm high over the North Sea I think of you safe, going about your life, doing everyday things. It gives me such strength and now, with Clare, we are a family no matter how far away I am. When I hold you both, I can forget what tomorrow may bring, the fear I may not return in one piece or that there may be no happy ever after for us.'

Ella wept at his words. How could he say such things?

'Don't cry, you're the best thing in my life, everything I ever wanted. You light up a room with your smile, your hands create beautiful things and you care for people. How can I not love you? When I think how easy it would have been never to have conked out in that field, never to have met you. I feel so lucky, so blessed. Many chaps never got the chance to be loved by a woman. We'll pull through, we will, so don't worry.'

'You've done your tours. It'll be a training post soon, surely?' she asked.

'I hope so, but only for a while, darling. I can't sit at a desk, knowing what I know.'

'Promise me you'll come back to us,' she pleaded, clinging to him.

'If I don't, I want you to get on with your life, your art, find another chap. Don't become a nun. My parents will see to Clare's education. You are not to worry about money,' he insisted.

'Stop it. Just keep yourself safe for us.' She hated him talking like this. It was bad luck to talk about dying. She felt as if someone had walked over her own grave.

'You have to face facts, Ella. The odds are stacked against us. Sometimes I get a feeling in my bones . . .' Ella flung her arms round him and halted his words with her kiss.

'Come on, let's go for a walk. You're just tense about leaving. Fresh air will do us all good. We can walk down the towpath and take the baby to feed the ducks.'

As they walked slowly, they heard planes droning overhead on their way back to the Operational Training Unit at Lichfield, returning from doing 'circuits and bumps', the routine training flights around the district, getting the hang of how to work as a crew, testing their skills. She could never escape from the roar of their engines. They even haunted her dreams.

So much had happened so quickly for them. Clare was a honeymoon baby. Love in a war was indeed love in a rush but she wouldn't change a day of it. Anthony must survive for Clare's sake. She must have a father. Clare must have what Ella had never known, a proper family with two parents to love and provide for her. Nothing else would do.

109

The summer picnic for the evacuee children had been exhausting. The WVS had organized an outing to Hopwas Wood for sports, games and fresh air, with extra hands provided by mothers, grandparents and able-bodied volunteers in the city. Celeste was helping to organize the picnic tables, ready for the bun fight when the hordes of city children made a dash for the sandwiches and cakes they would wash down with bottles of fizzy pop, which had been carted up the hill in wooden crates. The pent-up enthusiasm of these boisterous children was exhausting just to witness.

Ella and little Clare were entertaining the few young mothers who had stayed with their children, most of whom were finding Lichfield too quiet, sleepy and remote to their liking.

At the back of Celeste's mind she was still chewing the cud over Roddy's last letter. He'd revealed his training was over and he'd got a commission into the army and was looking forward to seeing action in the Far East. Now she had no idea on earth where he was in the world.

They'd had an influx of American troops into the local barracks at Whittington. What with the boys in blue at the air base at Fradley, Lichfield was now a busy garrison town. She only wished Roddy were here.

At night they crowded into the public houses; raucous, noisy boys, accompanied by some Waafs in uniform, spilling out onto the streets, drunk, making the most of their leave. The whole city was geared up for war with convoys once again trundling down the main streets. The traffic passing Red House was so loud at night, it made the windows rattle, and overhead was the ever-present drone of planes on night-time bombing missions.

Celeste couldn't believe they'd had nearly three years of war, three years of rationing and coupons, travel restrictions and blackouts, with no sign of an end. Sometimes she felt every one of her fifty years, her legs constantly aching from standing, and the drabness of make-do-and-mend shabbiness had taken its toll on her spirits.

It worried her that Clare wouldn't know anything but black-out curtains and gas masks, home-made toys and cut-down clothes. She was the one bright spark in their day with a ready smile to light up their darkness. Ella had proved to be a natural mother. She also found time to work on her sculpting and she'd made pen and ink drawings of Clare to send to Anthony. One of Anthony's friends had introduced her to some of the leading artists in the Midlands, and a gallery in London had bought two pieces, which was such a boost to her confidence. The war wasn't dampening her talent, even if her materials were harder to come by.

The picnic was going so well. It was as if there was no war in the woods, just the screams of children enjoying themselves. The sun was shining and it was a perfect summer day until they heard the roar of engines overhead as if a dogfight was breaking out above them. They whipped up the children, dragging them under the cover of the woods just in case there was strafing. To her relief Celeste saw it was no more than a Wellington limping slowly back to Fradley with smoke coming out of its backside.

But then she watched in horror as it stuttered and spluttered lower and lower. There was nothing they could do for the stricken plane but pray. It was still too far off the runway to make a safe landing. It was too low, and the barracks at Whittington had some sort of landing strip. Celeste willed the pilot might make it down safely, but then it dropped out of sight, and they heard a sickening explosion as it burst into the ground, a great pall of smoke rising up. Those poor men in that bomber were doomed.

Death had marred a beautiful holiday. Celeste wanted to scream out loud, and then she saw Ella's face, white with fear in the agony of wondering if this was how Anthony and his crew might end their lives one night.

'Come on, everyone,' shouted the committee chairman, rallying her troops. 'Home, James; let's pack up. Time to head back. There'll be lots to do at HQ.'

Keep busy was their motto when things were dire. Keep busy, keep calm and keep going, no matter what. Everyone scurried about packing baskets, folding tables and chairs, finding blankets and making the silent children pick up litter, distracting them from the stench of smoke and what they had all witnessed.

There was nothing they could do for those men in the wreckage. The fire service would see to their bodies. Tonight some poor mother would receive a telegram telling her the worst had happened. All over the world such telegrams were winging their way to families. What if her Roddy ended up like that?

They drove back into Lichfield in silence. The outing that had begun with such jollity had now ended in sadness.

'Are you all right?' Celeste whispered to Ella. 'It can't be Anthony. He's transferred to Coastal Command now.' Not that this was any comfort to Ella. He was being stationed further north and she couldn't stay with him often.

'I know, but to be so close to such a horrible thing. It brings it all home. I've forgotten what it's like to live a normal life.' Ella was close to tears.

'It'll end one day and we'll soon forget the bad times, you'll see,' Celeste lied, knowing she'd never forgotten those terrible images of the *Titanic* splitting in two and the screams of the dying in the water. They still haunted her dreams.

When they reached Red House, the door was wide open and Selwyn was hovering in the doorway with a strange look on his face.

'What's happened?' Celeste asked. 'Is it Archie?' She felt weak at the knees, fearing the worst.

Selwyn broke into a grin. 'Nothing like that. We've got a visitor.'

'But I've got nothing in the house but leftovers,' she began. She was so tired she couldn't be bothered with entertaining, not after what they had just witnessed.

But there, standing in the hall, she glimpsed a tall officer in American uniform, his cap cocked over his eyes at a rakish angle.

'Hi, Mom.'

'Roddy, oh, Roddy.' She fell into his arms, all weariness instantly forgotten. My son has come home at last. Oh, thank you, thank you, she prayed.

'The last time I saw you, you were in short pants,' Ella laughed. 'Look at you now, the all-American Boy. I can't believe it's over twenty years ago.'

'And you were a pain in pigtails,' he quipped, eyeing her up and down. 'And who is this little beauty?'

'This is Clare. Say hello to your uncle Roddy.' But Clare clung onto her, burying her face in her shoulder. 'She's just shy; she'll get used to you. I can't believe it's you! How did you pitch up here?'

'By courtesy of Uncle Sam, First Class all the way across the Atlantic, zigzagging to avoid the U-boats. What a trip! Half the guys spent it retching over the side. Not quite the Cunard liner-style in luxury but we got to Liverpool in one piece. My God, what a sight for sore eyes that was, battered but still standing, like most of Britain, from what I've seen. I pulled a string or two, and got some leave to see my folks. I just had to see Mom.'

'I could've walked past you in the street. You're so American. Nothing wrong with that, of course,' she added hurriedly, 'but some of the guys stationed here are a bit rich. Candy for the kids, and nylons for the girls . . . with conditions,' she winked, 'if you catch my drift?'

'Don't worry, I bought candy for the baby but nothing for you.' He held out some chocolate in his hand. Clare didn't need any persuading to grab it from him, her shyness miraculously gone.

Later, they walked down Market Street, pushing Clare in her folding pushchair.

'I've never seen Celeste so happy as when she walked through the door and saw you,' said Ella. 'You are the best gift of all for her. She worries about you.'

'I know, but I'm here now. Don't know where next.' Roddy looked round in amazement. 'Nothing seems to change much but it's all so much smaller than I recall.'

'How could it change? There's a war on. We're all routine bound. Funny how life just goes on, war or not.'

'And your new husband?' Roddy smiled. 'You were pretty quick off the mark,' pointing to the pushchair.

'Why not? Babies are our future, our hope for a better future. Are any of yours on the streets of Akron?'

He looked down at her with a sheepish grin. 'Not that I know of,' he replied. 'You've changed too.'

'I should hope so. I'm a mother now.' They were ambling in the direction of Cathedral Close. 'Remember this? We used to come in here to hear you sing.'

'Sure. It feels like that was a lifetime ago. Reading our newspapers, I was expecting the whole country to be flattened. This looks untouched.'

'Don't be fooled, we'll all be touched before this is over. At least we're doing something across the Channel now, giving the enemy a dose of their own medicine. But let's not talk about the war. How long do we have to put up with your bad jokes?'

They paused to look up at the familiar façade of the West Front.

'I'll be off tomorrow. I don't know where, of course, all hush-hush.'

'So soon?' Ella felt sad as she made for the West Door. 'Want to go in, for old times' sake?'

'Why not? Who knows when I'm back again? Might as well have a last look at the old place. Do you remember how Grandpa Forester always had sweets in his cassock pocket? If you fidgeted, he gave you a mint ball to suck on.'

'I liked his liquorice Imps, those tiny tic-tacs that hit the back of your throat to help you sing better. He was such a nice old man and he was so kind to my mother.'

'Mom wrote to me about May. I should have written but I didn't know what to say.'

'I'm glad she told you. I do miss her, especially here,' Ella added, walking along the aisle.

'I miss not having Mom in my life too,' he replied as he followed her.

'I feel so happy to have Clare and Anthony, and the Foresters too,' she continued. 'Your mother's been wonderful.' She stopped and turned to face him, looking him straight in the eye. 'Why did you leave us?' She asked the question that had been unspoken for years.

'I didn't. I never intended to go with Pa but it all got out of hand, and I was too young to realize what he was doing until it was too late.'

'But you could have come back with Celeste. We missed you.'

'I know, I was young and didn't think, and later on it wasn't that simple. There was Grandma. She was having a rough time with my father's drinking. I just stayed until it was too late to return and now I have my business to go back to.'

'So I hear, and very successful too. Never thought of you as a truck driver.'

'Don't be such an English snob,' he laughed. 'I'm an officer now,' he tapped his lapels. 'So behave yourself.'

They walked around the rest of the cathedral in silence, just like any other tourists, feet echoing on the stone slabs. Everything of value had been boarded up and removed, and it felt cold and empty. Ella was glad to be back outside in the sunshine.

'Time to go back. Mrs Allen's Woolton pie awaits us, I fear. You have been warned.'

'Haven't you forgotten something?' Roddy said.

She looked up at him, puzzled. 'What?'

He was pointing across the Close to the narrow entrance on Beacon Street. 'We have to complete the tour, if I'm not mistaken, and go to Museum Gardens to see that old sea dog.'

'Captain Smith! I thought you would have forgotten him by now?'

'Never. We must do the whole tour. Without him, neither of us would be here to tell the tale,' he insisted.

It was as if they'd taken up where they had left off all those years ago. Her big brother was back on form. 'Now let me tell you how I met the captain's real daughter. You'll never believe this.'

Roddy pushed Clare as Ella filled him in with her story, unaware that he was eyeing her with renewed interest. She would stop the traffic at his base with those looks. Perhaps if he'd stayed in England who knew . . . he sighed. Now she was spoken for and out of bounds. Served him right for leaving his return so long.

110

The Italian Campaign, 1943–44

'Hit the dirt, Padre!' yelled a voice from a foxhole as a mine detonated close by. Frank jumped, automatically covering his head, his face flat down in the mud as he prayed. He knew combat was no respecter of dog collars. He was well blooded now, and bone-achingly tired. The Anzio landings had been easier than they thought, but now they were bogged down after a German counterattack, pinned down against strong defence lines.

The fighting to liberate North Africa seemed a long time ago and so many of his comrades had been lost along the way, blown up, shelled and ground down by overwhelming fatigue. Now a quick route from Naples to Rome was not going to happen. It was going to cost them dear.

His colonel often joked that Frank had taken to battle like a monk to prayer. But he was so numb and felt more and more like an automaton as he jumped from one muddy foxhole to the next, bent double in case of snipers. He'd taken to wearing a Red Cross brassard around his arm. It had already saved the lives of men stuck out there alone, wounded or dying, when he went to give them the last rites, or carry them back. Not all the enemy was heartless. Some infantry soldiers respected the skill and sacrifices made by the other side and held their fire. Others didn't.

Now, after the last bombardment, he must scour the battle-field for dead and wounded on both sides, dragging the living on his back to safety. It was the least he could do. They were family, brothers in arms, they needed him, but he wondered how long he could keep up his strength, not to mention his courage. The shells of Anzio Annie were coming closer, and his prayers were getting more fervent as he crouched. 'Better pray us out of here, Father,' someone yelled.

This was his life. Side by side with the men as they fought their way northwards in clothes that never dried, sodden boots, sleeping on mud, fortified only by dried 'C' rations, since they arrived in Italy. How could anyone sleep in a blanket and shelter when they were waistdeep in water and mud, gunfire their lullaby?

Later he would perform his daily ritual of removing dog tags from the corpses, trying to match their identity, sometimes with so few remains. Ever present was that overwhelming sweet stench of death in his nostrils. Waiting with the bodies as trenches were dug was the worst bit. There were so many sometimes that they were stacked up like logs. They laid the remains in neat rows, arms and legs buried as best they could, adding them to bodies that were limbless. Each burial service got harder when so many young boys he knew were snuffed out in a split second of mortar shelling or by a sniper's bullet. The slaughter here was more like a massacre.

Sometimes there was only a thumb left with which he could make a decent print for identification. Looking over the row, Frank felt a part of his heart was dying with each burial, each familiar face. How could he say blessings over such a waste of youth? But it was his job. When the canvas covered over the temporary grave it was time to face the mountains of condo-lence letters he must write. Sometimes he was so weary his pen just wouldn't move and he stared into space for hours on end, praying for the strength to repeat this baleful duty all over again.

They were hunkered down under the mighty guns from the Alban Hills, unable to break through. Only an aerial bombardment would destroy the menace of this advantageous placement. The enemy's sights were fixed on any movement on the beachhead, making progress impossible.

If he managed to sleep, nightmares would haunt his dreams; he'd see a boy clutching the Union flag, pleading to live. 'Don't let me die, Padre. I don't want to die.' There was nothing he could do but hold the boy's hand as his eyes glazed over into blessed unconsciousness. Frank saw once more the German soldier who had held a photo of his child to his lips, crying. 'Father, help me, hear my confession.' He had prayed over him, giving him the last rites as he would to any of his men. How did he know whether the man was here out of choice or drafted, coerced, sick of war and pain and battle?

Some of his troops cursed when they saw him approaching – 'Get out! Go some place else. We want none of you' – but they were the exception. Mostly they were relieved when he turned up like a dog sniffing the scent of where they were hiding, handing over mail, delivering messages, listening to their complaints or just sitting with them, having a smoke.

The toll on his fellow chaplains was beginning to show and there were few replacements. The Catholic priests never filled their quota. Those remaining felt they weren't doing enough, unable to reach all the men who needed them. For every moment of action there was an hour of boredom and waiting, when services could be held to give men strength and hope.

Frank was hoping the next push would lead them north. He wanted to visit the Holy See, listen to Italian voices delirious at their liberation. His father's language rang in his ears. There would be a few precious days of leave and recuperation while they caught up with all the bureaucracy that was demanded of them. But while he was away, who would take his place? There was no time for the luxury of grand silences and spiritual retreat into some monasteries. He would take off only as much time as these men, not an hour more. How could he look them in the eye if he returned well fed, in clean uniform, refreshed when they were exhausted?

He wondered how Paul, one of the Jesuit fathers whom he'd met on training, was faring further up the line. He envied the Jesuits their military discipline. They had a head start over him and they were the largest cohort of Catholic priests out here, close to the men yet set apart by their calling. He'd seen such bravery from them, such sacrifices. They were just human, after all, fallible, fearful men, wondering who would make it to the next Mass or how many of their men would ever return back home. Fear was a great leveller.

As he ducked into his foxhole he felt ashamed to find himself touching the little talisman deep in his pocket, the *scarpetta d'Angelo,* the baby shoe. At first it had smelled of home and the scent of Mamma's soap. Now it was grubby with dust and mud from his fingers, but it was still there and so was he.

His men viewed him as indestructible. 'Stick with Father Frank, he'll see you right,' they'd say, introducing rookie replacements to him with a grin.

They looked on him as a kindly parent, even though he was not much older than many of them. The Cross on his lapel set him apart but not so far apart that they couldn't joke and fool around in his presence. There was time for personal stuff, talking about a letter from home with bad news, a boy with a niggle in his groin that meant a trip to the VD clinic and subsequent confession. He looked over them as they prepared to defend their trench, knowing mothers had laboured to bring these boys into the world, had brought them up with care.

There must be a better way than this, he prayed. When this war was over he'd work to make sure no more boys had to pay such a price as the lads at the Anzio beachhead. Being in the forefront of battle had changed all his views, opened his mind to the possibility that just because a man wasn't born a Catholic he was destined for Hell. There were good men of all faiths and none, living brave lives here. They were on the right road too. Nothing was black or white any more. If he got out of here alive, how would he ever be able to settle back into the old rigid beliefs?

'Anzio Annie is giving us hell again, Padre,' yelled another voice, suddenly blotted out by a huge explosion and cries for help. It was time to go over the top and search them out. Frank scrambled to his task, trying not to let his hand shake as he crossed himself. '*In mano tuo, Domine,*' he prayed, crawling on his belly for what seemed miles in the direction of the moaning.

If there was one thing he hated it was to hear a boy crying out in pain with no one to administer morphine. Dying alone in a crater didn't happen on his watch if he could help it.

Bullets whizzed past him, but on he crawled. His men said he was their bird dog, able to sniff out the wounded by instinct. He didn't know about that. It was more dogged fear and determination that made Frank crawl on as the voice in front of him grew weaker even as he drew closer. He saw two boys hunkered down, one shot through the head, his eyes staring at the sky in surprise, the other shivering in shock and clutching his belly.

There was no time to waste. Pressing the first-aid pad onto the wound and giving him a shot of morphine, Frank just had time to close the eyes of the dead boy and say a few words of prayer as best he could. 'No, Father, he's Jewish,' the injured boy whispered only half conscious. So Frank prayed the Shema over him, suddenly aware of a shadow blocking his light. When he looked up he saw the muzzle of a rifle and the grey-green pants of an enemy soldier, watching him. Then he heard the words that chilled his heart: 'For you, Father, the war is over.'

111

Captain Roderick Parkes stared up at Death Mountain, his hands frozen to his binoculars, eyes half shut with fatigue after night upon night of a sleepless bombardment. For two months they'd been stuck here right in the firing line from the fortress on the Apennines. What a hellhole of slaughter it had been with some battalions now down to single figures. How much more punishment could they stand before they snatched Santa Maria Infante, the surrounding hills and moved northwards?

Now the roar of engines roused a thin cheer as bombers flattened the ancient fort, buildings crumbling to dust and ashes before them. It was the only way.

Roddy was hoping for news of a breakthrough at Anzio, but they were pinned down and Rome hadn't fallen yet. Their own push had ground to a halt, stuck in this godforsaken mud, scrabbling for cover, but just glad to be alive.

He stared up at the barrier of mountains, knowing it would take weeks to clear them. Why had he volunteered when he could have been sitting safe back home? Was it for just this moment, for the chance to look death in the face, to lead his men to slaughter, to live like filthy animals exposed to frost and snow and covered in vermin? Was this what it was all about? This Italian campaign felt like a forgotten front, all mud, mules and mountains. They'd spent a miserable Christmas holed up in a bombed-out chapel and someone had started out playing 'Silent Night' on a mouth organ. He'd felt such a pain of sadness and longing for home. As these weary troops bowed their heads, he sensed tears flowing, the fear that so many would never see home again.

Above them, the peaks loomed like a Cyclops's eye. A diligent muzzle searched out any movement, ready to pounce if they gave themselves away. As they watched the air attack and every explosion of orange flame, there was no feeling for anything but relief that they had been spared. War did this to a man, stripped him of humanity and pity. Monasteries, churches, castles, beautiful hilltop villages crushed by guns, testaments to the glory of God; all must be destroyed if they were ever to chase the enemy back over the Alps.

As the dust, smoke and the mist cleared Roddy could see they'd hit their target and knew they must take advantage of the hill and move forward ready to reclaim the ground they'd already lost. But in the scrum and rocks of the shattered village there might be Allied troops waiting, ready to join forces and seize more positions. If only they could link up and move as one unit.

'Forward,' waved their commander. 'We've got a hold up there,' he yelled as they formed a ragged line, pulling the mules up the craggy path, sure of a welcome from Allied troops.

It was the colonel who took the shot in his chest as he yelled, 'Hold your bloody fire. We're Americans!' The bullets whizzed by as they hit the ground, ambushed, surrounded, outnumbered. Roddy felt sweat on his brow, his hands clammy with fear. So this was it, a futile end on a filthy ledge in a foreign country where he couldn't even speak the language.

What a bloody mess. They'd led their men right into a trap. Now they were all going to be shot and there was not a thing he could do but pray.

112

December 1943

Another wartime Christmas was coming, another make-do-and-mend affair. Each year it got harder to raise enthusiasm, except now there was Clare. A child's excitement lifted the festive season. December was a month of celebration with Clare's birthday, and then Christmas to follow. Clare was too young to understand much, but nevertheless out came the decorations, tired and torn as they were; the paper chains and tissue bells and all the Christmas tree baubles. They'd hoarded enough dried fruit, sugar and precious lemon peel to attempt a half-decent fruitcake.

All Ella was praying for was good enough weather for Anthony to snatch a few days at home. His leaves had become more haphazard. He'd been transferred to Coastal Command, 144 Squadron in the far north of Scotland. All he told her was that he was now on anti-submarine patrols, preventing attacks on Allied shipping coming from Scotland. His last letter hadn't sounded promising.

Darling,
    Don't be disappointed if I can't make it back in time. You know how these things are by now. Hardly time to throw my hat in the door and it's time to turn round again, but I'll try.

Sorry about last time. What could I do? The boys were so keen to see you and have a change of scene. I knew you wouldn't mind entertaining them for a couple of nights. I should have given you more warning; they did get rather noisy, waking Clare and spoiling our night. You were quite right to be angry that we spent so little time alone. I promise I won't be so thoughtless again, but my crew and I are a family of sorts and I hate to see them stuck up there at a loose end. I sometimes forget I have a real family to cherish on leave. I have also neglected my parents, but they will be coming to join you for Christmas, I hear. All of us under one roof. It's going to be magical.

It's frightful here. The wind and rain must be endured, bleak Scotland at its worst is so cold but we're doing sterling work out on patrol and reconnaissance. Can't say where but you can guess. Been doing some extra training and I just wish the conditions were a bit more hospitable. If only I had you to warm my bed each night. Not a lot for the boys to do but drink, read and flirt with the Waafs. (Don't worry, none of them could hold a candle to you.) I'm counting the weeks till I'm on the sleeper south. Pray there's no snow to hold us up.

There's talk of a ground job coming up for me. I suppose a third tour of ops is pushing it, but experience is what helps get the younger chaps through their first sorties. Firing torpedoes into submarines on a stinking night needs training and practice. You get protective of these young boys straight out of school, so green, so enthusiastic and so quickly lost without proper tactical training. Yes, I can do some of this in an OTU but we'll see how things are in the new year.

By the way, I heard Simon Russell-Cooke is somewhere up here too. Small world. Do send his mother a card. I shall never forget our precious honeymoon down there.

Good night, my darling. God willing, see you soon. Best love to all the Foresters. Did you hear anything from Roddy? I

think the Yanks and Brits are having a tough road through Italy.
Give Clare a kiss from her 'Daddy in the Sky'.

Not long now.

Always and forever yours,

Anthony

Time was so short together. He'd leap off the train south, race to
Red House for a long soak in the bath, a stiff whisky with
Selwyn, a long walk, just the two of them, and then early to bed.
Sometimes he was so tired he slept most of his leave. She watched
him playing with Clare in a detached way as if his mind was still
in the air. He'd aged in the last year; the frown lines over his
brow were deep furrows and he would drop asleep at any time.

She felt ashamed of how furious, how jealous she'd become. 'You
have your bloody crew day in and out; we barely get to see you. It's
not fair. It's me you married, not them,' she screamed one night.

It was hard to swallow the jealousy. She wanted to spend every
second with him. It was all she had to get her through the weeks
to come. But in some ways she had to admit that his crew were
his family now.

He'd survived two tours. It was good there was a ground job
coming up but she feared he would turn it down in favour of a
third tour. 'No one survives three tours,' she cried to him on the
phone only last week.

'There's always an exception to the rule,' he'd replied. 'I'm
feeling lucky.'

She dreaded to think what he risked each night flying low
over a dark sea, looking for targets, taking photographs, dodging
flak or wandering in thick fog with hardly any vision, low on
fuel, praying for lights to guide him to land.

'It's what I do,' he argued, 'all I've ever wanted to do since I
saw Uncle Gerald's bi-plane landing in our field and he took me
out for a spin. And I'd go to Cobham's Flying Circus in the
summer holidays when I was a boy. I got to fly an Avro 504. I

would cycle miles to sit outside the RAF base just to watch the aeroplanes taking off. It gets into your veins.'

But fear stalked her. If he didn't ring or write for days she couldn't work, settle, eat or concentrate until the phone rang with news. Now there was so much to do preparing work for school, ordering groceries for Christmas, making the house look festive and tracking down little bits for Clare's stocking. Ella had ordered a capon from the farm. She loved it when the house was full of guests. Their lodger was a young teacher from school who would be visiting her own family, leaving a bedroom free for when Anthony's parents came to stay.

Shopping was always a rushed affair, especially with a toddler in tow, and Clare was being tiresome again, stamping her feet whenever they passed the little sweet shop. There were queues at the Maypole grocery store and at the butcher's round the corner. The bus was late and Ella had to sit with Clare on her knee until they were dropped off at Streethay.

She was hurrying towards the house when she saw a strange car parked in the drive. Anthony had come home without telling her! How wonderful. He'd obviously borrowed someone's car and petrol coupons to get here quicker, she thought, pushing open the door with excitement. 'Daddy's home, darling!'

Selwyn was standing by the telephone. 'You're back.' There was something in the way he was looking at her that made her knees quiver and her heartbeat quicken.

'What's up? Who's our visitor?' She unstrapped Clare from her pushchair.

'Ella, they've come to see you. I've put them in the drawing room. Shall I take Clare?'

She knew that second, from the look on his face, the gentle way he said her name, what was coming. Oh, no! Dear God, no, she prayed as she opened the door and saw familiar blue uniforms rising up at her entrance.

★   ★   ★

'He's missing. There's always hope.' That was what they said. Anthony and his crew had been on a routine mission from Wick, looking for enemy shipping. The plane didn't return but they may have had to make a forced landing in enemy-held territory. They could be prisoners of war. He was only an MIA. There had been no sighting or wreckage, nothing to indicate they had ditched into the sea. She was glad the officers had come and told her in person, softening the blow of a telegram to come. 'We must pray that it is good news,' the padre offered.

Ella sat, numbed, unable to take in much of what was said, unable to breathe. *You wouldn't want me to be hysterical or to break down. You would want me to hold up and be positive for Clare's sake. She's too young to understand any of this. Be brave, hundreds of forces wives are going through this.* This was the worst day of her life but how cool and logical she was being, how sensible and correct, setting an example just as an officer's wife must.

She'd given them tea with shaking hands, acted the hostess, playing her role like an actress in a play. They didn't linger. They'd seen it hundreds of times before, no doubt.

It was only when they left that she found herself doubled up with agony. She couldn't think, couldn't move or cry out, frozen by this awful news. It just couldn't be true, not for her – for others, perhaps, but not for her. There was a mistake, the telephone would ring in a minute. She'd hear his voice: 'Darling, I'm fine. It's just some stupid mess up at HQ. Got the wrong chappie, another Harcourt, poor fellow bought it, not me. I'll be home soon. Give Clare kisses from Daddy.'

Selwyn appeared and shoved a brandy in her hand. 'Get that down you. I've rung Celeste. She's coming straight away.'

They would all fuss over her as if she was sick, commandeer Clare to take her out of her hair. She didn't want Celeste coming, or anyone. She wanted Anthony. He couldn't be gone, missing, overdue. Any of the words no one dared say: KIA – killed in action – drowned in the sea, blown out of the sky. They were just words. They weren't real. None of this was real. She would go to bed and wake up tomorrow and this would all be just a bad dream.

But when the morning came there was no phone call, nor on the day after that. Ella began to write a diary, reasoning that if he was a prisoner of war he'd want to know all that he'd missed while he was away. She'd speak to him on the page, make sure he knew all her thoughts. It would keep him alive, knowing every night she would fill in the journal as if they were talking on the telephone. It would make Christmas bearable knowing she could tell him how they'd tried to celebrate the coming of light into this dark, dark world.

Of course it can't be the same if you're not here. Nothing is the same now. I can't seem to pick up a tool or a piece of charcoal or a chisel. We made a snowman and Clare called him 'Daddy in the sky'. She's called you that for so long. Are you in the sky or in the sea? It's so cold in the sea. Where are you, my dearest? I have to know you are safe. Surely I would have known if you'd been taken from us. I have to believe you are safe somewhere and one day you'll come back to us. That's why I'm keeping up this chatter. It fills in the awful hole I find in my heart. Not to feel your arms round me ever again, not to touch your lips, is not to be borne. Why have you left us? Why did you keep putting yourself in danger?

I'm sorry. I shouldn't be angry with you but I am. I have the letter you left in a safe place but I won't be opening it yet. It is too soon and there's always hope, isn't there? You might be hiding out somewhere with Norwegian partisans, or rescued by fishermen, sheltered by good people, unable to let anyone know in case they are compromised. I do understand your silence. You are such a strong person. You wouldn't put anyone else's life in danger.

Tom and Sybil are bearing up. They came down at once. They looked at me with pity when I told them you were only missing. Now I know how my mother felt when she lost her Joe and her baby, why she clung to me and wouldn't let me go. I was her reason to keep on living. Why do we not understand how parents feel until we are parents ourselves?

Clare prattles on unaware of your absence. She has seen so little of you, it breaks my heart to think she may never see you again. We kiss your picture and say night-night to Daddy in the sky. It will do for now. Please come back to us, darling, and if you can't then let me know you're safe.

I am praying night and day that this confidence I have that you are still alive isn't false. It would be so cruel to go on in false hope. Oh, Anthony, where are you now?

Celeste felt hopeless, watching Ella's grief strip the flesh from her bones and the light from her eyes. She kept busy, so busy, never pausing to take breath, her days filled with teaching, meetings, anything but dwelling on her loss. There was no reaching behind her bright, brittle smile. Hazel kept calling in just to see how her friend was doing but she was hardly ever at home. There was no further news, but as the weeks turned into months it did not augur well for Anthony's survival.

What was worse was there was no outlet for her grief. The studio was shut up, gathering dust as if, with Anthony's death, all her creative spirit had withered. She would not even look at her unfinished work. She prepared her college work and nothing else. The rest of her focus was on Clare. No one was allowed to take her out of her sight. Clare was going through a strong-willed stage, raging if she didn't get her own way but Celeste suspected Ella was in danger of ruining her temperament by giving into her too often. It was only a phase but Celeste felt the child needed discipline, but how best to give advice when it was not sought? She thought of that old saying, 'A granny should keep her purse open and her mouth shut.' But you are not her grandmother, just an old aunt, she thought.

One morning Clare was sitting at the breakfast table refusing to eat her boiled egg and soldiers. 'No want,' she said, shaking her head.

'But, darling, you must eat,' Ella pleaded, 'or you'll have a poorly tummy.'

'If she doesn't eat she will be hungry. Let her go hungry, but don't give her anything else until luncheon,' Celeste offered, hoping it didn't sound too strict.

'Poor thing will be starving by then,' Ella replied.

'Good, then she'll eat. Think of all those children who never see an egg from one month to the next. She mustn't waste food,' Celeste continued.

'But she's only a baby,' Ella argued back.

'She's not too young to be checked. It's for the best.'

Ella stared at her coldly. 'You're so old-fashioned. Clare knows what's best for her.'

'Does she? Who's in charge then, her or you?' It was time to challenge her. 'You must take control on some things. Just because ...' Celeste paused. Should she dare raise his sacred name? 'Just because Anthony is missing doesn't mean you must spoil Clare.'

Now she had Ella's attention. 'What you mean by that?'

'Life has to go on, and if Anthony can't come home, you will be her sole parent. I know you'd want to do things as he would have wished.'

'It's all right for you, you have Archie,' Ella snapped.

'You forget, I brought up Roddy on my own and it was hard. I had to work for both of us. Let's face it, Ella, Clare is at a difficult age, but it will pass soon enough. You'll blink and she'll be in silk stockings.' She tried to make light of things.

'Oh, don't say that. She's all I have.' Ella began to cry.

'You're doing a wonderful job but let us all help you and

share the strain sometimes. The more she's with other adults, the more you'll have to rest and do things for yourself.'

'I don't want time to think or do. I just want to know Anthony is safe,' she cried.

'I know that, dear, but if he's not coming back . . .' The words hung in the air.

'Don't say that, I won't have it. Don't be so cruel.'

'But it's been nearly five months now. You have to face the possibility that—'

'I can't and I won't. How can I go on living if it's true?'

'You will, you are and you must, for Clare's sake, like your own mother carried on because of you.'

'That was different,' Ella argued, not looking at her, bristling with indignation.

'No, it's not. This is your *Titanic* moment, you must face the biggest loss of your life like thousands of others. But you'll go on living because Anthony would want you to. How could you ever think of leaving his child? He'd want you to do all the things you did before you met him, to pick up the threads and weave something wonderful again. That's the only thing we can do after such a tragedy. You keep going forward one day at a time. There's a big push coming. Haven't you seen all the convoys going south? The road's lined with tanks, lorries, troops heading out goodness knows where. They say it's coming soon and please God there'll be an end to this madness.'

'You don't think he is alive, do you?' Ella sat down, her head in her hands.

'We should have heard something by now. It doesn't look good, but I may be wrong. I hope I am,' Celeste said without conviction as Ella picked up the plates and rose from the table, watching Clare tucking into her toast with relish.

Celeste looked up and smiled. 'See, a child knows when it's well off. Out of the spotlight and she just got on with it all by herself.'

They were still clattering about when the front doorbell rang. Ella sprang up like a gazelle. 'The post!'

Celeste was making more tea when Ella placed a telegram on the table. 'It's for you.'

'Not Archie?' Celeste tore at it, all fingers and thumbs. She blinked in disbelief as she read the words, then threw it across the table. 'It's Roddy. He's missing in Italy, presumed killed.'

Clare looked up, puzzled, crunching her toast as the two women clung together. 'More soldiers?'

113

Italy, 1944

You get used to anything given time, Roddy thought as he stumbled out of the cattle truck, blinking in the harsh sunshine, at another camp somewhere in the hills of Italy. He hoped it was better than the last transit camp, the one they called the 'Film Studio' somewhere outside Rome, and about as near as he would ever get to the Holy City.

After the ambush, it was hands up and a long march with dogs snarling at his heels. They were lucky not to have been shot on the spot but the German officer was an aristocrat of the old Prussian military school with some respect for the Geneva Conventions. Nevertheless, they'd been stripped of valuables – watches, cigarette lighters, rings – and kicked around as they stumbled through the rocky terrain, before being herded into cattle trucks and driven for miles without food or water until they'd arrived, exhausted, at a holding camp. Men were standing around looking at the new arrivals with bored curiosity.

There was a roll call of sorts, dividing them into sections: British, American, French and others. It was like some rancher's roundup, being corralled into compounds. All he could think of was food and water.

They didn't stay long before it was back into rail trucks heading north to yet another camp, smaller this time, remote with a stunning view of the mountains. This view was masked by barbed wire fencing, guard posts and guns, reminding everyone they were going nowhere fast. Roddy gathered that they were near a battered city called Arezzo, famous for its paintings, but that meant nothing to him. He was just glad to be out in the fresh air, trying to get used to the idea of being a prisoner of war.

To be in the power of the enemy, reliant on him for food and shelter, to have to obey his orders and his whims and fancies, was a constant humiliation. There were rumours of escapees being shot and any peasants who helped them meeting a similar fate; a grim prospect that wouldn't change until the invading troops pushed the enemy back north out of Italy. Easier said than done, as Roddy knew only too well.

The faces of his fellow officers said it all: suntanned, lean, gaunt and edgy. How would he cope with the boredom of it all? How long before they went further north to Austria or Germany? He looked round to see if there were any others from his division, any familiar faces from the landings, from training days, accents from Akron or Ohio, even. No one.

Roddy was glad he didn't have a girl back home, worried sick by him being posted missing. Will and his mother would know some time soon. That was enough. He trusted that she would write on receiving his Red Cross postcard telling them he was a prisoner of war but not injured. He'd been lucky. His colonel still lay on the mountainside where he fell. He would never leave Italy. What Roddy would give to be driving some huge truck down an interstate highway, king of the road, stopping at a diner for steak and fries. Will and the Freight Express business felt a thousand miles from where he was standing.

Their chow was some sort of pasta soup slop, topped up with rations from their Red Cross tins. Funny how food, however meagre, becomes the focus of all your thoughts when you're hungry, he sighed. There was so much time to fill. Time and boredom were the enemies now.

Books sent in were passed around carefully, but they were instructional, religious, classical literature, not the sort of books most of the men wanted to read. Any port in a storm, though; anything to take the mind away from the present had to be welcome.

He was messed in the officer compound. They were a mixed bunch with stories to tell of their campaigns that after a week or two you could reel off word for word. Everyone had plans to escape, but without a decent smattering of the lingo it would be impossible to make a run for it. No one would get further than the road end before being recaptured. In fact, they'd have a better chance dressed in German uniform, so many of them being tall, fair, blue-eyed, but would then run the risk of getting their throats cut in some dark lane by the partisans known to be lurking in the hills.

There were classes in everything, from chess, Italian, Hebrew and Polish, animal husbandry, beekeeping, nautical knots and kite flying. If you had some sort of specialist knowledge, it was shared with someone to keep their minds off flinging themselves at the wiring and getting shot.

What could he offer but stories of trucking round the States, the best stopovers, tyre manufacturing and the history of the rubber industry in Akron? Surprisingly, he did have an audience at his talk. There were church services for the devout but they did not appeal to Roddy. After what he'd seen in battle he doubted any universal deity was in overall control of this war. All he could think of was getting out of this pen.

He did go to the Italian lessons on offer because he never knew when it might come in handy. The Italian-American priest who took the class was more American than Italian, but he made a decent stab at it.

Despite his misgivings about religion, Roddy liked what he saw about the padre, Father Frank. He was short and dark, younger than he, but with a gentle calm way about him. He'd saved the lives of two soldiers in a dugout. Even German soldiers drew the line at shooting priests giving the last rites. His latest idea had been to start up a music club with some records and a wind-up gramophone that had been sent into the camp. The music was mostly classical, of course, but it did the spirit good to listen and let the images roll over in one's mind.

Today, they were listening to Dvorak's *New World' Symphony*, full of folksy tunes and spirituals that made Roddy yearn for the wide-open spaces of Ohio.

'I'm thinking we should start a choir,' said the padre. 'We're hoping to have a concert, a show of sorts. If I can get ten or twenty voices together, we could do a spot or two.'

'Count me out,' said the guy next to him. 'Tone deaf, I'm afraid.' Why then was he listening to music? Roddy pondered.

'Can't read music,' said the next man, rising to leave.

'Who said anything about music?' laughed the priest. 'We'll just sing from memory until we get some sheet music sent over.' He turned to Roddy. 'How about you, Captain Parkes?'

Roddy was halfway through the door and held his hands up in horror. 'The last time I did any singing in public I was in short pants,' he laughed.

'Where was that?'

'Lichfield.'

'Litchfield, Connecticut?'

'No, Lichfield Cathedral in England. Be seeing you ...'

'Hold your horses. Sounds like I've got my first recruit, a choral scholar, no less.' The padre went after him.

'Hell – I mean, sorry – no, Padre. I'm not sure what will come out if I open my mouth now.'

'None of us does, that's the challenge. We'll take what comes, Captain, and work on it.'

Suddenly it had become 'we'. Roddy groaned. 'Call me, Roddy, Padre.'

'See you tonight at sundown, Captain Roddy. Might as well

make a start. You never know what tomorrow will bring. We may have a Caruso hidden in our midst,' he laughed, pleased with his new recruit.

How did I get myself into this? Roddy grumbled, knowing he'd turn up. What else was there to do in this hellhole?

Frank had finished his sick visits. There was a hospital of sorts, not very well equipped, but the doc eked out his first-aid kit and demanded they got their due supplies from Red Cross stores. He looked exhausted, in need of a rest himself.

'You go and have a smoke,' said Frank. 'I can take over if you point out the ones who need attention.'

He'd heard confessions and written a brief note home for a guy who was flat on his back with fever. He was glad to be useful. The latrines here were a disgrace, little more than a board with holes in it, and the faeces were carried on the duckboards and into the huts no matter how careful they were.

'It's the infection I fear most, the big T, typhus,' said the doc. It was hot. There were flies. The work parties in the fields came back sunburned, bitten and exhausted, but it gave the fittest men a chance to work off their frustration. Boredom was the true enemy here. No one knew anything of the outside world and what was going on. The latest arrivals to the camp were pounced upon for news of the coming Allied advance, but the push north was slow, too slow ever to overtake this place and set them free.

Frank was curious about the surrounding district. It was tantalizingly close to where his father had been born. He could not be far from the Bartolini farmstead. He tried to recall the letters that had come from his father's family in Tuscany, how his father had said they had a smallholding clinging to the hillside near to the famous walled city of Anghiari, somewhere close to where Michelangelo was born. To be so near and yet so far . . . Why hadn't he taken more notice of his family history?

There were a few locals in the employ of the camp after the

declaration in September 1943 that split the Axis partners from each other. It had been a lax regime until the Germans had taken over and tightened security. There was a stand-off between the two sides now. There was an old priest who called on the commandant and was allowed to make contact with Frank. When he'd heard his surname was Bartolini, he'd offered, at great risk to himself, to make contact with the family through a secret network.

What was the point, though? Unless the Allies came soon the prisoners would be shipped north in trucks and he'd never get a chance to meet his father's relatives. His choir was coming together, at least, with a bit of arm twisting, slow to gel in harmony. Captain Roddy had a decent bass voice, much to his surprise, and they'd found a few tenors. He was enjoying licking this motley crew into shape for the concert party, aiming for a barbershop harmony. They sang 'Swing Low, Sweet Chariot' and 'Alexander's Ragtime Band'. Corny, but everybody knew those tunes.

He was getting along well with Roddy Parkes. They'd met at the lecture on the *Titanic* by some guy whose uncle had been on board, reeling off all sorts of facts and figures about the disaster. Most of the men had long forgotten the sinking. His lecture was as dry as dust until Roddy stood up and said, 'My mom was on board,' telling them the story of how she had befriended a woman and her baby in a lifeboat and how they had all ended up living in England together, and how he'd met the real 'unsinkable Molly Brown' in Washington, DC. They discussed how the First Class passengers got the best treatment while the Third Class men never stood a chance once the ship began to sink.

Frank had then chipped in with his own story. 'I'm here too because of the *Titanic*. My father's first wife, Maria, was lost on that ship.' Frank added, 'And his baby. They were never found, but my papa was convinced the baby lived because he found this.' He pulled out the lace boot, grubby and crushed. 'He still believes this was hers.' He passed it round the men. 'It was given to me for safekeeping. My papa says if it could survive the Atlantic it might stop me being seasick.' He paused and then laughed. 'It didn't. I threw up all the way. I should throw it away, but I won't. It was some little kid's shoe.'

'Shoes are lucky. They put them in the roof of a house for protection. Don't ask me why, they just do,' said one of the men in the audience.

Everyone began to talk about the myths and legends of that ship. How there was supposed to be a mysterious cursed Egyptian mummy on board, a safe full of stolen diamonds, and the ghosts of the riveters of Belfast hammering in the hold, accidentally trapped after their shift. It was after the lecture that Frank found himself in step with Roddy again.

'Funny how we both have the *Titanic* in our lives,' he remarked. 'My mother is Irish and she lost her sister, my auntie Lou, on that ship. My parents met in church on one of the anniversaries.'

'My mom left her husband and took me to England for a while to get away. She said it was seeing that ship go down that made her face facts and walk away. I know your Church doesn't hold with divorce, but my father was cruel.'

'It's the Church that teaches against divorce, in theory, but I'm not sure I'd want to see my mum living with a wife beater. It was bad enough living with the portrait of my father's first family on the wall like a precious icon. For years I thought we kids were second best. How can you ever compete with a dead baby?'

'Is that why you became a priest?' asked Roddy. He raised his eyebrows. This question was a bit of a cheek but he was curious.

'Who knows? Could be. I never wanted to be anything else. My sister escaped into the theatre on Broadway; she's just in the chorus but Patti's got talent. Jack, on the other hand . . . well, that's another story. We're chalk and cheese. I suppose one of us brothers had to be the good guy. He's out somewhere in the Pacific last time I heard.'

It was strange how camp living had made him share the sort of private stuff he'd not shared with his parishioners. Roddy was a fellow officer, someone he could identify with, an outsider with a glint of life still left in his eye, determined to survive.

'I need to get out of here soon before they ship us north. I want to get back to my men. There's still some fight left in me. I reckon if I walk south, I might make it,' said the captain one night after rehearsal.

'Not looking like that,' replied Frank. 'Locals can be slow coming over to our side. You look too American to get past the square, though it would be good for morale for someone to make a run for it.'

There was just a chance someone might help them find a safe place for Roddy and give Frank a chance to see his folks, if only for an hour or two. He couldn't leave the camp. He wouldn't leave his post, but to be so near and yet so far ... Surely they could cover for him for an hour or two, if they were in the fields. It would take some plausible bribery and prayer to find Roddy a way out but it wasn't impossible, given outside help. It was worth a try but he'd say nothing to raise hopes until he was sure.

114

Ella's students were being clumsy this November morning, none of them grasping what she was demonstrating. All they could talk about was the huge explosion that had rocked the Midlands two days before, shattering windows everywhere, causing people to fear a rocket attack. Someone said an arsenal had been bombed. Others said a whole city had been blasted away. Lichfield shuddered with its impact as if an earthquake had struck, but there was nothing reported on the news.

Ella looked up at the skylight of the studio. A pool of light was streaming down onto the floor. It was funny how she no longer felt comfortable in this space, or in her own studio, both of which had been her boltholes, her creative space. Her studio at Red House was a mess now, an empty workshop, just a chilly, broken barn. Her own half-finished work stood accusingly but she shut her eyes to it. It was no longer a place to linger, and now that much of her work had fallen on the floor, smashed by the quake, it summed up her feelings.

Here was her proper work, instructing young students in the rudiments of stonemasonry and carving at the art school. It paid the bills and she didn't have to deviate from the syllabus: basic tool work, stone recognition, and carving and copying basic motifs. Her time was spent supervising and correcting the errors of the novices whilst watching the clock to see when it was time to return home. She would count down the days until the college holidays, looking forward to spending more time with Clare.

It was many months since that first news of Anthony and the return of his personal belongings that had been packed so neatly in a box.

Every item still smelled of his Players cigarettes: photos in silver frames with smudged fingerprints where he'd touched them, his books, socks, shaving kit. What a pitiable collection of objects to sum up a life. She still couldn't bear to open the two letters he'd left: one for Clare and one for herself.

Condolence letters were still arriving from his friends' parents and old schoolmasters; letters she painstakingly answered.

The hardest one to answer was from Captain Smith's daughter, Mel Russell-Cooke, whose own son, Simon, had perished in the sea on a similar exercise to Anthony's in March. How brave, stoic and resolved his mother was, accepting that there was little hope of rescue after ditching in the sea in winter.

> The best resource we find, and I'm sure you'll do is in keeping busy. I'm driving ambulances in London, digging for victory in the garden and helping out in the village, but you must know only too well how to deal with such a terrible loss, my dear.

I am not dealing with it, Ella sighed. I'm just putting it out of mind, pretending it never happened, pretending that my husband will walk through the door any minute and that all this is just a nightmare. She paced up and down trying not to get exasperated by the feeble efforts in front of her. Work, work, work, yes, that was the answer. At least Roddy was safe, even if he was in a POW camp somewhere in Italy. They'd received only two post-cards but had sent Red Cross comforts parcels as often as they could.

When would this bloody war end? Hadn't they all suffered enough? The Allies had landed in Normandy, in Italy, in the

South of France, but still the wretched battles kept raging. Would Clare ever know any other life? Ella felt so bitter inside, so angry and frustrated that the colour had gone out of her world. The joy of being loved and cherished was over. It was so unfair. How would she ever thaw out into a semblance of the woman she had once been?

Archie was returned from Portsmouth to Celeste. Selwyn went on his own merry way, drinking far more than was good for him. Hazel was counting the days until her husband returned from the Far East. Ella felt resentful and jealous of them all.

Catching a glimpse of herself in the glass of the cupboard was a shock. *I don't like you very much.* She sighed realizing sadness had aged her. There were dark circles under her eyes, lines across her brow. The first grey hairs were streaking through her unruly mane, habitually tortured into a severe bun. What was the point? There was no one to dress up for and Clare didn't mind how she looked. She'd stopped visiting Museum Gardens and Captain Smith. He was only a lump of bronze, after all. How stupid to make a statue the recipient of all your hopes and dreams as her mother had done.

Oh, Mum, I know now how you must have felt in losing Joe and Ellen. You lost them both. I still have my child but it is so hard. I think I understand now why you did what you did.

Death was death. There was no coming back. She didn't attend the cathedral with Celeste. She was still too angry to pray. No, she really didn't like the person staring back at her. She felt as if she was the only one to be feeling as she did, like a frightened little girl stamping her feet against her losses, not knowing what to do next.

'Miss, miss?' a voice broke her reverie. 'Is this all right?'

It was Jimmy Brogan, one of the Birmingham Irish scholarship boys, short and slight, pinched in the face. She'd forgotten to look at his efforts. He'd carved a Celtic cross into the stone, and for a beginner was showing a firm hand and a neat execution. In fact it was an excellent piece of work.

'This is good. I like the way you've finished it off,' Ella said, smiling. At least someone had taken her advice.

'Do you think they'll let me take it home?'

'I'm not sure,' she cautioned. 'Isn't it part of your assessment for a place at the art college?'

'I ain't doing that, miss. This is for Peg, a grave marker,' he replied, not looking at her.

'Peg is your dog?' she said, surprised.

'Oh, no, miss, Peg's my sister. She got run over by a bus in the blackout. She was going to get a jug from the milk cart.' He bent his head to hide his tears. 'I'd like to give it to me mam.'

'You take it then. I'll make sure the cost's covered. How is your mother?' she continued as if she needed to ask after such a tragedy.

'Bad, since we were bombed out, miss. We're living with her sister and they don't get on, and me dad's with the Eighth Army in Italy. It's all a bit of a crush.'

Ella looked at his work with admiration. 'You know there are more scholarships for boys like you to go on further,' she said, realizing she could be losing a talented pupil.

'Not for the likes of me. I've got a job in a foundry with my uncle Pat. I can always carry on at night school,' he said, shaking his head. 'I'm glad you like it, miss.'

'It comes from the heart, Jimmy. Good work always begins inside here.' She tapped her chest, feeling the sadness well up. 'Remember, not from your head, from your heart. Stick to that and you'll not go wrong. Good luck.'

Why on earth was she complaining when this boy had no home, no father and had lost a sister? Now his talent would go untrained. She had a roof over her head, a darling daughter and caring friends. She had a job, a modicum of talent. She must help Jimmy realize his potential somehow. What about an apprenticeship with Bridgeman & Sons, the masons in Lichfield? It might just be possible.

She spun round, sensing a presence just over her shoulder and heard a familiar voice. 'Good show, I knew you'd see sense, darling. Just get on with it, don't waste your gift.' She could hear Anthony's voice so clearly, piercing her frozen defences. 'I'll never leave you.'

The pain of recognition was almost too much for her to bear, standing there in the studio classroom, watching the bent heads of these young people with so much hope before them. Then, mercifully, the bell rang and she told them to down tools and ushered them through the door with as much haste as was decent. Only then did she sit at her desk and break down, sobbing, her head buried in her hands. Anthony was never coming back to her, yet there was a bit of him inside if she could only listen.

She thought of Jimmy's Celtic cross and the pride and love that he had put into it as she sat on the bus going home, staring out of the window, feeling strangely light-headed. She'd heard his voice again: 'You can do something for that boy.' Anthony knew her grief and had come to comfort her. As long as she lived she could touch that bit of him within her.

After supper that night, Ella rushed upstairs to pull out the box of his things with the precious letter inside. She hugged it to herself before she opened it. Through her tears she managed to read:

> This is a letter I hope you will never have to read but if you are, then the worst will have happened. Have no regrets. I haven't. I have been blessed in finding you and knowing part of me lives on for you through Clare. Children are our immortality. Please give Clare her letter when you think she is old enough to understand.
>
> She will know her parents even if neither of us got that chance.

Don't be bitter that fate hasn't allowed me to survive. I always knew this day might come. Better to live one day as a tiger ... goes the proverb, and we flyers are tigers in the air. Someone has to stop that madman over the Channel.

I wish I could write a poem, a sonnet to express how much I love you, but all I keep thinking of is how lucky I am to know you and be loved by you. No one can take away those precious days alone in the cottage, our hilltop rides from Thorpe Cross, making love high on the rocks, those sweet walks down the tow path and the sight of you walking down the aisle of the cathedral. In time, feel free to let go of me and find someone else to cherish you. I don't want you to be lonely.

Chin up. Be British.

Goodbye, my darling.

115

During the following weeks Roddy and Father Frank took to patrolling the perimeter fence every morning and evening, a ritual often carried out in silence, a chance to walk off their frustrations. From their first tentative steps together a friendship grew.

'If you are going to escape, you need to be fit. Walk and work, build up your legs,' Frank whispered one day. 'You must discuss it with other officers in case someone wants out with you.'

'I'd prefer to try on my own.'

'Forget it then. You wouldn't last two minutes.'

'You come then,' Roddy challenged him.

'This is where I stay, tempted as I am to sneak off for a couple of hours and find the Bartolini clan.'

Roddy liked Frank's honesty, the way he could grumble and curse with the best of them. He wasn't like any other vicar he had met. He fought for better food rations, the sharing out of Red Cross parcels, more medical supplies. He'd found the commandant was a good Catholic and allowed a local priest in to bring consecrated wafers and hear his confession.

Their mail was hit and miss, but one morning Roddy found Frank pacing round the fence, unable to speak, holding out a letter from his mother telling him his brother had been killed in the Pacific, his ship torpedoed.

'Jack was the bad one. I was the good guy. But my father loved his bad boy. He will take it hard, two of his children lost now.'

Only weeks later came news of Ella's husband, months out of date. Roddy was now up to running round their trodden path. He stopped. 'Why do we do this, all this killing to each other?' he asked Frank, who was puffing to catch him up.

'Because we're animals, territorial animals out of the jungle, I reckon. It's bred in us to hunt and scavenge and fight. We forget we're all the same under the skin, a fallen race.'

'Are we? I'm not so sure,' Roddy replied. 'I've seen some terrible things from our side and some decent things from the enemy. Get me outta here, I'm going to explode.' He could feel the frustration tearing inside him.

'Did you talk to the escape committee?'

'They want an organized break-out. They say it was easier when the camp was run by the Italians. The guards now are much more thorough.'

'I've heard there is still a secret hole dug under the outer perimeter fence and the field workers aren't guarded all the time. There's a priest in the town. He says if we can find the right spot in the fields, there are ways to walk out but you'll need to work on your Italian. The dialect here is unfathomable and we need to get those legs in better shape if they are to do twenty miles a day uphill.'

Roddy felt his thighs; they were still weak and thin. 'I'll double the circuit.'

'Put rocks in your pockets to add some weight and I'll try to get you extra rations.'

'Why are you doing this for me?' Roddy asked. 'I'm not even a Catholic.'

'We can work on that later,' Frank quipped.

That's what Roddy liked about him: no bullshit, just honest talk and a big heart.

'I think one decent escape is worth twenty half-hearted attempts. If you can walk yourself through enemy lines to the Allies, send us a postcard.'

'You?'

Frankie shook his head. 'Though I might have a day excursion to see my father's family. As long as I'm back before roll call. I could pick up supplies. Father Mario is to be trusted, I'm sure.'

'So when do we go?' Roddy felt the excitement surge through him.

'When it is time. Be patient, get fitter. It'll be no walk in the park, especially for you. You know the risks.'

'You've got it all planned, haven't you?'

Frank tapped the side of his nose and smiled. 'Only in my head. First we need to get you supplies, bribes, smokes and, most of all, good luck.'

'You'd better get on your knees then,' Roddy laughed back.

'You and me both, brother. Two voices are louder than one.'

116

By some miracle Father Mario and Frank made contact with a network of sympathizers who were setting up a chain of messages to the Bartolinis to expect secret visitors. It sounded a crazy scheme, all the more so when Roddy realized they were to filter out of a field working party. He would put on a cassock and claim to be another padre on pilgrimage. This meant stripping off his officer rank, disguising himself among the field gang and bribing one of the weaker guards with smokes and souvenirs to smooth their escape.

The night before the plan, he took Frank aside. 'It's too risky for you,' Roddy whispered. 'You go another day after I'm gone.' If the escape was discovered, the padre would be in danger himself. But Frank would hear none of it.

'I owe it to my father to seek out his family before we're sent north, like all the rest. It is only a matter of time before we're moved. The nearer the Allies get, the further we'll be sent from joining them. You making a run for it will have nothing to do with my extraordinary visit. I'll be back on time. No one will connect us. I know how to get back in now.'

On the appointed morning, Roddy slipped out to the other compound on a pretext, ripped off his insignia, trying to transform his uniform into more peasant clothing, and filled his knapsack with tins, smokes, anything that could be bartered. He shivered as they opened the gates, knowing every one of them would be culpable if his disappearance was discovered too soon. He tried to look calm as he edged as far as he could to the far side of the field for their short rest break. Some of the boys were planning to distract the guard while Frank darted first into the woody copse where he hoped some partisans might be waiting.

It was a scorching day and the men were stripped to the waist, glad of any makeshift cap to deflect the sun's glare from their faces and necks. The guards in their uniforms slunk off for a smoke in the shade. Two men picked a fight and soon everyone was brawling and Roddy seized his chance to dart out of sight and make for the spot where he hoped someone would be waiting for him.

True to his word, an old man and a young priest pulled him into the bush, pulled a cassock over his sweating body and shoved a biretta on his head to hide his sun-bleached hair. He was rushed to an ancient truck and unceremoniously dumped under a load of sacks. Frank was already lying in the back, sweating. They rode through narrow twisting cart tracks for what seemed miles, including past one roadblock.

It seemed Father Mario was a familiar sight with his round pebble-glass spectacles, acknowledging the local militia guards cheerily as they waved him through.

'The Bartolinis will keep you for a few days only. Everyone here is afraid of reprisals. There are Fascist sympathizers in every village with tongues as big as the Grand Canyon. You must head south to the Allies as best you can, only at night, of course. The cassock may help you – or not. This area is very mixed.'

The truck jolted to a stop outside a small farmhouse with golden stone outbuildings and a red tiled roof. It nestled in the hillside with a good view of the track. Hearing the sound of the truck, an old man and woman stood in the doorway, blinking into the sun and watching as Frank and the priest got out and then pulled Roddy out.

'This is Father Francesco Bartolini, and his comrade, the captain'

Their leathery faces stared as they shook hands with the priest and gabbled in Italian. They stood politely eyeing them cautiously but pointed to the door.

Roddy was blinded for a second as they were ushered into a dark room with a smoking fire, a polished table, and stucco walls lined with fading portraits. The first thing he noticed, though, was lace. It was everywhere: lining the mantelpiece, the back of the old armchairs, the edge of the tablecloth, the panels on the curtain netting. Everything was pristine, though the room was humble and smoke filled. They were given a thick soup of pasta and vegetables and slices of hard cheese with deliciously ripe peaches that melted into their mouths.

Frankie was stumbling, trying to understand their dialect, nodding, waving his hands and pointing to the photographs. Roddy noticed a very old lady was weeping in the corner as she listened to his story, shaking her head, and crossing herself, and when it came to the bit about the lucky shoe, which he'd pulled out from under his cassock, she almost collapsed. '*Merletto d'Anghiari*, Salvatore, look.' She was so excited. The atmosphere in the room suddenly changed. '*Il bambino d'Angelo, Francesco!*'

Frank was shaking his head, trying to explain why she was in such a state. 'She says my father brought this many years ago. Now she knows I am truly his son. They thought we might be spies. It's from one of the Marcelli patterns, a pattern of the *paese*, the local district. She says it is a miracle. Look over there at her lace maker's stool and cushion. I've seen those in New York. This is my grandmother and my cousin and his wife. They must have no name, just in case . . . I must be dreaming this. Wait until I tell the folks back home.' He smiled and sipped a rough country wine, which was as sweet as liquorice.

All too soon the sun crossed over the ridge and it was time for them to return. Father Mario was especially anxious to be off.

'You must get back to the camp. We mustn't be out by curfew.' But Frank was reluctant to part from his family with so many questions still to ask and so much to tell them.

Roddy felt moved to have witnessed such a reunion. He would stay the night in their attic, their hidden guest, stripped of his cassock now. All he could give them was cigarettes and a few Red Cross tins, muttering his *grazie*s as best he could.

Once outside he dared not show his fair skin and hair in case there were other eyes watching. Nothing would remain secret in these valleys by sundown. He shook Frank's hand. 'If and when I get back, I'll make sure your folks know you're safe and that you met up with your father's family at long last. I promise.'

Frank edged towards the door and his cousin offered him the shoe back but he refused it. 'It belongs here. It joins us back together, proof of my visit,' he said, shoving it back into her hand. 'My father wishes it.'

There was something about this act that moved Roddy so much he found himself doing a strange thing. He bent down on one knee. 'Give me a blessing, Father. I may need it where I'm going,' he whispered. 'When this is over we'll dine out on the stories for many a year. How can I thank you all for what you are risking, my friends?' he added. 'Tell them what I'm saying, Frank.'

Frank translated and then whispered in his ear, 'Just get the hell out of here tomorrow and make a home run.'

The truck hit a puncture somewhere close to Arezzo. It was getting late and Frank knew he would be late for roll call. They would be in trouble now. The commandant was a decent man but he would not stand for this deception and by now would realize that another man was missing. Frank sighed, knowing he'd have to walk the rest of the way back. The old priest was not up to his faster pace but he knew where the entrance was on the perimeter wire.

'Stay with the truck and the driver. You can say you were going to give the last rites somewhere. No one will ever query it. I will walk back to camp, take a short cut across the fields. It can't be more than a mile or two. Thank you for giving me this chance to see my family. We'll not risk this again. You've done enough. I'll never forget your kindness.'

Mario held on to him. 'Stay, you can escape too,' pleaded the old man. 'The *capitano* will not last three days on the run without you to help him. You are one of us, you look like one of us. You can pass as a native, who has come back from America. Your accent will give you away but we can make up a good story for you. Stay, Francesco.'

'No, I gave my word. There are sick men who need me; the doc needs my help.' He shook Mario's hand firmly. 'I'll get back late, the only POW begging to get back into his prison. That will amuse them and I shall bore everyone with the story of my secret pilgrimage. My knowledge of the terrain may be useful next time.'

He didn't tell him he had a compass hidden in a button of his uniform beneath his cassock. It was a warm night as he ripped off the button of his uniform to set the directions.

How different a wood seemed in the dusk, the shade of the leaves, a drone of mosquitoes aiming for his face, the croak of frogs and a hint of mist. It would be so easy to get lost, but with the aid of his lighter, he checked his bearings, still feeling uneasy. It had been an indulgence to escape for a day. Now he must pay for the risk.

He'd played on the commandant's faith in letting Father Mario in to see him. Had he put men's lives at risk? He lingered, feeling the freedom of the open space, the smell of pines. Who would not want to dally in such a haven?

As it grew ever darker in the wood, the path grew less distinct, but a path he trusted led out onto the fields where he and Roddy had made their exits only that morning. He hadn't gone far when he heard the barking of approaching dogs and glimpsed a flash of light. Hunters looking for deer or wild boar perhaps? But it took only a moment for him to realize he was the quarry, and it wasn't hunters but the *Feldgendarmerie,* tough militia types hunting for escaped prisoners of war.

He stopped to put his cassock back on, hiding his uniform just as a torch flashed upon him. 'Stop!'

Frank put his hands up and tried to explain. 'I am Father Francesco Bartolini. I have been out for a walk and lost my way. *Sono Padre Americano,*' pointing to the Cross and his insignia.

A voice spoke in broken English. 'You are an escaping prisoner. He is seen dressed as a priest. This is the prisoner.'

'No I am not. I am Father Bartolini. I was coming back to the camp. The commandant knows me ... Take me to the camp commandant. *Capisce?* I can explain.'

'You are an American spy, an escaping prisoner. You will not go back to the camp,' the military policeman sneered, his voice hard and threatening now. Frank carried on walking towards them, bracing himself when he heard the click of their rifles. There was no time to pray as the bullets sprayed into his chest.

117

Roddy woke on a mattress of straw covered by a horse blanket. He could hear rustling in the hayloft, and was alert to any strange noise and the beautiful birdsong outside. Where was he? Everything was a blur: his escape hidden in the truck, the smell of the farmyard, the scent of pasta sauce on his fingers. The sun was up and he was itching like mad, but lying back he tried to assess his chances of making a home run.

Blond, blue-eyed, speaking only a few words of the language and here only by the mercy of Frank's grandparents and uncles were not the greatest of assets. He wouldn't be able to stay long, but a good night's sleep and supper had worked miracles. He was ordered to stay hidden until it was safe to appear in the dark, knowing every moment he lingered would put their lives at risk.

What was all that business about the little shoe? Could Frank's father be right? Could it be true that it was from the *Titanic*, and indeed from this very region? It sounded too much of a coincidence but Frank had been determined to give it to them.

He'd taken a huge risk in bringing him here. Roddy only hoped he'd got back before curfew. The *milizia* would be out combing the hillsides with dogs to sniff out the sweat of a man on the run.

Surely if he walked south by night he'd run into the Allies somewhere. If only there were facts and not just rumours to go on. He wondered if somewhere in the villages sympathizers were listening to BBC broadcasts on their hidden wirelesses. Maybe Frank's cousins could find out the truth without alerting suspicion. He was at their mercy, dependent on their generosity and humanity to shelter him for the rest of the day. He needed his wits if he were to survive.

It was Frank's cousin Giovanni who called him down for a breakfast of cold ham, cheese and fruit served with acorn coffee and lashings of warm milk. The young man had a few words of English and drew a map for him out in the yard in the dust. 'You walk over hill in *mezzo notte*. No stop, long way. *Americanos* come, *si*? No more bam bam,' he said, pretending to fire. '*Allora, vieni.*'

The family sheltered him for four nights, fed him, showed him letters from New York and snapshots of Frank as a child, his brother, Jack, and his little sister Patricia with pride. He wanted to give them money, but they pushed it away. Poor as they were, this pride was one of the Bartolinis' few luxuries.

It was Giovanni's father who mimed that he must go up the hills where a shepherd he called Mani would guide Roddy down to the next valley. 'Mani will find you.'

They sent him on his way with a blanket, cheese and ham, dried fruit in his pocket and a phial of some oil that smelled strongly of lemons.

'*Zanzara,*' cackled the ancient lady, indicating he should put it on his face and neck. It was foul-smelling insect repellent. '*Grazie, molto grazie, io non dimenticato,*' was all he had managed in response. How could he thank those who'd shown such kindness and given him his freedom back?

They dressed him in old trousers and a shirt, but his disguise wasn't convincing. He would have to evade all travellers, scavenge as best he could from the land. He had no papers, just his identity round his neck. It was a crazy scheme, a game of cat and mouse, but he was willing to take the risk.

He walked for miles uphill, following a trail, listening for any telltale signs, but there were only the night sounds of the forest to comfort him. It was warm, too warm, and he searched out springs to quench his dusty thirst, making a bed hidden by branches and leaves. He spent his first night on the run under the stars.

In the weeks that followed he tramped down ever southward, thankful for the mercies of shepherds, guides and partisan sympathizers who passed him from valley to valley. They had a no-names policy, of course. What he didn't know he couldn't betray. He had nothing but a compass pointing south and west. His skin turned into tanned leather punctured with the red wheals of mosquito bites, despite the Bartolinis' lemon oil, but his boots held out despite the blisters on his heels. He smelled of farmyards and dung heaps; no hobo could have reeked like he did. Once he found a lake and threw himself naked into it, washing out his shirt and spreading it to dry over a bush. His beard grew a foxy red, a giveaway to anyone who saw it. He could pass for a German deserter but his luck held. He ate what was offered, which was all that could be spared. Others went hungry because of him, he feared. His frame grew lean and muscular and he was always hungry.

He wouldn't survive the winter in the open, and any fool could see it would snow here on high ground. Then a shepherd showed him a cave where he could shelter and make a rough fire when it was wet. One morning after a terrible night of hunger, his spirits were so low he wondered whether to hand himself in to the nearest militia. It felt as if he was getting nowhere. He'd made more than forty miles of progress cross country. Weak and disheartened, sick of living rough, he longed to be back in Akron, on his front porch, supping a beer. Why had he put himself through such agonies?

The past months had changed him. All the luxuries of life in Akron now seemed so meaningless. Here he'd been doing an important job. He was fighting for the people who mattered to him most and for his men, who'd already paid the price so that ordinary folk could choose how and where they lived their lives, free from the tyranny of fear and bombardment. He owed all these local farmers so much and one day, if he made it home, he would pay them back. He had to survive. He'd promised Frank but just how he had no idea.

It was time to move on, hungry or not, when he heard twigs crackling. He wasn't alone. He hid at the back of the cave, fearing the worst. Then he heard voices: '*Americano, Americano, buon giorno.*' There were two dark-eyed little girls in headscarves, one with a basket strapped to her back, peering into the darkness. 'Ella?' he croaked, thinking one of them was his sister. Was this a dream?

'No, signor, Agnese,' she said, smiling. 'Come, eat.'

Roddy made his way into the light, blinking as if two angels had suddenly appeared. The basket was loaded with cold meat, cheese, bread, a bottle of *vino lavorato* and a bunch of grapes. They must have walked from dawn to bring him his feast.

They sat silently watching him fill his face with all these treats, refusing to eat anything he held out to them. Then they beckoned and pointed down into the valley. '*Vieni a casa, mezze notte, vieni?*'

Later Roddy made his way down the valley in the darkness to a cowshed, where the cattle were lined up for morning milking. He could spend the night tucked up in the manger covered in straw. He could only sleep there at night, but at first light crept out to hide back in the woods or in the cave until it was safe to return.

He never met the rest of the family, only the two little girls who tried to teach him their dialect. One morning he heard the dreaded word *Tedeschi*, Germans, and feared the worst. He spent that day perched high, ready to dive into the cave at the first sound of troops on their manhunt. Perhaps he had been betrayed.

After all this time the thought of being captured and brought back to camp or worse, after the selfless generosity of so many people, filled Roddy with despair, but the silence held until nightfall when he crept back to his itchy billet. He was met by a large man who threw his arms round him with excitement: '*Americano amici, Inghilterra, Americano . . . Tedeschi . . . kaput, vieni . . . amice.* The women darted round in the shadows and he saw them all smiling. He was ushered into the farmhouse to a table lit with candles and the smell of roasting meat. He could just make out enough to know that there'd been a breakthrough. The enemy had moved further north in retreat and American troops were close by. A look of pure relief and joy flooded over their faces: *Liberazione!*

'You are free.' The girl who still reminded him of Ella looked at him with a big smile. 'You are free.'

If only it were that simple. It was one thing to know that the troops were gone, but there was still local militia and collaborators in every village. He didn't know who he could trust. But somehow the atmosphere was different. Italian flags were flying proudly. He still didn't want to show himself in public so kept walking parallel with the tracks out of sight, under cover, until he saw an army Jeep in the distance.

Roddy shot out of the woods waving his arms. 'Stop, stop!' He ran in front of the Jeep in case the troops missed seeing him.

He was searched in case he was a spy, but he told them his rank and number, finally convincing them he was genuine. They handed him a shirt and some real cigarettes. They were a British reconnaissance party, checking the road ahead was clear of ambushes. They took his ID particulars and the address of the Italian family who were sheltering him, telling him to return there until further notice.

It was all such a letdown after being in hiding for so long. But English cigarettes were like gold dust and he shared them out on the farm. Now he would repay them by working out in the fields. There was time now to shave, to smarten himself up and write letters. Two weeks later he received a letter from Rome telling him to report to Allied screening for probable repatriation. He ought to feel glad that he was on his way home, but somehow it didn't feel right. There was still a war going on, the enemy were not yet beaten, there was no way he would return stateside with a job half done. He would write to Father Frank, though, and tell him he'd kept his promise. Roddy's war was not over yet.

118

The crowds in Cathedral Close watched the floodlights beaming up onto the Three Spires. The blackout was finally over. The war was ending at long last but Ella felt numb, indifferent, going through the motions of celebrations at their village street party. She'd watched the bands parading in the city with the flags and bunting everywhere, but felt nothing. She could see Clare was jumping up and down, pointing to the lights. Celeste and Archie had taken her off to see friends leaving Ella alone with her thoughts.

The city was ablaze with light. Her hometown had seen her through good times and bad, and she felt such affection for the cobbled streets and spires, but now, she also felt empty, drained of emotion. The letter from the Air Ministry had finally ended any hope of Anthony's return.

In view of the lapse of time and the absence of any further news regarding your husband, Squadron Leader A. G. C. Harcourt DFC, since the date on which he was reported missing, we must regretfully conclude that he has lost his life and for official purposes his death has now been presumed to have occurred on 10 December 1943.

Now it was official, she was a widow, just like her mother all those years ago. How strange that history was repeating itself.

Life felt bleak and uncertain. At least in the war there'd been so much to fight for. It had been a team effort to keep life as normal as possible for the children. Now what?

She found herself wandering around the cathedral again, looking up at it with tired cynical eyes. It never disappointed, with its lofty arching roof, its gargoyles and brass wall plaques. Unlike some of the vaster cathedrals, Lichfield was intimate, quirky, so much a part of her younger life. She sat down on a chair, wanting to weep for all that she'd lost, but here was not the place, not in front of people passing by, chattering so excitedly. Ella forced herself up and wandered round to the Lady Chapel at the rear, her eyes alighting on the marble effigy of *The Sleeping Children*. Despite herself, she was moved to see it again. Not through the eyes of a child all those years ago but as a woman bereft and bewildered by who she'd become.

Her professional eye roamed over its contours, the romance of its curves, the perfection of line and execution. The detail of the mattress caught her eye, so real and soft she could lie on it herself. Yet she knew even in its perfection Francis Chantrey had left his mark: a small block of marble under a foot was uncarved, solid, a reminder that this was only a piece of art, flawed by this deliberate omission. How beautiful it was. No wonder it had caused such a sensation when first exhibited.

Death did not always come peacefully and she knew one of those children died as a result of a fire, burned, choked, like so many of the Blitz victims. The blow of death has to be softened with effigies and monuments, she mused. How many memorials had there been erected to the victims and crew of the *Titanic* across the globe? How many after the war? The world had to know and remember such terrible losses and try to make some meaning out of such tragedy.

The thought of how Anthony had faced his end, fighting his engine, trying to keep it afloat, was torture. There was no body to mourn and no goodbyes, no grave. This must have been how

May had felt too. No wonder they had come here to Smith's statue in the park. Her own parents had no grave but the ocean bed and she had given them so little heed over the years, but seeing this effigy again had stirred something inside her. Who were they and where did they come from?

Don't think about that now, she thought, turning away. It'll drag you down even further. Life must go on. Even though there was no grave to stand over, Anthony's life must be celebrated. Clare must have something to remember her father by, something tangible, more than just his letter.

This effigy had been made to comfort the parents of those two little girls, so she must make something to comfort herself, something only she could do, something permanent, beautiful and meaningful for Clare and herself.

Suddenly she felt a flood of excitement rush through her body like a current of electricity; an idea, a feeling of certainty rose in her mind's eye. How strange after she had walked into the cathedral with leaden shoes. Now she strode briskly out into the crowd. It was time to go home and face her studio.

The studio was damp and musty, full of clay shards from the explosion that had shattered her plasterwork. There were dead flies on the shelves and a pervading smell of neglect and abandonment. But this June morning was sunny and it was time to brush the cobwebs from the dirty windowpanes and spring-clean the place.

She needed light – strong northern light – fresh air and space to work her ideas into drawings capturing all she felt about her husband. First she must clear out all the dross for a fresh start. Ella picked up the drawing board and smiled.

Anthony, I'm back home and this is where I'll begin again.

119

1946

Roddy hung over the side of the troopship taking him home. He felt like an old man, so different from the guy who'd followed the flag in 1942. His head was full of memories he wanted to forget: the grim fighting north from Italy and on into Germany, sights of horror they'd encountered there, the forced marches of the dispossessed, exhausted troops, the camp prisoners. He never wanted to see another bombsite again. He'd joined another unit of the Fifth Army. There was nothing left of his old troop. He was a stranger among strangers who soon melded into a band of fighting brothers.

He would never forget the kindness of the Italian peasant farmers, those *contadini* who'd given him another chance to join the Allies. Those strange months in the foothills would stay with him for the rest of his life.

It was halfway through the journey that he found himself at the officers' dining table with two chaplains, one Jewish and one Catholic, judging from their insignia. He recognized the look of exhausted men, their eyes sunk deep with tiredness. The priest had an insistent twitch on his cheek. They got into conversation and he told him about his friend and chaplain Frank Bartolini in the camp near Arezzo, how the priest had helped get him out to his own family, and asked them if they'd heard where he was.

The priest, a Jesuit brother, Paul, looked at him with interest. 'Francesco Bartolini? He was in my training group at Harvard, a little dark chap. He was . . .' He paused, peering over his rimless glasses at him. 'Didn't you know?'

Roddy felt his heart skip a beat as he shook his head. 'You've seen him?'

Paul shook his head. 'I'm afraid he was shot. We heard on the grapevine. They've awarded him a Purple Heart, posthumously.'

'When? Where?' Roddy was shaking. He couldn't comprehend what he was hearing.

'Many chaplains lost their lives in the front lines. I just recall his name in prayers, knowing we'd met somewhere.'

'But he was a prisoner when I last saw him in Italy. How do I find out more?'

'The Chaplains Corps will have all the details. I am sorry. He was a friend?'

Roddy nodded. 'I owe that man so much.' He was no longer hungry, just in need of fresh air.

Later, walking on deck, Roddy was troubled by an instinct that Frank's death might have had something to do with his own escape. What about his poor family? Oh God, what about those kids he'd met. Were they safe? He just had to find out more. He couldn't go back to Akron and his old life without discovering exactly what had happened to his dear friend. He'd been so looking forward to meeting him again.

Then he recalled a conversation with Frank about the new church in New Jersey, one that was built as a replica of a church in Italy. That wouldn't be difficult to find. It took only a few phone calls to find St Rocco's on Hunterton Street and the address of Frank's family in New York. He wrote a short note introducing himself, asking for a visit of condolence before he headed back to Ohio. He told them he owed Father Frank his life.

Two days later he found himself knocking on the door of a

brownstone apartment in the Italian quarter of Lower Manhattan. A grey-haired woman opened it, smiling. 'Please come in, Captain. I'm Kathleen Bartolini.'

Roddy found he was shaking at the thought of meeting Frank's parents. He would just say his piece and leave. They wouldn't want reminders of him and the consequences of Frank helping him.

'You must be Roderick Parkes. Frank wrote about you. You joined his choir. His "English choirboy", he called you,' she said, immediately putting him at ease with her Irish lilt.

He followed her into the parlour full of pictures and ornaments and Holy Statues of the Madonna and Child. Sitting on the sofa was an old man and the most stunning girl he'd ever seen, with a head of glorious wavy auburn hair and green eyes. She stood up, tall and slender, as her mother introduced them. 'This is my husband, Angelo, and our daughter, Patricia.'

The old man made to struggle to his feet. 'No sit, please, sir,' Roddy insisted.

'My husband has not been well for many months,' his wife offered. Roddy was struck by his dark piercing eyes, the same as those of his boys, Frank and Jack, who peered across the room from their photograph on the shelf.

'Please call me, Patti,' said the vision in a green silk blouse, stretching out her hand. 'Sit down, Captain.'

'Thanks, ma'am. I must tell you, I saw a picture of you all in your grandmother's house,' he said. 'But you were only this high.' He smiled and Patti smiled back. He knew he was already lost in the loveliness of her smile.

The old man stared at him. 'You met my family, the Bartolinis? When?'

'I did, but please tell me first what happened to Frank.' He looked across again to his portrait. He'd not looked so smart in the camp, none of them did. 'I only heard on the ship that he died.'

'He was shot and left to die. They say he was trying to escape. That's all we were told.' They all stared in Frank's direction as if expecting the portrait to chip in and give his side of the story.

Roddy shook his head vehemently, holding his hands up in horror. 'That's not true. He was going back to camp to be with the men. Frank helped *me* escape. Your family sheltered me. I saw him leave in the truck with the priest to return before curfew. That's all I know. He was offered a chance to escape but he didn't accept. He wouldn't go. I was there. You must believe me.' He found to his horror he was crying. 'He was a good man, my friend. If I had known what risk he was taking . . .'

The family stared at him in amazement. 'You were with him near Anghiari?'

'To be honest, I never knew where I was, but Frank made contact through the Church with his father's family. That I do know. They took me in and gave me my freedom. Are they safe?'

'We've not heard anything. Maybe we can write now the war is over. You went there with my son and you saw him leave?' Kathleen looked at him again.

Roddy told them every detail he could remember of the secret visit, even the story of the little shoe and what had happened when they showed it to the old grandma.

'Alessia's shoe?' gasped the old man.

'I don't know any Alessia but when he showed it to them, the old lady knew it was you who had sent it, proof that the young priest was Frank and not a spy. She did say something about the lacework but I'm afraid one piece of lace looks much like any other to me,' he offered, seeing the reaction on their faces.

Kathleen crossed herself. 'Oh, Angelo, you were right to give it to him. My husband had a daughter and wife who died.'

Roddy knew what was to come next. 'On the *Titanic*, Frank told me. My mother was on that ship too but she lived. What a strange coincidence.'

'Did he tell you my sister drowned also?' said Kathleen. 'All three us connected by that terrible disaster ... you say he gave the shoe to the family as proof. When he gave away his talisman, his sister's shoe, he gave away his luck,' Kathleen cried, and Patti folded her into her arms.

'This is too much to take in, but thank you,' Patti said. 'You were sent to us for comfort,' she wept.

Roddy jumped up, not wanting to intrude any longer. 'I'd better go now,' he said.

'No, please stay, we have so many questions for you. You've brought us strange news and talking about Frank helps bring him alive again. I'll make us something to eat.' Kathleen disappeared.

'I'll have to go soon.' Patti wiped the tears from her eyes. 'I've got a show tonight.'

'My daughter's in the chorus on Broadway as an understudy: Patti Barr is her stage name,' Angelo smiled with pride.

Roddy eyed her again. He wouldn't have been surprised if she was on the silver screen. 'Which show is that?'

'*Annie Get Your Gun.* I can always get you tickets.'

'You bet,' he answered with just a little bit too much enthusiasm. 'I'm sorry, I didn't mean to offend at such a time.'

'No, no, we've gotten used to the idea of Frank not coming home. He's not our first loss. Our other son, Jack, was killed in the Pacific,' Angelo explained.

'Frank told me. I saw the letter. Both your sons, I'm so sorry.' Roddy didn't know what to say. The old man shrugged and held up his hands.

'Frank would say, it's God's will, He gives and He takes. It's a test of faith but here you come and bring him back to us with your news. Please stay and tell us everything you know. You were sent to us for a reason. Now tell me about my *famiglia.* Were they well? It is so long since I was there.'

Roddy pondered that question for many weeks afterwards as he conducted a cross-country courtship of the beautiful Patti

Bartolini. He had never believed in love at first sight, but one glimpse of that face and he had been lost. Roddy had always known what he was looking for but had never found it until that moment in New York.

He hadn't walked through Italy and fought his way through Europe to fall at those first hurdles of distance, of different faiths and backgrounds. What was more amazing was that Patti responded to him just as enthusiastically.

So what if their union would mean taking instructions in her faith, Frank's faith? That was good enough for him if it had made men like his friend. Where would they live? It didn't matter. What was important was that Frank had brought them together in the strangest of ways. Roddy would be forever in his debt.

All that was left was to write to his mom and tell her this good news. He'd found his match. He'd found his wife and life was just beginning.

Angelo couldn't sleep that night, not because of the usual ache in his legs but for a strange feeling of joy. The shoe had done its work again. Lost, found, given, taken, received, a curious journey it had had. Now a stranger comes and claims his daughter. He had seen the thunderclap of recognition between them; a half-English Protestant soldier had stolen his daughter's heart from under his nose. He should forbid such a match, but this was the very last man to see his son alive, a good man with good prospects. No, it was all a mystery. Here they were, battered, bruised and tossed on the rocks of life, and now there was talk of weddings and celebrations to come.

None of it would bring his children back but these young ones might bring others into this world for him to love.

Part 5

A NIGHT TO REMEMBER

1958–1959

120

England

'They're making a film about the *Titanic*,' said Clare, scouring the latest issue of *Picturegoer* magazine. 'A big one in London, starring Kenneth More.'

'Oh, yes, dear?' said Ella, who was hard at work on her latest commission and didn't want to be distracted.

'No, really, it says here, it's going to be an epic tale: a true story based on a true book.'

'I very much doubt it,' Ella replied. 'In all honesty, who knows what really happened that night?'

'Oh, don't be such a stickler, you know what they mean,' Clare snapped, flouncing off, not waiting for her explanation.

Ella sighed, wondering if she had been so touchy at that age. Clare was home from her boarding school near York. It always took them time to get back into their comfortable rapport. It wasn't easy bringing up a girl on her own, not one as sparky and bright as Clare, who played rock 'n' roll records on her Dansette, driving Ella out into the studio for peace and quiet.

An artist needed uninterrupted hours, and the school holidays were always a chaotic time for both of them. Clare wanted attention, outings, one-to-one time with her mother, but Ella's work piled up, holidays or not. Since that first exhibition after the war when she'd presented a series of sculptures of airmen, aviators, weary figures dragging jackets over slumped shoulders, and the bust of Anthony, alongside a series of studies of war-ravaged faces, she'd never been out of work: monuments, memorial plaques and private commissions for busts of lost men and women from the war.

She had been part of the Festival of Britain artistic exhibition representing the figurative side of modern sculpture rather than the startling abstract sculptures of Henry Moore and Barbara Hepworth. Their avant-garde work had stolen the show at the Battersea Exhibition Centre in 1951.

Sometimes Ella was so busy, it was hard to settle to anything else. Her private life was Clare, work and the Foresters. She still lived at Red House with Selwyn. It suited them, sharing the expenses. He was older and frail now, his old war wounds weakening his constitution, his drinking ravaging his liver.

She had never found anyone to replace Anthony. He was her one true love and besides, she was content to put all her passion into her work. There were men who'd taken her out, offered romantic interludes, but Clare and work were her priorities.

She'd fallen in love with her art all over again after those fallow wartime years when all she had done was copy, repair, teach and learn to breathe. Now it was as if all that pent-up energy had been released. Poor Clare was feeling neglected so she must make time to take her out for lunch.

Clare knew about her *Titanic* past in a vague disinterested way. She'd found the suitcase full of baby clothes in the linen cupboard after the war, played with the bonnet for her doll and one day Ella had come home to find the lace border cut off the night-dress and sewn onto a little underslip for her tennis dress.

Ella hadn't minded about the lace. What was the point of letting it all moulder in the top of the airing cupboard, slowly turning yellow? But the rest of her baby layette she kept in a suitcase for old times' sake. It would all get thrown out if she ever moved house.

There was a real story in there, one this new film would not be telling, but she was curious. She didn't know what to make of another *Titanic* film. How could they make such a story on a film set? She'd like to see them try. It was funny how Walter Lord's book had become a bestseller. A *Night to Remember*, it was called. A night to forget, more like.

Renewed interest in the ship had led to articles about the great disaster in the paper, survivors telling their stories. No one would ever believe her story and she couldn't recall a single memory of the event. She wondered what Mrs Russell-Cooke would make of someone playing her father. They'd kept in touch after the war, linked forever by the loss of their airmen. Her companion now was an artist and she'd seen them in London across the room at an art gallery cocktail party. She hadn't wanted to intrude as they were deep in conversation with the owner. When she turned to catch up with them they'd disappeared.

Perhaps that was for the best. So many people wanted to forget the war and the loss of so much that was precious in their lives. But grief, someone once said, was like an ever-present lodger hogging the fireside and blocking any heat from getting to you. You learned to put on an extra jumper to stop the shivers. She'd never pursued the quest to learn the identity of her real parents after promising herself to make the effort after the war. Her work and other distractions got in the way. You make time for what you want to do, she sighed. Somehow the quest for information was always bottom of the list. It was all too late now.

Life was about now, the present and the future and yet . . . What was the point of looking back to what she could never change? But still she felt a niggle of guilt that she'd never even tried.

Celeste was just back from Roddy's in the States. They'd gone to see their grandchildren for one of their birthdays. She still couldn't get over Roddy settling down with his Italian-Irish wife, becoming a Roman Catholic and opening a chain of diners across the highways of America. Roddy's businesses had hit the big time. He'd had a good war. Ella and Clare had been invited to his lavish wedding, of course, but the trip was too time-consuming to make: that was her feeble excuse. Celeste and Archie had dined out on their experience for months afterwards. No expense was spared. Patti had looked like Maureen O'Hara in her lace bridal gown and veil imported from Italy. Everyone had danced until dawn, the food was piled high and after wartime British austerity each course made Celeste's mouth water. There was talk of their moving over to the States permanently, but Celeste knew Archie would never leave Britain.

It was strange how life had worked out. If Roddy hadn't met that chaplain whose family had helped him escape, he would never have met Patti.

Ella forgot about the film until, a few months later, out of the blue, an unusual invitation arrived from Mel Russell-Cooke, who was hosting a private dinner to celebrate the premiere in Leicester Square of *A Night to Remember.* She hoped that Ella and her family would attend with Celeste, as guests of the film company in July.

'You've got to go.' Clare pranced around, delighted. 'You just have to. You'll meet all the stars. It's not fair, though, I shall be still at school.'

'It's not really my idea of a night's entertainment, watching people drown,' Ella began, but when she talked it over with Celeste she knew it wouldn't be an easy invitation to refuse.

'We were there, my dear. It'll be interesting to see how they muck up the storylines. We owe it to those who didn't survive to represent them. I heard they built half a ship on a lake and sliced a decommissioned one in two to get the angles right. It's the first time there has ever been any real public interest in the *Titanic* since the war. I wonder if there's even a mention of you, or the story of how Captain Smith rescued a child and put it in the lifeboat. You never know, you might find out something to your advantage,' she argued.

Ella was not convinced. 'I don't want my story all over the papers. I'm not going.'

Celeste was not easily dissuaded. 'When do you and I get a free trip to London, all expenses paid, dinner and the best seats at a West End premiere? Think about it. It sounds fun to me.'

'Fun? How can you say that? You were there, you saw it all happen.' Ella was shocked at Celeste's breeziness.

'It's all history now, all so long ago. It's become a famous drama all of its own. We could talk to other survivors but, Ella, I couldn't go on my own.'

It was that heartfelt plea that made Ella change her mind. She owed Celeste so much; to deny her this trip would be churlish and ungrateful.

'I'll go on one condition. I go as Ella Smith, Ella Smith Harcourt, not as Ellen God only knows who. That knowledge must stay in the family for my mother's sake.'

'May wanted you to find out more. It was her dying wish.' Celeste lifted up May's picture as if to emphasize this. 'Her dying wish. That's why she told me, I'm sure.'

'I know, but I don't want history rewritten or any sensational stuff. I can see the headlines: "Mother of British artist steals *Titanic* baby girl. The lost baby of the *Titanic* found at last! Do you know this child?" That's not going to happen.'

'You drive a hard bargain. I take it you've never told Clare your true history? She's so like you, so determined when she gets an idea in her head.'

'Why, what has she been telling you?' Ella was curious.

'She's given me an autograph album to collect signatures. She hopes to sell them at a pound a time for her travelling fund. So you see, we have to go now.'

121

Roddy and Patti made sure Kathleen was sitting between the two of them at the premiere of *A Night to Remember*. Angelo was advised not to go as it might destabilize his heart murmur. There'd been mixed feelings in the American press about this low-budget British attempt. William MacQuitty, the producer, had done his homework and invited some of the *Titanic* survivors, officers and crew to flesh out the human stories behind his epic. His radio appeals asked for Americans survivors to come forward with their own tales. Immigrants, now well-established matrons from all over the world, answered the call and Kathleen received an invitation as a sister of one of the Irish victims.

Patti, with her Broadway connections, made sure they got good seats and met all the VIPs. Roddy ensured they had a wonderful weekend in New York visiting friends and relatives, shopping in Macy's for presents for Frankie Junior and little Tina, who were at home with their nanny.

Prosperity sat easy on Roddy, but he'd worked hard to develop the Express Diner end of the business. Will Morgan headed up Freight Express, and with Patti's flare for décor and the theatrical, they'd cornered the market for reasonably priced roadside comfort stations where you could dine at 'Mamma Joe's' Italian style, or 'Murphy's Irish kitchen'.

They bought up old rolling stock and pitched them by the state highways in fields or close to gas stations. They'd hacked out the interiors using the carriages as dining rooms decked out with pretty curtains and furnishings.

Like many veterans, Roddy found it hard to believe he had survived with hardly a scar. The scars he had were invisible to the eye, but his dreams told other stories.

When the film was over he had a sudden urge to phone his mom in England. How had she managed to survive such an experience and remain so calm all her life? The music score kept drumming in his head like rolling waves. It was a simple well-told storyline of different families coping with the sudden disaster: the fate of the officer in the lifeboat and the women trying to keep spirits alive, the stoicism of the great industrialists as they watched their wives leaving the ship without them, the frustration caused by the absence of rescue boats, resulting in so many unanswered questions.

The whole audience was moved. This was no great Hollywood biopic with stars flaunting themselves before the camera, just ordinary faces, good acting and a convincing enough set that gave a sense of the scale of the ship.

Moviegoers left in silence, deep in thought, moved by the enormity of the disaster. Roddy knew it was going to be a box-office hit.

'What did you think then?' he said, holding on to Kathleen's arm.

'I want to light a candle for Louise, and Angelo's poor wife. If what he once believed about his little girl is true, do you think she could be out there watching this, not knowing who she really is? All this time, we just pushed his dream away. It's not right, is it? We could go to the papers, tell them the story. They would investigate for us.'

'We have to be sure of the facts first. Papa has accepted that the shoe belonged to someone else. Don't raise his hopes only to dash them,' offered Patti. 'I kept thinking of the young mother and her children, the little boy sleeping through it all, and the look on his father's face as he waved him goodbye. It makes me never want to go to sea again with the children. How did those men bear to let them go, knowing they'd never see them again?'

Roddy shrugged. 'You do what you have to do, it's instinct.' He shivered, thinking of the sights he'd witnessed during the war, children strafed with bullets, their mothers clinging to them in desperation. Men murdered before their families for helping the Allies' advance.

'What got me was that so many lifeboats were virtually empty, so many more passengers could have been saved, like my sister, Maria and Alessia. They were the real victims, those in steerage. I'm glad Angelo wasn't allowed to watch this. That ship was doomed, wasn't it? Unsinkable indeed! What arrogance in tempting Providence.'

Later they sat in a restaurant, the gloom still heavy upon them. Roddy was trying to lighten their mood, desperate to think of something to cheer them up. It was one of their favourite trattorias in Mulberry Street with pictures of Italian scenes on the walls, familiar scenes of poplar trees, fine churches with hills in the background. How they brought back memories of his escape. Then he smiled. He'd just had the most brilliant idea.

Celeste leaned back in bed, laughing. 'Just listen to this, Archie. Roddy and his big ideas.

I've booked us all a trip to Europe next July. I've reserved a big house with room for all the family to share a few weeks under the Tuscan sun. I know it sounds crazy but I want all of you over there to join me. Don't worry about the cost; I would like to cover that. I mean everyone: Ella and Clare, of course, and Selwyn, if you can drag him out of 'The Anchor'.

Kathleen, Patti and the kids are dying to meet everyone and see where Grandpa Angelo came from. We hope he will be well enough to fly with us too. Of course we all want to see

Frank's final resting place and meet those dear people who sheltered me during the war. It's all arranged, flights, car hire, everything. You know me, once I've decided it's a done deal. I can't wait, this is going to be one hell of a vacation.

She turned to her husband. 'Do you fancy driving to Italy?'

'No, I'd prefer to go by train. At least there are plenty of loos. You know my bladder,' Archie laughed. 'Do you think Ella will come?'

'Clare will give her no peace if she doesn't. She's such a recluse these days, stuck in that studio till all hours.'

'It's what she does. It's her world, but artists and Italy are a good combination. I think she could be persuaded. I wonder what's brought this on. Roddy seems very determined.'

Celeste sank back into the pillow, thinking. 'Guilt at surviving the war. I guess he has a lot of people to thank,' she sighed. 'You and I both know about that.'

Ever since the film premiere her dreams had been full of that terrible night; the awful screams and then the even worse silence. They'd got one bit wrong. The *Titanic* didn't slip silently into the sea all of a piece. It had broken in two and crumpled before it disappeared, such an abiding memory.

The likeness of Captain Smith had been uncanny. Mrs Russell-Cooke remarked on how the actor had unnerved her at first. She'd been an excellent hostess, taking time to talk to all the survivors, just as charming as her own father was at the captain's table, Celeste noted.

Ella whispered that not only had the captain's daughter lost her son in the war but her only daughter, Priscilla, had died from polio as a young bride. It was rumoured her husband was killed in a tragic 'shooting accident' in his office six months before her own mother was killed in a road accident. This brave woman was a fine example of British grit sitting round the table that night.

They'd all made new lives for themselves just as so many were having to do after the war. Celeste would have loved to throw a grenade into the table by saying that the striking woman sitting next to her was really an orphan from the ship who never knew her parentage. But she would never break the promise made to Ella to remain silent. How many other secrets would never be told about the passengers on the *Titanic*? She shuddered, thinking how she'd wished her first husband, Grover, dead that night. Now he too had passed away, just after the war. She no longer felt any bitterness towards him, just pity for his unmourned passing within the family.

Watching the film was like watching the world a lifetime ago, the clothes, the manners, the graciousness of an era that would never return. The Great War had seen to that. She was part of that time, born a Victorian but living in the Elizabethan age, and Britain was prosperous and peaceful once more.

They would take a cross-channel ferry, a train to Milan and hire a car for the rest of the journey to Tuscany. It would be a once-in-a-lifetime opportunity for them all to be together, with a chance to pay respects too. She was proud of her son for planning such a splendid treat.

122

There had never been any choice in the matter once Clare took control. She could be such a bossy madam at times, Ella smiled. 'This will be my grand tour before university, Mummy,' she announced. 'I want to see Paris, the Swiss Alps, the South of France, and go round the bay to Florence, of course. And you could show me the galleries and then we can go inland to Arezzo and see the paintings of Piero della Francesca. We can share the driving now I've passed my test. I've one condition, though. You are going to buy some decent clothes for once. I'm not being seen dead with you looking like a tramp.'

That was the trouble with daughters. They told it like it was, not like Roddy, who cherished his mom and treated her like bone china. Still, it would be good to go away. Selwyn refused to budge. No surprises there. He would guard the house, feed the cats and dog, and see to the garden, or so he said. Ella was curious to meet Patti, a beautiful Irish colleen, judging by the look of her wedding photographs.

Celeste said they were a loving family and Roddy was a very proud father. If Ella felt tinges of envy, she brushed them aside. Each to his own, and Anthony's clever daughter was all she could wish for, even if she was growing up too fast. Soon she'd be off to university and then Ella really would be on her own, a prospect suddenly filling her with uncertainty and fear. At times she felt cast adrift, unwilling to let go of Clare, but when she started nagging she couldn't wait to see the back of her.

This time together would be precious. The funny thing was she'd never had any intention of not going to Italy. Ella was not that bothered about getting there, but driving down French roads together in the shooting brake would be fun. If only Anthony could be by their side. He seemed so far away now. She'd given Clare his letter on her fourteenth birthday and it was always in her bedside drawer under the photo of him in his uniform.

'I don't look like him, do I?' she sighed, looking at her passport photograph. 'We're so dark. Why's that?'

'I don't know,' was the only answer she could come up with on the spot. It had troubled her, this lack of curiosity about finding her true identity. This ambivalence was tinged with fear, apprehension and not a little laziness. What was she afraid of? If she didn't look, she wouldn't be disappointed if there was nothing to find, but hadn't Clare a right to know the truth by now?

Perhaps on the journey down she would broach the subject. It wouldn't hurt May now. Since the film, more information was coming out about *Titanic* survivors. It would not be impossible to track down some of the truth. If she was too scared to do it for herself, she ought to do it for her daughter's sake. It was her heritage too.

The bust she'd made of Anthony for Clare showed him forever young while she was ageing not very gracefully. Her black curls were dusted with grey, but her eyes were still jet-black and her jaw firm, if a bit saggy in the middle.

Perhaps a few new tops and slacks would not go amiss. Clare refused to compromise, insisting Ella bought a fitted swimming costume and decent underwear, two sundresses, some Capri pants and a smart evening dress. 'You could look really glam, if you just tried a little harder.'

'I shall stay out of the sun or my skin will end up like crinkled leather after a few weeks in the heat. It did last time.'

How strange to be wandering across Europe again, this time in style and comfort, staying in a mini palazzo rather than some flea-bitten mattress in an attic. Ella smiled, thinking of her old self, free-spirited, fancy free, strolling through the French markets with just a few centimes in her pocket. The young have no fear, no cause to doubt the future, she mused. She'd once been confident, gregarious, so sure of herself, but not any more. She envied her daughter. How beautiful was the bloom on Clare's young face. She hoped no Italian Lothario would wipe that shine away: war had taken its toll on her generation. It mustn't scar the next.

War had been exciting and dangerous at first, and Ella had relished living for the moment, her life full of passion and risk, but grief and loss had been its unavoidable consequences. How she wanted to protect Clare from heartbreak. She was glad she was finished with romance and the agonies of being in love, but Clare had it all ahead of her.

123

Roddy stood dumbstruck by the sheer number of white crosses in the American War Cemetery outside Florence. He paced along the granite panels lined with the names of the missing, looked up at the tall stone pylon and saluted his comrades before the hillside chapel. He thought of all the men he had known who were buried here, and with that thought came the inevitable flashbacks to faces, smells and explosions.

Here, everything was so clean, so beautifully preserved, so quiet, so American in its efficiency and detail, and so very moving. Angelo was not up to the long journey so Kathleen wept at her son's grave alone and Roddy held young Frankie's hand, praying he'd never have to know such a life-changing experience. He was too young to understand much of it, but the atmosphere touched both his children just the same as they tiptoed round the graves, curious but respectful.

He wanted them all to see what sacrifice looked like. Every one of those crosses was a life unlived, a lighted candle stubbed out before its time. We make death clean and peaceful, clinical and safe here, he thought, but it was not like that the first time they crossed this country. Battle was a filthy business.

They'd arrived in Rome and made as many of the cultural tours as they could. Jetlagged, after many hours of flight, they had stood in St Peter's Square soaking up the atmosphere of Vatican City, before driving to Florence so Kathleen and the family could pay their respects. Now she knew where her boy lay it would help her to rest her own sadness.

Roddy hadn't expected to cry, to feel the tears running down his cheeks at the sight of such vast fields of the dead. Memories flooded over him and he wondered if such emotion would spoil the rest of their vacation.

'Why's Daddy crying?' asked Tina as Patti held him.

'Because this is where his friends lie. They never got to go home with him. Your uncle Frank is here too.'

'Did we win the war then?' Frankie asked.

'No one wins a war, honey. They just think they do.'

Two days later they arrived in Tuscany to find an old rambling country house on the edge of the medieval walled town of Anghiari. It was perched high on a wooded slope with a magnificent view over the plain, and the scent of cypresses, pine and herbs perfumed the air, taking Roddy right back to his time on the run. He recalled those fearful nights hiding in the woods by day, and the smell of the farmyard, the sweaty stench of the cattle shed and oil lamps by night.

He couldn't wait to visit all those outlying *contadini* who'd sheltered him. Over the years he'd made sure Patti's Italian relatives and friends received gifts in kind: fresh tyres for their trucks, clothing in parcels. The Bartolinis knew they were coming and he'd brought gifts from Angelo, his old uncle Salvi and his children. They were going to host the biggest party for everyone later on when the British contingent arrived.

He wondered how his mom and Archie would cope with the travelling, and if Ella would turn up late or not at all. They'd not met since Clare was a baby when he had briefly touched down in England on his way home.

Ella was such an unknown to him now. She chose not to come to his wedding, which had hurt, he admitted. She was modest about her success and reputation as a sculptor. Her infrequent letters were full of Clare, never herself. She was the nearest thing he had to a sister and he hoped there would be time for them to get to know each other all over again. He wanted her to like Patti and Kathleen and feel they were all one big family.

She'd always been a loner, an outsider, brought into their midst through the kindness of his grandfather and mother. She had no one but Clare, no family to call her own but his. He hoped she'd soften to the idea of them all mucking in together. He really didn't understand artists very much, but this was the birthplace of so many and down the road was the very birthplace of the famous Michelangelo. He wanted everyone to feel at home here as much as he did.

Celeste gazed up at Villa Collina with amazement. It was picture-postcard pretty with golden stone, and painted shutters and a terracotta pantiled roof. It stood tall, majestic in a setting of olive groves surrounded by woods with a gracious drive up to the castellated house. Trust Roddy to find the most beautiful spot. They had lunched in the Piazza Baldacci in Anghiari, marvelling at the high walls of the medieval streets, the wonderful ancient buildings. It was all so very Italian and well worth the long journey, even if the dry heat was not what she was used to. It was like a fairytale setting. She expected men in doublet and hose to leap out onto the cobbles and start duelling and to see Juliet sitting on a balcony waiting for her Romeo.

Later, after unpacking in a beautiful bedroom with the most exquisite gilded mirror she'd ever seen, Celeste joined the others who were sipping wine in the shade, watching the sun slowly sinking across to the west.

She watched Frankie and Tina playing games on the sloping lawn. Frankie was all legs, had braces on his teeth, and dark hair, not a bit like Roddy. It was Tina, with red curls like her mother and grandmother, who was going to be the beauty. Frankie reminded her of somebody but no one she could bring to mind at that moment. They were polite but lively children and a credit to their parents. She was going to make the most of her time with her grandchildren and spoil them as much as she dared.

What a mixed bunch they all were. Archie was sitting back with some historical tome on his lap, soaking in the sun. Kathleen had produced her knitting and Patti was rushing round making sure the housekeeper and staff knew that there were other guests still to arrive before they served a candlelight dinner on the terrace.

How would they all get on for three weeks? It was the longest holiday she'd ever had but there was enough land and space for them not to get on top of each other.

Kathleen said there was a lovely shop in Sansepolcro nearby where you could buy local lace. 'The lace for Patti's wedding dress came from there but the handmade veil, the Bartolini family sent as a gift. I think it was Maria's. It has such a beautiful patterns, very distinctive.'

She daren't let on that she'd never really noticed the motifs or any detail of the wedding dress, being so in awe of the whole event, nervous at meeting more Irish and Italian families and trying to fit into their wedding customs. Patti had looked like a film star.

She glanced at her watch. Ella and Clare were late again. She hoped the journey hadn't been too much for them. Perhaps they had got lost. This visit had been planned with Forester military precision, down to their itinerary: where to find the best churches, restaurants and overnight stops, route maps and must-see sites. Dear Roddy had set such store on this reunion. She hoped Ella would rise to the occasion and not let them down.

124

There was so much to see and so little time if they wanted to find Villa Collina in time for supper. Ella resented the rush southwards, wanting this time alone with Clare to last for ever. They'd driven slowly down through France and lingered around Florence, taking in all the sites, including the Uffizi with its famous statue of David. It was wonderful to share her old haunts with her child, to see the magic through her eyes, to wander the streets and gawp at all the magnificent architecture. They'd fallen in love with Siena and Arezzo, the food and wine especially, and had relished living off salads and fish and wonderful pasta.

As they'd climbed up towards Anghiari, Ella found herself slowing down, reluctant to give up this precious time, unsure how she felt about being tagged on to Celeste's expanding family once again. She'd not plucked up the courage to tell Clare about May's confession either. Every time she thought about it, her heart skipped a beat. Perhaps later, after a glass or three of wine.

Roddy was being so generous and it felt mean-spirited to be resentful. If only she had a larger family of her own to share. It was funny how, as the years went on, she was feeling more and more awkward. She and May had been dependent on the kindness of strangers all their lives, for shelter and education. Celeste had been like a mother to her but her whole life had been shrouded in mystery and now it was almost too late to discover the truth. No one had ever claimed her, that was for sure.

Interest in the *Titanic* and its memorabilia was still growing. There were books and articles, even societies forming. It wasn't too late to share her mysterious history and discover more herself, but in a funny way she felt ashamed of being a nobody. As Anthony's widow, she had a secure standing, and if Clare had children one day, she'd be a grandma in her own right. Surely that was enough?

'You're going the wrong way, Mummy!' yelled Clare. 'It's to the left, not to the right.'

'Damn, are you sure?' The lanes were steep and narrow. 'Let me see.' She stopped the car to look at the map. How on earth was she going to turn round here?

A sports car stopped behind them, seeing their dilemma, and a man came to the window. 'Please ... inglese? You are lost, I can help?'

'*Dove e Villa Collina, per favore?*' Ella asked, trying her best Italian on the stranger.

'Ah, Signor Forester, yes? Turn around.' He pointed, smiling. 'No, better follow me. I will take you.'

'There's no need,' Ella protested.

'I take you. Follow,' he commanded as if there was no argument.

'Wow,' said Clare. 'He looks just like Vittorio de Sica.'

'Who?' Ella snapped, reversing down the lane, aware she was swerving.

'The film star ... Oh, never mind, just follow him. You're hopeless, Mummy,' said Clare, exasperated. They were both tired. It was almost dusk and they were nearly there. Ella mustered her flagging spirits for one last effort. You will enjoy this holiday whether you like it or not, she muttered inwardly as the entrance to Villa Collina came into view.

* * *

As the days turned into weeks, they fell easily into a pattern of lazy mornings, lunch in the nearest café, siestas, sightseeing and long suppers under the stars, each relating their day's activities.

They drove into Arezzo to see the frescoes of Piera della Franscesca, marvelling at his *Legends of the True Cross*. They enjoyed lazy picnics by the river and Roddy visited as many of the old haunts as he could find. Some farmsteads were sadly now nothing but ruins, their inhabitants scattered. Other families had built new villas, and white stuccoed houses rose up from new sites on hillsides. But signs of neglect and poverty were everywhere. Life had been tough here after the war and local children were leaving for cities and the States.

There was always a royal welcome of recognition from these kind people, older and more weathered by the sun and wind, their children now married with children of their own. The highlight was taking Kathleen, Patti and their children to the Bartolinis' farmhouse. The reunion was tearful as they passed around precious photographs.

It was here that Roddy heard what had really happened to Father Frank, mistaken for an escaping prisoner by renegade militia deserters, murdered in cold blood. His body had been left to rot, but had been found by a hunter and taken back to camp. There'd been an inquiry and the German commandant was removed for letting the old priest into the camp. But when the local partisans found out what had happened to one of their own, they'd taken it upon themselves to finish off each of these militiamen in cold revenge.

Only then did Roddy realize the full cost of his escape. It was hard to take in the news without breaking down. Giovanni took his arm. 'It was war, *amico*, these things happen. It will not happen again.'

Roddy wasn't sure. Human nature was both kind and cruel. He thought of Frank's words all those years ago. The families that had sheltered him were quite capable of turning their guns on each other if crossed, the animal instinct in all of them was plain to see. The meaner streets of New York and Chicago were no different. He'd seen enough violence to last a lifetime. He wanted only peace for his kids.

'We didn't come here to be miserable, honey. We came here to celebrate and thank these kind people. We must invite all of you to our villa to dine with us and meet the rest of our family,' Patti ordered, seizing the moment and saving the day. 'We'll send cars to fetch you all.'

125

Clare was watching the chattering lace makers with interest as they sat in their doorways with their cushions and stools along the narrow streets of Sansepolcro. The tall buildings sheltered the ladies from the heat of the sun as they wandered round the ancient city, examining the shop windows, sitting in the piazza and watching the world pass by. They had dined in the Albergo Fiorentini the night before, savouring its wonderful dishes, aware that its high walls were full of souvenirs from Napoleonic times. When they heard the story of how one of Napoleon's officers had defected and married a local girl, to establish this restaurant, Archie had nodded. 'You can see why a soldier would prefer this to a route march, and the women are so beautiful here.'

Celeste looked up in mock horror. 'So I am to be abandoned here?'

'There are far worse places on earth,' laughed Ella, her skin bronzed like a local. She felt layers of tension slip away as she soaked in all the colours of the town: ochres, burnt sienna, terracotta ... Everything blended into each other, the street, the walls and the rooftops a harmony of colours so easy on the eye.

Sitting in the piazza now with the warmth of the sun on her skin, she felt relaxed for the first time in years. This place was having a magical effect on her. As she soaked in the ambience of this beautiful place, she sighed, knowing she'd left her sketch-book in the car.

'Ah, signora, signorina.' A man in sunglasses stopped at their table. 'You are enjoying your stay in Villa Collina?'

'*Sì, grazie.*' It was their knight in the white Lancia who'd escorted them to the gates of the villa. He introduced himself as Piero Marcellini, a notary, a lawyer in Sansepolcro.

'I am glad you like it. It was my family home,' he smiled. 'It still is, but now we, how you say, rent to visitors in the season.'

'It's a beautiful home, Signor Marcellini.' Ella blinked up at his tall frame.

'Please call me Piero, Signora Forester.' He whipped off his glasses and smiled.

'I am Ella Harcourt, Mrs Harcourt, and this is my daughter, Clare.'

'Ah, *la bella Clara*, she has been noticed. And Signor Arkot . . . ?'

Ella shook her head and raised her hand. 'Killed in the war.' It was strange how she could say this quite calmly without shaking.

'*La guerra, sì, mi dispiace.* I'm sorry, so many sad things. How long you stay here?'

'Only another week and then we are driving back. I'm going to university,' Clare chipped in.

'Will your mother have dinner with me before you leave perhaps?'

'Perhaps,' Ella replied, shocked to be asked and feeling herself blushing.

'I will call then,' Piero smiled, and with that he promptly strode across the square.

'Mummy, you've got a date. He fancies you.'

'Don't be ridiculous. Continental men are all like that.'

Clare was laughing. 'Why shouldn't you have a date? You're not that old. How exciting. What will you wear?'

'Enough, it's time to go.' Ella jumped up, embarrassed.

'But I wanted to find the lace shop,' Clare said.

'Another time. We're supposed to be helping get dinner ready for tonight. It's the Bartolini feast, remember?'

Ella was anxious to be off, unnerved by Piero's unexpected attention. It was such a long time since she'd been noticed by a man. They were usually too old, or too young, but Piero was in his fifties, maybe younger, handsome in that dark Italian way, with a strong profile. He would make a good subject to sculpt with his firm jaw and aquiline nose, long neck and wide eyes. She smiled, sensing she was more than a little attracted to his profile. Why not enjoy a night out? The sun had clearly gone to her head, softening her brain, but when you travel anything can happen, she mused. Now it was time to peel potatoes and set up tables and make sure Roddy's special guests had a night to remember.

There was no hurry, they were on holiday and soon they would be homeward bound, back to the humdrum old life. Yet the thought of leaving this sun was hard with only grey skies and harsh winters to come, cold nights and rain. Poor Selwyn would be waiting for her to tidy up his mess. Clare would be off to university soon. All that was left for Ella at Red House was work.

If Piero Marcellini rang (and she doubted that he would) she would accept his invitation just because it would add a little colour to her life.

Patti, Kathleen and the housekeeper were busy setting the long tables out on the terrace with white cloths and finding an assortment of chairs and benches to accommodate all their guests. There was going to be a crowd of villagers as well as the Bartolini relatives. Ella made for the kitchen to help prepare salads and Clare was ordered to pick fresh flowers for the table. It was going to be such a feast: *zuppa di cipolle, tonno e fagioli salata, pollo alla campagna, ricciarelli, gelati*, to name but a few of the dishes. Every course was to be accompanied by a fine wine.

'What do you think, Sis?' Roddy said, surveying the table with pride. 'Will it do?' Ella liked it when he called her 'Sis'. It

made her feel part of the family even if she wasn't. 'Best bib and
tucker tonight, you know my mom's rule: collar and tie after six.
But no ties in this heat.'

'You'd better tell me who everyone is. Do any of them speak
English?' she asked.

'Don't worry, we brought in our own translators and a few
extra guests to help out. You don't know what this means to me,
having everyone together. For Patti and Kathleen to meet
Angelo's relatives is so very special. If it wasn't for Frank ... I
just want everyone to enjoy the get-together. You won't disappear, will you?'

'What do you mean?' She prickled at the insinuation.

'Sometimes I look at you and you look so far away. I know
you miss Anthony. It makes me feel so guilty to be here and him
not.'

Ella reached out for his hand. 'It's not that, it's just I envy you
having such a big family.'

'You are family too, you know that,' he replied.

'I know, but sometimes ...' She shook her head, unable to
explain.

'None of that. Tonight is for singing and dancing and making
it a night to remember.'

She looked at him and smiled. 'You saw the film then?'

'Of course. I wouldn't have missed it. There's still so much we
don't know about that night, isn't there?'

'You can say that again.' Ella mused silently. 'Let's not think
about *that*. This is your night, and if the food is anything to go
by, it's going to be a feast. I can't wait to get stuck in.'

Ella took extra care to dress for the occasion, coiling her hair
up in a French plait with her best gold earrings. Thank goodness,
Clare had made her bring a decent dress, a deep turquoise cotton
with a full skirt that showed off her suntan, and the stone neck-
lace they had chosen in Arezzo. She'd also bought espadrilles
with straps round her ankles. She looked at herself in the

dressing table mirror and smiled. 'You've scrubbed up well, old girl, not bad for your age.'

There was a lightness inside her, something she hadn't felt for years as if she was a girl going to her first dance. She hoped it would be a night to remember.

126

Celeste sat with her champagne, watching the guests walk up the track to Villa Collina by the light of the setting sun. Everyone ate later in Italy. It was almost dark and the lanterns flickered along the path. First came the neighbours from the farm who tended the olive trees, dressed in dark suits and bright cotton frocks. Then a car brought old Nonna Bartolini to the door. The Ancient of Days was dressed head to toe in black, with a headscarf like a nun, edged with black lace. She bent over a stick, leaning on her grandson Giovanni for support, surrounded by his children in pretty cotton frilly dresses also edged with lace. Next came the local priest, Father Michael, and a tall, distinguished-looking man, who was the owner of the property. More Bartolinis and villagers arrived in pickup trucks and three-wheeled scooters. The noise grew as Patti and Kathleen greeted everyone with kisses, and Celeste felt so very English in her reticence. Archie was mingling and she looked for things to do to keep busy. Clare was handing round drinks on a tray and Ella had appeared looking so very continental and beautiful. It brought a lump into Celeste's throat to see her so bright-eyed and relaxed. This holiday had done her so much good, it was as if the years had dropped off her. It was going to be a special evening and Celeste smiled with excitement. It was the sort of night when anything could happen.

★　★　★

There was toast after noisy toast as glasses were raised and laughter and wine flowed; not rough wine this time but fine Italian Chiantis, Barolos. Local cheeses and chocolates were passed around during the neverending Italian speeches. Ella had the urge to capture the scene in a drawing but cameras were snapping to record the event. She was storing it all up in her mind's eye.

She found herself distracted when seated next to Piero Marcellini, who appeared as if by magic by her side. There was no getting away from the man. Why shouldn't Roddy invite the owner of the villa? She'd had to confess to him her profession and he proved to be a man knowledgeable about art. He was hard to ignore and Clare kept giving her knowing looks and whispering. 'Vittorio de Sica has no chance against him,' she hissed, which was all rather silly, but after a few glasses of excellent red wine Ella was past caring.

The oldest of the Bartolini men got to his feet and made a toast to absent friends and Father Francesco, Patti's brother, who had saved Roddy's life. Piero was translating as much as he could. He said that the country dialect was so thick you could only catch the gist. 'He says war divided us for a while. Now we are united. The great Atlantico parted the Bartolini brothers all those years ago, but families are strong and now we are united never to part. It is what Francesco would have wanted, and Angelo. We wish him long life and good health!'

'Who are they?' she whispered, close enough to admire the subtlety of his aftershave.

'Maria was Angelo's first wife, before Kathleen. She was lost on the *Titanic* with her baby.'

'Yet another of the *Titanic*'s victims ... how sad,' she murmured.

'Alessia wasn't lost, though,' Patti chipped in. 'No, she was lost only to our family, mislaid, or so my father used to believe. Uncle Giovanni,' she shouted in her most theatrical voice, 'tell them all about the shoe, Frank's shoe!'

The old man rose up again and was waving something at the far end of the table in the candlelight.

'What is he saying?' Ella was straining to hear but he spoke too fast.

'Something about a *scarpetta,* found by Francesco's father at the dock when the ship brought the rescued passengers, a baby shoe he always believed was his child's,' Piero added.

'That's the shoe we gave to Frank for good luck, but it didn't work,' whispered Kathleen, shaking her head across the table.

'Because he gave it to them, to Nonna Elisabetta there. I saw him do it,' added Roddy. 'Frank told me she said it was proof he was his father's son. She said it was made around here. He refused to take it away with him on the day he died.'

There was silence as the old man passed the little shoe round the table and their guests handed it along, shaking their heads. 'It kept us safe, though,' said Giovanni. 'So many were betrayed and ruined but we survived.'

Piero handed it to Ella, and Clare leaned over and grabbed it. 'It's just like the one in that case, the one—'

'Let me look at it.' Celeste fingered it, shaking her head. 'I've seen one like this before.' Realization dawned. 'Good Lord! Ella, it can't be?'

Everyone was looking in her direction. She couldn't speak. How could this possibly be the same one?

'It's now or never,' Celeste said.

Ella drew a deep breath, flushed with wine, heat and amazement. 'No, please, say nothing yet, I have to be sure.' She paused, looking round the table for the old woman, standing up holding the tiny shoe. 'I have seen a shoe like this before. Its partner was in a suitcase of baby clothes with a nightdress edged with fine lace. It was rescued from the sea ...' She felt herself breaking down. 'I can't say any more.'

No one spoke for a moment.

'Can this be true?' said the priest. 'Then it is indeed a sacred shoe. Does Nonna hear what is being said?' They looked to the old woman, who was crying.

'This is too much,' Ella cried, shooting up out of her chair.

'Stop, stay.' Piero grasped her wrist but she shook him off, fleeing to the safety of her room.

What have I done? This was my mother's secret, not for sharing amongst strangers. It was a story best left unspoken like the secrets in any woman's heart, better left undisturbed like the wreck on the ocean bed. This strange coincidence is too much for me to understand. Could it be true? And if it is, what happens next?

'How do you know about this, Mom? What's all the mystery?' Roddy sat back on his chair smoking a cigar in the flickering candlelight, staring at the empty table, the spilled wine, amaretti crumbs, the crumpled table linen.

'All I'm saying is we have some lace baby clothes in the airing cupboard at home that came from the *Titanic*, and the shoe, well, there's one of them too.'

'Not any more. I cut them up for my dolls,' Clare said.

'So whose clothes were they?' Patti asked. 'I don't get it. Why the disappearing act?'

Celeste sipped her umpteenth espresso and sighed. What a strange evening, everyone wondering what was going on, curious, asking questions. Ella had hidden in her room refusing to return, overwhelmed by the turn of events.

'I was there the night a baby was rescued. I believed what I was told, that it was the captain who put the baby into the lifeboat. May grabbed on to her as her own. That is certain, but memory is such a strange thing. It plays tricks and a person can see what they've seen or what they think they've seen. Now I can't recall any of it. The rest . . .'

'But what baby?' Patti turned to Kathleen. 'What is going on here?'

'Are you saying what I think you are saying, Mom?' asked Roddy.

'Oh, I don't know. I'm not sure now, but when I saw the little shoe . . . It may be just a coincidence.'

'There's one thing that won't lie and that's those baby clothes, what's left of them,' Archie said. 'I'm surprised the mice haven't got to them by now.'

'Surely there'll be something left in the case,' she said, turning to Clare, who shrugged.

'What do we do now?'

'Nothing,' Celeste said. 'It's not our history, or at least it's not mine. Your mother will know what to do. Let her sleep on it all. She'll do what's right. We must give her space to work this out for herself. She has always been so loyal to May. She will tell us the rest when she's ready.'

'Come on, it's time for bed. Tomorrow could be an interesting day,' Archie said.

'But what is going on, what with the baby shoe? Whose is it?' Patti cried impatiently.

'Let's see what tomorrow brings,' said her husband.

127

Ella woke with the vestiges of the strangest dream still in her mind. She was in a large empty house, walking along a gallery filled with pictures on the walls, of ships and churches and land-scapes. As she walked around these treasures of memory, her feet echoed on the marble floor. It was cold, the wind rattled the doors and she was afraid. She saw a picture of an aeroplane skimming over the water and another of a great ship sinking into the ocean. She could taste the salt water in her mouth and feel the chill. She was thrashing and bobbing and then swimming along this neverending gallery until she found herself pulled towards a secret corner where a woman was smiling, opening a door. She knew that face, a face she'd cherished all her life. May was nodding and smiling as she opened the door to wave her through to safety and daybreak.

She made her way to Clare's room.

'Now you know everything,' Ella said as she lay on the bed next to her daughter. 'I did want to tell you earlier but it's such a sad story. Then that business with the shoe last night . . .'

'Do you think they're a pair?'

'I don't know, they're very similar. There's a way we might find out, though.'

'It's all a bit spooky. Could we really be Bartolinis? That would make Patti your stepsister . . . Wait till we tell everyone we're Italian.'

'No! This is a private matter between us for the moment. There must be no fuss in the papers. This is our secret. It may be all just a coincidence,' Ella warned, not wanting to raise false hopes. 'We have to find out more about the lace.'

'There's not much left, I'm afraid, but that border on my tennis slip.'

'There'll be enough. We'll go into Sansepolcro and check out the lace shops, take a closer look. We might find the key to it all there.'

After a breakfast of leftover puddings and cake, they piled into two cars and set off for the walled city. Patti and Kathleen were curious, dying to ask more questions, but Ella just smiled and kept saying, 'Wait and see.' How different she felt this morning after the dream; free to look round at the hazy beauty of the hillsides, the golden light on the houses as if looking at it for the first time. Could this really be her birthplace?

How many other Tuscan wives from the district were on the *Titanic*? It would be easy enough to trace through the records, and the knowledge that her own father might be alive made her heart leap with excitement, but she must be sure. No point in raising his hopes only to dash them again.

There were many small lace shops off the piazzas but the biggest one had windows full of drapes, tablecloths, sheets edged with lace borders, napkins, and baby linens.

Patti was in like a shot, wanting to buy up all the stock, rattling away in broken Italian making herself understood.

'Ask about the designs,' Ella asked. 'Who does this work?'

The lady was fulsome, pleased that the tourists were purchasing souvenirs. 'You must go to the *scuola di merletto*. Speak to Signora Petri and her husband. They set up the school many years ago. The girls win many gold medals, their work is the best in Italy. She will tell you their story.'

Celeste caught up with Ella as they made for the little school. 'Are you all right? Did you sleep? I didn't, not when I saw that shoe. It has to be the same as yours.'

'Who knows?' Ella whispered. 'The truth is in the lace some-where. Without any of ours, we can't prove anything. You've seen it more times than I have, I never liked to look. It reminded me of May being ill. Do you think you can recognize any of the patterns? My mind's gone blank but I've told Clare all I know this morning.'

'Thank goodness for that. If nothing else, she knows now. I remember how angry you were—'

'Shush, I know. I was so upset but now it's time we laid all this to rest one way or another.'

They stopped off for coffee, regrouped and made their way to the school where girls were sitting round the room twisting their bobbins on their cushions, looking up at this strange posse of foreigners. The room dripped with lace panels, tablecloths, collars, displays in cabinets, certificates on the walls, pictures of lace dresses. It was the finest work Ella had ever seen.

Patti explained their mission to learn about lace making and the history of the patterns on display. They were shown motifs and pattern books, and one of the girls demonstrated how the lace was pricked out according to Signor Petri's designs. Ella could see animals, flowers, stars, even people in their borders. She asked Kathleen to show them the shoe they had kept from last night.

'Is this from the region?' Patti asked.

'Yes, our girls do this fine work for special shoes, baptisms, sometimes for funerals. It's an old one.'

Patti explained its strange history. 'Do you know who might have made it?'

Signora Petri shook her head. 'Sadly, no. It's a common design, the edging looks local but there's not enough to identify one of our designs. You have more?'

Patti nodded. 'There's my wedding veil in the States, and in England perhaps . . . ?' She looked to Ella, who nodded.

'If you can send me some examples, I might be able to trace

it through our records. There's nothing distinctive in this, I'm sorry,' she added.

Ella looked around the room with a fluttering feeling inside her stomach. *Did my mother work here? If they had stayed in Italy, would this be where I would be working too?*

They left feeling flat. 'Let's cheer ourselves up with ice cream,' suggested Celeste. 'My legs are telling me it's time to sit down.'

Ella's mind was racing. It would take months for their samples to be posted and checked and she was impatient to find out more.

There must be someone who could help. They were halfway back to the car when the answer shot into her head. Of course, how simple! There might still be samples closer than theirs to be found but this time they must go alone.

128

The next morning Ella took the car back down to the walled town to find the office of Piero Marcellini. If he was surprised to see her, he showed no sign of it, sending out for espresso and seating her in a comfortable old leather chair.

'To what do I owe the honour?' he smiled.

She told him everything she knew about her history and why the little shoe had upset her so much. She told him about the lacework and how she had tried to identify it.

'I can't say any more to the Bartolinis until I am sure. Angelo, Patti's father in New York, knows nothing of this. I need someone to find Maria Caprese's family, Angelo's first wife. There may be some lace still here that might be identified as hers. I want to know if there is anything that might link us to her. Whatever we find out must remain in the family. It is not for public consumption, ever.' She looked up at him. 'If you would translate for us and be our witness, I would be most grateful.'

'I would be delighted to help. The family will be easy enough to trace. We're very good at registering people, Il Duce saw to that. Tonight perhaps, we can drive out ...'

Ella could see where this was leading. 'Clare must come too. It is important she be part of this. I have kept her in the dark too long.'

'Of course,' he replied. 'Shall I call for you?'

'No, we will come to you.'

★ ★ ★

'Why all the mystery?' Clare laughed as they sneaked out after their siesta into the car.

'Just an idea to speed up things, I hope. We're going on a visit, not sure where yet, but Piero is taking us.'

'I'm not playing gooseberry, am I? I wondered why you're all dressed up ...'

'Nothing like that,' Ella smiled, knowing Clare missed nothing. 'But this is important and we need a witness, just in case ...'

'Now you are intriguing me.'

'We are going to visit Maria Bartolini's family home. There may be some of her lace there. It's worth a try.'

Piero drove them into the hills in his sleek car that purred its way to just outside Anghiari, not far from where they had visited Patti's grandparents, the ones who had sheltered Roddy in the war. Higher and higher they rose to a small hamlet, a cluster of little stone houses clinging onto the side of a hill. Hens and ducks scattered at their approach, dogs barked and faces appeared at the doors. Piero asked directions to the Caprese house and was pointed to a tiny cottage, little more than a room with stairs into a loft. A women in black opened the door, listened to Piero rattling off their story and beckoned them through the door with a toothless grin.

Inside it was so dark it was hard to make out more than a table, a stove and someone stirring in the corner. It was an ancient lady bent double.

'This is Maria's mother, Alessia. She's very deaf now and her eyesight is not what it was, and Katerina here is her late son's wife. She says she never knew her sister-in-law. I am trying to establish if they have anything of Maria's to show you but I don't think the old lady can hear me.' Piero was doing his best but it was not looking hopeful.

'Do they have any photographs?' Ella asked him to translate.

Katerina pointed to a rough wall full of sepia portraits of

long-departed ancestors, men in uniforms, matrons in stiff dresses. The family had seen better days and now the two widows were scratching a living, as so many had to since the war.

In the far corner was a photo of a young girl with dried flowers pinned round the frame like a halo. Dangling from the end was a postcard with a picture Ella recognized only too well. Her heart was beating faster as she drew closer, sensing she was looking towards something she'd never dared to dream of before.

It was Maria's eyes that drew her into the face, eyes she would have known anywhere, eyes she'd seen so many times in the mirror and the shape of the lips and the narrow dent above them. It was the face that once had been her own face that now was her daughter's.

Piero peered too and then stepped back, looking at both of them, smiling. 'You don't need any lace, do you? Just look at the three of you. Look, Katerina, what do you see?'

Katerina looked and smiled, and took the picture off the wall to hand to the old woman shouting in her ear. They crossed themselves, shaking their heads, crying, laughing. Ella felt the tears rising as she kneeled before the old woman. 'Nonna? I am Maria's daughter ...' Her grandmother stretched out a bony claw to greet her.

She stared across at Piero, grateful for his intervention, breathless at this discovery. Katerina was rushing for cups and a bottle of wine.

Clare kept looking at the picture amazed. 'This is where it all began,' she said. 'It's amazing.'

Ella nodded. But not where it ends, she thought.

129

New York, December 1959

'Come on, Papa, get dressed. We don't want to be late for our guests,' Patti was chivvying her father from his fireside. 'Into your suit and new shirt. It's cold outside so wrap up.'

'Plenty of time yet,' Angelo muttered, reluctant to get out of his chair. He didn't want to go down to the docks to meet the *Queen Mary* from Southampton, even if Roddy's relatives were on board. Why couldn't he just stay here in the warm and let them all get on with it? It was bad enough they had to decamp to Patti's house for a traditional Christmas in the country. What a fuss they were all making.

Ever since their return from Italy in the fall, there'd been talk of nothing else but the vacation, and who they met and what they did, and what a pity he hadn't been able to join them. The house was full of fancy lace and expensive glass souvenirs. It was bad enough he didn't go with them and now his heart was playing tricks again. Winter was coming and his bones ached. Did they want to kill him off, sending him down to the water's edge? What he needed at his time of life was peace and quiet, not a house full of noisy kids and strangers who didn't speak his language.

The harbour held nothing but bad memories. One ship was the same as any other. Why couldn't they just pick him up on the way out to Springfield or, better still, leave him here to sulk?

★   ★   ★

Now he was bundled into the station wagon, piled with presents and food, all the festive fuss Kathleen had been cooking up. He caught her winking at him. 'It's gonna be a Christmas Eve to remember this year.'

What was so different from any other year? They'd eat too much, drink too much, get indigestion, sleep it off and then it would be back to feet of hard snow for months. Much as he loved his wife and daughter, they sure were playing up today.

'Have you shaved properly? We want you looking your best.'

'Huh!' he snapped. 'What's so special about today? But if I catch my death standing at the dock, then it'll be one for your calendar right enough.'

'And a Merry Christmas to you, Papa,' Patti laughed.

Ella and Clare hung over the rails waiting for the liner to make its way through New York harbour, staring up at the Statue of Liberty and Ellis Island, speechless at the sights before them. So much had changed since their return from Italy.

Clare was now reading History at Durham and on her Christmas holiday. Ella had returned to Lichfield knowing she would not be staying there much longer now she had found the other part of herself.

Celeste, Archie and Selwyn were thrilled by their discoveries, and Roddy and Patti, along with Kathleen, were being kindness itself, keeping the secret under wraps for the sake of the one man who would complete their story.

Ella had wanted to jump on a plane to meet him right away but there were commissions to fulfil and she had needed time to settle into her new identity and find out more about her heritage in private.

Her Italian lessons were proving useful. She'd sent the lace pieces for verification and for confirmation of what she already knew. Patti had sent Maria's wedding veil, as further proof that they were made by one and the same person.

Ella had seen for herself the *Titanic* passenger list. There was no other Tuscan woman on board but Maria Bartolini with a baby daughter, Alessia Elisabetta, no one of the same age or description. To her delight she found she was younger by months than she'd first thought.

Piero Marcellini was being a good friend in all of this, translating her letters to Katerina and old Alessia, passing on her gifts and photographs taken of them all together. In fact, he was becoming far more than a friend to her but that was for the future, not now.

This was the moment she'd been waiting for. But as she hung over the side taking in all the sights and sounds of the busy waterway, she thought of that first voyage she'd made in a stranger's arms, in borrowed clothes on the saddest of all arrivals back in 1912. How could they not pass close to the *Titanic*'s last sighting without praying for all those lost souls, for her mother and her foster mother, and all the love that had brought them to this moment? What had been done by May had been done out of love and she'd long forgiven her, as she'd forgiven Anthony for leaving her.

That time was past. It had been an emotional journey and now it would reach a climax. Ella shivered at the thought of meeting her real father. She'd rehearsed it so many times, had practiced over and over in her head the words she would say.

Would Angelo be disappointed? Or confused or disbelieving? She hoped the shock would not be too much for him.

The story had been in the lace all along; finding who she was had taken almost a lifetime of strange happenings that threaded them all together. Captain Smith had saved a baby, May had taken her in and Angelo had never given up hope. Frank had sacrificed his life for Roddy's freedom and had brought him to Patti: all these twisting threads made up her story and it had all begun with those little shoes.

* * *

Angelo stared up at the liner without emotion at first, but the smells of the dock, the oil and fumes, the gulls crying and the general bustle brought back such a terrible feeling of desolation. Why were they making him come here when they knew how much it distressed him? Why hadn't these English visitors come by plane?

He stood between Kathleen and Patti, each with an arm in his, holding him up, his feet chilled as the passengers trickled out slowly from the arrivals hall. Passengers were waving, smiling, rushing forward to greet their families just like all those years ago when he had stood alone in despair. At least this was a happier arrival.

'Here they are, Papa!'

He saw a striking woman in a fur coat and a brilliant pink scarf, with a girl in a duffel coat – a pretty dark-haired girl with a ponytail, smiling as if she knew him. There was something about her smile that reminded him of someone, something warm and familiar.

'Now, Papa, this is Ella and her daughter, Clare, from England. Ella has something for you.' Patti pushed him forward.

The woman smiled as she pulled a little package out of her handbag. 'I believe you have the other one to this,' she said, looking into his eyes. 'One shoe without the other is no use if you have two legs,' she added.

Angelo fingered the shoe, puzzled, turning to Kathleen for support. 'What is this? Why has she got my shoe?'

'She hasn't. Ours is at home. We brought Frankie's shoe back from Italy, remember?'

Then he turned to the young girl, his heart thumping as he studied her features, as if something long lost was coming into focus, a faded photograph coming into life. 'She has Maria's face and so do you. Is this true? How can it be true? Alessia? All these years I have hoped. Is it really you?'

Ella was smiling back. 'I hope so . . . I think so.'

He felt her arms around him and tears on his cheeks. Patti and Kathleen stepped back. Angelo turned to them for support. 'You all knew?'

Kathleen smiled and nodded. 'We wanted to make it special. It's taken a lifetime to bring you two together. Where better for you to meet than where it all began?'

'But how?' he said. 'How is this miracle happening?'

His two daughters took an arm each to escort him out into the winter light.

'It's a long story, Papa. It may take some time.'

A Note from the Author

'It is a rash man indeed who would set himself up as final arbiter on all that happened on the incredible night the Titanic went down,'

wrote Walter Lord in his book, *A Night To Remember.*

This story evolved from reading survivors' accounts of their experiences in the lifeboats and afterwards. There were reports of Captain E.J. Smith's rescue of a child in the water but nothing ever proven. Had this been so it might have mitigated the swift decline of his reputation that made the unveiling of his statue in Lichfield such a contentious event in July 1914.

The trail to find out more about the *Titanic* and its passengers took me from Liverpool's National Maritime Museum, where I was able to view the very medals I describe given to the crew of the rescue ship, *Carpathia*, and much more, to the Titanic Historical Society of America's Museum in Indian Orchard, Springfield, Massachusetts: a shrine to many intimate relics donated by families of passengers. It has a wonderful atmosphere thanks to the owners Edward and Karen Kermuda.

I am grateful for the enthusiasm of so many *Titanic* aficionados who loaned books and argued different theories as to what might have really happened if the mystery ship had come to the rescue. Thank you to my friend, David Croll, for sharing his books and ideas, to my son, Josh Wiggin for chauffeuring me up the Eastern seaboard and checking out some of the other

American museums and helping me flesh out a brief visit to Akron, to my ever-patient husband, David, always ready with the camera, to Margaret Brothwell for guiding me re the history of Lichfield Theological College and all my Lichfield friends for their hospitality; researching is thirsty work!

Although this is fiction and my main characters are entirely fictitious, I did need the presence of many real passengers, crew, cathedral clergy and relatives to have walk- on parts. The famous 'unsinkable' Margaret Brown and the Captain E J appear as does an imaginary visit to his daughter, Helen Melville Russell-Cooke (née Smith) with reference to her son, Squadron Leader Simon Russell- Cooke killed in 1944 and his twin sister, the late Priscilla Phipps.

In every case I have tried to adhere to what was known of the people involved. Of course there is no evidence that what I describe could have happened, but with some slight adjustments to their lives and itineraries there's no reason why such events couldn't have been possible either . . . However, any mistakes in the narrative concerning them are entirely my own.

For further information about Helen 'Mel' Smith I am indebted to the article by John Pladdys in The Titanic Historical Society of America's magazine, *Commutator. Vol. 17. 1992*. I am also indebted to the following books for specific information: *The Man Who Sank the Titanic? The Life and Times of Edward J Smith*, G Cooper, 2nd edition, Cotes Heath, 1998; *Rubber's Home Town*, Hugh Allen; *Lichfield in the First World War, The Diaries of W.E. Pead*; *The History of St Matthew's Hospital Burntwood*, David Budden 1989; *Memories of A Cathedral City*, Cuthbert Brown, 1991. *Universal Aunts*, Kate Herbert-Hunting, 1986; *No Moon Tonight*, Don Charlwood; *The Cinderella Service: RAF Coastal Command*, Andrew Hendrie; *A Small place in Italy*, Eric Newby. On the U.S. Chaplains Corps: *Soldiers of God*, Christopher Cross, 1945. I would also like to recommend Lichfield Archive Office's excellent collection of Titanic information where I read the account of the unveiling of the Captain's statue in the *Lichfield Mercury.*

Further on the trail when lace became an important factor, I was helped by Audrey Pemberton and the Settle lacemakers in understanding the process and later took a detour to Sansepolchro in Italy to visit its wonderful Lace Museum which was opened especially for me. Thank you to Leila Riguccini (President of Associazione Il Merletto nella citta del Piero) and Anna Nespoli. Their enthusiasm and help knew no bounds and despite me having only a little Italian to hand, they produced just the articles I needed and more. This visit was made possible by the generosity of my brother and sister-in-law, Chris and Cerys Wiggin who placed their Tuscan home at our disposal.

So the story was drafted among the winter snowdrifts and shown to my editor, Maxine Hitchcock, who made some wonderful suggestions and encouraged me to pull out all the stops with her immaculate editing. Thank you to Jessica Leeke and all the team at Simon & Schuster, along with my agent, Judith Murdoch, for giving me the opportunity and challenge to explore one of the great dramas of the twentieth century.

Leah Fleming.
Crete, 2011